Geo. D. Bent
Rec. Sep. 8 / 09
After meeting the author
at the "Cliff Dwellers Club"
of which he is Prest — C.E. Nixon
introduced us — They joint
toured Yellowstone Park together.
The author used to attend
circuses at Burr Oak
& left Hesper just about
the time I left Burr oak — 1869.
G.D.B.

HESPER

A Novel

BY

HAMLIN GARLAND

AUTHOR OF
"THE CAPTAIN OF THE GRAY-HORSE TROOP" ETC.

HARPER & BROTHERS
NEW YORK AND LONDON

Contents

Contents

Hesper

Hesper

I

The Emigrants

NEARLY the entire boat-load of passengers was jammed along the forward gates, ready to spring out upon the Jersey wharf, restive to reach the waiting trains. But quite apart from all these whose faces were set westward, three people—a girl, a man nearing forty, and a slim lad—lingered on the after-deck as though loath to take their leave of the imperial city whose singular sky-line was becoming each moment more impressive, more unaccountable to those who were looking upon it for the first time.

As the big barge drew out into mid-stream, the wharfs, the four-story tenements, and the business blocks rose in dim terraces, one behind the other, till the highest of them all loomed like the crest of a mist-hid mesa, and the lights in the dusk of the lower levels allured like camp-fires in the deeps of wooded vales, while between the little group on the stern of the boat and this smoke-hid range of mysterious peaks the cold, gray water rolled, ever widening, menacing, inexorable as death in its power to divide the fortunes of men.

The resemblance of this monstrous hive of human-kind to a height of land was so marked, so singular, that the girl remarked upon it, and the boy, a pale lad of seventeen, cried out, in shrill staccato,

"Yes; but think of the real mountains we're going to climb!"

The girl did not speak for a moment, and when she did her voice was distinctly sorrowful. "I feel as though I were saying good-bye to everything worth while."

"Including me?" asked her escort.

She did not smile, but her accent was kindly as she answered, "Yes, Wayne, including you."

"Oh, sis, you make me tired!" cried the boy. "Just as if going West were bidding good-bye to everything!" He beat his thin chest. "I'm just beginning to live, now. I'm glad to get away from the stuffy old town. I want to see something besides Fifth Avenue and Central Park."

Wayne Peabody laughed good-naturedly down at the boy. "You wouldn't care if civilization did stop at the west bank of the Hudson River, would you?"

"I should say not. I'm tired of it all—the noise and the pavements and the heat and the wetness. I want to get out where the wolves and the cranes and the cow-boys are; I want to hit the trail and find where father's camps were."

Ann smiled a little. "All of that we've heard before, Louis. Wayne knows all about your ambitions."

The city was by this time a vast, blue bank of cloud, an indefinite mass, out of which only the larger lamps still dimly shone. It might have been a mining-town scattered along a hill-side. Around the *Hopatcong*, scuttling to and fro, other deep-laden craft were plying like prodigious water-beetles, confusing to the spectator, yet pursuing each his predestined course, palpitating with power, thronged with other human beings eager to find rest and shelter for the night.

The girl spoke musingly. "It's singular, but I have a premonition of some dark fate—some vague sorrow. I never felt so before—not even on my trip to Egypt. If I don't come back I want you to note that I was forewarned."

Peabody smiled. "That isn't very flattering to the West. You will not find a desert waste exactly, even in Valley Springs. There are some millions of people between here and there—"

"But such people! Just a welter of commonplace personalities. The more we have of such creatures the worse for our country."

"You're a little severe. There are a few commonplace personalities on our little island." He nodded at the receding city. "I fear I shall find it an especially dreary collection to-night as I go back to jostle elbows with them, while you are being carried out of my reach."

His attempt to make a personal application of her own misgiving silenced the girl, and as her brother cried out, imperiously, "Come, let's go forward!" she turned with a sigh and followed him.

Peabody remarked, in a low voice: "Louis is transformed already. It will do him all kinds of good to go West."

"I hope so," she replied, rather drearily; "but he seems unwholesomely excited at the present moment."

"He'll get over that."

"I fear he will be disappointed. Father's trip was made nearly twenty-five years ago, when it was a really wonderful land."

"He is young. He will reimagine it."

The boy stood like some beautiful animal poised for a spring as the ferry shouldered its clumsy way into the Jersey dock. He was of less bulk than his strong, composed, modish sister, and his face was as dark, as mobile, and as eager as hers was fair and impassive. Peabody experienced once again a twinge of keen regret that Ann had not some of her brother's radiant enthusiasm.

Surrounded by porters and wearing an air of command, Louis led the way to the sleeping-car, impatient of his sister's deliberation. On one hip he carried a pair of large field-glasses, and over the other a costly camera, while half-concealed cases of pencils and pads of drawing-paper bulging from his pockets announced his artistic intention. He was comically prepared to "jot down" at a moment's notice any wild man or animal he might encounter, or any good story he might hear.

As the time for the train to start drew near, Peabody strove to win some softer word from Ann; but she was not of those who manifest emotion — her training and her temperament were alike opposed to easy expression. When he tried to take her hand a second time, with eyes that entreated, she recoiled.

"No! No! You have no right to expect that!"

He was no longer a boy, and he was bred to self-control; therefore, though his voice trembled a little, he spoke quietly. "Good-bye, Ann. Write every day, won't you?"

In a voice which chilled him, she replied: "Every day is pretty often—but you will hear from me. Go and see mother, please. She will not say so, but she will be glad to have you come."

"Depend upon me," he said, lifting his hat. His bearded face betrayed no emotion, but his eyes were hot with pain and grief. How cold and unresponsive she had been, and how desirable she was!

The girl, on her part, felt a sudden twinge of remorse as she left him there, a fine, strong, manly suitor, who uttered no complaint though she wounded him. The twitching of his lips troubled her, but she did not relent. In her heart she said: "I can't help it—it isn't in me. He shouldn't ask it."

Louis threw himself flat on the couch in their state-room and said, boyishly: "Gee! we're off at last. Now let her whiz. This old train can't go fast enough for me."

Looking down at him at that moment, Ann's bosom swelled with an emotion almost maternal. "How thin he is," she thought, as her eyes took in his slight body. "I'll go; I'll do anything for him—if only he can grow strong and well."

She loved that slender lad, and assumed for him a greater weight of care and hope and fear than for any other human being. He was so like his father—the soul restless as flame, the slender body racked, worn with endless enthusiasms, the burning, mesmeric eyes and the delicate mouth. All these she had known and valued in her father, and when the doctor seriously advised the Rocky Mountains she readily gave up her

5

own plans—and here and now she sat, rushing towards the West, to a town as repulsive to her as Hoboken or Coney Island, a place of emptiness and weariness, a social desert, where no one lived but her cousins the Barnetts, to whose hospitable door they were bound as voyagers on a wide sea to a snug harbor — without that home, as a point of arrival, she would have been in such uncertainty of mind as besets a sailor on a chartless sea.

Her patriotism was not excessive, even when confined to New York. Patriotism was to her a word of small weight. Hers had been a narrow life—narrow without being intense—and she knew little of her native city; and as for the great inland valley towns, they were unworthy of mention even in a jest. It did not matter to her whether the States contained one or a hundred millions of people. They had no distinction — and distinction was a great word with Ann Rupert. The only personalities worth while were necessarily in the East. "And yet," she was accustomed to add, "New York is a village compared to London. There is but one really satisfactory city, and that is Paris."

Louis held hot arguments with her on all these points, but they usually ended in substantial agreement that Paris possessed all that was really worth while in art, but was sadly lacking in mountains, wild animals, Indians, and cow - boys, for which he had developed a most unreasoning passion. He was all for the free, untrodden spaces, the primitive types. He longed to companion those who approached the bear in strength, the wolf in cunning, and the antelope in lightness of foot.

The Emigrants

In listening to this conversation a stranger would not have suspected Ann of fervent self - sacrifice— she was so calm, so cold, so irreproachable in every line—and yet she was making this abhorrent trip in order that her brother might thrive in his physical well - being as well as in his art. He had recently determined on being an illustrator of wild - animal books. " I'm going to study them at first hand," he repeated often, " the way Melborn Foster has done. And, besides, I want to illustrate father's journal." This journal, the record of a trip into the West made by Philip Rupert before his marriage, had come to be the most powerful influence in the lad's life. It was a worn, little red book in which the father had written the daily happenings and impressions of his trip and its discovery by Louis, in a box of old papers, had quite transformed his life. It had made him an American, filling him with a longing for the "Hesperean Mountains," as the father called the romantic land he had seen but once, but whose splendor lived with him throughout the remainder of his short life.

As they sat at table in the dining-car, Ann again listened indulgently to her brother's plans, and permitted him to order the dinner and assume all the manners of a grown man, honestly trying to conceal her own weariness of spirit, sincerely regretful of her bitter words on the ferry.

Louis was not weary; he eyed every man who came in, avid to discover some Western trait, some outward sign of inward difference between himself and his companions, but could not. They were all quite commonplace business men, well dressed, close-clipped, and urbane of manner. Some of them were evidently

7

salesmen going over to Philadelphia or out to Chicago, and they all ate long and with every evidence of enjoyment. Some of the women were young and pretty —students returning to the West for their summer vacations.

Once more in the privacy of her state-room and looking out at the landscape reeling past, Ann sank back in her seat wholly dismayed. "What in the world can I do out there?" she asked herself, most poignantly. "Of course they don't play golf or tennis, and I can't ride; and, besides, whom could I play with? Jeannette is not a bit athletic." And again the small round of her interests—she had no gayeties—was borne in upon her. "I shall die of inactivity."

Louis excused himself quite formally and went back into the smoking compartment to sit with the men, while Ann, left alone, gave herself up to a close, half-ironic study of the absurdity of her position. With a dozen most desirable invitations to distinguished London homes, with everything before her that a girl of her age and tastes could desire, she had turned away to face the crude conditions of a Western State in a warm glow of sisterly affection; but now with Louis deserting her for the nondescript crowd of men in the smoking-room, her flame of duty began to flicker and to emit smoke. "Why not Switzerland?—or the Adirondacks? Either would have done as well for him," she thought; but added: "No, they would not. Nothing but the Rocky Mountains will satisfy him, now that he has the journal. I can only hope that this enthusiasm will die out like the rest; only, the trip must do him good."

She took up the little red book, in which she had

The Emigrants

taken only a languid interest before, and, turning the leaves at random, fell upon bits of description that stirred her unaccountably. Now that she was about to enter this land of her father's delight, the words took on passion and power. Why should unknown rivers and endless forests and high, lonely valleys so allure a man? Where did this singular passion spring from? Was it a reversal to his pioneer grandsires?

Louis came back to her, much excited.

"Sis, there is a man in there who has a mine in New Mexico. He wants us to visit his camp when we get time. He says there's a mine in Colorado so high up that you can only bring the ore down by an 'aërial tramway.' Jupiter! but I would like to see that! I told him about the places father wrote about, and he says he knows lots of 'em."

"You are over-exciting yourself, boy," she said, severely. "Now you lie down and be quiet for a while. The bad air has started you coughing."

When she used that tone he generally obeyed, and, stretching himself out on the couch opposite her, he pretended to rest, eying her abstractedly.

Perceiving his disappointment, she asked, gently, "Was he a Colorado man?"

His tone showed a little disgust. "No; he lives in Pittsburg; but he's been all over the Rockies," he added in qualification.

"Well, never mind; you'll see Western men with stories all day to-morrow."

For a year or two this high-bred, excitable lad had been reading every obtainable book which treated of cow-boys and miners. He had read and remembered all the stories by Welland and Ridgely and Gough—

9

he knew every illustrator of the wild life, and had come to believe that the entire West swarmed with long-haired desperadoes and lonesome men in chase of splendid wild animals. "After we leave Chicago we'll meet 'em," he said. "You know father says 'the West begins at Chicago.' All this country is East," and he went to sleep early in order to be up at dawn to meet the real West.

They woke next morning in Ohio; and as they sat at breakfast, Ann, looking out on the nameless little towns whizzing backward in a blur of clanging switch-gongs, shuddered and cried out, "Think of living here!"

The boy was reflective. "Pretty slow, aren't they? But it's different on the other side of Chicago."

"Oh, of course. No one would want to come here—not even a crazy boy like you," she said, in a tone he could not quite fathom.

He was disposed to be generous, even towards Ohio. "This isn't so bad. It looks a little like Surrey; don't you think so?"

As the morning wore on, Ann settled down to her reading, refusing to look out even once upon the landscape. She ate her lunch in gloomy silence, and even the boy's spirits began to flag. "I wish this old train ran two miles a minute," he grumbled. "I want to reach the Hesperean Mountains."

"They will wait for us," replied Ann.

They arrived in Chicago behind their schedule time, and had but a few minutes in which to make their transfer, and so they saw little of the great central metropolis. To them it was only a gloomy, clangorous shed, fitted with long strings of railway coaches all marked with strange names—names that meant little to her, but which excited Louis almost to tears. "See," he cried, "there is a car from Oregon and one from Wyoming!" The people who filled the coaches were not markedly different at first glance from those she had been travelling with; but Louis, more keenly discerning, began to distinguish types at once, and when one or two big men came in wearing wide hats and chin beards, he trembled with joy. "There are some cattlemen—I'm sure of it," he whispered, hoarsely.

A crowd of laughing college girls blew in, half filling the car. Some of them were going home from school, and the others were classmates bidding them good-bye. They were very gay, very lovely, and very fervent, and Ann, looking upon them, recalled that she once looked like that. A little hush fell on the group as one of them said, with a little catch in her voice, "Girls, when will we seven meet again?"

In that hush came thoughts of courtship, marriage, death—and the first chill touch of Time's inexorable hand. They would never meet again. Two would, three might, but four or five—no—they were parting forever—some of them. Their sweet, careless faces clouded; tears sprang to their laughing eyes. For some of them womanhood and duty—that is to say, life—began at that moment. To them Ann was no longer young.

At length one of them, irrepressible of spirit, cried out, in jocular, defiant way, "Why, how solemn we all are! This is not a funeral." And then their birdlike chatter broke forth again; but it was no longer carelessly gay, it was forced, spasmodic. With kisses and tears they parted, while Ann, letting her book fall in her lap, attained a new realization that her own careless girlhood was over. "I used to feel things like that," she said to herself. "Now I neither love nor hate," and her thought of Wayne Peabody had no glow of tenderness in it.

Louis did not return to the Pullman till after the train had left the city, and she was just beginning to wonder thereat, when he came in with eyes ablaze. "I've struck 'em at last," he fairly shouted in her ear. "They're all up in the reclining-chairs. Chin-bearders, spitters, and all. I'm just crazy to sketch two or three of them. It don't pay to ride in a state-room if you want to see types," he ended, in conclusive discontent.

"You can go and ride among the 'spitters,' whatever they may be, but you can't expect me to do so."

"Of course not. But there are two men up there that are stories. One has his whiskers cut exactly like Alkali Ike—you know what I mean—to make his mustache look fierce. I'm going to tackle him later. He's just what I need to illustrate my story of the man who killed another because the other man was robbing a girl of her mine. Oh, I've got a bully scheme for a story."

Ann saw nothing more of her fellow-passengers, and not much of Louis, till next morning at breakfast. The dining service was surprisingly good, and their dainty meal was made really wonderful by contrast with the plains country through which they were rushing. Louis had been up an hour, and fairly boiled and bubbled with talk about the people in the coaches ahead. "Do you know, sis, they slept in their chairs all night. Think o' that! I didn't know they did that sort of thing, did you? I suppose they were too poor to buy berths. Don't you think so?"

"Perhaps the berths were all full."

"That's so," he replied, a little disappointed. "But we're on the edge of the cattle-country. All the talk is about cattle, and I struck one old man who lives away out in the real cattle-country. He wanted me to come out and see him."

And this was true. Every one liked him, he was so genuine, so lyric in his enthusiasms. His candid, boyish eyes glowed as he listened to their braggart praise of their own State or county; his interest had no undercurrent of distrust or ridicule in it, and young and old opened their hearts to him. He, on his part, went so far as to invite the man with the Alkali Ike mustache back to see his sister. "She'd like to know you, Mr. Barse."

The rancher shifted uneasily in his chair, and said, with instinctive delicacy: "I'm just as much obliged, youngster, but, to tell the truth, I've been on with some cattle and knockin' around Chicago for several days, and I ain't in no fit condition to meet ladies. You can't do such work as mine and not carry off some of the smell."

Louis insisted that his sister would make all allowances, but the rancher remained firm in his resolution, and so Ann missed seeing those wonderful whiskers. However, she was forced to look at prairie-dogs and owls, and once she feared Louis was going out of the window in mad pursuit of a wolf. His interest was deeply pathetic, and confirmed her in her good resolution to do whatsoever she could to make him happy.

As the day wore on the boy began to burn with a

new phase of his fever. He commenced to count the hours till he might be able to discern Mogalyon, the great peak of the Rampart Range, whose fame is world-wide. On the railway map was a point marked "First view of the peaks here." Thereafter Louis no longer scanned the plains for coyotes. He rushed from one side of the car to the other, resolute to register the exact moment when the great dome could be seen mounting above the sod, and Ann once again, for the thousandth time, wondered at the difference which lay between his temperament and hers. She was nine years older as the clock ticks, but measured in the cooling-down of her loves and hates she was more than twice his age. That she was her mother's child she knew; but she could not give up the hope that something of her beautiful, poetic father lay dormant in her somewhere.

A shrill whoop from Louis, who was hanging from the window, roused her from her deep musing. How like his father he was at that moment! His eyes were blazing, and his long, black hair, blown back by the wind, disclosed his high, pale forehead; his sweet lips were parted in an ecstatic smile.

"There she is! Just as father saw it! And there's snow on it!" he shouted, as he turned towards her. "I'm going out on the platform. There's a curve ahead, and then we can see it perfectly."

Ann experienced her first decided flush of interest as the swinging, reeling rush of the train brought the great peak into view, a dim, blue dome against the western sky. Above the strange, desolate sweep of plain he rose to a low, slate-blue cloud, and then, soaring above the vapor, appeared far in the clear, upper sky, triumphant and unassailable, his crest glittering with snow. As she peered through her field-glass her heart gave a sudden leap. "That is strange," she thought. "Why should I be so moved? Mont Blanc did not give me such a throb," and she turned again to the passionate praise of "the portals" in her father's journal.

There was no rest for Louis thereafter. He saw and tried to estimate every herd of cattle, he waved his hat in greeting to every cow-boy. He called to Ann to observe how much those herdsmen resembled the illustrations in Welland's books. His trips to the common coaches ahead lengthened, and each time he returned he seemed more heavily burdened with newly acquired information. Ann now began to long for the journey's end on his account, rather than on her own. "He is wearing himself out with the joy of it all, and will collapse if he does not rest soon," she thought, anxiously.

At last, just as the red was paling out of the sky, the train swung to the left on its southerly course, and the whole Rampart Range began to stretch and wind away to northward and southward, while between the plain and the foot - hills rolled a tawny sea of sod, deeply marked with ravines and dotted with pine-clad buttes. The whole land, magnificent in breadth and dignity, made no dramatic appeal, but expressed a colossal reserve—even the mountains seemed remote. So quietly vast was this wall of peaks it dwarfed everything which intervened, reducing towns to soundless flecks of color and streams to strips of brass. Its mystery and its essential majesty touched the poetic lad to tears, and Ann, imperturbable as she seemed, experienced a singular swelling of the throat. For the first time she acknowledged that possibly the nature-side of the West might interest her, after all.

The range grew dimmer as they gazed, and at last even Louis was content to sink back in his seat and wait.

"It isn't a bit as I expected it to be," he said; "but it is glorious. That purple-green was wonderful. I'm going to try and get that sometime. It isn't as precipitous as the Alps, but it's superb just the same; and just think how much wilder it was when father came here!"

"I'm glad you were not disappointed, boy," she replied, laying her hand on his shoulder and caressing his cheek. "But you need rest. You're seeing too much."

The train was now winding down towards Valley Springs, and only the splendid sky-line of the range could be distinguished as the lights of the town began to sparkle out of the obscure murk.

The porter, with brush in hand, came down the aisle. "This is Valley Springs, miss."

They were met at the car door by a big, smiling man in modish summer dress, while behind him stood a pale, sweet-faced woman in blue.

"Hello, Don!" shouted Louis.

"Hello, laddie! How do you do, Ann?" replied Barnett; and as Ann and her cousin embraced, the big man caught Louis by the hand. "How's your muscle, my boy? Got all your traps? Here, Tom!" he called to a colored footman, "look out for these things. Now give me a chance, Jeannette," he called, jovially, but Ann put up her hand warningly.

"Don, you forget. Respect my age."

"Age nothing—you're tasty as a peach," and he gave her a smack.

"Donnelly is the same old irrepressible," said Mrs. Barnett.

"So I see," replied Ann, dryly.

"Welcome to the West!" called Barnett, as he opened the carriage door. "The land of gold, ozone, and—"

"Brag," interrupted his wife, with an inflection which made them all laugh.

II

The Health-seekers

ANN'S entrance into the Barnett home cut her off
from all contact with life distinctly Western. She
found herself still amid the velvet and silver of the
parlor-car, and saw only remotely those who slept all
night in the cramped corners of the ordinary coaches.
Her cousins were not native; they were, indeed, only
translated Philadelphians who had gone West in search
of health—at least Mrs. Barnett was there for that reason; her husband made the change for love of his wife.

A certain percentage of the towns-people, and the
members of the special circle in which the Barnetts
moved, were health-seekers, and Ann was deeply relieved to find that all the comforts of an Eastern home
were to be enjoyed in the big, gray-stone houses on
Rampart Avenue. Indeed, the Barnetts lived quite as
they would have done in Seabright or Lenox. They
had a dozen horses, a suitable assortment of vehicles,
saddles, and bridles, and were enthusiasts concerning
polo and golf. Their neighbors and friends were un-
failingly ecstatic in praise of the climate and the views,
and seemed illogically anxious to placate the prejudices
of this haughty, pale-faced, scarlet-lipped young girl,
who looked with calm eyes upon the great peak gloom-
ing to the westward. They formed, in fact, a colony

18

of alien health-seekers, busied with pleasures, set distinctly apart from the toilers and traders of the place.

Ann was puzzled and a bit bored by their insistence on winning her admiration of the mountains, and, being naturally perverse, withheld the expressions of pleasure she might otherwise have uttered, for she was profoundly moved by what she saw. The very first day of her stay offered a titanic combat of clouds and peaks, which recalled some of the descriptions in her father's journal. The morning opened dazzlingly bright and very still, and the pitiless light seemed to search out every prosaic line and color-note in the mountains till they shrank, diminished and humbled, as if ashamed of their disfigurements. But towards mid-day a single shining, white-edged cloud appeared behind Mogalyon, clear-cut, radiant as a moon, and swiftly rose and silently shook out prodigious wings until it covered the summit with a most portentous shadow. Out of its dark folds flashed a yellow lance of lightning, and then the cloud called to its fellows, called imperiously, and they came, suddenly, like warriors from ambush, and, massing side by side, charged to and fro, hurtling over the desolate ridges in a frenzy of warfare, till their battle-vapor hid the whole majestic wall. The noise of their onset was majestic. At two o'clock the valley was darkened with the smoke of the tumult, and timorous women in the town trembled with dread. It seemed that all who dwelt below were in peril of their lives.

They were needlessly alarmed. The sturdy peaks receiving the shock remained unmoved. At four o'clock the legions of the air suddenly withdrew, and

Mogalyon's crown soared aloft unchanged save by the transcendently beautiful robe of new-fallen snow with which the storm had covered him as if in acknowledgment of his kingship. He flamed with a high lustre that humbled the proudest heart, and swept the passing plainsman into such emotion as those of old felt when the heavens opened and the walls of the celestial city appeared.

Louis' poetic soul was strung to most intense pitch by this first day's display. He scarcely ate, so eager was he to witness every stage of the struggle. The Barnett dining-room commanded a view of the mountains, and the host, observing the boy's enthusiasm, said, indulgently:

"Don't feel that you're losing anything, Louis; this comes every day regularly between 11 A.M. and 4 P.M."

"Oh, don't put it that way, Donnelly; it vulgarizes it!" cried Mrs. Barnett.

"Nothing can vulgarize that peak — not even the railway," remarked a guest.

"I never did understand that girl," said Barnett to his wife one night after a superb drive up into the great Bear Cañon. "She has everything to make her happy, and yet she goes about torpid as an oyster. What's the matter with her?"

Jeannette sighed. "That's her mother's blood. She's like her mother in a hundred ways. Louis is exactly like his father." I remember when he came back from his first and only trip to the West. I was only a child, but I recall his enthusiasm."

He was a lovable fellow, but I never could stand Alicia. She was positively stony. I have hopes of

Ann. Her hand is strong and warm—human, in fact. Don't you think her indifference a pose?

"I wish it were. No, it's genuine."

"She needs to be shaken up by a good, hot love affair. Some man will come—"

"That's what I've been saying, but the man don't come. She's twenty-six."

"How awful!"

"That's the part I don't understand about Ann. She has money, is handsome, and yet here she is quite *disengaged*—if we except her affair with Peabody, which Adney writes is quite as tepid as any of Ann's other affairs."

"Well, now, I'll tell you. She's come to the right place to have men ride up and demand attention. If she don't have at least an offer a week it will not be my fault. I'm going to invite all the young fellows home to dinner while she's here. Now watch things 'bile.'"

"You don't suppose she's going to fall in love with a mining engineer or the clerk in a bank, do you?"

"Now, that's the funny thing about us. I am all for romance, hot blood, love at first sight, and the like, while you are calculating—coldly calculating. Madam, I am shocked at your self-restraint!"

There was a certain truth in his jocular accusation. For with all her delicacy of mind and body, Jeannette Barnett was deliberate and judicial. She wanted to marry Ann off, but she did not hope for, and did not desire, a romantic marriage. However, she acquiesced in Don's hospitable and cousinly plan, and their table was filled each night with young people deftly paired off so that Ann was always seated beside some promising candidate — generally a tourist like herself, eager to discuss the differences between his idea of the West and its reality.

Barnett, nominally a mining broker, was, in fact, president of the polo club, secretary of the Sage Grass Golf Association—in short, financial nurse to every collection of amiable sports in the town. He knew all "the best fellows" in the State and now became more popular than ever. The young men accepted his dinner invitations with gratitude, and each and all paid prompt and undisguised court to "the proud Eastern beauty," as one young fellow called her. But they soon acknowledged failure. Her reserve led to a sense of injury, and was reported to be arrogance. They were seldom flattered by the slightest unbending on her part.

However, several of these young fellows turned out on acquaintance to be socially related to some of her friends in Boston and New York, and in that way won a certain acceptance which no mere civil-engineer from Omaha or professor from St. Louis could hope to attain. They were met on the conventional plane, and they got no further at any time.

Ann wrote her mother a coldly satirical description of the Springs.

"There are a few nice people here, mostly health-seekers—'one-lungers,' Louis calls them—a vulgar phrase he has picked up—but for the most part, of course, the townspeople are impossible. The Barnetts practically control the social situation, but they are altogether too catholic to please you. Don Barnett always was indiscriminate in his friends, and all manner of queer people turn up at his table. Naturally, Louis is ecstatic, and is securing a vast fund of useless information about mining and cattle and timber culture. I'm bored most of the time, but the mountains are really very grand and solemn. The cañons would be most impressive, only they swarm with tourists. The town is absurd—and pathetic. So many are trying, as I am, to interest themselves for the sake of the climate. How long I shall stay I cannot say—probably till November; all depends on Louis' health, of course. He is, at present, unwholesomely excited. Every long-haired, broad-hatted man he sees is a story to him, poor boy, and he is on the trot every hour of the day."

To Wayne Peabody she wrote:

"It is a strange thing, but I feel as if I were on an island out here—a social island—with two thousand miles of arid nothingness rolling between New York and our little group. What do you suppose all those millions on the prairie think about? What are their ambitions? I never even considered them before, but being on this side of them has brought them nearer to me. What is the good of all these cheap little men and women?"

Meanwhile she was really troubled about Louis. He was eating less and less each day, and his sleep was broken, and at the end of the first week fell in a state of collapse. The excitement, the late hours, the contact with new types, and, above all, the attempt to understand the country and his relationship with it had worn him out. Then Ann said, in her decisive way: "I don't believe this altitude is good for Louis. I think I will take him home again."

"Oh, don't do that. It isn't the altitude; it's the social whirl. Send him down to my ranch. It's a hole of a place, but it's just what he needs. Nothing to see but coyotes and cow-boys. We'll put him under Rob Raymond's wing. Rob's my foreman, and a good chap; he'll take to the boy like anything. I'm sure of it."

Louis sat up with a jerk when told of this plan to send him among real cow-boys—he had only seen one or two thus far, and they were galloping out of town—and was all for starting at once, but Ann was firm. "You stay quietly in bed for a few days and get rested, and then we will see."

As soon as he was able to ride down-town the boy began again to mix with the ranchers on the street, and to strike hands with every "character" he discovered. He came home to lunch each day full of talk of some picturesque miner or hairy cattle-man whom he had met on the corner, and whose heart had been opened to him. His room began to fill with specimens of ore, and his keen and relentless memory acquired a still more wonderful collection of phrases and scraps of what seemed to him useful information. He began to plead for his visit to the ranch.

"Everybody cottons to the lad," said Barnett to his wife. "He tackled old man Sandefer to-day and had him telling the story of his life before he knew what he was about. He'd make a wonderful broker; he could sell stock, even the stock of the Red Star," which was his own mine.

"He's very lovable," replied she, "but he is terribly intense. He will wear himself out, just like his father."

"Oh no; he'll begin to harden up pretty soon. Besides, he's bound to lose interest finally."

"That would be a pity. His enthusiasm's are beautiful to me. When do we go to the ranch?"

The Health-seekers

The plan as worked out by Barnett involved a trip on his automobile for the four of them; but he delayed too long. Mrs. Barnett entered upon one of her "poor spells," and Donnelly, faithful as a big dog, promptly told Louis to go ahead and not wait for the party. "I must stay and nurse Jeannette."

Ann was afraid to let Louis go alone, but Barnett pooh-poohed her. "He'll get on all right; in fact, he'll rejoice to be free of us for a day or two. I'll wire the mail-carrier to meet him and take him down, and I'll send a letter to Raymond to look out for him. He'll be more than safe; he'll be happy, and he won't miss us in the least."

Ann insisted on going down herself. "I want to see him properly settled," she said.

"It's a dreary ride," murmured Mrs. Barnett from the bed where she lay, weak and wan, "but you are so strong—you can do anything; perhaps you'll enjoy it It will be a new experience for you as well as for Louis."

Barnett slyly winked at his wife. He really wanted to see Ann "jarred." "It 'll do her good to rough it a little," he said, privately. Thereupon, Louis, trembling with eagerness, began to "rustle his outfit." He bought a pistol, a rifle, and a broad-rimmed hat. He rolled some blankets and tied them, under the instruction of the hostler, who was experienced in such manner of life. He also purchased the most highly ornamental cattle-man's saddle in the Springs, and glowingly explained to Ann what each string and strap was called and what its services were.

"What a child you are!" she exclaimed, as she watched him, her eyes warming with love and pride. "You're a dear boy!" she added, as he came to her side.

He looked up at her tenderly. "You're good to me, Hesper," he said, fervently.

"Sh! don't ever call me by that absurd name."

"It isn't absurd. I like it," he said.

Barnett, seated at his telephone, made every arrangement for them. "You'll be met by old Jones, and when you get there Mrs. Jones will look after you. She's a very good cook, so don't get nervous when you see her. She's not pretty. Raymond will do his best to entertain you, and when you come back you'd better ask Raymond to put his own horses in the cart and drive you out—he'll be better company than Jones."

As the train drew out from the depot and began to climb the hill, Louis stood on the rear platform and swung his cap at Barnett and the coachman; and both made reply, for the boy was on good terms with master and man.

Ann, again in the Pullman coach, looked out on the tawny landscape and said, "I wish we were on our way home."

Louis looked up with scared eyes. "You don't mean that, sis. Why, I'm just beginning to see things."

III

Raymond of the Goldfish Ranch

BARNETT'S ranch, one of his chief amusements, lay at the head of a valley surrounding a spring which was the source of Wild Cat Creek. The buildings stood just where the ravine opened out upon a grassy meadow. It was a comfortable place, shielded from the desert winds by the low hills to the north, while a small, artificial pond, gravelled and rimmed with cottonwoods and willows, gave it enviable distinction among the bleak and barren farmsteads. It seemed a very beautiful spot to those who dwelt on the unrelieved plain, for the pond overflowing upon the bog kept it green perennially; and the house, though built of cottonwood logs, was unusually large and well-kept. In brief, it was a show place—a shady spot to which lovers drove on a Sunday as to a bower. It was known as the "Goldfish Ranch," for the reason that at one time Barnett had filled the pond with ornamental fish.

At about five o'clock of a hot and windless July day, a horseman galloped swiftly up the valley into the yard, and was met at the door of the house by a tall, composed young fellow in broad hat and spurs.

"Hello, Perry!" he said, quietly. "You made good time."

Perry, a young Mexican, showed a score of his white

27

teeth in a grin. "Here is letter. Some people coming to rancho to-night."

The young man tore the end from the long envelope, and read the letter in silence. His face darkened. "Well, that's a nice case o' beans. So they're on the road, are they?"

"Yes; 'bout fo' miles back."

The young foreman turned towards the house, from which the faint strains of "Annie Laurie" came. A plump, light-haired young fellow of about thirty sat tilted back in his chair, with one leg thrown across the corner of the table, playing a mouth-organ. His eyes were closed in a musical ecstasy, and his hands, modulating the tone of the instrument, were just opening into a quavering crescendo when the man with the letter slammed it on the table with such force that the player started to his feet.

"Hello, Rob! I didn't hear you come in."

Raymond was in bad humor. "Put up your plaything, you monkey, and listen to me a moment."

The musician wiped his instrument with his neckerchief while studying his foreman's face.

"What's up?"

Raymond pointed at the letter. "Read that. Nice thing the old man works on us." His indignation and disgust deepened into a growl. "This settles it. I'm going to pull out."

The other man composedly took up the letter. "What's he done now?"

"Going to quarter a crazy kid on us, a New York degenerate, who'll be a confounded nuisance every hour of the day; and that isn't all—the kid's sister is coming down to stay a few days." Here his

28

dismay was fairly comical. "'To get the lad settled.'"

Baker's eyes widened and his fat face lengthened. "Not comin' to-day?"

"That's what!"

"And us without no woman 'round."

Raymond broke forth again: "That's it, now. You'd suppose Barnett would at least read my letters. I told him last week that old Jonesy and his wife were going up to Sky-Town," He turned to the Mexican, who still stood in the door, broadly grinning: "How far behind did you say they were?"

"'Bout fo' miles."

"Well, we're in for it. We can't turn a woman out on the plain. Jack, you slovenly whelp, set to work and clean up the mess you've made. Perry, go rope some snags for a fire. Hustle now!"

Baker opened the letter. "What kind of a girl do you reckon—"

"It don't matter. Any kind is a nuisance just now. She's more than likely to be one of Barnett's Eastern relatives who think we're all half-brothers to red Injuns out here."

Baker began to read the letter aloud in a monotonous, painful way, while Raymond moved about the room picking up the litter.

"'My dear Rob,—I'm sending you a new hand and a visitor—'"

"Thinks I'm running a summer resort," Raymond interrupted, bitterly.

"'They are cousins, and nice people. The lad is not very strong, and I'm sending him down to you to get an upward turn.'"

Raymond turned. "See! You thought we were running a cattle-ranch; but we're not—it's a sanitarium."

Baker went on, calmly, "'He's crazy on the subject of wild animals and cow-boys—'"

"Don't you see the meaning of that?" sneered Raymond. "We're a holy show—a 'Wild West' to these people."

"'And is a very clever artist. He'll want to have you pose for him.'"

Raymond came over and seized the stove-lid lifter as if to break Baker's head. "We're to cook and purvey like boarding-house keepers, and doctor like a nurse at a health resort, and in addition we're to pose for a delicate youth who thinks we're 'material.' That settles me. I'm going up to Sky and take a shy at mining." Baker listened with a fat smile, which exasperated his boss to danger-point. "Grin, you jack-rabbit. If your chin made a little more noise, you'd keep yourself company."

Baker broke forth into a slow drawl: "Hadn't you better strike a few attitudes so's to be in practice when the boy comes?"

Raymond throttled him half in earnest. "I've a mind to wring your neck," he said, through his teeth. Then, suddenly releasing him, he again commanded him to clear away his dishes.

Baker was not yet finished with the letter. "Hold on. Don't be in a rush. I hain't got to the girl yet—that's what interests me. 'Miss Rupert will only stay a few days to get the lad settled.'"

"She can't stay too quick to suit me."

Baker's voice took on a little more expression as he read Barnett's appeal. "'Now, don't be cranky, old

man; the Ruperts are good stuff, and on Mrs. Barnett's
account—'"

"Ends up by laying me under obligation to his wife,
knowing mighty well I'd do anything for her. Well,
I'll do it, but I reckon the atmosphere won't bake a
cake while she's here. I'll leave you and Dutch to
do the talking; that 'll chill her cold."

Baker began to show alarm. "Not by a hatful.
Right here is where I take a sneak."

Raymond's brow darkened and his eyes threatened.
"No you don't, my Christian friend and neighbor; you
remain right here and do the honors. You will pass
for the boss. I've got to cook."

"Great Peter! you mustn't do that! I can't carry it
through. I'm no spieler."

"Play the mouth-organ for her."

"Oh, see here, you're joshin'."

"You won't find it any 'josh.' You've been getting
gay with me lately and need discipline. You pass for
the foreman—understand? You amuse the girl and
pose for the boy, while I knock pots; that is settled.
Now take the pail and rustle some water, and don't you
peep."

Perry, entering at the door with an armful of brush,
called out, with quiet joy, "The señora has come."

Raymond seized him by the arm. "Listen here,
Perry. The old man has written down to say that
he has made Jack the boss. I'm going to cook a few
days, and then I leave. You tell the other boys that
Jack Baker is made foreman, and they've got to obey
him—you sabbe?"

Perry grew solemn of face. "I sabbe. If you go,
I go."

"Never mind that. Get out there and help take care of the team; and, Jack, you go too—" He laid a hand on his back and pushed him through the doorway, just as the two-seated hack rounded the corral and drew up to the door.

"Oh, isn't this fine!" called a clear, boyish voice, and a moment later the cool, deliberate voice of a girl replied:

"Oh, what a blessed relief, after the hot sun of the plain!"

Then Baker was heard to say, with elaborate courtesy: "Shall I help you out, miss? I reckon you are the friends of the old man—I mean Barnett?" And a moment later the young girl stood in the doorway looking out at the plain. Raymond gave her but one glance from the corner of his eyes, but her firm, well-balanced body and calm, high-bred face touched him with admiration. His resolution to be disagreeable weakened, though he kept about his work. There was no mistaking the modishness of her skirt and hat. She was Parisian from crown to toe, and perfectly cool and sweet, in spite of her long and dusty ride.

"I never knew how grateful the shade of a tree could be," Ann said, partly to Louis and partly to Baker. "The prophet must have had such a country in mind when he spoke of 'the shadow of a great rock in a weary land.'"

"I'm a little weak on poetry, miss," remarked Baker, hesitatingly, "but I know something about the way the sun wallops a man between here and Wallace. But lay off your things—ma-make yourself to home." He was twisting his hat into ruin in his agitation.

Ann began to draw off her gloves. "Is it always so fiercely bright here?"

"Oh no, this is an unusual spell. I mean it is rather—"

She was now aware of Raymond moving sullenly about in the gloom wherein the stove sat. He was dressed in a light-tan, loosely fitting shirt, and brown trousers without braces. His spurs rattled at his heels as he walked to and fro, lithe and powerful. He did not look up—did not appear to notice what was going on, but came and went at his work, deft and absorbed.

Louis was instantly delighted with the room. "Isn't this ripping!" he exclaimed, as he studied its furnishings. "Won't this make a strong background for an illustration? Only that stove—isn't it too bad?—that's all out of key. Why don't you have a fireplace, Mr. Raymond?" he asked, turning to Baker.

Raymond gave Baker a glance, and the plump one waded in: "Too little wood in this country. Cook, draw up a chair for the lady."

Raymond's eyes flashed with a silent menace, but he did as he was told, and, as he put the chair down for Ann, he dusted it with his hat.

Louis was husky-voiced with joy. "Did you see that, Ann? I'll have to work that in somewhere."

Baker continued, in the same tone, "Can't you rustle a little grub for the company, Jack?"

Raymond curtly replied, "I'll try hard."

Baker, who was gaining self-control, turned to Ann. "We have to humor our cooks out here. They're scarce and mighty uncertain in their minds—stop and shy at nothin', like a locoed steer."

Louis clapped his hands. "Oh, isn't the talk good, Ann? And these chairs—aren't they fine?"

"Cook made 'em," said Baker. "He's handy as a bootjack with tools."

Ann ignored the chairs, but studied the cook, whose curiously absorbed, sullen, yet deft movements interested her. He appeared to be about thirty years of age, and his lean, powerful figure dignified the rough and dust-stained clothes he wore. His profile was stern and manly, but his chin was youthful. His eyes she had not yet seen.

Raymond, on his part, was fairly abashed by the grace and youthful charm of his visitor. She reminded him, as she stood there calmly looking about the grimy walls, of the stories he had read of princesses visiting the huts of their peasantry. She was of good height, but the proud lift of her head made her seem taller than she was, and the cut of her gown, the color of her gloves and hat, told of good taste and the service of the best tailors and milliners. "Great Scot!" he said to himself, "she's an up-to-date beauty. What will I do to feed her?" And, imperturbable as he looked, his heart sank within him, and if he could have fled honorably he would have done so instantly; but as this was out of the question, he screwed his brows into a still more savage frown and bent to his task.

Ann was not at her ease for other reasons. Ordinarily the only color in her rather impassive face lay in the vivid scarlet of her lips and the deep gray of her eyes, but the dry wind, playing upon her delicate skin, had filled it with a sense of heat. She believed herself to be scorched to the color of a brick, when, in fact, she was radiant with the most delicate pink. With a

34

sense of appearing ill she was as dazzling as the bride in the songs of Solomon, and the young ranchers were awed and humbled. They wanted to go away and exclaim over their wonderful good-fortune. Baker feared to look at her—could not think of anything to say. For a time Louis alone broke the silence. At length Ann turned. "I never was so tired in my life, and my face is burned to a crisp. That wind has fairly stiffened my lips."

Louis looked at the backs of his hands. "I like it. A few days here will give me a dandy burn. It's just the thing I need. I want to be brown like these men."

Raymond took no pains to be noiseless or dainty in his work; but every movement told. He sloshed out the coffee-pot and sliced the bacon and stirred up the fire, all with a grace and quiet dignity which opened Ann's eyes in an effort to understand him. His hands were noticeably fine, and the poise of his head expressed strength and pride. He was very brown, almost as brown as the leather cuffs he wore on his arms.

Once, when he passed out of hearing, she turned to Baker suddenly and asked: "Why does your cook wear spurs? An affectation, I suppose."

Baker flushed and stammered. "Well, no; he has to help with the cattle once in a while."

Raymond called to Perry, who was seated on the doorstep. "Perry, jump your horse and round up a dry cottonwood snag; this brush is of no sort of use. I want a hot fire."

Louis beamed at Ann. "He's talking just like Walter Owen's heroes."

Ann silenced him. "Hush! He'll hear you."

Baker, quite ready to take a fall out of Raymond,

interposed: "He's a little hard at first, but reel sociable when you git him started. But he's shy as a rabbit when they's any company round."

Raymond uttered a cough which made Baker start. "I guess I'll go out and see what that driver has done with his horses."

Louis sprang up. "I'll go, too, if you don't mind, sis."

Ann sat with closed lids, resting her aching senses. The ride, after the first moment of exultant joy of the immeasurable tawny plain and the far, translucent-blue mountains, had been an utter weariness. She had stepped from the parlor-car into a rusty, little, two-seated wagon, and almost before she could realize it had been shot into the midst of a wide, empty, expressionless land—a land of jack-rabbits and rattle-snakes, of barbed and bitter weeds, miserable cabins, and wire fences—a land whose grass was scant, hot, and brittle as hair, whose springs were few—a land without a tree or a stream, a desert on which the horned toad and the prairie-dog alone seemed cheerful and at peace.

Her first fleeting interest in the strange blooms and plants, in the delicate color and wonderful lines of the hills, gave way to a sinking of the heart, a deep dismay, as she penetrated farther and farther into this flaming desert. The unkempt men, the slattern women, the desolate huts, the bones of cattle—these had at last filled her thought to the exclusion of the glories which Louis was continually discovering. Only when she looked away to the pink-gray and purple domes of the Rampart Range had she been able to find relief from the endless, gray monotony.

Raymond of the Goldfish Ranch

The lad, however, had taken note of everything. He saw every jack-rabbit, every bird. He discovered innumerable little lizards fleeing before the horses' hoofs in the dust. He made the driver wait while he caught a horned toad, and once he killed a rattlesnake. He was wild with delight at the intelligence of a jack-rabbit, which kept under the wire fence in order to escape the swoop of a hawk.

It had been to Ann not merely an entrance into the life of the common coach; it had been a sudden plunge into the smoking-car, where ranchers, negroes, Chinamen, Mexicans, and dowdy and unlovely women sat discussing the price of cattle and the hay-crop.

As she looked round the low-ceiled room, in which the flies buzzed, her eyes fell upon a little case of books in the corner. For lack of something better to do, she rose to inspect them. She was surprised to find them mainly essays, and wondered who of these men read Emerson and Burroughs. One of them was a book of verse. Raymond's name was on the fly-leaf.

"How handsome the cook is!" was her inward exclamation as she returned to her seat. She was not one of those who sit in silence when they wish information, and, lifting her voice a little, she said:

"I understood Mr. Barnett to say that you had a woman to cook for you?"

Raymond shifted a stove-lid. "We did."

"Where is she?"

"Gone—a week ago."

"Isn't there *any* woman about the place?"

He peered into the coffee-pot. "No one but you."

Ann sat in silence for a moment. "I don't understand. Mr. Barnett said—"

Raymond straightened and looked at her sombrely. "If Barnett paid a little more attention to his ranch and less to polo— I wrote him, more than a week ago, that Jonesy was pullin' his freight." He returned to his cooking.

Ann composedly went on, "Was Jones the name of the foreman?"

"No, he was assistant; but he was married, and his wife was our dough-twister. He's gone to Sky-Town gold camp. The whole country is full o' the fever."

Ann began to feel that she was a little in the way. "I'm sorry to trouble you. If I had known, of course, I shouldn't have come down. In fact, if I had realized how desolate it is, I would not have permitted Louis to come. May I take off my hat?"

Raymond turned quickly. "I beg your pardon—I didn't observe—why, sure thing!" He wiped his hands on a rod-towel and came forward. "Let me hang it up for you. Mebbe you'd like to go in the other room and lie down. I'm hustling some grub as fast as I can, and afterwards"—he looked about at the bunks— "we'll fix a place for you."

Ann smiled sweetly. "Oh, don't trouble; I'll be glad to sit here. I am feeling better already." To herself she said, "He has nice eyes." Turning towards him, she quietly said: "You must not bother about me. Can't I help you? I can cook a little. I once went to cooking-school. Won't you let me try?"

Raymond looked at her delicately colored hands and fleckless linen. "No, thank you; you'd get yourself all tangled up with soot and bacon grease. Besides, it's about ready—what there is of it—and 'nough of it, such as 'tis, as the fello' says."

Ann, with a note of sympathy in her voice, said: "I don't like to see a big, strong man cook. Do you get extra pay for it?"

"Not a cent. We all take turns at it, to tell the honest truth."

"I hope you're the best cook?"

"That wouldn't be saying much, lady. I cook in self-defence."

Ann opened her eyes at the significance of this phrase. "Then you don't do it as a—a business."

"Not by a whole row o' steers. Do you like prunes and rice?" he asked, hastily.

Ann looked into the dish which he held out towards her and gravely replied: "I don't think I ever ate any. You don't mean they're cooked together?"

"That's what. It sure makes a filling combination," said he, dishing some out before her.

"I can well believe it," she replied, with a humorous intonation. "Let me taste it; perhaps I'll like it." As she nibbled a little of the mess from the spoon, she glanced up at him with a queer little smile that made the room whirl before his eyes. "It seems a nutritious mixture."

He recovered himself. "Oh, it's a hearty mess, all right. If you're on the lookout for experiences, you'll get 'em this trip. We're more than half-Injun here, especially since Mrs. Jones pulled out. Anything that will sustain life goes. My cooking isn't fancy—"

"I beg your pardon," Ann hastened to explain, "I didn't mean to criticise. I didn't intend to hurt your feelings. I'm sure it's a very tasty dish."

"Oh, I don't blame you; but, you see, we're not

39

running a summer hotel exactly; still, we'll make you as comfortable as we can while you stay—"

"By which you mean to hint you hope I won't stay long." She was frankly amused.

He became very sincerely grave. "I didn't say that, lady."

"But you meant it."

Raymond scorned to lie. "Well, sit up and do the best you can. The grub isn't as tough as it looks. This coffee I buy myself. We aren't in anywise fitted to cater to delicate appetites, but, as I say, our intentions are of the best."

Ann took her seat, filled with singular enjoyment of the cook's embarrassment. "No one ever accused me of having a delicate appetite. It isn't fashionable in these days of golf and tennis."

Raymond shifted a bowl of sugar her way. "Sorry we have no cut-loaf. Where's the invalid?"

"Do you mean my brother?"

"Yes."

"He's not an invalid. He's only a strenuous youngster who needs a change of air."

"He'll get it." Going to the door, Raymond raised a loud, shrill, quavering call. As he stood on the threshold waiting an answer, his eyes again sought the charming figure at the table, and his blood awoke. He became aware, even through the mist of his resentment and embarrassment, of his amazing good-luck. Ann's eyes being demurely fixed upon her plate, he had opportunity to absorb every detail of her vigorous, well-rounded figure, her dainty yet serviceable clothing, and the graceful and womanly poise of her head. When he spoke again his voice had softened, and Ann—experienced in the ways of men—well understood his change of heart.

He coughed a little as he weakly began his apology: "As I say, we're not keeping summer boarders, but I'll make you as comfortable as possible, and I hope you'll stay as long as you feel like—I mean as long as you think necessary."

Ann turned a dangerously sweet and winning look upon him. "Thank you. I'm not obtuse. I know when I am out of place. I shall flee to-morrow."

She was forcing his hand, as he well knew, but he remained gravely simple. "I'll be sorry if our grub, or anything else, should scare you out."

"Oh, it isn't that. But I don't like to be a burden to any one."

"Did any one say you were a burden?"

"No, but you looked it."

Raymond set his back against the wall and, with a quizzical light in his eyes, replied, "I didn't know you so well when I took that attitude."

"You mean you didn't know how vigorous my appetite was?" She changed the subject quickly. "I can see that Louis is to be perfectly happy down here. I am glad I came. I shall feel much more resigned to his being here, now that I have met Mr. Raymond and you."

Raymond remained inexpressive. "Your brother is an enthusiast, I believe you said. He'll be more charitable than—than you, for instance."

Ann didn't like his emphasis. "I don't wonder at your resentment. Our coming is an imposition, but if I had known— Please be kind enough to admit that I didn't know how you were situated."

41

Raymond resumed his cow-boy manner. "Now, lady, you let that go. I don't blame you a hair. You're here, and I'll see—I mean, the boss will see—we'll all see—that the boy is treated right, and I'll guarantee that he gets a fair share of what's going. I'm not apologizing, but I hope you won't take us on the wrong slant. I hope you'll come often—you brighten up the place wonderfully."

Ann drew herself up. "I don't understand you, Mr.—"

"Call me cook—Mr. Cook; anything goes out here."

They were now squared before each other, he with a malicious smile lurking at the corner of his mouth, she with dark and puzzled brow.

"Of course, you cow-boys are all strange to me—I mean your manners and customs—but my room-mate at college told me a good deal about this life. She was from Colorado."

He betrayed new interest. "What was your college—Smith?"

Ann lifted her eyebrows in surprise. "No. What made you think it was?"

Raymond began to retreat. "Oh, I don't know; you seemed about that style. I mean to say, you carry yourself like a Smith College girl that came down here once with Mrs. Barnett." He caught up the water-bucket. "Excuse me a minute; I'll run down to the spring and get some water." His going was equivalent to flight.

Ann smiled composedly as she sipped her coffee, which was very good indeed.

Louis burst in at the door. "Sis, you ought to see

the corrals out here. They have ninety head of horses —think of that! And I'm to ride all I want to."

Baker, who appeared just behind him, put in a drawling word: " 'Peared like he wanted to ride four to once, like a circus-man. Are you gettin' somethin' to eat, miss?"

"Oh yes, indeed."

Louis, throwing down his cap in imitation of Raymond, cried out, "I'm hungry."

Ann turned to Baker. "Mr. Foreman, isn't there something mysterious about your cook? Part of the time he speaks like a man of the world and part of the time like a rancher. I think he's playing a part, and playing it badly."

"What makes you think so?" asked Louis. "They say he's a bully rider."

"They ain't none better, miss," replied Baker, who began to look a little uneasy.

Ann pursued her point. "I think he's one of those romantic cow-boys who have seen better days—perhaps an English nobleman in disguise."

Baker was always ready when a chance to get even with Raymond offered itself. He puckered his plump face into a frown of deep concern. "I guess you're some right, miss; but he ain't no English lord, I don't think. We never inquire very close into a man's pedigree out here if he can ride a cayuse and flip a gun; but he's American, all right, and a good cook."

"Is Cook his real name?"

Baker became cautious. "Did he say his name was Cook? If he did, that goes. I'm not in the habit of disputing him."

"No, he didn't tell his name, but he intimated that

43

I might call him Cook. Your name is Raymond, isn't it?"

Baker was again slow to answer. "Did he intimate that my name was Raymond?"

"No, but Mr. Barnett said the foreman's name was Raymond, and you're the foreman, aren't you?"

Baker seemed resigned. "We'll let it go at that. We don't mind little things out here, miss. Never go behind the returns anywhere in this Western country."

Ann, after looking at him in silence, remarked, gravely, "Of course, you're both having fun with us, because we're from the East, and I don't think it quite nice in you."

Baker began to look distressed. "Oh, see here, miss, you mustn't think— You're all wrong! Why, we're delighted—we—you see—"

Ann turned to Louis. "Louis, you are living out one of Owen's stories this very minute. I want you to stay here until you can meet these people on their own ground." She faced Baker again. "Tell me more about this cook. He's a college man, and there's some hidden mystery—as the story-books say. What brought him to this pass? Is he a fugitive from justice?"

Baker took a seat and appeared to ponder. "Well, now, I don't like to say. You see, it ain't safe to tell tales on Cook. If you'll swear not to breathe a word—"

"Hold up your hands, Louis, and swear!" cried Ann. "Of course, we won't tell."

Baker settled into his chair. "You mustn't blame him till you hear the hull story, but he killed a feller back East, somewhere in Illinois."

Ann started melodramatically. "Really?"

Baker, pleased with his success, added, "Two of 'em, in fact."

Louis, wide-eyed with interest, "What did he do it for?"

Baker, glowing with pleasure in the work of his own imagination, cut loose from his moorings. "It was this way. He was courting a girl—the daughter of a rich farmer—and her family was hot because Rob was poor, and her dad put another feller on to tell lies about Rob's drinkin' and all that, and Rob met up with this feller and just naturally piped him full of soft-nose bullets; that led him to seek higher altitudes, as the newspapers say. Now that's the plain truth of the whole business, as I heard it."

Ann pretended to shudder. "He doesn't look like that sort of desperado."

"He don't now, does he? But that's the way it goes. Couldn't meet a peaceabler man when he's sober. Set here and read them books all day long; but you let him get red-headed once, and *whisp*, out comes his gun, and then everybody hunts a hole, I tell you."

Louis pursued the inquiry, "Who was the other man he killed?"

"The deppity-sherf. Had to do *that* to get away."

Ann looked about. "You say he reads these books?"

"When he has time—he dotes on 'em."

"Do you read them?"

"Great Scot, no! I'd go to sleep over such things. *The Boy's Own* is about my size."

Ann's tone was reflective. "That's queer. Mr. Barnett said you were a great reader."

Baker paled, then got red. He had walked into a

clever little trap. He wriggled in his chair. "Did he say that? Well—I—I used to, but lately—"

Ann looked at him keenly and said, calmly: "You also are an impostor. Your name isn't Raymond— you're not the foreman. You are all bandits and have stolen my cousin's ranch, and are running it to suit yourselves. I believe you killed poor old Mr. Jones and his wife."

Louis sprang to his feet. "Ann, what do you mean?"

Baker threw up both hands. "Hold on! Don't shoot. I'll come down. I knew I couldn't keep the game going." He rose, and his manner changed. "Now listen. I'll tell you the square-toed truth. It was my turn to cook, and Raymond—that's our boss— when he heard you was comin', knowin' I couldn't cook sour-bran mash, says: 'Baker, you'll have to play boss while the company's here. I've got to toss up the ba- con and prunes. Now that's the God's fact, lady."

Ann, with conviction, turned to Louis: "Now I be- lieve he's telling the truth. What *is* your name?"

"John Edwin Baker — Jack, the boys call me. I never had any other name, I'm sorry to say, and I came here from Kansas. I never killed anything bigger 'n a coyote. I'm just a plain cow-puncher at twenty-six per month."

Ann was deeply moved by this honesty. "Won- derful!"

"Furthermore, I don't want to kill anybody," ex- claimed Baker.

"Louis, this is your opportunity. Do a picture of a good, honest, sober cow-boy and send it to *Puck*." She turned to Jack. "Thank you very much, Mr. Baker. I think I understand the situation now."

Louis looked relieved, for Baker had not appealed to him very strongly. He was fat, and a fat cow-boy seemed out of conformity with all his preconceived notions.

Raymond, reappearing at the door, put them all into guilty confusion. His eyes were too keen to be withstood, and Ann's lashes fell for a moment as he offered the dipper. "Like a cool drink, lady?"

She recovered herself instantly. "Thank you, if you will be so kind."

Raymond threw a glance at Baker that propelled him through the doorway as palpably as a kick, then turned to Louis. "How does the grub go, youngster?"

"Bully!" replied the boy, as he took up a spoonful of rice. His eyes followed the lithe figure of the rancher with joy.

Raymond abruptly inquired, "What are you squintin' at me for, boy?"

"I'm going to draw you."

"Well, draw me purty, or there'll be war."

"My, but you're built for a rider! Can you throw a lariat?"

"We call it a rope out here. Yes, I can do a trick or two with it; but our days of roping cattle are just about done with."

Ann cut in with a grave face, belied by something in her voice. "I didn't suppose a foreman would stoop to cook."

The young fellow frowned. "What's that?"

Ann went on, "I think it's nice of you, Mr. Raymond, to abase yourself to the rim of a kettle."

"Excuse me, lady, but —" He looked about for Baker.

47

Ann interposed: "That's twice you've called me 'lady.' No real cow-boy ever does that, I'm told, so you must be an impostor."

Raymond's face flushed with anger. "See here! What has that fat jackass been saying to you about me?"

Ann, calmly smiling, made her charges specific. "You're not the cook. You're called Robert Raymond. You're the foreman and a graduate of Harvard University, like all superior cow-boys, and you have gallantly volunteered to cook, in order that we might eat. Now, isn't this true?"

Raymond was stunned for a moment, but as she went on his head lifted and into his eyes leaped a spark of red light. "Wait till I sight that scoundrel. You'll have a fine chance to study a cow-boy in action. What else did he say?"

Louis was becoming alarmed. "Don't tell, Ann; he'll hurt him."

Raymond turned to Louis. "Now I *know* he needs killing. Did he tell you I had a private graveyard, and that I had a stage name?"

"Oh yes," replied Ann, sweetly. "He told us all about your fight with your rival. It was very thrilling. It's like being a character in a novel one's self. I'm quite exalted by the thought."

Raymond's eyes ceased to glower, a faint smile quivered at the corners of his lips as he bowed gracefully. "Miss Rupert, permit me to astonish you still more. My name, though alliterative, is my own. I have never killed a man"—he looked towards the door—"that incredible ass will be my first. I am not a graduate of Harvard, and I did not leave my native town between two days. Does this disappoint you?"

"Most deeply. Are there no mitigating circumstances?"

"None whatever. I am hopelessly commonplace. I'm not even a cow-boy. I'm foreman of a hay-ranch."

"You destroy our dreams. But these books are yours?"

Raymond's eyes wavered. "Well, yes — some of them; but I don't care to pose as the student-rancher. The boys respect me now because I can ride a horse and pitch hay. I make it a point not to air my other accomplishments—"

He was interrupted by a series of faint yells, and as they all listened the swift trample of horses' hoofs could be heard. Louis sprang up, all excitement, his eyes glowing.

"What is that—Indians?"

Raymond smiled at Ann. "No, only a bunch of cow-boys passing." He stepped to the door to study their approach. "It's a mob of Williams's men. I don't know what they're doing here." The rush and trample of hoofs swept nearer, and a group of five drab-colored horsemen drew up at the hitching-pole with loud outcries, each man setting his pony on end with a wrench at the reins.

"Hello, Bob!" shouted the leader.

"Howdy, boys—howdy?" he replied, coldly. It was plain he was not well pleased by their inopportune call.

"Got anything to eat?" asked one of them, as he swaggered up.

"Sure thing. Tidy up and come in." Raymond, turning to Ann, said, gently, "Perhaps you and the boy had better step into the other room; this gang is coming in."

"They're not dangerous?"

"No, but some of them are not fit to eat in the presence of a lady."

"Louis will want to see your guests."

"Very well," replied Raymond, and turned to meet his visitors, who appeared fresh from a hasty toilet. "Come right in, boys. What's the best word from over the ridge?"

The man who entered first was a big, raw-boned, wide-mouthed, freckle-faced fellow, who gaped in amazement as he caught sight of Ann. "Hello, what's all this?" he asked, hunching the man next him.

The insolent vulgarity of his tone brought a flush of anger to Raymond's face. "Shut up!" he commanded, in a low voice. Then added, in explanation, "Some of Barnett's folks visiting the ranch." At the moment he hated them all with a sudden realization of their essential cheapness and their filthy manners.

As they took seats each man glanced at Ann with furtive, devouring eyes, and she thrilled under the scrutiny as she would have done beneath the glare of a wolf. She had a sudden sense of danger. "I am getting close to the elemental man," she thought, and by contrast Raymond assumed new interest. Though his clothing was almost as rough as theirs, his face and voice betrayed good blood and refinement. She wondered whether Wayne Peabody could stand between such a mob of ruffians and a woman. This man Raymond dominated them easily. She imagined them worse than they were, for they were only a group of mongrel, misbegotten types, ludicrously egotistic, jealous of their reputations, and careless of the rights of others. Each fellow talked boisterously, in order to show that he was as good as anybody else.

Louis sat as one entranced, studying the groupings in the sunset light, which had begun to dim a little. To him these men were heroic. Their physical hardihood, their slouching grace, their rumpled hair, their tag-ends of kerchiefs, and greasy belts and cuffs were all "bang-up material." The avid glare under which Ann shivered was hidden from the eyes of the boy; but Raymond took note of every nudge, every wink that passed, and once or twice he fixed his eyes on the man they called Speckle in a look which stayed a coarse jest upon his lawless lips.

They talked of the great, new mining-camp on the side of Mogalyon, whereto they were all bound. "They're strikin' it rich in the grass-roots, and we're going up to take a hand in it. Why, last week they made three strikes on Pine Mountain within fifteen feet of the surface. They say the placer is turning out ten dollars a day. So we're riding up to turn a rock on our own account. The cattle business is done for. Gold-chasing is the game now."

"Say, Raymond," called out a little man down by the stove, "you'd better hustle out your gang and meet that fire; it's comin' right over the ridge this way, and is getting worse every minute."

Raymond's face betrayed keen interest. "I've been trying to locate that fire all day. It's over about Round Top, isn't it?"

"Oh no. It's away this side. Look's like it's sure

to take Williams's hay, if he don't watch out, and yours, too."

"Why didn't you ride over and see just where it was?" asked Raymond.

"Too busy," Speckle replied, loudly, and the others laughed. "I'm after gold now. I'm sick o' forkin' hay."

Raymond's voice grew sterner. "You didn't leave Williams short-handed to fight that fire?"

"No matter whether we did or not; we've got done. Our time was up; we've got our pay. He can fight his own fire; we're not responsible." They all laughed as though this were a good joke.

Raymond's next words were as cold and calm as they were unexpected. "You get up and get out o' here, every man of you. I mean *now*." His anger broke out as they stared. "I don't feed men who leave a rancher short-handed with a fire rampin' down on him." He rose and stood beside the door.

Speckle rose and stared in silence, coffee dripping from his jaws. "You want 'o go easy with me, Rob Raymond; you've done me dirt enough already."

Raymond's face was pallid with passion. "Get out!"

They perceived his deadly earnestness, and tramped out, but Speckle blustered: "I see you again. I get you for this. You crawl for this."

Raymond's hand dropped upon his shoulder, and he landed outside the door on all-fours. With his hand on his revolver, the young foreman stepped out and watched them mount.

Ann could hear their threats as they rode away, and Louis, breathless, absorbed, his mouth open, stood in the doorway.

"What's the matter, Rob?" asked some one outside.

"Those mangy curs have deserted, leaving Williams short-handed, with a fire over on Porcupine Creek and coming his way. I wouldn't feed them when I found out what they had done."

"That's like Speck. He has no more honor than a wild-cat."

Raymond did not acknowledge, even to himself, that the attitude of the ruffians towards Ann was also a sufficient cause for kicking them out, and the worst of the whole affair was, he now stood in the foolish attitude of a man who has bullied a crowd of cowards in order to display his own honor and courage before a woman. When he came back into the room he was again sullen and silent.

IV

Life and Death

ANN had been absorbed in a study of the cow-boys. In her own walk of life, even the basest of men approached her clad in linen and broadcloth — sleek beasts—with civility; but here were males whose lean jaws clamped upon food with the eager haste of wolves, men primitive as Picts, with less of law than Zulus. They were not outlaws from society, for they had never known society. They were desperadoes for diversion.

Raymond's motive in thrusting them out appeared more and more a deed to win applause. It lowered him, made him less admirable in every way, and when he spoke to her she withdrew into herself with a glance which chilled and depressed him.

"Of course his character is of no consequence to me," she thought, "except in so far as he is likely to influence Louis." The situation suddenly lost its spirit of comedy and took on a very serious cast. The plan of leaving a sensitive, poetic boy to the company and influence of men like these became questionable, even dangerous. Baker was a foolish and stupid person, and these rough riders troubled her; but Raymond, to whom the boy's eyes already turned with fervent admiration, was more corrupting still, for whatever weaknesses he might have would surely come to be active

54

and vital forces in debasing others. The whole design, in the light of this encounter, assumed the face of folly.

"I will not leave him here," she resolved, "to be coarsened and perhaps attainted by these savage men. Why, it were better to send him among the Choctaws."

She was deeply shaken, rendered unwontedly timid by this turn of affairs. What madness to have exposed herself to the flare of withering sunshine on that long ride! What insanity to have isolated herself from her friends, her protectors! and yet this thrill of fear was not without a singular sort of pleasure.

She could feel once more—"My fear, at least, is vivid." Life being stripped of its forms, its silken covering, took on power, just as storms are more vital than calms. This powerful young rancher, a mixture of barbarism and culture, engrossed her quite as a mountain-lion might have done. His action could not be foretold, and she was amazed to find herself carried entirely outside herself, shaken and dismayed. As he set to work to put the table in order, silent and sullen as before, she watched him from her corner with intent gaze. "How deeply can I trust him?" she asked herself. "Don admires him, and he certainly is a man of intelligence."

Louis, who had gone to see the sunset, called to her excitedly, and as she stepped outside the door she, too, caught her breath in wonder and admiration, finding herself face to face with a new world—a world so big and bare and lonely that her native city seemed but a fleck on the mind's horizon. Far to the southeast a tower of smoke rose. This was the burning grass of Porcupine Creek.. Over a swell from the north a couple of horsemen were loping steadily, homing animals, weary with their long day's ride over the range. Their ponies' feet made no sound. The smoke of the far-off fire rose silently. The wind lay flat and breathless along the sod, like a runner utterly spent. A nut-like flavor filled the air — a smell of ripened grass, dusty yet aromatic.

"If we had hunted the world over, we could not have found a place more remote from all we have ever known," she said to Louis.

The boy turned, his eyes ablaze. "I like it!" he exclaimed, almost defiantly. "I don't know why, but it is beautiful to me! It is magnificent! And those mountains — I want to climb them the way father did. I want to explore their cañons. I want to tell our friends how beautiful they are."

Ann turned to the dim purple range, crumpled into ridges and slashed with deep valleys. "They may be alluring to you, laddie, but they scare me—a little. Well, perhaps you'll be able to go and see what they are like by-and-by, when you are stronger."

"Perhaps Rob will take me. I wouldn't be afraid of anything with him. He's a splendid type. Don't you think so?"

Ann smiled, but answered, doubtfully, "He seems a fine, resolute fellow." Her sisterly anxiety reappeared. "But I don't like to leave you here, Buddie. These men, the best of them, seem rough and reckless. I think you'd better go back with me—really I do."

"Oh no! I'm all right here, sis. Rob will look after me. It's just what I need."

"Maybe it *is* for the best, but I have a feeling that something is going to happen to you. I don't like to go back without you. I'll stay on a day or two longer, anyhow. I want to find out more about conditions here. I have a queer feeling at my heart. I don't want to leave you."

She was not given to presentiments, but as she imagined that pale and fragile boy surrounded by rude and unsympathetic cow - herders, the keen point of some mysterious, almost maternal, pain touched her. The loneliness and silence of this majestic world ceased to allure; they became a menace. "Let us go in," she said, putting her arm about his neck. "I am tired. I was never so tired in my life."

"Lean on me. I'm feeling fine," he stoutly replied.

A kerosene-lamp stood among the dishes, and the driver of their team and the two late-coming horsemen and the Mexican boy were all eating together. Raymond was not to be seen, and Ann realized, with a pang of dismay, how wholly she was depending upon him. "Without him I shall be scared," she admitted to herself. The other men paid very little direct attention to her beyond a moment's awkward pause and a lowering of their voices. They continued to discuss the fire and their day's work. It was plain that they were of different temper from the crowd Raymond had thrown from the door, and yet they were not prepossesing.

The liveryman, a short, dirty, and very assertive man of small wit, was maintaining himself against one of the riders in an argument. "I punched cattle all over them hills," he was saying. "I know it's all another fake like that old Mount Horeb business in '70. It's nothin' but a cattle-range—a lot o' smooth hills—"

"But they've found the gold; they can't be no question about it now. I've got a brother up there, and he writes me—"

"They told the same kind o' yarns about Horeb, and see how it turned out. They ain't an ounce o' gold in this whole Rampart Range. It ain't the right kind of formation."

"Well, I'm goin' up there, anyhow," said Baker, "as soon as Barnett can fill my place."

"So am I," said one of the other cow-boys, a dark, smileless fellow of nearly forty years of age.

"They're talking about Sky-Camp," whispered Louis, "the new mining-town."

Ann nodded, and again the unimaginable strangeness of her position swept over her. The action and accents of the characters before her were more unreal, more alien, than any play she had ever seen. They were more unaccountable than figures seen in a dream. The yellow flame of the lamp, shooting straight into their uncouth faces, transformed them into wind-worn masks —only their eyes remained unclouded of the weather. The flaming sunlight of the long day had produced in each a habit of squinting, and left a fine clutch of lines at the outer corner of each lid. Every garment they wore was tanned and faded. They lounged on the table with their elbows, like tired men, and their spurs clattered and rasped along the floor with every uneasy shifting of their aching feet. They were engines wrought into adaptation to certain uses—hardly human to her. They were loyal and respectful—she could see that—and yet the mere thought of remaining in the house unprotected troubled her. There was very little comfort in the sight of Baker's fat, inert face, but something chivalrous and considerate went out from Raymond in spite of his moody silences and abrupt ways.

The talk among the men shifted again to a discussion

of the fire. "I hope Bob won't order us out to fight it to-night. I'm tired as a dog," said one of the men.

"The way I put it up is this," bleated the liveryman. "That fire started from somebody campin' over on Birch Creek, and it's 'way beyond the ridge. It's got to cross that rocky wash before it can do any damage."

"Well, we'll know when Rob gets back," replied Baker, and Ann inferred from this that Raymond had ridden away to locate the fire, and heartily hoped he would not be gone long.

The men shoved back, one by one, and with sly, curious glances at the girl, sitting so cold and white and still against the wall, went out to smoke and discuss her with the driver. Baker, mindful of his duties, remained. "Don't be uneasy, miss; one of us will stay here, anyhow."

Ann was thinking. "A year ago I was in the Tyrol, and now—oh, it is incredible! Did any one ever do such a foolish, such an insane thing as this?"

Louis was looking over his sketching material, his mind busy with plans for work, when a shout outside announced Raymond's return. The lad rushed to the door. "Oh, Ann, come quick!" he called, a moment later. "Here he comes—oh, can't he ride!"

Ann reached the door just as Raymond dashed up and swung from his saddle; his voice was not loud, but it was stirring. "Boys, the fire is climbing the ridge, and we've got to fight it. Gather up your blankets and gunny-sacks. We'll find Williams over there with some water-barrels. Hustle now! I'll be along a little later. Tom, you take charge till I come."

With groans and half-jocular curses, the weary men, loyal to their duty, scattered to rope fresh ponies and gather up such material as they had for fighting flame, while Raymond came to the door and brusquely said to Ann: "I'll leave Baker to look after you, Miss Rupert. I hope you won't mind."

"Oh, certainly not," said Ann, as firmly as she could.

"I'd like to go along," cried Louis. "May I?"

"You're needed right here," Raymond sternly replied. "We're likely to be out all night, and your sister needs you."

"Couldn't Baker go in your place?" asked Ann, very quietly.

"Jack isn't very energetic. No, it's my duty."

"That's why I'd rather you stayed," Ann said. "If we should be attacked by Indians, or anything, Mr. Baker might be asleep."

He laughed. "Indians! There aren't any within two hundred miles of here."

"But you said you'd take care of us, and Mr. Barnett has consigned us to your care."

He warmed beneath the allurement of her glance. "But how would it look for the boss to remain comfortably at home while a fire—"

"You're not the boss—you're only the cook."

His face lighted up. "True enough!" After a moment's hesitation he added: "Very well, consider me your protector—and cook. Baker is in for it," and he went away, filled with a delicious sense of having suddenly been honored above his desert.

Ann was accustomed to men who flew to do her bidding, but this instant victory over the big rancher pleased her unaccountably, and she laughed softly, acknowledging a glow of confidence and relief in the promise of his presence.

Louis turned a sorrowful look on her. "I wish I could go, sis; it's just the kind of thing I want to see; but, of course, I can't."

"No, you are my knight, Buddie, and I can't spare you. Is your revolver loaded? This may be your time of trial. I feel very weak and defenceless here in this lonely, horrible land."

He took a small, shining weapon from his pocket and gazed at it ruefully. "I showed this to Jack, and he laughed. He said such a popper as that wouldn't kill a jay-bird."

"Perhaps he was joking you. It looks very formidable to me. Anyhow, it's all you have, and we must prize it. I'll send you down a larger one next week."

Out by the corrals, the trampling and snorting of excited ponies could be heard mingled with the muttered oaths of the men as they hurriedly roped and saddled. The sky was darkening rapidly, and the pillar of smoke already glowed like a brazen tower. It rose straight into the air for hundreds of feet, then spread away into a long, level cloud, showing that the wind had not yet begun to fan the flame.

At last the men were all mounted, and, with a final command from the boss, spurred away into the gloom, complaining, weary, but faithful. Raymond felt a little foolish as he faced the liveryman from Wallace.

"No, I'm not going—at least not till I get Barnett's people fixed for the night. You'll have to bunk in the tool-shed, I reckon."

"That's all right. I'll curl down close to my team. I don't want to run any risks with a lot of toughs like that Williams's gang cavortin' around. They had just liquor enough aboard to make 'em reckless. I'd advise you to look out for old Turkey Egg there; he has it in for you."

Raymond was unimpressed. "They're half-way to Wallace by this time, and, besides, Speck is a big bluff, anyway. We're rid of him forever."

"Well, all is, when you meet him next you pull first," the little man replied, very seriously.

Raymond walked slowly towards the house, filled with a guilty joy. Instead of a night of hard riding and laborious wet-bag swinging, he had given himself the pleasure of sitting in conversation with a beautiful and cultured girl. "I haven't earned this," he admitted. "I don't deserve it. It's too good to be true, but Barnett will approve. Anyhow, I'm going to enjoy it while I can."

Nevertheless, this sense of being a sneak and a cheat threw over him a gloomy and preoccupied air which vexed Ann, who began to question him very much as she would have done had she discovered unusual powers in her coachman. "How do you happen to be out here, Mr. Raymond?"

He replied, bluntly: "I don't know. I came here six years ago, because I hadn't any trade and the cattle business was attractive, and I've been here ever since."

"But you are wasting your time and talents."

For a moment he meditated a jocular reply, but at last gravely said: "I know it; at least I've begun to feel so lately, but I've drifted along from year to year. The fact is, I don't know what else I could go into, and then there's something fine about this life, after all. It's free and wholesome. No man is my master. I'm afraid I couldn't stand any sort of confinement now. In short, it's easier to drift than to row."

There was a note of despondency in his voice, in violent contrast with the power and decision of his splendid body, and Ann began to regret having started him on that line of thought.

"Yes, it's always easier to go with the tide," she said, musingly. "But in a big, strong man like you it seems less admirable than in a woman."

"I don't admire myself," he replied. "I've felt like a dough-boy for some time, and — well, I'm just about decided to try my luck up at the big camp. I wish you would take a letter to Barnett, and be sure that he reads it. I want him to send another man down here to take my place. But, see here, you're both tired and want to go to bed." He rose and lighted a second lamp. "Mrs. Barnett's bed is in this room" —he opened a door on the side opposite—"I'll see if it is prepared."

Ann interposed. "Oh no! I'm not so helpless as that. Let me take the light. I will do very well, never fear."

He yielded to her. "I'll get you some water, and I hope there are some clean towels. Let me know if there is anything else I can do."

"You are very thoughtful."

"We try to keep that room ready, so that when the folks come down it will be tolerable."

"I'm quite sure it will do," she said, definitely, and entered the room.

Raymond turned to Louis. "Youngster, can you shoot?"

"Not very well."

"Learn. A man going round this country with a young woman wants to be prepared for war. He may never have any need of a gun, and then again, unexpected, he may. A gang of hoboes like that to-day is dangerous when they get to drinking, and it stands a man in hand—" He made a sign commanding silence.

Ann reappeared with a pitcher in her hands. "If you'll fill this for me?"

"With pleasure," he quickly replied. After filling it and placing it in her room, he asked: "Now, which bag is yours? I'll pass that in."

"This one. But where are you and Louis to sleep?"

"Right here." He caught at a sort of frame hung upon the wall. It fell and was transformed into a bunk. "Right here, close beside your door, I'll put the youngster. I'll not take much sleep to-night. The boys will need some hot coffee when they come in." He walked to the door and stood there looking away towards the fire. "I'm afraid they've an all-night job of it. The mountain wind is springing up."

"If you really feel that you ought to go—" she began, rather feebly.

"Would you feel safer if I stayed?" His voice possessed a note of tenderness as he asked this question. His tall form, outlined on the outer darkness, again appealed to her with power.

She hesitated. "I never was among—I mean I have never been separated from my kind in this way before. I am a city dweller, and, I confess, I am a little nervous."

"Then you'd like me to stay?" he insisted.

"Yes, I wish you would."

"Then I will do so. I'm sure Barnett will excuse me when he knows—"

Something—a whip, a pistol—snapped far out in the darkness, a little slapping sound, a puff of dust rose from Raymond's broad breast, and he put his hand to his heart with a quick, indrawn gasp of pain. "Oh!"

"What was that?" asked Ann.

He swayed back against the door-frame, and a yellow-white pallor came to his face. "Some one has touched me," he said, slowly, through his set teeth. "It's that cowardly hound Speck. Go call your driver. I'm shot." He tried to walk to a chair, but reeled and fell.

Ann's first impulse was towards laughter. It was so absurd, so melodramatic, so perfectly impossible. "He is trying to frighten us," she thought, looking down at him, but Louis ran out screaming for Watson.

Raymond partly rose and faced her. Big drops of agony-sweat gleamed on his forehead. "It's no joke," he gasped, seeming to divine her feeling. "He's put it right through, just above my heart. Don't let me bleed to death," he ended, with guttural harshness, and began to tear at his coat in the effort to get it off. "Damn him—to shoot—in the dark—" And as he took away his hand and studied his palm, which was red with blood, Ann's heart grew sick with horror. Her limbs grew numb and weak. Then, as she watched him tearing feebly at his coat, the long-dormant woman in her awoke. She ceased to tremble and fell on her knees beside him.

"Let me help you," she said, and her voice was calm and clear, her fingers firm. When his coat was off, he sank again exhausted, breathing hard.

"Cut away my shirt—get at that hole and plug it," he commanded. "Anything that will fill it. You'll find some scissors there in that box—in the window—"

His shirt was wet with blood, and yet the girl clipped it away with steady hands. He looked down at the wound and then smiled up at her. "I'm all right. It was a steel-jacketed 30-30; it won't bleed much, and it's above my lung. I'll fool him yet."

The driver, wild of eye and much crumpled of hair, scrambled into the room. "Who did it? My God! who did it?"

"Never mind who did it. Plug this hole," commanded Raymond. "Bring some cold water and pour on it."

Ann saw that the driver's wits were too muddled to permit of proper action, and while her tense nerves quivered she bathed the wound, which was already ceasing to bleed.

"Turn me over, Cap," called Raymond. "You'll find another vent on the other side."

Louis and the driver turned him gently on his face, and Ann was horrified to find an uglier wound than the other. Sick with horror as she was, she contrived to cut away the shirt, and stanched the blood as before.

Raymond was recovering from the first shock of the wound, and, though his breathing was troubled, his mind was clear. "Now, Watson," he said to the driver, "spread some blankets under me—and then you go out to the corral and take my brown mare—with the saddle on—and slide out for Wallace and bring a doctor. Don't urge the mare—just let her take her gait; —and don't ride her back. Leave her there—"

After the driver had helped him to a bed on a blanket,

Life and Death

Raymond added, "Now I've got to be quiet and wait, that's all there is about it." He looked at Ann. "You can go to bed and sleep. Youngster, you're in for sentinel duty to-night—"

Ann interrupted him. "You must not talk, not another word! Lie perfectly still. We will keep cool bandages on your wound till the doctor comes."

He submitted to her directions and lay quiet, moving only to allow her to change the compress. Louis, when he knew what was needed, became almost as deft as Ann, and relieved her of the painful task of replacing the bandages. But the powerful frame of the ranchman grew each moment more inert, and at last they could not dress the wound at his back.

Ann sat in a sort of stupor, oppressed with this sudden contact with murder and sudden death. She longed to escape, to recover the care-free, clean, and peaceful life she had put aside. She resented it all. "Why have I been brought to such a brutal and disgusting country?" she said to herself, and at the moment this cowardly assault seemed typical of the West. "I shall return to the East at once."

Louis, for his part, was exalted by the suddenness with which he had been brought into contact with what he considered real life, and into service to a man dying of a gun-shot. These were the experiences he had hoped to take part in, and in his mind this incident began to take shape as a story of revenge.

V

Ann's Vigil

FOR a long time the silence remained unbroken, except now and then when the girl bent over the silent figure to ask, "Can I do anything for you?" Each time she listened with added fear, hoping eagerly for his voice. To have him die there would be too horrible. Looking down on a wounded man she found to be a deeply moving point of view. Merely to see the closed eyes and the hollow, haggard face, was a transforming experience, but to feel that his life-blood was ebbing away while she sat helplessly by was akin to murder.

"Oh, I wish we could do something," she whispered now and again to Louis.

The boy, worn out with his day's excitement, struggled manfully to keep awake, but, as the night deepened, slumber rose about him like a wreath of benumbing incense. His sense of what had taken place dulled, his head nodded and drooped, and at last Ann lowered him to the floor, where he slept, his cheek pillowed upon her feet.

Again the singularity of the chance, the absurd unreality of the situation, came upon the self-contained girl, inciting her to a sort of hysterical laughter. Here now she sat—Ann Rupert—most conventional of persons, in a rude ranch - house, alone with a strange, rough man sleeping in deathlike trance before her. "I to whom nothing unexpected ever came," she added. Truly this was a domineering land. Outside a weird yapping and howling arose—some spiteful dog. Dog! No, it was a wolf; and a creeping movement of her hair followed.

The wind in the big cottonwood advanced upon her with hissing, stealthy motion. Voices sibilant and prophetic spoke to her out of the darkness, and invisible arms seemed reaching through the open window. The wounded man, with tightly clinched teeth, drew his breath slowly, irregularly, stifling his pain for her sake, but the boy's breathing was tranquil as that of a babe. The minutes elongated like bands of rubber, attaining the length of quarter-hours, and the night stretched away into horrifying distance as she sat tensely waiting, hoping each moment for deliverance, expecting each instant to hear the swift beating of hoofs, the hoarse laughter of the men; but only the wind-serpents hissed and the wolf howled.

At last immobility became intolerable, and, lowering Louis' head to the floor, she gently placed his doubled coat beneath it, and with a mighty effort of the will bent again above the pallid man, so tragic in his supineness, and whispered:

"Are you still suffering? Can I do anything for you?"

He turned his head slowly, and with a glance which made her shiver, answered: "No—I have ceased to bleed—I am going to pull through—if my pulse keeps down. Won't you take it?"

Timidly taking his brown wrist in her soft finger-tips she tried to count the pulsing of his blood.

He waited a little time in silence, then said: "It's there, but it's weak. Don't you feel it?"

"Yes, it is more regular now," she answered, though her throat filled with the pity and the fear of his dying there before her eyes. He was a splendid figure as he lay motionless, straight as a carven figure on a tomb. She had never in her life looked down upon a man lying supine, disabled, and it added to her woman's instinctive fear a singular tenderness, an almost maternal yearning to help, to minister to his needs.

He seemed to understand something of this feeling, and, with a little touch of mocking humor, he slowly said: "This is a new experience for you, isn't it? If the boy were awake this would be a good subject for a sketch—the dying rancher and the lady."

"Don't—please don't!" she pleaded.

"Oh, I'm not going to die," he continued, in a hoarse, flat tone. "I could get up and mount a horse right now, only I'd bleed if I did. It's hard to keep quiet, but I'm going to do it. I can't afford to die now. You've roused me. There's something in the world for me to do." His breath came a little quicker. "The Lord gave me a talent—I haven't buried it. I've only hid it in a napkin—if I ever get up again that talent gets burnished."

"You must not talk," she whispered. "Please—it will do you harm."

She put her hand impulsively on his forehead as if he were a child, and he closed his eyes and lay in silence for several minutes. When she withdrew her palm he muttered, "Leave it there, it—is so cool and soft."

"Would you like a wet cloth on your head?"

"No—only your hand—if you don't mind—"

Ann's Vigil

Her feeling towards him at the moment was like that she manifested towards her brother. "I don't mind, if it helps you," she answered, but a flush rose to her face.

He had a fine brow — she could not help noticing that—full and white, and his neck was very fair below the red-brown mask which the fierce sun and withering wind had put upon him. It was not a gentle face, but it was handsome and interesting. The lips were refined and the eyes sincere. Some one must have loved him deeply—a sister, a mother. This gave her a new thought. "Would you like us to send word to anybody in the East—to your mother?"

He hesitated. "No; not unless the doctor advises it." His thought turned towards her perplexities again. "The boys will come in soon, and then you can go to bed and rest. I'm sorry to trouble you. You can go now. I'm all right."

"I shall not leave you," she firmly replied.

"You're mighty good," he said, simply.

The night wore on interminably. Once a fierce yapping and howling broke forth close to the corral, and the girl started visibly, but the wounded man whispered, "Don't be scared—coyotes—perfectly harmless," and she was instantly relieved. He knew the wild and its danger.

Strange to say, she no longer bemoaned her folly in having been dragged into this world. She no longer thought of herself as an alien. Something of the exaltation which irradiates the faces of the devoted Sisters of Charity came to her. She glowed with a species of pleasure born of the conviction that she was doing a little of Christ's work in the world. She had never been a visitor of slums, had never enacted the rôle of Lady Bountiful, and yet her life had not been sensual. She had simply avoided responsibility. Suffering, guilt, death had not come near her. Aside from her sense of duty towards her brother she had never acknowledged obligation, and this sudden reaching call of a stricken human soul filled her with new conceptions of human need. Suppose this man were about to die? What comfort could she give?

She had never been a devout Christian, though she formally attended church and tepidly read her prayers with the congregation; but now she wished for some power to solace—to prepare a soul for death. This splendid youth, lying along the brink of the grave, caused her to grasp at the known and to question the unseen. She was amazed to find herself nearing him, desiring to help him, and her anxiety became a benumbing pain.

After some hours of troubled dozing, the wounded man opened his eyes and said, thickly, in a tone he had not used before, "Nell, I thought you were in Europe?"

Ann's blood froze with a new terror. She read in these words the delirium which precedes death. The fevers of the man's breast had reached his brain! His breathing indicated growing pain.

His voice was reproachful. "Won't you speak to me, Nellie. I don't blame you. I disgraced you all, but I didn't mean to do so."

She laid her hand gently on his forehead. "Hush! You must not talk. Be very quiet."

He raised his big, brown right hand, and brought her palm to his lips and kissed it.

"No, no!" she cried, putting his hand down by his

side again. "You must not move. You are hurt.
Don't you remember? You must not stir till the doctor comes."

His eyes became troubled and wondering. "I—I
thought you were Nellie." He raised his head and
cleared his eyes. "What's the matter with me?"

In terror she fell upon her knees at his side. "Please
don't!" She put both her hands to his face and pressed
his head back upon his pillow. "You must *not* move.
You will open your wounds again."

He smiled curiously. "All right; I feel as if I'd
been punishin' wet 'boodle.' My head is hot. Nothing so good as a wet towel—pounded ice—"

"If you'll be very still I'll go get some water. Do
you promise?"

"Oh yes, I'll promise."

Hastily sopping her handkerchief in water, she laid
it on his brow, which was burning with heat. His face
and neck were now flushed and swollen, and his eyes
very bright. Putting her hand over them, she said,
firmly, "Now shut your eyes and go to sleep."

He grew still—deathly still—once more. Only the
throbbing of the fevered veins of his temples told of his
laboring heart's continued action. For a long time
Ann sat thus, her outstretched arms aching with the
constraint, but at last he seemed to sleep, and she
was free. Rising, she took from her hand-bag a little
medicine-case, and from one of the phials marked "Fevers" she poured a few pellets. These she dropped into
a glass with a little water, and returned to her seat beside the sleeping man with a feeling of power, a sense of
being prepared to deal with his rising pulse; his wound
was beyond her skill.

Hesper

At a little past three, faint and far, arose the cheerful crowing of a cock.   Her heart burned with joy—the morning was near!   Hastening to the window, she was able to detect a faint golden refulgence overspreading the eastern sky.   As she exulted, the cock's call was repeated, and then a long, sharp, wailing howl answered it.   It was the morning song of the wolf.

As she waited the light came, and voices faint and far away touched her ear, and then slowly, moving in a disorderly squad, the weary fighters of flames came riding down the slope and across the meadow.   Their words, even as sounds, seemed weary and spiritless. So impatient of their slow approach was she, the girl leaned far out of the window, eager to scream; but her better judgment deterred her, and with both hands clinched on the window-sill, her white face ghastly pale in the growing light of the morning, she awaited their approach.   "Why do they not hurry?"

The herders did not ride up to the house as she expected them to do, but turned aside towards the stables, and she could hear them as they dropped their saddles and turned their tired ponies loose.   "Surely they will come now."   Then all was still save the crowing of the cocks and that sad howling of the wolf on the hill.

Unable to endure the suspense, she tiptoed across the floor and hurried out towards the corrals, her heart in her throat with fear of the body on the floor.   She ran as silently as possible, as if to avoid rousing some fierce animal, and was close upon the men before they saw her.

"What's that!" she heard one quick, keen voice cry out.

Ann's Vigil

Then each man rose from the heap of blankets wherein he lay curled like an Arctic dog.

Ann answered them breathlessly. "Come to the house, quick. Mr. Raymond is shot!"

Their responses were like bullets: "Shot! Who shot him?"

"Some one fired out of the darkness—he was standing in the doorway. He is delirious. I'm all alone. He must have help!"

"Where's Watson?"

"Gone for the doctor."

Shaking loose from his bed, Baker started on the run for the house, but Ann cried out, sharply: "Wait! Go quietly. You must not excite him;" and, walking beside him, she returned to the house, and in a sort of daze the other herders silently followed. The jangle of Baker's big spurs, familiar and penetrating, called Raymond to a knowledge of his surroundings.

He turned his head and looked at the men in a way that made them shrink, and asked: "How's the fire? Did you stop it?"

Baker replied, "Yes, we got her under."

Raymond half closed his eyes. "I'm glad you're here. This lady needs a rest. Somebody did for me."

Perry, the Mexican boy, with a face white with passion, uttered a sobbing moan, and, rushing across the room, fell on his knees beside his boss.

"Who did it? Tell me! I will hunt him! I will kill him!"

His voice, tense, muffled with passion, thrust Ann to the heart; but Raymond, putting his hand on the boy's head, said, gently: "Keep cool, boy. Baker, you and Jones and Skuttle stay here. Perry, you saddle a

horse and get Abe and his wife. Miss Rupert, you go
to bed; the boys will look after me now. I can't let
you wear yourself out for me."

But Ann could not so easily be put aside from her
plain duty. "No, I will stay till the doctor comes.
Men"—she turned to the cow-boys—"he ought to have
an easier bed. Can't you lift him—"

Raymond spoke again: "No, don't bother. I'm
used to hard beds."

The herders recovered from their awe as they listened
to the sound of their foreman's voice. Though weak
and broken, it was, after all, that of the master, and
familiar.

Baker, hardly able to speak, hoarsely murmured,
"What can we do, miss?"

"I don't know — nothing except to put something
soft beneath him."

And so, to her own wonderment, Ann found herself
in direct and full control of a gang of clumsy, rough, but
resolute men—men who could break a savage horse or
fight flame all night long, but who knew not how to lay
hands upon a wounded comrade. And, stranger yet,
she found herself warming under their naïve admiration
of her skill and judgment.

At last, when the wounded man was lying comfortably on a thick pile of blankets, and the white light of
the morning filled the cabin, Ann yielded to his entreaties, went to her room, and threw herself down upon her
bed with a sense of having put all her easeful, careless
girlhood behind her. It was as if she had suddenly
been flung into a gray and bitter sea far from shore.

Louis, who had been roused by the return of the
herders, and who sat watching their slow and painfully

cautious handling of the sufferer with the mute, unemotional gaze of a sleepy kitten, followed his sister into the inner room and stood in silence till his bewilderment left him and his perplexity crystallized into words. Then he said:

"Jupiter! I didn't know you could do such things. What do you think? Is he going to die?"

"I don't know, laddie. I hope not. I've done all I can."

Ann must have dropped asleep thereafter, for when she woke the horizontal rays of the flaming sun filled the room, and the loud and hearty voice of a woman could be heard out in the kitchen. Her words came distinctly to Ann's ears. "Now, Rob, you've got me to deal with. I'll cuff your ears if you don't do as I say. You've got to eat to keep your strength up."

Ann rose hastily, but paused before the closed door with a new and singular timidity. The coming of another woman made her own position embarrassing. With a return of resolution she opened the door and met the big, gray eyes of a tall, broad-shouldered, slatternly woman, who stood over Raymond with a bowl of steaming broth in her hand. She was neither deft nor dainty, but Ann perceived that she was capable and good-tempered, a natural nurse, experienced in the ways of the border.

"Good-morning," she called, and her inflections and many of her phrases were masculine. "You must 'a' had a right hard night of it. Friend of the Barnetts, Rob tells me."

Her familiarity and the essential commonness of her

77

tone repelled Ann, who asked, with cool dignity, " Can I do anything?"

"Not a thing. I'm Mrs. Scribbins, Rob's nighest neighbor. We come a-runnin' the moment we heerd of this thing, for Rob's a mighty good man and neighbor."

Ann repented and held out her hand. "I'm glad to see you, Mrs. Scribbins. I'm Miss Rupert, and this is my brother." She turned to Louis, who had crept to her side, pale and silent.

Mrs. Scribbins shook hands carefully, guarding her broth. "I don't see how in hell you kept Rob down. I've had to just about throttle him once or twice since I came. He's a headstrong cuss, and hates being bossed or nussed."

"Has the doctor come?"

"Good Lord! no; but I've sent Abe up the road. That fool Watson is more 'n likely to get lost and never get in; even if he did he couldn't get a doctor here before noon, and that Wallace doctor ain't worth the powder to blow him to hell, anyway. We need a bone-doctor from Valley Springs. As soon as Don Barnett hears of this he'll come a-runnin' with the best there is in the Springs—" She broke off suddenly to say: "Boys, you'll have to kill a critter. I can't feed the people that 'll come a-rackin' in here, if you don't. Seems like you've lost all the sense you ever *did* have. Hustle out o' here, you're in the way."

Raymond lay on his pile of blankets, his face expressionless as that of a dead man, but his eyes called to the girl, and she bent to ask, "Are you better?"

His lips moved a little. She bowed lower, and he whispered, "Yes—bring Don—"

Ann's Vigil

"They have gone for him."

"They must hurry." Then he added, "Don't leave me."

With a conviction that he knew he was about to die, she spoke, and her tone was tense with a desire to help him, "I will not leave you—do not worry."

He closed his eyes again, and lay so still, so breathless, it seemed that he had entered upon the last coma, beyond the reach of any medicine.

Louis, awed quite out of his sprightly self, drew Ann aside and whispered, "How is he?"

"He is worse. Oh, I wish the doctor would come!"

"The boys say that big, speckled-faced fellow did it. He had it in for Mr. Raymond. Do you know, Perry, the Mexican boy, took a horse and was going to chase them up, but the boys wouldn't let him. They've sent word to the railway, and they'll have Speckle before night. Uncle Don said that these fellows were only hired men, but seems to me they're a good deal like the old-time cow-boys. I consider I'm in great luck."

Ann looked at him in astonishment. "What do you mean?"

"Why, it isn't often you can see a man shot, even out here."

"Louis, I don't believe you realize how heartless that sounds."

"I'm seeing life," he said, triumphantly.

Ann did not say what she thought, but in her heart she replied, "You are seeing death."

Barnett to the Rescue

BARNETT was at breakfast when a telegram was laid at his elbow by the maid. He opened it leisurely, thinking it some matter of business, but his hands stiffened as he read:

" Bob Raymond is shot. Send best doctor in town, quick.
                                      WATSON."

For just a moment he sat in silence, then rose and walked slowly to his library. Seating himself before the little desk on which stood a movable telephone-receiver, he began to "make things hum." He reached his friend, Dr. Braide, and set him in motion. He ordered out his racing automobile. He telegraphed Watson to take fresh horses and return by way of Junction and get best doctor there. "Burn the air as you go," he added.

After giving orders for his valise to be packed, he walked up to Mrs. Barnett's room and kissed her good-morning without betraying his excitement.

"I'm going out to the ranch," he said. "The boys are having trouble with the hay, and I want to see how they're coming on. You won't mind, will you?"

"Of course not, Don. I'm going to be all right in a few hours. I'm glad you're going. You can bring

Ann home. You should have gone with her yesterday."

"I see that now," he answered, dryly. "It will be a startling world for her. Well, I'm off. Better stay in bed to-day. I'll be back by to-morrow night, I think."

When he took his seat in his big, flat, powerful autocar, his face was set in grim lines. "Is she all right, Henry?" he asked of his engineer.

"In perfect order, sir."

"She needs to be. This is to be a record-breaker."

With his big goggles over his eyes and his cap drawn low down on his forehead, Barnett seized the wheel, and the ponderous, panting organism began to move. Wheeling into the street, he let on the full power of the engine, and when he drew up at Braide's gate the mechanism was hot with speed, its joints oiled and frictionless—in racing trim.

Braide, a small, smiling, trig young fellow, came out. "What is it all about, Don?"

"Got your tools?"

He pointed at his bag, "Emergency kit."

"Then all aboard!"

Henry leaped out and caught up the bag, while the doctor climbed in beside Barnett on the front seat.

"This looks ominous. How much of a trip is it going to be?"

"Just a short run," answered Barnett, as he swung the shining red bulk of the car into Mogalyon Avenue, which led directly east over the plain.

Beneath their feet the puff and click of the piston and the purr of cogs grew each moment more furious, until all sounds fused into a humming roar. The keen air of the morning smote the riders jovially. The

flaming sunlight slanted upon them with growing heat,
and backward, beneath them, the sod swept like a
tawny carpet, while Barnett, watchful, intent, composed, worked the levers and valves with the skill of a
practical engineer. When they had crossed the two
railroads, and were climbing the long, low ridge, he
casually remarked,

"My foreman, Raymond, is shot, and you've got to
pull him through."

"Great Scot, Don, I can't afford the time! It 'll
take all day. If I'd known—"

"You'd have gone just the same," asserted Barnett,
calmly. The machine was again running very swiftly.
"You're here, and you daren't jump out, and you
might as well enjoy yourself. This is to be a record
run. I'm going to pull in by noon."

Braide was young and a man of red blood and shining eyes. "Very well; go it, old sport! I can stand it
if you can. I'll make it a holiday, and charge you
double for every hour."

"That's like you doctors; your meat is another man's
poison."

When they had reached the top of the pass between
two piñon-spotted hills, the road could be seen for
miles, driving straight into the mist of the mighty
Missouri Valley.

"It's all the way down-grade from here to Omaha,"
remarked Barnett. "I could make the run in two
hours—only, I mustn't invite a break-down."

"You seem to value your foreman."

"He's something more than my foreman. He's a
splendid chap. You've met him—the fellow who went
on the 'coyote drive' with us."

"Why, certainly I remember him. I've met him at the club. But he was very reticent. I didn't get at him. Who is he? How does he come to be your foreman?"

"He's a little slow about telling his own life story, but he's all right. I think I know the cause of this shooting. He got into trouble with a couple of fellows out there, and one of them has done him. It was this way: I am postmaster at my ranch, and Raymond is deputy. One day when he was about to send out the mail a fellow called Speckle rode up with three letters to register. Rob laid the letters down on the table in the room—the post-office is in one corner of the dining-room—and slipped out to speak to one of the boys. When he came back, Speck was gone. Rob caught up the letters hurriedly, for the carrier was waiting, and thrust them into the bag. Some days later he received notice that the letters arrived at the post-office in Denver without enclosure. Each envelope had been neatly slit with a knife and the money taken."

"Well," said Braide—"Speckle did it, of course?"

"That's what Raymond thought. But Speckle made counter-accusation: 'Would I rob myself? One of them letters contained money I was sending home.' Moreover, his friends go on to say, 'One of those letters contained silver, and it is nonsense to say that Raymond didn't feel the difference in weight.'"

"They might have been opened on the route."

"No, the bag went through to Denver without being opened. The authorities came down and investigated, but haven't come to any conclusion. This shooting is likely to be an outcome of the dispute."

The road was now merely a trail across the prairie. The farm-houses were left behind; only the long reaches of wire fence denoted the presence of ranchers. It was a big, bare land, covered with a short, dry grass, with occasional shallow ravines in which minute streams of water percolated. Cattle were scattered over the range, but sparsely. Occasionally they passed a prairie-dog town, and Don laughed to see them disappear at sight of the big, red monster. Once in ten or fifteen minutes Henry was forced to leap down and open a wire gate, and these delays brought a deeper frown to Barnett's face. At last they swept out upon the open range, with only the dry and russet sod basing the hemisphere of flaming sky.

As they came sweeping down on the "Bar O" ranch-house, half hidden in a narrow valley, all the hands and every child of the family, including the dogs, rushed out, eager to see the new machine, shouting for Barnett to stop; but he only shook his head and bent resolutely to his levers, leaving them all behind in a whir of dust.

Twice he met a little squad of whooping cow-boys, and the bucking and the plunging of their terrified ponies gave rise to splendid feats of horsemanship; but Barnett, busy bringing out of the great red beast every ounce of power that was in her, did not even glance their way.

The doctor, looking often at his watch, shouted, "We are running more than thirty miles an hour!"

"We have a sand-flat to cross," replied Barnett.

As they entered upon a particularly smooth stretch of road, the man at the wheel relaxed his hold and said, with deep feeling: "I don't mind saying that I'm anxious about Rob. I've grown mighty fond of him. He's not one given to confidences, and I've respected his reticence. I don't know quite why he is here, but I trust him and count myself fortunate to have him on the place. He made forty thousand dollars for me last year on hay and cattle, and must have a little bunch laid up for himself. It would be devilish to have him snuffed out by that wide-mouthed blackguard."

"I thought him a little different from the ordinary cow-boy."

"Cow-boy! Good Heavens, the man is a gentleman."

"Couldn't he be both?"

"This cow-boy nonsense is no longer humorous to me. The cattle business is on a new basis now, and what I want is not a woolly jack who shoots off his mouth and his pistol on the slightest provocation. I want steady, decent workmen. Rob is invaluable to me for the reason that he controls these trifling 'bad boys' of Missouri and Kansas. It's a cursed shame to have such a man disabled by a hobo like Speck Hanson. It's murder, pure murder, for he must have shot him from ambush. He wouldn't face him."

Braide was vastly astonished to observe the self-contained Don Barnett growing red with wrath. "Maybe it was an accident."

"Oh no, it was one of that Hanson gang. They terrorize Williams. Saturday night he hides out and they run riot." After a silence he said, slowly: "I've felt for a year that I ought to put Rob into something better; I owed it to him. Now if he dies—" He broke off and bent to his wheel to hide the emotion that made his lips quiver.

"It may be only a flesh wound. Anyhow, we'll do our best for him," replied the doctor.

"Here's our sand-flat," called Barnett. "Henry, we're in for it."

The machine, hitherto joyous, began to labor and lag. Her master turned a cock here, opened a valve there, threw on the hill-climbing device, and under these stimulants she crawled slowly through. The men bent forward involuntarily, as if trying to push, and the helmsman took advantage of every streak of sod, every patch of gumbo, and at last, with a whoop of joy, struck the hard soil of the opposite hill, and up the slope they went with a sense of victory.

"We're all right now, except for the bridge at the Goldfish Ranch," said Barnett, with a sigh of deep relief.

The speed of the splendid chariot now rose to nearly twenty-five miles an hour, and on the down-grade touched railroad speed—and the young surgeon took off his hat and yelled with delight.

"Whirroo! turn on the juice!" Then he shouted: "There go some antelope! Oh, for a chance to race with them!"

For an interval of several minutes the antelope—three does and two fawns—ran parallel to the auto's course, as if curious to test its speed and understand its motives; then veered off and drifted, light as cottonwood down, across a swell and out of sight.

It lacked ten minutes of noon as Barnett rose above the last great wave of the tawny sea and sighted the clump of cottonwoods in which his ranch buildings sat, and two minutes later he swept into the yard and up to the door, amid a throng of singularly silent cow-boys and ranchers. The first one to speak was Mrs. Scribbins, who exclaimed:

Barnett to the Rescue

"Jerusalem the golden! You hain't come from home this mornin' in that doggone thunder-cart, have ye?"

"That's what. How's Rob?"

"Quiet as mice; but I hope ye brought help."

Barnett rose from his seat stiffly and climbed painfully down, while Braide seized his case of tools and hurried into the cabin.

Barnett, feeling a small hand gripping his arm, turned to meet Louis. "Hello," said he. "How is Ann?"

"She's all right. She saved Rob's life," answered the boy.

Ann, who stood just outside the door, answered, very quietly: "I am quite well. How is Jeannette?"

"I left her feeling very well— But tell me the truth, is Rob dying?"

"No," said Ann. "But he needs help. He was shot last evening—and has lain all night in pain—he is very weak now."

Barnett hurried into the hot dusk of the ranch-house, smelling of the dinner which was cooking, and bent above his foreman.

"Hello, Rob. How do you feel?"

Raymond whispered, "Oh, I'm all right — a little weak—"

The doctor interposed. "Clear the room of everybody but the woman." He indicated Mrs. Scribbins. "We must find this bullet!"

Barnett turned to the men who filled the doorway. "Clear out, boys; the doctor wants to be alone now."

Raymond smiled a little. "The bullet went on. It's in the wall somewhere!"

Hesper

Barnett came to the door and said to Ann, "You better go out under the trees and rest; you look tired."

"I will stay if I can be of any use."

"We don't need you—Mrs. Scribbins will help us. Please go. Louis, take her away till this is over."

Released from her benumbing load of responsibility, Ann laid her hand on her brother's arm. "Come, Louis," and together they went out along the little winding path which led to the spring.

"What do you suppose they will do to him?" asked Louis.

Ann turned sick. "Oh, I don't know. Don't speak of it—it's too horrible!"

They took seats in the long, matted grass under the willows which rose out of the moist earth beside the spring, and looked away at the pink-brown domes of the range warmed by the morning sun and diminished by the absence of clouds. There was balm and healing in the sight of them, and, with passionate voice, Ann cried out:

"Oh, to get back to the Springs—to be rid of these horrible, prying people! It's like a nightmare! I hate them all!"

Louis' sensitive soul quivered with sympathetic pain at sight of her tears. "I'm awfully sorry, sis. I didn't intend to get you into this scrape."

"I know you didn't, but I feel as if my soul had been scourged. I'm not fitted for such life — such work. I can't let you stay here, laddie. These men are too savage; they are not suitable companions for a boy like you."

"I don't want to stay if Rob dies," he said.

"He won't die," she said, with conviction. "His frame is accustomed to hardship—it will throw this off. But you are too young to be mixed up in these wild scenes."

He was silent for a moment, peering away across the meadow, where a crawling object appeared, curving down like a dark-brown serpent. "There come some cattle. The cow-boys are riding ahead. See! They're coming down to the pond. Let's go up there and meet them."

Ann followed him down along the wire fence to a mound which overlooked the marshy pool just above the stables, and there stood watching the cattle as they descended in an endless, thin file, from where the crest of the ridge cut into the burning sky, to the green valley. They approached in single file, their heads held high, their nostrils wide-spread. Even the leaders were gaunt and poor, and all trotted with long, eager, jolting steps, and as they came they cried out with voices hoarse and weak and high-keyed, like those of women worn with pleading. A dust arose from their feet—a dust that drifted like smoke.

"They are starving for water," cried Ann, with sudden realization of the meaning of their moaning.

Louis stood like one smitten dumb, his big eyes fixed like the lenses of a camera — eager to absorb every detail of the strange scene.

As the big, bony leaders neared the pool, they plunged in, catching at the water as wolves snap at meat. Those behind forced those in front ever deeper into the cool liquid, while later - comers encircled the little pool, crushing and crowding one another till those in the centre swam, and those behind, unable to find place, swirled madly on the outer edge, moaning most piteously. All were lamentably gaunt and wild-eyed.

They soon formed a huge bowl or pit wherein they moved—a crater paved with clashing horns and muddy, up-raised nostrils. The water beneath them became inky black with churned slime, and yet they drank, gulping this liquid mud. And still they came. The air was filled with the sound of their hoarse breathing, their whining and muttering. Those in the rear seemed to stagger as they ran down the hill. Turning to one of the cow-boys, who sat composedly on his horse, Ann asked, "Why are they so thirsty?"

"We're moving 'em across country, miss, and the water is mighty scarce on the divide between Wild Cat and the North Fork."

His calm unconcern dismayed and angered the girl. "Come away, Louis. I hate this cruel land and all its people."

Louis followed her reluctantly. To him it was all drama—a splendid, robust play. He admired the cowboy who sat so calmly watching his thirsty cattle battle for a mouthful of wet slime. To Ann it was barbarism—unhallowed and unnecessary. "Oh, what a terrible country!" she repeated, as the horror grew. "No wonder its women swear and its men kill one another."

When she re-entered the cabin, Barnett met her with a smile. "The doctor says Rob's all right. He insists that you saved his life. You poor girl! What a night that boy let you in for! I didn't know till ten minutes ago that you were here all alone, and that Jones and his wife had vamoosed. I hope you'll forgive me, Ann?"

"Oh, I blame no one but myself," she wearily replied. "I shouldn't have come to this miserable, ghastly region."

"Rob wants to see you. Will you come in and speak to him?"

Ann reluctantly followed Barnett into the inner room where Raymond, with his wounds dressed and limbs properly clothed, lay stretched on the bed. He was very pale, but his eyes were calm and quiet. He reached a feeble right hand towards her, saying, painfully: "You've been mighty good to me. By-and-by I will try to thank you. Without you I would have bled to death."

"I beg you not to give it a moment's thought. I did very little," Ann coldly replied.

His eyes were round and soft and appealing, like those of a big, wounded dog. "Don't leave me now. I want you—"

She glanced at the young doctor, who stood listening. He nodded, as if to say, "Grant his request." And so she put his hand away gently, as if the clinging fingers were those of a sleeping babe, and said, with a return of pity: "I will stay till to-morrow. Now please go to sleep."

He closed his eyes under her palm, and tears of gratitude came stealing down from his brown lashes. For the moment she forgot that she had known him but a day, that she, too, was a stranger—far removed from him in every thought and purpose—and consented to stay because he clung to her and needed her. A hand seized her throat, and an emotion which alienated her from her old self rose within her bosom and for a moment frightened her. In the end it irritated her, this pity, and yet it could not be shaken off. A deeper self, which she had not known, insisted that she keep her word to the wounded man; and so for two days she oscillated between a pitying tenderness for him and a disgust and bitterness with herself and her weakness.

On the third day Braide pronounced his patient out of danger, and then Ann's pity died.

"I am going home," she said to Louis, "and you must go with me. They are going to take the foreman to the Springs, and I cannot leave you here."

Ann said good-bye to the wounded man in Barnett's presence, and a sense of irritation caused her to be very distant with him.

"I hope you will soon be able to be removed," she said, evading his glance. "This is a distressing place in which to be sick, and now I must say good-bye."

He took her hand in both of his. "I shall miss you, but I won't ask you to stay any longer. You've been very sweet and helpful to me, and I hate to have you go. You will let me see you again—won't you?"

"My cousin intends to take you to his house as soon as you can be moved," she answered, formally. "No doubt we shall meet again there."

"I will live in hope of that," he answered, gallantly.

VII

The New Life

ONCE more in Valley Springs, Ann's old self returned, and the scenes through which she had passed became as unreal as the happenings of a dream; but her sense of injury deepened into dislike of Raymond and the life he represented. Therefore she took care not to see him as he was borne into Barnett's house. "He is nothing to me, and I must decline to be troubled by him further," she said, as she was dressing to go out.

Mrs. Barnett, however, was waiting, and when the carriage in which he lay came to the door, hastened to take his hand in both of hers and make him welcome. "I'm glad you came, Rob. We are going to have you out in a few days. How do you feel?"

In his weak state he could only boyishly say: "Oh, I'm on the up-grade. You and Don are mighty good to me."

"Not a word about that," she cheerily cried.

As the men bore him through the doorway, he said, with a faint smile, "I cut as wide a swath as a piano, don't I?"

Barnett, piloting the way, called out, "No more heavy jokes; it's all the pall-bearers can stagger under now"; and in such fashion they rumbled up the stairs, the helpers on the broad grin.

As he sank into the cool, delicious bed, soft and fragrant, tears of gratitude filled the strong young man's eyes.

"I don't deserve such treatment, old man—a tramp like me—"

"Rats!" roared Barnett, to conceal his own emotion. "In the phrase of the great statesman from Wisconsin, 'I seen my duty, and I done it.' I've got you now right where I want you. You do just as we tell you."

"I submit," he answered, and thereafter abandoned himself to the joy of travelling back to life along such ways of wanton luxury as he had never known. He permitted himself to be waited upon, even by Mrs. Barnett, without protest, and when Louis came stealing into the room in awe and love his heart went out to the boy as to a brother.

"Hello, younker!" he called. "You needn't walk so soft-voiced; I'm worth a dozen dead men yet."

The boy's face shone. "I thought you were asleep. Can I do anything for you?"

"No, only come and sit down and talk to me. What have you been doing since you came back to the Springs?"

Louis took a seat. "Nothing of any consequence, except to make some drawings of the ranch. It's dull here. I want to go into the mountains."

"You're a wonderful youngster. Wait till I'm able to travel, and we'll go up into the high country together."

Louis clapped his hands. "Won't that be glorious! I'd rather do that than anything else in the world."

The New Life

"How is your sister?" asked Raymond, with abrupt change of tone.

"She is well—she's always well. We just came in from a drive; that's the reason I wasn't here to help you. Did it hurt you going up-stairs?"

"Not a bit. The boys handled me as tenderly as a side o' pork. Let me see your drawings, will you?"

The boy's face glowed. "Well, you just wait," and he rushed away to get them.

Mrs. Barnett, upon meeting Ann, said, with deep feeling: "Rob's illness has transformed him. He said to me a few moments ago, 'If you can find the man who shot me, reward him. He has done me a great service. I am lost in a dream of luxury.' There was a beautiful light in his face. I wish you could have seen it. I have known there was a great deal more to him than he was willing to give out, but I didn't know he had such delicacy of sentiment. He asked after you with emotion, and said he would like to thank you for your service to him."

Ann, listening intently, remained coldly impassive of face. "Mrs. Scribbins was the really efficient person. I have a horror of sick people, and as for wounds—" She shuddered for lack of words.

Mrs. Barnett went on: "I like to do for him, he's so grateful and so obedient. He says just the right thing always. There must be good breeding back of the man, although he never mentions his family. There's some love affair to account for his being here. He's too handsome not to have had entanglements. Don't you think so?"

"He insisted not," replied Ann. "He begged me to consider that his life had been quite commonplace."

"I don't believe it. He couldn't be commonplace. He said to me just now, 'Sometimes a man must hear the wash of the river of death to realize how futile he has allowed his life to become.' His gratitude towards you is pathetic."

Ann frowned. "It's worse—it's oppressive. I did so little, and that little was not done with a gracious spirit. I didn't enjoy it then—nor in retrospect."

"You mustn't let him know that. His worship of you positively irradiates his face, and he's very handsome."

"Yes, he is handsome," said Ann, slowly. "I thought him the most superb animal I had ever seen as he went about sullenly cooking our suppper that night. He resented our coming, and I couldn't blame him for that. I assure you he glowered at us."

"His point of view is quite different now. You may make light of that night's experience, but he regards it as the greatest moment of his life. He insists that you were heroic."

Ann grew a little petulant. "I wish you wouldn't try to make mountains out of mole-hills. It was a most unpleasant experience, and I wish to forget it—not to have it dinned in my ears forever. My going was folly, and my stay in that ghastly place was a torment. Please allow me to put it out of my memory."

Mrs. Barnett looked at her friend in amazement. "Ann Rupert, do you realize what you've done? You've almost lost your temper. Wouldn't I rejoice if that night's vigil with death had shaken you out of your indifferentism. I tell you, life isn't the tepid thing you think it is. You're bored with things that once seemed worth while, but there are emotional facts in the world, my serene lady."

Ann rose. "I must go dress for dinner. Are we to have the usual collection of civil-engineers and English adventurers? You never had any subtlety of method, Jeannette. I don't mind your flinging these young men at my head, but, for Heaven's sake, don't be so obvious, or I shall begin to hate your horde of nondescripts."

Mrs. Barnett sank back in her chair. "Your egotism is insufferable. Sometimes I think you're not worthy the least of your suitors; but you'll meet your master one of these days."

Ann disdained to reply, and walked away really angry. "If she is going to take that tone, life here will be intolerable. I don't see why my friends should all be so eager to marry me off without my consent."

She had a moment of bitter homesickness, a feeling she had never known before. This mad trip into the West with a reckless and supersensitive boy grew each moment more disastrous. At the moment she fairly hated her cousins and all the guests at their table, and longed, with unspeakable hunger, for the roll of carriages on Fifth Avenue and the glitter and tumult of Broadway. The stony, uninterested stare of her mother was better than this prying, this overstrained interest on the part of Jeannette.

As for Raymond, he had been momentarily interesting as a cow-boy, and when he was lying at the brink of the grave he had assumed tragic value; but now that he was on the way to recovery he ceased to interest. "He is merely one of the thousands of other commonplace young Eastern men who have tried their fortunes in the West and failed," she said. "Why should I be burdened with any further care of him?"

Her resentment still sat upon her face as she went down to dinner, and though she was more than usually white and impassive she was also more alluring to the young engineers and college professors who bowed before her with hearts of wax. The man on her right, a government botanist, just returned from a four-months' trip in the dearth and desolation of Arizona, had all his fingers turned into thumbs by her beauty, and every attempt to serve her threatened disfigurement to furniture and to table-ware.

Don told again, for the fortieth time, the story of Raymond's shooting, and in spite of Ann's protests put her in as the heroine, which reinfuriated her almost to the point of leaving the table. The "Ah's!" and "Dear me's!" and "By Jove's!" volleying from the listeners were quite insupportable. One lady said, "Poor fellow!"

"Not at all," said Dr. Braide. "He was a lucky dog. I'd be shot any day to get such a nurse."

Jeannette saw the angry flush on Ann's face, and hastily turned the conversation into less personal channels.

Thus every influence swept her towards a dislike of the wounded man's very name, and thereafter she ignored his presence in the house—his being in the world—as though he did not exist. She neither asked after his health nor replied to any report or question made by her brother concerning him.

Louis brought to Raymond one day a small, limp book in red leather, which he proffered with the air of giving a gem.

The New Life

"What's this?" asked Raymond. "Your diary?"

"No; my father's. He was out here before I was born—when the Indians were here."

Raymond opened the volume with languid interest, but soon realized that he was looking into the past through the eyes of a poet. Part of it was written in ink, very legibly, but in a fine, running hand, while other of the pages were hastily scribbled in pencil, and not to be easily deciphered. Plainly the record had been made under great disadvantages and in the field. The inks were of various colors, some watery blue, some dusty black.

"Can you read this?" asked the rancher.

"Every word of it," the boy proudly answered.

"Decipher this for me—this one in pencil."

Louis took the book and read, reverently: "'I am sitting on a stone beside an overturned coach at the foot of Gooseneck Hill. Happily our coach is upright. Accidents do happen, it seems. Wonderful to say, no one was killed—not even the driver, who was responsible for the accident. He lost control of his team someway. We could see it all from the opposite side of the valley. It was tremendously exciting to watch them sweeping down the trail like a bead on a wire. It made me think of De Quincey. Our driver has hardly spoken a word since. We've all been busy getting the people out of the coach and disentangling the team.'"

"That must have been the hill coming down to Clear Creek," remarked Raymond. "Go on."

"It ends right there," said Louis, regretfully. "He got on the coach and didn't have time to write again till he reached Midgely's Ranch." He resumed reading. "'At first sight I was deeply impressed and a little alarmed by the rough dress and heavy arms of the men at this "half-way house." The walls were festooned with glittering new revolvers; but on closer inspection I discovered that most of these men were as harmless and as timid as myself. But there was something wildly grand in arriving as we did in the biting dusk at this lonely ranch, with its barking dogs, its big sheds swarming with horses. As I write here by the great open hearth, the roar of an icy, swift mountain stream mingles with the voice of the fire. There is something gloriously primeval in it all. I feel as though I were about to enter upon the actualities of a great American epic. I wish I had the power to express this scene in verse.'"

The boy stopped, this time from emotion. "I wish I could find that place. Do you suppose we could?"

"Yes; but it wouldn't be the same. The valley is full of cattle now, the trees are all cut down—irrigating ditches everywhere. The glory has gone, boy. Stick to the little red book. Have you any idea how your father looked at that time?"

Louis glowed again. "See here!" He extended the book again, opened at the front, wherein the picture of a slender, smiling, handsome young fellow in sombrero and hunting-clothes had been pasted.

"He enjoyed his new hat, didn't he?" said Raymond, to whom the essential incongruity of the refined face and border-ruffian toggery first appealed. "You're the image of your father," he added, looking keenly at the boy. "He don't look much older in this picture— taken at Sylvanite. Well, Sylvanite was a wild town in those days. Is there much about it in the book?"

"Ten pages. He wrote a page of fine script every

day; but I don't care so much for that—these stage-rides, and the big cañons, and crossing the rivers, and the Indians — he saw lots of Indians — the Utes—these are what interest me."

Raymond became profoundly interested in this book. Without conscious literary taste himself, he was able to perceive the unusual power with which the young traveller marshalled words. He read on, absorbed by the passion and purity of the young man's spirit. It was unaccountable that he should have this love and longing for the wilderness. What sort of a man was he? It was plain that Louis, and not Ann, had received the father's inheritance of romantic love for the untracked spaces.

There was an appeal in the closing entry of this journal which touched Raymond profoundly, for his love of the high country and its sunshine and starshine, though less poetic in expression, was deeper in the grain. The entry was headed "The Last View." "I can still see the purple peaks lording over the plain. The portals of the West are closing behind me. In an hour my mountains of Hesper will have sunk beneath the plains. I love my home and my friends in the East, but this primeval world has laid its spell upon me. I shall come again next year."

"Did he come again?" asked Raymond of the boy.

"No," answered Louis, sadly. And it was soon evident to Raymond that the lad knew very little of his father beyond the message in the worn little book.

"Leave this with me, Louis. I want to read it all," he said, and the boy was glad of this interest.

Mrs. Barnett came in later and asked, "What are you reading?"

"It is a journal kept by Louis' father Did you know him?"

"Oh, very well. He was my favorite uncle."

"Tell me of him. Who was he—how did he come to make this trip?"

Mrs. Barnett took a comfortable seat. "I don't know where Uncle Phil got his streak of sentiment. He was one of six brothers, all successful business-men; keen, practical—you know the kind. But Phil— Well, he was the odd sheep — he always seemed a boy to me. He worked in the bank, but his mind was on other things. I don't remember how they came to send him out here, but I can recall perfectly the effect he had on me when talking of his trip. He glorified this country. He saw the mountains as the old-time landscapists pictured them. When I first came I wept with disappointment, the range seemed so prosaic by contrast. He talked of nothing else for a year. Then he married, and gradually ceased referring to his experiences."

"He never came again, Louis tells me."

"No. His wife was not the kind of girl to go West. I don't want to say anything severe about Alicia, but she made Phil very unhappy. When Ann was born, Phil wanted to call her Hesper—in memory of his trip to the West—but Alicia cried out against it. It *was* an odd name, but it was pretty, and there was no reason why the father shouldn't have had his wish; but that was her way. She was cold and selfish even in her honeymoon. I never saw such a girl. Phil went with her to every fashionable resort in Europe, but she not merely refused to make a trip into his Hesperean Mountains, but she wouldn't let him go. He used to get up into the Adirondacks now and then, I remember, but only for a day or two. Oh, how exacting she was! After Louis was born she grew worse. She became morbid. I never could see that she had a particle of maternal affection. If Ann isn't like her, it is because Phil's blood is in her veins. Louis is exactly as Phil was, as I recall him when I saw him first."

"You say the father called her Hesper?" pursued Raymond, acutely interested in all that concerned Ann.

"It was his pet name for her. Few people know it. I don't think Louis knows it—for Ann considered the name absurd as she grew older, and never refers to it. I think it is a pretty name—don't you?"

"Yes. It is beautiful." His eyes took on a musing look. "I can understand how he felt, for, in those days the Crestones were fabled mountains. All this country seemed a great way off—almost as remote as the place where the evening-star goes down—I suppose that is what he meant. It's all quite commonplace now."

"Not to Louis."

"That's true. He sees it as a boy sees the world, and then he's read this little book till his father's thought adds the glory of the past to it. I suppose his sister takes her mother's view."

"Yes; she's her mother's daughter," answered Mrs. Barnett, significantly. "I don't know what to think of the girl. There are times when I love her dearly, and then again she exasperates me so I want to box her ears."

Hesper! Somehow the name expressed the poetry of the father's conception, and with little else to do the wounded man gave long hours to recalling and reliving his experiences with her as his nurse.

He longed with a great longing to see her again, but to his curious shyness had been added the humility of one who feels himself unworthy to ask any favor, and the troubled look which came now and again into the lines of his face made Louis sad. The boy idealized him, made of him a wonderful being, better worth serving than any monarch, and in this strain he talked to Ann till she impatiently begged him to stop.

"You must not fix upon such a man as your ideal, Louis. What has he done that you should exalt him? You don't even know his real name."

This the boy was compelled to admit. "Of course I don't know much about him, but I like him, all the same. I know he would make a brave fight, if he were called upon to do so. You can't always tell why you like a person. He's awfully gentle and considerate when you come to know him, and he's a bully story-teller."

"All that may be true, and he still be unworthy your adoration. You must remember, laddie, that your passion for the wild West is of recent development. You may change. Father returned from his trip and settled down, you remember, and never went back."

"Yes, but he didn't forget. He was always talking about it, and you can tell what it meant to him by what he wrote. If I had known about his journal earlier, I would have been out here before this. I didn't like England, I didn't care for Europe. I do love this, and I don't see why you can't leave me here and go back," he ended, at the brink of tears.

The New Life

"Now, now, what are you complaining about?" she asked, with sharp inflection. "I haven't asked you to go home. I was only trying to correct your absurd estimate of Mr. Raymond."

"You needn't bother," he cried out, hurt and saddened. "I can take care of myself."

In her secret heart Ann admitted that she, too, had been touched by the indefinable charm of Raymond's voice and manner; but the question of how best to check his growing power over her brother's life had become a very serious problem, for as the days wore on he put her aside as completely as she ignored his hero.

Together Raymond and the boy read the little red book, mapping the points described as best they could— a task of some difficulty, for the traveller had purposely given mythical names to the towns, rivers, and peaks. It had all been a wonderland to Philip Rupert, and he took care to have no stupid or vulgar name mar the perfect effect.

There was something in all this which refined and softened the young rancher. Joined with his love for "Hesper" (as he loved to call Ann in secret), this boyish father's enthusiasms transmuted every reckless, bitter impulse into stern resolutions to enter upon a new life — a life with purpose and devotion in its course.

Everything conspired to make Ann alluring. The rough walls of the ranch-house had been a foil for her exquisite color, her daintiness, her calm beauty. Then, through the long night, as she softened, growing wan and sorrowful over him, he had watched her, absorbing every detail of her presence; even in his pain and while facing death he had taken account of the sweet line of her quivering lips, her graceful hands, so soft and strong, and of her deep, serious eyes. She had come to stand for something more than a woman to him. She was clothed in light by his gratitude and his passionate, adoring love.

VIII

Raymond Vanishes

AT last there came a day when the doctor permitted his patient to be clothed and seated in an easy-chair, and, calling Mrs. Barnett to him, Raymond asked, "Do you think Miss Rupert will see me now?"

"I will ask her," replied Jeannette, with due appreciation of the romantic situation.

Ann rose to comply, with a little thrill of unpleasant excitement. She did not want to see him, and yet she could not decently refuse.

At the door of the sitting-room Mrs. Barnett stopped, and the girl walked in alone, her face set in lines of cold disdain.

Raymond sat in a big, padded chair, with his back to the window and the sunlight streaming over his head. He wore a handsome, gray dressing-gown, and the linen at his neck and wrists was spotlessly clean. His hands were refined—almost delicate in effect, and his clean-shaven face and his well-brushed, abundant brown hair gave evidence of a most careful toilet. Something mystically solemn and sweet was in his eyes, and his lips trembled as he greeted her. "This is very good of you. Pardon me, won't you? I am forbidden to stand."

"I beg you, do not think of it."

"Dare I ask you to be seated? I want to thank you more suitably than I have been able to do for what you did for me."

"Please don't, Mr. Raymond. I assure you I deserve no credit. I went out there under compulsion, and what I did was determined by pressure of circumstances. I'm not a bit of a heroine, and I do not like praise."

He was chilled by her tone, and for a moment hesitated. "A sick man may be forgiven some things," he began to say at last. "I may as well confess that I have been longing to see you. I have been trying for many days to rise and dress, in order that I might have you come in. You must let me ask your forgiveness for the rude way in which I received you that day. All that I did seems incredible to me now—like the action of another man."

A gleam of amusement crossed Ann's face. "I didn't blame you. I'm willing to admit that your position was trying."

He was too exalted of mood to respond to her quizzical tone. "I had lived for years quite apart from any—from association with cultivated people, and, besides, I had begun to feel that I was wasting my life, and had become irritable. I went to the ranch to pay off a debt, and I—well, I had fallen into a groove. You recalled me to better things."

"I and the bullet," she said, rather flippantly, for she was becoming apprehensive of the trend of his confidences.

He ignored her interruption, or, rather, he ploughed across it with something like his old-time resolution. "It is due to you to know—or, at any rate, I desire you to know, that I am not a fugitive from justice. Baker thought he was being funny."

"I am not so dull as you think, Mr. Raymond. I understood him perfectly."

"I am glad you did. It is true I am estranged from my family, but it is not due— My faults have never been criminal."

"Please do not feel it necessary to explain," interrupted Ann. "It is painful to you, and — and it is wholly unnecessary. I beg you to desist. I hope you will understand that I am in no sense doubting you."

A shadow of pain crossed his face. Somehow the reality of their meeting was not as he had imagined it.

She, on her part, was angry and displeased with herself, and resentful of his implied social equality, and yet he looked the gentleman, and his face was very handsome, very moving in its clear pallor; suffering had infinitely refined its lines, but she could not forget his services as cook and cow-boy, and, besides, she hated being perturbed. She resolutely changed the subject.

"Dr. Braide says you are getting on splendidly, and that you will soon be returning to the ranch."

Checked and chilled by her manner, he plainly abandoned all further thought of confiding in her and answered, wearily and sadly, "It will be a long time before I return to the life on the ranch. I have other plans now."

Ann half regretted her action, and, as she rose, said, with a smiling assumption of easy, friendly interest, which hurt him worse than anything she had hitherto spoken, "I think it wonderful, the way you are coming on. We will see you at dinner in a few days."

"Thank you. I shall be down at the earliest moment," he quietly replied, and leaned back in his chair, white and suffering, his eyes closed, his lips quivering.

Ann was well aware that she had not lived up to her higher self in this interview, and that she had been cruelly unresponsive and distant with him. "And yet I don't see how I could have acted differently," she argued with her better self. "He must not go on thinking me more deeply interested in his life than I really am. He must be taught that a mere accidental meeting, such as ours has been, is not the working-out of fate—at least, not with me. It is better for him to suffer a little now than a great deal further on."

Mrs. Barnett was impatiently waiting for her return. "What did he say?" she breathlessly asked. "I'm dying to know."

Ann answered with evasive indifference. "He thanked me again for my heroic action, and begged pardon for his rudeness; all of which he might have spared himself the trouble of repeating."

Mrs. Barnett was on the scent for romance. "What else?"

"Nothing else."

"Poor fellow! He has been struggling towards this event for days. Only the doctor's express orders kept him from getting up ten days ago. He has been all the morning dressing for it, and now you tell me, in that supercilious tone, that nothing happened."

Ann fired into anger. "What could happen? You needn't speak in riddles, Jeannette Ward. What do you think should have happened — come, now, you silly, romantic thing?"

Mrs. Barnett became evasive in her turn. "He might have told you the story of his life."

Raymond Vanishes

"Why should he do that, and why should I listen to it?" Ann replied, with more of heat and bitterness than the case seemed to demand. "I am not his father-confessor. I always knew you were absurdly romantic, but this is beyond anything. I warn you, if you go any further in this direction, we shall fight."

Some note in her voice touched Mrs. Barnett, and she slowly replied: "Ann Rupert, you are the coldest, cruelest creature I ever knew. I know what you did to that poor fellow—you unmercifully snubbed him—you froze his gratitude on his lips. Of course, you are infinitely his superior"—she became weakly sarcastic at this point—"but you are not justified in stabbing a sick man to the heart."

"You're quite mistaken. I was very nice to him."

"Nice! I've seen you *nice* to young men before. Oh, I'd like to see some man crush you! I'd enjoy seeing you *crawl!*"

Ann, quite restored to good-humor, smiled, and the gleam of her beautiful teeth brought back her girlish charm. "I like your kind heart, Jeannette. Anger is becoming to you," and she took up a book and retired to her favorite chair.

Mrs. Barnett went immediately to Raymond's door and knocked. At his word she entered. He sat where Ann had left him, but Louis was beside him, showing him a new drawing.

"Isn't that wonderful!" said Raymond, holding the sketch in the air, his eyes aglow with pride in the boy. "If I could do that I would never be lonesome or restless. I wish I knew my use in the world as certainly as Louis does."

The young artist flushed with the pleasure. "It's

just as wonderful to ride the way you do—and throw a rope—and all that. I'll teach you to draw if you want me to."

Raymond turned to Mrs. Barnett with a look in which amusement and a certain sorrow met. "I'm long past such instruction, lad. I haven't sense enough to keep out of mischief. You draw and I'll do the posing. I'm a good poser; don't you think so, Mrs. Barnett?"

"I don't know what you mean?" said she, feeling vaguely his pain and discouragement—his disillusionment.

"I posed as a farmer and deceived good Don Barnett. I made up for a cow-boy and fooled Baker and the rest of the squad. And now I'm posing as an invalid when I ought to be out on the ranch again. It's time I rode away to a new range."

Mrs. Barnett was alarmed at the undertone of bitterness in his words. "You must not think of even walking down-stairs for a week."

"But I can't sit here and sink deeper and deeper into obligation to you," he answered. "What rights have I in this room? I'm only a poor, wandering ne'er-do-well, and your beautiful home makes me ashamed—more than ashamed—it fills me with a sense of guilt. I can walk now, and I ought not stay another day."

Mrs. Barnett knew very well that his mood was due to Ann's icy disdain, and she realized, too, how difficult the task of diverting his mind from this foolish purpose would be. She said, gently: "You were injured in our service, Robert, and it is our duty to look after you. You must not utter another word of this sort of talk to me, or I will call Don, and *then* you will hear a voice that will make you quake."

He smiled. "Men don't make me quake, but girls have always scared me blue, I admit it." He returned to his original thought. "But I've been such a burden to you all these days, that troubles me. Your kindness has been out of all proportion to my deserving."

"There's only one way in which to repay our kindness."

"How is that?"

"By keeping in a heavenly temper, and getting well and strong. I tell you, frankly, I will not listen to your walking out of this room for a week."

Louis, who had been sitting in some wonder, trying to catch the undercurrent of this talk, put his hand on Raymond's knee and said, "When you go, I go, too; remember that."

Raymond, looking down into the boy's admiring, shining face, slowly replied: "I can't promise that, Louis. I've cut loose from the old life. What my new life will be I can't tell. It's all uncertainty now."

"There's time to settle all that," said Mrs. Barnett, decisively, "after you are able to walk. For the present you are our guest, or, if not that, our prisoner, and I appoint Louis turnkey."

"Hah!" cried Louis, melodramatically. "The boy turnkey is on your trail; escape if you can!"

Mrs. Barnett left the room while yet it echoed to their laughter. "He's too good for Ann Rupert, and that's the truth," she said to her husband. "He's a splendid fellow. I don't care what his mystery is."

It was interesting to Jeannette to observe that evening-dress changed Ann's estimate of Raymond's character. He was not a boor, that the girl already knew; but she was conventional enough to welcome a chance to see this unaccountable ranchman in the garb of polite society. She had to admit that he looked surprisingly well as he came slowly into the library just before the little Chinese chime sounded for dinner. Every trace of the cow-boy, the man of sun-smit, wind-swept plain, was gone. He was pale, languid, but self-contained, and wore his dinner-suit with easy grace.

Mrs. Barnett ran to him with outstretched hands. "Why, Mr. Raymond, are you sure the doctor will sanction this? Please don't stand — take a chair. Does Don know of this?"

"Oh yes. He sent me on ahead in order to surprise you."

"You certainly have succeeded in doing *that*. I'm so glad to have you down, only you must not overdo it. Isn't he looking well, Ann?"

His manner towards Ann was that of a polite acquaintance merely, and her fear of something — she hardly knew what—instantly vanished. Her imagination was stirred by the vivid contrast between the figure he now made and the lithe, sullen, booted and spurred rancher cooking that rank and odorous supper. "He plays the part well," she thought. "I wonder who and what he really is." And she half wished at the moment that she had permitted him to confide to her his life's history.

His bearing during dinner and throughout the evening made her forget the kind of person he had hitherto seemed to her, and she began to study him in his true character. He dropped all his ranch-life phrases, and, putting aside his reserve, talked with entire intellectual freedom, showing a knowledge of books and of communities remarkable in any man. He assumed nothing, but grew frank and gay almost to boyishness, and his eyes, when they met hers, were as politely deferential and as distantly admiring as those of the college professor who sat opposite. Once or twice, as she encountered his glance, a mysterious movement ran about her heart, and her breath quickened.

As they rose from dinner, and while he stood to allow her to pass, he said: "You are very beautiful to-night. Mountain air has done wonders for you."

"You are very courteous," she responded, and her eyes fell, exasperatingly, and she walked away with a sense of having revealed a weakness.

He came into the drawing-room half an hour later to say good-night to his hostess, looking very tired and pale, and when he took Ann's hand his eyes were burning with deep, inner passion. "Good-night," he said, "and forgive me for any impertinence." She scarcely had time to reply, to ask his meaning, for Mrs. Barnett ordered him instantly to bed.

No sooner was he safely out of hearing than the ladies began to discuss him, and turned to Ann in the hope that she would recount the story of her eventful night on the ranch, but Ann shrugged her shoulders, and a perceptible frown gathered on her brow. "Oh, please don't ask me to go over that dreadful experience again," she protested, and her displeasure was too genuine to be mistaken.

With instant good-will the guests fell upon a discussion of the merits of the new Hungarian band which had but recently been engaged for the Casino, while

Ann sat in silence, a perplexed abstraction in her eyes.

Louis became restless as soon as Raymond left the dining-room—the talk of the men did not interest him—and after a few minutes slipped out and, mounting the stairs, knocked timidly at Rob's door. He was on the point of turning away when Raymond called, "Come!" As Louis entered, the young rancher looked up from his writing absent-mindedly. "Hullo, artist!" he said, with an effort at his usual camaraderie. "Have you finished your cigar?"

Louis, almost as embarrassed as a girl, twisted on his heel. There was no reason for his visit, except that he would rather be with his hero than with his cousin. Raymond, on his part, was disturbed by the boy's coming, and for a moment an awkwardness, hitherto unknown, silenced them both. At last the man spoke. "Well, laddie, what can I do for you?"

Louis searched his mind for some excuse. "Can't you go riding with me to-morrow. I want to be the first one to go out with you."

"I don't believe I'll be able to ride for some time. I have a notion that I'll walk a good while before I ride. I feel pretty tired just from climbing the stairs."

"Well, then, let's take a walk to-morrow morning."

"We'll see what the doctor says. Good-night," Raymond replied, and Louis went reluctantly away, promising to call him at seven.

No voice responded to his knock next morning, and, hurrying to Barnett's room, Louis called, excitedly, "Cousin Don, have you seen Rob?"

Raymond Vanishes

Barnett, splashing in his tub, shouted, "No; can't you find him?"

"He isn't in his room."

"He's gone down to breakfast, then. Hurry along and keep him company. Don't let him go out."

Louis rushed into the breakfast-room, but found it empty. The maid said: "Are you looking for Mr. Raymond? He came down very early and said he was going out for a walk."

The boy hurried out-doors, filled with dismay. "He shouldn't be out alone. He might get dizzy and fall." He ran round the block, eagerly seeking Raymond, who was nowhere in sight. When Barnett entered Rob's room he found three letters lying on the little desk. One was addressed to Don, one to Ann, and one to "Turnkey Louis."

Barnett broke the seal and read his note almost at a glance.

"DEAR BARNETT,—I'm sorry to pull out in this way, but I am afraid it's my only way. I have been very uncomfortable because of my growing indebtedness to you and Mrs. Barnett, and so I have cut loose. Please don't think me ungrateful. It is because I feel so deeply your kindness that I go. Don't look for me. I'm going to hole-up for a few days till I get strong. If you happen to get any clew to where I've gone, don't tell the boy. I can see that his sister does not approve of his fondness for me, and she is quite right. I'm not a proper companion for a boy of his sort. I enclose a check, which squares us so far as money can, but your kindness in other ways, and especially Mrs. Barnett's care and assistance, I am in despair of ever paying. I slide out because it would be difficult and painful to say good-bye, and, besides, I feel that I *must* cut loose from the boy."

Raymond's note to Ann was short, almost curt:

"Since my thanks are a burden to you, the least I can do is to take myself out of your life and beg pardon for having entered it. Had I attended to my duties that night of the fire, you would not have been troubled by me. I stayed because you were beautiful, and that is the whole truth. It is not the first time a man has neglected his duties for a woman, and the pain I now suffer in giving up all hope of meeting you again is a just punishment for my presumption. I am sorry to go without saying good-bye to Louis, but it is best. I know you do not like his growing regard for me, and you are quite right."

Ann's first feeling was one of resentment. "He is putting me in the wrong." Then came a distinct sense of guilt. As she recalled his words and glances of the night before, she was able to interpret what had puzzled her. Had she made life intolerable for him? For a moment she suffered with a sense of having driven him into danger, and returned to the letter. No, it was too firm, too decided, to even remotely suggest a fleeing from life.

Louis came to her door and cried out, dolefully, "Ann, Rob has gone away."

"I know it. Come in."

He entered with troubled, tearful face, and, in deeply aggrieved tone, said: "He went without saying good-bye. I want to go hunt him and bring him back; but Uncle Don says that we must respect his wish. All the same, I like him, and I want him back. No, I don't—I want to go with him."

"And leave me?"

His resentment, long smouldering, burst forth: "Yes,

Raymond Vanishes

I would! Don't you suppose I have seen how you
treated him? You think because you're from New
York you can snub a man like Rob; but you're not
up to him—you're not half as good as he is. I'm going
away, and I'm never coming back. You're a hateful,
miserable thing. You don't do anything but look
down on people." He stamped his foot. "I despise
you. I don't care if you are my sister. I wish the
devil would get you."

Ann listened in astonishment to this outburst from
her brother, and then cuttingly remarked:

"One would think I had taken away some plaything
of yours. Go out of my room, and stay out till you
can treat me with respect."

"I'm going, and you'll never see me again. I'm going to follow Rob. I don't care what you say." With
this defiant cry he rushed from the room.

Ann remained seated before her dressing-table for a
long time in silence. Louis' utterance, while of a piece
with his occasional emotional outbreaks, had gone beyond all bounds, all reason. Never before had his
anger reached black rage. What was there in Raymond to win and wear such devotion? He had dis-
played himself not at all. Since his wound he had been
able to do little except to lie on his bed and permit
Louis to read to him and prattle of plans for the future;
and yet he had taken first place in the boy's life. "He
has turned my brother's love to hate."

A keen ache of jealousy ran through the proud girl's
heart. The one soul of vital interest in her life—her
sweet little brother—seemed about to pass from her
hands to that of an adventurer. Her resentment of his
influence blazed hot within her. "I will defeat him

with his own weapons," she said. "I will win him back to me. I will go wherever he wishes to go."

But Louis did not return to lunch, and she was greatly troubled. He did not appear at dinner, and at last, openly alarmed, Ann told Mrs. Barnett of Louis' bitter accusation and of his threat that he would never return.

"The man has bewitched him. He was fairly beside himself. Where can he have gone?"

"Don't worry. Don will find him. He'll get tired of it and come back. These boyish tantrums don't last."

"It scares me to think of that poor, innocent lad spending the night alone in a big, wicked Western city. I wish Don would hurry home. Can't I go down to his office?"

"Oh no; there's no need of you're going. I'll telephone him at once."

When Barnett returned, Ann, white with anxiety, poured out her story. He comforted her by saying, "You take it too seriously. I will notify the police at Cinnabar and Mogalyon. They'll locate him in an hour."

They did not find him, and Ann passed a miserable night, imagining all sorts of ill adventures into which Louis might be led, and would have accompanied Barnett on his quest next day but for his firm command: "Don't be absurd. I can find him alone much quicker."

"Bring him back, if you have to use force," she cried. And then, with a knowledge of Raymond's power, she added, "If you find Mr. Raymond, please tell him to send laddie home—say I wish it."

Raymond Vanishes

With these words in his ear Barnett took his way to his office. At lunch he was more concerned. "He's not in Cinnabar, nor any of the surrounding towns. He may have gone back to the ranch. I will wire out there this afternoon. Did he have any money?"

"Yes. I had just given him his allowance. He must have had nearly two hundred dollars."

Don whistled. "A smart boy can hide-out a good while on that. However, he'll come back when his pet wears off."

Even though Raymond had taken himself bodily out of her life, his power to disturb and thwart Ann's will remained. She began to fear him a little. He was bigger, more powerful, than she had thought him. Could she have found him in the days which followed— days of increasing unrest and anxiety—she would have humbly asked him to find the runaway and bring him back to her; but he had disappeared as utterly as if he had never been.

Barnett visited several of the neighboring towns, including Bozle, the great mining town, but without result, and Ann began to distrust even her brother, and to wonder whether he and Raymond had not planned this desertion together; and this thought gave her a painful sense of being alone and loveless in the world.

IX

Raymond Enters Sky-Town

MEANWHILE, during Raymond's days on the ranch, while the cattle were withering away on the plains, and the long trail from the south was filling with grass, a most notable settlement had been forming like some new kind of parasitic growth on the westward shoulder of old Mogalyon, the mighty peak to the west. Originally the hunting-ground for the Utes, this land, after their withdrawal, became a mountain pasture whereto the herds from the rainless lower country were driven when the grass grew scant and sear. It was, in fact, a high park surrounded by secondary crests of the Rampart Range, but so suave, so fragrant of bloom, so velvet-soft of grass were these genial summits that the cow-boys, racing across them, thought of them and spoke of them only as hills. The vast, faraway peaks of the Crestones alone appealed to them as mountains.

In the midst of these hills, in the lap of two smooth, grassy domes, old Philip Le Beau established a cow-camp in the early seventies, and called it Belle Marie, after his wife. This, however, proved to be too fanciful for his cow-boy neighbors, who promptly called it "Le Beau's Hole," and in the end it was known among cattle-men as Bozle Creek.

Raymond Enters Sky-Town

Just west of Le Beau's Camp, and sentinel to the valley of the Loup, stood a symmetrical peak which some missionary to the red people had called Mount Horeb. About the year 1870 some persons not missionaries planted gold in the soil in convenient places at the base of this hill, and raised a mighty shout over the discovery of a new Eldorado. A rush took place, and to the outside world the region became known as "the Mount Horeb Mining District," and was alluded to with deep-seated resentment, with curses; for the sharp practices of those who made it known had caused much loss of time and money.

But there were miners whom neither the dogmatic opinions of geologists nor the tricks of schemers could turn aside from a faith that somewhere on the mighty slopes of Mogalyon lay veins of gold, and these continued to chip and to dig and to hammer, even while the cow-boys hallooed behind their rushing herds and branded their calves in Le Beau's weather-beaten corral. The world soon forgot Mount Horeb and its conscienceless swindlers, and the prospectors drifted to other and more promising fields in other ranges to the west.

But Valley Springs was becoming known as a pleasant health resort, and the waters of its springs were being bottled and shipped to the Eastern cities. Each year a larger number of stricken ones came to find respite, if not recovery, in its gloriously bright sunlight and pure air. For years it remained a village, and its business-men merely shopkeepers and resident ranchowners, but, as its fame spread, families of wealth and social position in the East began to settle along the bank of The Bear, and to build homes into which the sunlight streamed with healing magic; and the men of these families began to look about for business and for investment, and not a few of them were in the mood to listen when rough-bearded men began to plod down the trail from Bozle Creek bringing sacks of promising ore.

Returns from these samples, sent away to be assayed, started a flight of golden eagles east and west. Again the adventurous youth, the skilled prospector, the gambler, the harlot, and all the uneasy and shifting elements that follow such lures, poured into the valley and toiled over the trail to the grassy hills of Bozle and camped around old Le Beau's corrals to pick at the hills and to wait developments.

At first, though short of breath by reason of the altitude—two full miles above the sea—some of these incomers laughed, and some were angry. "Gold! In these grassy hills? Impossible!" And they went away again with bitter words. It was Mount Horeb repeated on a large scale.

But the assayers, the men of learning, persisted, and in their little mortars brayed the ore, and in tiny, portable furnaces smelted for many a sturdy miner minute buttons of shining metal. The gold was there, and at last even the most sceptical believed.

Then the inflow began in earnest. The trail was beaten smooth by swarming feet. It became a stage-road. A great railroad sent surveyors toiling up each of the deep and winding cañons in the attempt to reach the mighty camp whose fame was beginning to shine throughout the world. The beautiful, grassy hills were blotched with eruptions of red earth. Mounds of soil and broken rocks betrayed where soil-stained men burrowed like resolute moles beneath the sod. The rippling, shining groves of aspen disappeared, shaved away as with a prodigious scythe to provide walls for cabins, wood for fires, timber for windlasses, and stulls for mines. The tall, dark, martial - gestured firs followed, rank by rank. Paths appeared leading from burrow to burrow like runways in a town of prairie-dogs.

The main street of Bozle was ten thousand feet above the sea; but at last, on the top of Pine Mountain, a vein of ore running two thousand dollars to the ton was discovered, and another town arose—full eleven thousand feet above sea-level—the highest town in all America, and this became at once celebrated above all others, and was called Sky-Town.

To this camp, as towards a blazing beacon, the men who take chances came, and in its streets gold-hunters from Australia, South Africa, and California mingled with ox-eyed runaway plough-boys from Kansas and Iowa, wind-tanned herders from Texas and Wyoming, and tall planters from the valleys of Utah and Colorado. These gentle and unsophisticated fortune-seekers were called "alfalfa miners" by the hardened and self-confident men of hazards, and even after it became known that more than half of all the big strikes had been made by these same "tenderfeet" they were regarded with contempt. In the end, Sky-Town dominated the whole camp and gave name to it. Bozle, Grass Mountain, Pin Gulch, Hoffman, all were subordinated in fame as they were topographically, and the press alluded to the region as the Sky-Town Mining District.

It was the most accessible of all the camps of America. Its nearness to the plain and to the transcontinental railways made it possible for the greenest of green grocers, the most timid villager, to pack his valise and invade the mountains; and he came!—in tens of thousands; but as he commonly walked the streets for a week or two, looking on all the vice and hazard of the place with wonder-stricken eyes, and then faded away, returning to his hoe and his plough, his presence counted for little. The cow-boys, too, came loping in over the trails from the round-ups in the valleys to the west and from the plains to the east, but as they could not mine from the saddle, and as they loved their horses better than gold, they, too, filed away down the valley, leaving their savings with the faro-banks.

In those days the bar-room of the Mountain House in Bozle was the central stock-exchange of the whole camp. It swarmed of an evening with business-men from Denver, Kansas City, Chicago, Salt Lake, San Francisco, and New York. Every great newspaper had its representative there, alert and indefatigable, seeking the latest word of strikes and sales; and great artists, sent out by the Eastern magazines, sat about the mighty log fire taking mental note of its details, and studying the types gathered from the uttermost parts of the earth.

Notwithstanding Bozle's unprecedented accessibility, these Eastern men loved to imagine themselves exposed to dangers and to suffering—such hardships as the gold-hunters of California and Idaho had undergone. Some of them assumed the garb of wild Western desperadoes. They wore guns, and strapped leather leggings to their slender legs and clapped wide sombreros upon their bald heads. They played parts in this border drama, not merely for others like unto themselves, but for themselves. When, under the lead of Rocky Mountain Kelly, they rode forth upon the hills, it was with a sense of exploration, a seeking of adventure, a daring of danger; and when at sunset they re-entered the door of the hotel, it was with such joy as hunters hail the gleam of the camp-fire, where faithful comrades keep vigil.

Mingling with these genial actors, these boyish, fraudulent bad men and desperate characters, were a few investors from New York and Boston and London, who prided themselves on never for a moment losing their hold on a single habit or custom of their native towns. The Boston man tetered about in patent-leather shoes, with firm-set, pale jaw. The New-Yorker wore the latest cut of coat and the newest shape of pot-hat, while the Londoner querulously complained of the soap and towels, and gloomily turned his fried steak from end to end in hope of finding some part of it broiled.

At the time when Raymond entered it, Sky-Town was the busiest, most vital, and in some ways the most picturesque mining district in the world. It was at its height as a poor man's camp. New territory was being opened up each day. Each evening brought stories of strikes—scores of them. Each saloon was a miniature exchange and held a throng intently full of bargains and plans, but the great central hall of the Mountain House in Bozle was the chief meeting-place of expert, prospector, and investor.

With all its bustle and pressure of elbow to elbow, the streets were quiet. No man raised furious outcry, for no one did battle with the fist—the tradition of the revolver was still all powerful. Curses were polite and low-voiced, for the free miner, the gambler, the hunter, and the cow-boy each alike resented brawling as the cheap recreation of hired hands. To be quite fair, only now and then was a man killed—generally at the gaming-tables—so far had the camp recognized the change since the days of forty-nine and sixty-three.

As the district was made up of those who took chances, it followed that gaming was the chief amusement of the miner and the business of first magnitude even in the saloons. Every drinking-place had its long rows of devices calculated to induce the unwary or the self-confident to take instant hazard. Day and night the click of the marble in the bowl, rattle of " chips," the steady drone of the " crap-shooter " went on. A mountain-poet, writing from close-hand experience, said of a rival camp, "It is day all day in the daytime, and there is no night in Creede;" and this precisely applied to Sky-Town and Bozle. And yet old miners, who had seen Yuma, Pocatello, and Dead Pine, scornfully said: "This is a collection of tenderfeet—a town of punkin-rollers. The real thing is gone forever."

Admitting that they were right, it was vividly interesting to see this whirlpool absorb the grizzled and scarred veterans of the inland ranges as well as the truant sons of Kansas and Nebraska. It was a land of which anything might be predicted—a district as cosmopolitan as any in the world.

The streets of Bozle were graceless and grassless, but Valley Springs was a bower of trees and growing vines. The houses of the peak were tents, slab-shacks, and cabins of aspen poles, and remained so, while splendid stone palaces had already appeared in the valley, and every comfort and nearly every luxury of the East were obtainable, almost common. Both were made resplendent by their association with the great mountain, which for a hundred years had lured men across the dusty plain, beckoning with silent but ever-changing majesty throughout the seasons. Valley Springs sat at his feet. Bozle perched on his shoulder, pecking at his heart like a vulture.

The residents of these singular towns, diverse as they seemed, were, after all, of the same essential character. They were gamblers by nature—the men of the valley no less than those of the peak. As one of them said: "Gold is a priceless thing—only for the few. It is not a business—it is a venture."

In other ways the people of Bozle were peculiar. They took little account of the weather. Rains or snows were alike to them. They had no gardens to grow thirsty for water, no vegetables to be nipped by the frost. Stocks and the daily output of this or that mine formed their staple of interest, their chief anxiety. They could not endure the slow growth of grain, but they bore repeated failures of shafts or tunnels with smiling unconcern. Dreaming of sudden wealth and vast palaces in the future, they lived on bacon and beans in cabins of poles so low that only the women and children could walk erect.

The streets of this amazing camp were repulsive and barren, but the sky that roofed them was superb. Range after range of mountains lay to the west, serrate, illimitable, marble-white with sudden snow-falls; but no green thing grew in the little yards and open spaces —but what of that? The conical heaps of ore were better worth while than clumps of lilacs. What need had they of daisies in a land where the splash of ore in a seam was subtler than moss, and ingots of gold more glorious than poppies? These men, riding across the hills, looked upon the earth, not to discover flora, but the " float " of golden ledges. To them a bed of crumbled, white quartz was of greater beauty than lilies.

No one really lived in Sky-Town or Bozle—they were merely staying for a change of fortune. Strange to say, the most permanent of all the homes were built by the faro-dealers—the most impermanent, one would say, of the bankers of the town. For the most part, the streets consisted of a disorderly flock of cabins, many of them resembling the box-cars of a freight-train; but here and there a really picturesque log-house, with wide eaves, stood beneath a clump of firs, whose rigid, horizontal branches added something fine and austere to the picture. All paths fell into each other at last and ended in the saloons, the ways to the grocery being less deeply worn. Not that the camp was notably drunken, for it was not; but when the day's work was done each man sought diversion and the news. These commodities he found at "The Thirst Parlor" and "The Golden Horn."

Sky-Town was, therefore, the cupola of Sky-Camp. It surveyed the whole field, dominated only by the glittering crest of Mogalyon, which rose nearly four thousand feet higher into the thin and fleckless air. Bozle and Hoffman and Indian Creek and Eureka and a half-dozen other villages lay below.

As a mining-camp, Sky-Town had no fellow in the world. It had no cañons, no picturesque grouping of rocks and trees. It rose to the regions of clouds, and yet it had no streams, not even springs, and at times men suffered for lack of water to drink. It disordered all previous ideas of mines and prospecting ground, yet each day it amazed even the most sanguine by its output of ore.

Raymond Enters Sky-Town

The old Californian, the veterans from Africa and Australia, enjoyed no more favor than those who came into it straight from the ranch. Seemingly, it was everybody's game, with no distinction to the very wise and no discrimination against the foolish. The highest rules of mining were made of little account, every precedent seemed torn and cast away.

This was the town, the camp, towards which Raymond had been gazing in longing and irresolution for two years, and to which he directed his steps as soon as he was able to walk with something of his old-time vigor. The peak represented to him a chance to rise out of his slough. It was a hope, a possibility, an opportunity to begin the new life which some change in his heart now demanded of him. He was done with small things, with trivial affairs. Henceforth he resolved to live largely to retrieve himself in the eyes of those who loved him.

"In such a camp," he reasoned, "my luck is as good as any other man's."

For a week he did nothing but stroll slowly up and down the streets of Bozle, studying his surroundings, listening to all that was said, and asking searching questions of every man who seemed to know anything of mining matters. The altitude at first troubled him greatly, and to walk up the slightest incline gave him keen pain. Every air-passage distended rigidly, ached with fatigue. Deep breathing was especially painful to him because of his wound; but he ate well and slept well, and day by day his strength and native resolution expanded within him, and he began to definitely seek a place whereon to try his hands at labor.

One night, as he sat toasting his shins before the big

fire in the hotel, he became immensely interested in the grand physical proportions and easy, unstudied grace of a middle-aged miner who stood with his back to the fire replying to the rapid questions of a young reporter whose head was bent absorbedly above his note-book and pencil. The prospector satisfied every requisite of a mountaineer. His massive head, covered with grizzled hair, his handsome, weather-beaten, smiling face, his worn, laced boots, spattered with mud, his rusty-brown jacket, and his broad hat, worn with careless yet unfailing grace, made him easily the most picturesque figure in the room; and when some one clapped him on the back and called out, "Hello, Kelly!" Raymond realized, with a pleasant warming of the heart, that he was looking upon Rocky Mountain Kelly, who knew the ranges of the West as intimately as the lines on the palm of his hand.

Seeking opportunity, he touched the big man on the shoulder. "Are you Matthew Kelly?"

Kelly turned his keen, gray eyes on his questioner. "I am, sir. What can I do for ye?"

"I've heard you're a good-natured man," began Raymond.

Kelly slid his hand into his pocket. "How much is it?"

Raymond laughed. "Do I look like that?"

"You look like a sick man," replied Kelly, scrutinizing him. "And a hungry man."

"I'm neither," Raymond smilingly replied. "I've just eaten the supper they serve here, and I'm fairly comfortable; but I want to ask your advice about a business matter. If you had a little money and wanted to break into mining, what would you do?"

Raymond Enters Sky-Town

"Take out a lease," answered Kelly, promptly.

"Do you know of a promising property to lease?"

"I do."

"Will you show it to me?"

"I will."

Raymond was amused by the crisp succinctness of these replies. It was plain that the prospector was sizing him up, and favorably.

Kelly indicated a chair. "Sit down, man; ye look like a citizen with a lung faded."

Raymond took a seat and Kelly drew up another, a little facing him, and began to question in his turn.

"Where are ye from?"

"I'm a rancher from the plains."

"And ye want to mine?"

"Yes."

"It's ninety-nine chances to one ye lose y'r wad."

"I know it."

"Have ye a wife?"

"I have not."

"Any one dependin' on ye?"

"No one."

Kelly relaxed, and his eyes began to gleam friendlily. "Very well, then, I consent to rob ye. I'm the owner of one mine into which I've put me last dollar, but I know a dandy proposition which I'd like to display. I'll take ye with me over the hills when ye're a little better acquainted with me; and when ye've seen the mine we'll talk the terms of partnership. The bankers all know me, and the faro-dealers likewise—the more shame to me." A smile of singular charm curved his handsome lips. "But never mind that, Matt Kelly never tuck advantage of any man, and *that*, I think, ye'll find me neighbors agreed upon. I'll not say I like the looks of ye—that would sound like blarney—the truth bein' I'm seekin' a partner; but in a day or two I'll lay me scheme before ye."

Putting aside business, they talked of their personal affairs, Raymond guardedly, Kelly with entire freedom and some humor. "I'm no Dutchman," he said, "much as ye might think it from me accint. Frugality is not one of me strong points, as Nora, me little wife, can tell ye. Three times I've made a little stake, and lost it through me own foolishness; but this time I'm seeking a partner who can kape a grip on me elbow when I stand before the red spots on a faro-table. Ye do not look like a drinkin' man, and by yer manner of speech ye can read and write. I nade a man like that—not of me own kind. But there, we'll lave all that till to-morrow."

He seemed to know every mining-camp from Chihuahua to the Kootenai Lakes. He had struck a lead in the Savage Basin, and lost it in the Red Mountain Valley. He had retrieved himself at Creede, only to "blow his little wad into the game" at Sylvanite. He was married, and had two little boys, for whom he was now living. "Since Nora came," he said, with tenderness, "I drink no more; but gambling is in me blood. I play no more with cards or dice, but with lodes and shafts. I'm always taking on new chances. I load meself up with 'good things' till me back is broke and me hands fall empty."

There was something winning in the humorous glance of his big, gray eyes, and Raymond sat with him long. His vast experience, his indomitable good-nature, his physical pride, all appealed to the rancher with such power that he left him with a distinct exaltation "Here is the man to help me make my fortune, and I can be guide to him," he added, and he went to sleep that night with greater confidence in his future than at any time since taking Barnett's ranch. He set his teeth hard in the determination to win, and though he had put Ann quite out of his plans for the future, she remained an inspiration and a lure.

His feeling of confidence in Kelly was deepened by his ride with him next day. First of all, the big miner could sit a horse with easy grace, and that confirmed what he had said concerning his past life. Then, too, his eyes were clear and keen, untouched of gluttony or intemperance in drink. He strode a powerful bay horse, and his saddle, though worn, was of the best model and marked in Mexican silver. In everything he did, Matt Kelly satisfied the eye. He was effective.

Turning from the gulch road, he led the way up the side of Pine Mountain, along a trail which braided itself upon a grassy slope like a purple-brown ribbon. The air was keen, the sky a fleckless blue hemisphere. Far away to the west the great central range rose marble-white, and above the dark-green summit of pine loomed the yellow-white, rounded mass of Mogalyon. Raymond's blood leaped with the joy of it, and with a sense that his feet were set at last on the road to fortune.

All about him the miners were climbing, each his special way, swinging a tin bucket which sparkled like glass in the morning sun. Great wains loaded with ore rolled creaking on their downward course, while others of their kind, piled high with lumber and machinery, crawled slowly up the curving roads. On every side men were tunnelling into the hill-sides, trenching in gullies, and toiling at windlasses whose joints cried out resoundingly as the heavy ore-boxes rose. The whole scene set forth buoyant activity and hope. Each man had either struck ore or hoped to do so at any moment.

Many of the miners knew Kelly, and stopped him to show their ore and ask his opinion. To each one he was frank and kindly, but careful not to raise undue expectations. Once they passed a couple of men "witching" for their vein. One of them, with a forked willow withe in his outstretched palms, was ambling to and fro, his eyes fixed upon the upright end of the stick. Kelly, with an oily chuckle, called out: "Boys, are ye in need o' drinkin' water? I see ye witchin' for a well."

The necromancer paid no manner of attention, but his companion looked up with a broad grin.

"I don't go a cent on the darn thing myself," he explained.

The conjurer stopped, and, planting his foot firmly on a big bowlder, said, with conviction, "It's right under here."

"Good-luck to ye," called Kelly, over his horse's tail. "And when ye find it, lave no man credit but y'rself."

As they rose, Raymond began to comprehend the district. It was a group of hills semi-detached from Mogalyon and forming his raised right shoulder. To the west six distinctive but distant ranges of mountains rose, glittering with snow, blued by hundreds of miles of atmosphere. To the east the lesser heights of the Rampart Range shut off the view of the plain. To the north lay a small, parklike valley. To the south a series of cañons cutting deep into the ever-diminishing hills.

Here and there on the slope a tall and shapeless shaft-

house rose, with heaps of orange and blue-gray refuse
rock close beside it. The whole camp was as yet dis-
organized, formless, and debatable. Not one in a hundred of the mines was a paying property, all the others
were mere prospects.

As they left Baldy and turned to climb Pine Mountain, the dwellings thickened. They were nearly all built
of the smooth, straight trunks of the aspen, but nearer the summit were of fir, and a few of them stood in
picturesque nooks amid the rocks. Towards one of
these, more homelike than the others, Kelly directed
his horse, and as he neared the door a couple of lusty,
yellow-haired boys of six or seven years of age came
bounding out to meet him.

"Hello, nuggets!" he called, and turned to Raymond
with a proud look on his face. "Oh, the lungs of them!
This altitude makes no difference wid their diviltry.
They race and howl the whole day long. Aisy now,"
he said, warningly, as they began to swarm up his legs
like wild-cats. "Aisy now; ye'll sile me boots."

When they were seated, one behind and one before,
Kelly turned again with comical grin. "Negotiations
is suspended; three times around the house I go." And
so, while Raymond waited, the indulgent giant made
three circuits of the house with his shouting sons.

"Now, if ye'll light off, Robert, I will introduce you
to me superior officer."

Mrs. Kelly was unexpectedly lady-like, small, and
very pretty, with a skin that no wind could tan, and her
great, wistful, pathetic, gray eyes appealed to Raymond with instant power. She greeted him cordially,
and, while Kelly took the horses to the corral, he entered at her invitation. Her voice was as charming as

her pale face and hair of burnished gold, and the young
fellow looked upon her in surprise.

"How do you like living so high in the world?" he
asked, as he took a seat in the tiny little living-room.

"Not very well. The air is so thin up here."

"It *is* thin. I can hardly walk a block even down in
the Creek— How am I to do any work?" he asked
of Kelly, as he entered a few moments later.

Kelly laughed. "Ye'll develop lungs like a bull-
frog. Look at me!" and he struck his huge chest a
resounding blow.

"You don't look very well, sir," Mrs. Kelly said to
Raymond.

"I'm not very well, but I'm going to tear up the sod
just the same. Your husband is to show me how."

"Matt can find gold easy enough, but he can't keep
it."

"I've confessed as much, Nora, me girl, and if Raymond can help me on that score, I'll put him in the way
of makin' his pile. Can ye walk a few rods? If so, I'll
show ye the mine and the chance."

"Certainly. I'm far from being a 'one-lunger' yet."

The two men walked round the little grove of firs to
the west, and came upon some men busy with a very
small upright engine hoisting ore from a shaft.

"Here," said Kelly, "is where we tap 'the river of
life.' This is my own mine, but the wan I advise ye
to take is that just beyond. I have an offer for me
own prospect, but I shall not take it. If ye are agree-
able, we'll lease the Last Dollar together, and work
it to the limit, for I'm satisfied its vein is the same as
me own, which will keep; but if I strike ore, Curran,
who owns the Last Dollar, will jump his price to the

moon. Our lay is to bond and lease his mine, move my machinery over to his old shaft, and work like mad to open up ore to buy in the property. Ye see, no one has touched pay ore in this quarter, and Curran is anxious to sell. He offers it at fifteen thousand dollars. I believe we can open a vein that 'll pay fer it in less than six months. Will ye go in with me?"

"I will."

As their hands met, their hearts warmed to each other. Kelly removed his hat, and was almost solemn as he said, slowly: "This makes us both. Now let's go eat."

The Kelly home was as suited to its surroundings as a Swiss chalet. It had the dirt roof, the widely projecting eaves, and the Southern porch of a mountain cabin, and its latch-string and battened door were in keeping—only the windows, with their machine-made frames, were out of key. There were two small bedrooms, a living-room, which served also for dining-room, and a tiny kitchen; and yet it produced on Raymond's mind the most charming effect of unhesitating hospitality and homeliness. This was due as much to the charm of Mrs. Kelly's manner as to the deep-voiced, cordial invitation of the host himself. There was no lock on their door and no bar to their warm hearts.

But Raymond saw what Matt's loving eyes could not discern—Nora was overworked and losing heart. In spite of her ready smile and cordial seconding of her husband's invitation, "Ye must make your home with us," she was not strong enough to take on this extra care, and he resolved to stay in Bozle till he could build a cabin for himself.

As they finished their meal he said: "Now, Mrs.

Kelly, you must let me help you about the dishes;
please don't object. I won't listen to a word you say.
I used to be a cook in a cow-camp, and I'm handy as a
widower. If I can pull on a winze, I can help keep
house."

In the end he had his way, and she sat with tears in
her eyes and a smile on her lips while he washed and
wiped the dishes.

"Matt Kelly, you ought to be ashamed of yourself,"
said she, in admiration of Raymond's deftness.

"Should I be washin' dishes?" queried Matt, lifting
one big fist in the air. "Sure you'll need something
better than iron-stone chiny to withstand me. But
wait you; in six months you'll have a hired girl in every
corner of the room and a nickel-plated fly-trap. Sure!"

"Ye always were rich in fine words, Matt," she replied, with a gurgle of laughter.

X

Jack Munro

LATE in the afternoon, after they had talked long at the mouth of the mine, Kelly and Raymond left the house and walked out along the ridge towards Sky-Town, which was built where the ground rose from a pine-clad plateau to a rocky point overlooking the valley to the north. It had but one business street, which repeated in unpainted lumber all the shoddy architecture of a prairie town, whose flaming battlements pretend to a dignity which they do not fulfil. So far the place was without distinction; but here and there, even along Saloon Row, the original dwellings of the camp stood in testimony of the skilled handiwork of the pioneer. They were simple, dignified, significant of the life which admitted no shams.

The town, in short, set forth in its physical features the almost unexampled mixture of hunters, trappers, cow-boys, prairie-dwellers, slavish miners, and gamblers which made up its population. As the beautifully built log-cabins (snugly set beneath clumps of trees) alternated with the most slovenly shapeless shacks, so the drunken, spiritless tramp set his elbow to that of heroic prospectors like Kelly, and women of the unnameable sort called across the street to honest working-women—wives of newly arrived mechanics.

The chief business of the street was gambling. Next in order stood rum-selling, with assaying a close third. Exhibits of ore filled every window, and before these exhibits groups of greenhorns slowly moved. Nothing was ignored, every speck of "color," each new piece of rock was scanned by these tenderfeet, who roamed all day from door to door, and especially swarmed between supper-time and sundown. For all their trust, their imagination, they had no eyes for the transcendent sunsets which swept over the sky and the valley, night by night, with a flare of color that alarmed, like the sound of God's own trumpet. From the hill to the west, or the lookout to the east, sensitive souls bowed in humility before the passing of the day, so varied was the color, so majestic the spread of earth.

The men who sat at dice or lounged at the drinking-bars were not of those who weigh the gold of evening nor greet the crimson banners of the morning with song; but to Raymond these mountain-scenes were over-awing. He fell silent before the supremacy of the sun-set. He lingered now in the path, and Kelly, receiving no answer to a question, looked up, understood the ex-altation in his partner's face, and checked the word upon his lips.

At last Raymond said, "I thought the plains mighty, but that scene is mightier."

"I put me cabin so that Nora and the boys could see it," replied Kelly, simply, and they resumed their walk in silence.

The street was swarming as usual, but the talk was directed, for the moment, to one topic. A convention of miners had been called to meet in the Golden Horn saloon, and several who knew Kelly called out, "Hello, Matt, we're going to make you president of the union."

Kelly smiled as if all this were a joke, and introduced his friend and partner. Raymond shook hands with each man heartily, well knowing that if he were to remain in the camp, it would be well to be on friendly terms with all. Following the lead of others, they were soon wedged into a throng which filled the largest saloon of the street — a huge gambling establishment called the Golden Horn, of which Marvin Hanley, a celebrated gambler, was proprietor.

For the first time since the opening of the Golden Horn's door, gambling was suspended and the machines of chance set aside. The proprietor, a pale man with close-clipped, yellow hair—a man who looked like a Catholic priest—mounted a box at one end of the room and called the house to order. "You know the purposes of this meeting," said he. "Now, who will you have for chairman?"

"Kelly! Kelly!" cried a dozen men.

"Munro!" shouted those farther up the hall.

"Moved and seconded that Munro be chairman," said the smooth-faced man. "All who favor say 'Ay'!" A shout of many mingled voices answered. "Opposed, 'No'." Only an obvious minority voted "No." "Munro is elected. Jack, get up here!"

As the new chairman's head rose above the throng, Raymond experienced a shock. 'I know that man," he said, under his breath. Munro was a clean-shaven, boyish fellow, with black hair pushed back from his face. He was young and handsome, and began speaking in a clear, musical, and most persuasive voice. It was plain he was on good terms with his audience and quite certain of himself.

"I don't know why I should be made chairman of this meeting," he said, after some local allusions, "unless it be to open the way for the real speaker and man of the hour — the man who has a message for you — Tom Larned of Dead Pine." Cheers for Larned followed. Munro went on. "I'm a prospector, not a miner." A ripple of laughter arose. "But, of course, my sympathies are always with the heavy-handed sons of toil, and I'm glad to know Sky-Town is to have a union. I'll do all I can to further it. Brain and brawn should be united in this business." He raised one white, handsome, supple hand in the air. "I furnish the brawn"—again a roar of laughter burst forth, for there was a subtle twist in the speaker's voice which took hold of his audience—"and the brains will be furnished by Brother Larned, who will now address you, while I take a drink. Brother Larned, it's up to you."

While the crowd applauded, Larned climbed to his place and began to speak. He was a short man, with a forward thrust of the chin. His high forehead was smooth and pale, its calm lines in vivid contrast with his burning blue eyes. Plainly he was a vigorous, intense, and bigoted thinker, a man of far-seeing intelligence, but with narrow interests. His voice, harsh and penetrating, filled the hall with an effect of clamor, and his words were like pebbles from a sling. He ignored all of Munro's joking, and thrust his way into the middle of his contention.

"I hear some men say we don't need a union here, but I tell you you do. You're going the way of all mining-camps. As soon as the claims are all taken, consolidations begin, and wages will be cut. A big mining-camp must be run by union labor. 'Punkin rollers' and prospectors don't maintain a big, permanent, deep mine. The work has got to be done by men bred to the mine, and they must be organized; if they're not, they'll work for nothing. This camp is about to decline—"

"No! No!" shouted a dozen men.

The speaker held up a hand. "Wait a moment! I mean to say that this swarm of easy-going tramps scratching the surface, looking for a mine, will begin to melt away—it is already melting away. These men on horseback, these grub-stakers, these burro-punchers, will not dig gold for other men." ["You bet they won't," shouted a big-lunged fellow.] "The real miners have got to get underground and *stay there!* You understand? Stay there! And they will want somebody on top to look after their interests. They'll want a union, if you don't; but, I tell you, you short-term miners will want a union before February is out."

In such wise he argued, and even Kelly admitted the truth of what he said. Others spoke, grizzled old fellows from other districts, men who had given up all hope of discovering a lead for themselves; men with families to feed and educate, who had fallen to contentment with a good wage and a steady job. But in some of the speeches a note of bitterness towards Valley Springs made itself heard. Sky-Town had begun to hate the valley as the home of those who lived on the labor of others, and some of those in the valley, as Raymond well knew, expressed their contempt of those who dwelt in the Sky by calling them "red necks," in allusion to their tanned or drink-inflamed faces.

These citizens of Sky-Town (who suffered little on account of sickness) retaliated by calling their neighbors of the Springs "dudes" and "one-lungers," in allusion to their having settled in the West for the sake of their broken health. Politically the two towns were already as wide apart as the poles, and references to this division were numerous during the evening. The county was divided against itself and hopelessly embittered, and Bozle was eager to be free from the valley.

Kelly, weary of the wrangle, touched Raymond on the arm, and turned towards the door. A big miner, detecting this movement, shouted out, "Here's Kelly taking a sneak!"

Instantly Kelly was seized, a couple of brawny fellows lifted him to the bar, and so, towering over them all, the big prospector took off his hat and, with smiling composure, said: "Boys, I wish ye well. I make no objection to the plans; but why should I, an old burro-puncher, bother me head about a union? No one is cuttin' *my* wages. No one is shortening *my* hours of labor. Besides " — and here he broke into a broad smile—"I'm an employer of labor meself."

"Down wid 'im!" shouted Munro.

"To what extent?" asked another.

"To the whole of five men—not countin' meself," answered Kelly, with a roguish grin. "And I'm a har-r-rd master."

A roar of laughter responded to his jest.

"Down with the oppressor of labor!" shouted Munro. "Off with 's head!"

Jack Munro

Kelly playfully struck at him with his hat, and then became serious. "Now, boys, let me tell you. I honestly don't think you need a union. The landscape is wide up here; there's a chance for every man in the hills. I believe in the big, free land. When any man tries to corner me, I take me mule and strike out into the wild country. I have no fear of the Red Star Mining Company, nor any other, and you needn't. I do not oppose the union—mind what I'm sayin'; it's well enough for those who believe in it, and nade it, but lave me out of it. The Kellys will take care of themselves."

Larned was on his box before Kelly had time to get down, and, levelling his finger at him, cried out, sharply:

"That's all well and good for you, Matt Kelly, a skilled prospector, a man with a paying mine already, but how about these men who have no skill in finding gold, who are working for money to start themselves a home. How about those who are hoping to bring their families here and clothe and educate them? They are not so fond of all out-doors. They haven't even the mule and the grub-stake. They are holed-up five hundred or a thousand feet underground, working for a company, and this company, I tell you, has no regard for its hands. Their interests are not those of the miner. You may blarney all you like, but the miners must look out for their own interests, just as the employer hires lawyers and agents to look after his."

"Very true," replied Kelly, calmly. "I'm not objectin' to that. Organize and take care o' labor's interests, but don't ask me, an employer of labor, to throw up me hat when you vote to raise the wages of me five men. I'll fight scandalous—"

The crowd was amused. Plainly it did not take the contention seriously, and wished it to go on.

"Go it, Kelly! You have him on three legs and goin'!" shouted a wag, and, amid the laughter that followed, Kelly leaped down and made for the door.

When Raymond overtook him again he was in talk with a lean young fellow with large, bright eyes, who had the tone of an old and bitterly disappointed man. He was saying:

"A union! Of course we'll have a union. The glory of Ichabod is departed. I saw a fist-fight in the Creek to-day. This camp is on the decline right now. We'll have an ordinance against carrying guns next. Then I emigrate."

Kelly introduced him. "Rob, shake hands with Mr. Dolan, correspondent of the Valley Springs *News*. Jim, this is my new partner."

Dolan, as he clasped hands, remarked, "You've met up with a good man—a man that won't do ye—and there aren't many like him in this town."

"Ye must not mind what Dolan says, Rob," remarked Kelly. "He's always kickin' like a bay steer in harness. Nothin' suits him."

"Well, much obliged, Matt," said the reporter. "Mr. Raymond, I'll see you again."

Only long after did it come to Raymond's mind that Kelly had been giving Dolan a note concerning their plans, and that his whereabouts would be at once made known to Valley Springs and to Louis.

"Who is this man Munro?" asked Raymond, as they left the reporter and started for home.

"He's a devil-may-care chap from Red Cliff. He pretends to be a miner, and is a partner with an old fellow on the north side o' the hill, but he's workin' for Hanley—lookout for the roulette-wheel. The boys all think a heap of him. They say he always gives 'em a square deal."

"Does he?"

"I think so. I never heard to the contrary."

"Larned was right about the union," said Raymond. "The big owners in the Springs are sending East for their miners. They know that men like you and me will not do their deep work for them. He's right, too, in saying these cow-boys and farm-hands from the States won't make miners. They don't intend to work underground. We'll find ourselves left short some morning, if we depend on these fellows, who can hit the trail at ten minutes' notice."

"Sure thing," said Kelly. "This gettin' under the crust o' the earth and livin' there is unholy business— not for free men like ourselves. It's all goin' to be done by the Rooshians and the Dagoes."

"I didn't mean to say that a miner was a slave," replied Raymond. "I just meant that a man who is content to swing a pick in a mine all his life must be born and bred to it."

"Thank God, I was bred to the hills," exclaimed Kelly, "and have no fear of the open! Me father was a bog-trotter, but there must have been somethin' live stirrin' at his heart, for he pulled out at twenty and came to the hills of Idaho."

And in silence the two men looked abroad over the valley towards the dim line of peaks faintly lit by the big, silver-bright moon.

A sentence from Richter came into Raymond's mind: "In the presence of beauty, beneath the stars, men think of love," and his heart ached with a sense of loss.

Unconsciously, in spite of his attempt to put himself away from her presence, Ann had come to dominate his musing hours. At thought of her he grew resolute and hopeful, and, reaching forth a powerful hand, grappled the air as if it were the throat of a hitherto invincible opponent, and said, "I will win!" He acknowledged that wealth had power to aid him. "So long as I am unknown and poor and in disgrace she can only consider me what I am—a failure. Money is a measure of value—and wealth I must have first; then leisure and the higher life."

So while Kelly mused sombrely on the problems of labor, his partner looked away at the moonlit peaks and dreamed of one small woman's face. And with this secret hope his hunger grew in power

XI

Louis Finds Raymond

ON the second morning after his meeting with Dolan, Raymond, riding down the trail towards Bozle, discovered a small figure toiling towards him, pausing often to rest. "It can't be Louis," he said, "and yet there's something familiar in that walk. The hat, too, is of exceeding cleanliness—the kind he would wear." A few moments later the climber stopped, turned his back to the hill, and, with one hand resting on his hip, looked away over the valley.

"It *is* Louis!" exclaimed Raymond. "And he's on my trail."

When the boy, lifting his tired head, recognized the rider, he uttered a fierce shout of joy. "Hah! I've found you! Sammy the Sleuth never fails. My ears and whiskers! why don't you live in the moon? This air is so thin I can't breathe—" He fairly staggered with weakness.

Raymond slid from his horse and put his arm about the reeling lad. "When did you come to camp?"

Louis leaned against his big friend. "Oh, I've been here a week. I knew you were here somewhere, but I couldn't get track of you. Don was over here yesterday, but I dodged him, and he went back. I didn't sign my own name on the register." He grinned slyly. "See my boots—aren't they right?"

Raymond looked down at the boy's small legs clothed with miner's laced boots. "You believe in dressing the part—don't you? You *are* a kidlet." He laughed at the boy's chapfallen look (for Louis detested being called a boy), and added: "Well, what now? Does your sister know where you are?"

"No."

Raymond's whole expression changed. "Climb that horse!" he said, sternly. "You're going back to town, and you're going to send her a telegram at once."

The boy obeyed, stunned by the sudden disgust and anger in his friend's face and voice.

As he led the horse down the hill, Raymond comprehended something of the anxiety the runaway had brought to Ann, and that he, indirectly, was the cause of it, but at the door of the office he said, more gently: "Now, younker, hop off. You're going to send word to the folks that you're with me and safe."

"You're not going to drive me away?"

Raymond looked at him in silence. "No. I'm going to put you to work."

The boy's face threw off its shadow. "That's bully! Now I'm all right. Give me a pen." He wrote:

"I have found Rob. We're all O. K. Don't worry.
"Louis."

As he handed it over he said, gayly, "Will that do?"

"That's satisfactory. Now rush it."

As they walked out, Raymond sternly asked: "Want to stay with me, do you? Well, everybody works where I live. We don't allow idlers. If you had something to do, you'd keep out o' mischief."

Louis twisted his small right arm. "I'm ready for anything."

"Got your outfit—your whole kit?"

"I've got one camera and my drawing materials."

"All right, I'll find something for you to fill up your spare time with."

Raymond packed his hand-bags on the horse, and together they set out up the trail. At first the lad exulted and cried out like a blue-jay, but his breathing grew labored as they rose, and at last Raymond turned. "Now, see here, Louis, this air is pretty thin till a fellow gets used to it; you'd better mount. You'll enjoy the scenery better."

With a feeling that he was succumbing to an unmanly weakness, Louis clambered to the horse's back and perched among his possessions, while Raymond, striding ahead, led the way up and up, till the whole world seemed coming into view. "Oh, this is fine! Jupiter! this is the place for me."

He was unfeignedly delighted with everything, with the new shacks, with the slab tables and the plank chairs, and with the liberal and smoking dinner which Mrs. Kelly provided; but he drew a hissing breath of admiration over the grand figure of old Matthew Kelly. "Gee! but you are a wonder! I must do you."

Kelly was puzzled and a little embarrassed by this outspoken admiration, and regarded Louis with definite disfavor till he presented him with a pencil-drawing of the lads playing on the doorstep, and then he said: "The Lord God has made a power o' people that the Kellys have not seen; this is wan of them. Now isn't that a wonder? He put the whole thing together in five minutes." Thereafter he accepted the boy for the cunning that lay in his fingers.

Raymond wrote that night to Ann, as formally as the riot in his brain would permit:

"I planned to take myself out of your life as completely as if I were dead, but Louis would not have it so. When I met him on the hill to-day, and he told me how long he had been from home, I determined to hustle him back to the Springs, but he asked to stay a day or two, and here he is. Will you trust him with me? He will tire of it here by-and-by and go back to you of his own accord. Just now he is mad over the life and the scenery. As for myself, I am a new man, with new aspirations. They may not seem very high to you, for I am striving now to acquire gold; but that is only a means to an end. There is something else in the world for me to do. I don't know what it is to be—perhaps my care of this wonderful boy is a part of it. At any rate, he is here, and not to be driven away without great risk to him and deep pain to me. So, unless you object, I shall keep him. Our life is rough, but not contaminating. I will see that no harm comes to him."

There was nothing more personal in the letter than this, but Ann's heart warmed to the writer unaccountably. He was clean and manly—that she must admit; and very much of a gentleman considering his daily contact with gross men. And yet the thought of Louis in a mining-camp troubled her. "I ought to go and fetch him away," she said to Don.

"No! No! You remain here, and I will go over and see the little scamp and bring him back if possible."

The next morning Raymond put into action a measure he had formulated during the night. He called Louis to him, and together they ascended the "Lookout," as Kelly called the ledge back of his cabin. The wind was keen as a brier, but the sun shone full, and, sheltered by some low-growing firs, the man and boy took seats on an overhanging rock and looked away across the valley to the south.

"Isn't it magnificent!" breathed Louis. "It's grander than I ever imagined; but, oh, I long to see what lies over that big range! That must be father's ' Hesperean wall'; don't you think so? It makes me want to fly like the eagle."

Raymond brought him to earth. "See here, lad, I've brought you up here to ask you a few questions."

Louis braced himself. "Fire away!"

"As I understand it, you and—Ann are alone in the world—I mean you are closer to each other than to any one else—she's your best friend."

The boy sobered. "Yes, Ann's good to me."

"Well, now, she's taking a whole lot of trouble for you, and you ought to meet her half-way. Don't you think so? You oughtn't to go ricocheting off into the hills like this without letting her know. Think how she has worried over you for the past week."

Louis' lips quivered. "I didn't intend to worry her, but I hated it there, and I wanted to find you. I didn't intend to stay so long."

"You've given her a great deal of anxiety, my lad, and that isn't right. You must go straight back to her and apologize, and ask her permission to come back. If she consents, then I'll make a place for you here."

"She won't consent. I'd have to run away again; and I'd do it!" he added, defiantly.

"Well, that would be better than running off without letting her know. Suppose something had happened to her, or to you, while you were gone? Did you think of that?"

Tears were in the boy's eyes, and his sensitive face was palpitant with feeling as he replied, "No, I didn't."

Raymond, after a pause, slowly resumed: "Now I want to make a compact with you. If you'll go down and see her, I will write a letter interceding for you, and asking her to let you return."

The lad's face was suddenly illuminated. He threw out his small palm. "I'll do it!" he cried out, and his tone carried conviction.

Raymond continued. "You like me, and I like you. You can't live in the Springs, and your sister can't live here. So it seems that I must be your big brother, and look after you. And hark ye! You must mind what I say, or I'll take a birch to you."

This threat seemed not to appall the boy. "Can I work in the mine?"

"No, you can't work in the mine, but I'll find something on top for you to do. You must take care of those lungs of yours for a while; but come, let's see if we can't catch the stage."

"Oh, let me stay till to-morrow!" pleaded the boy. "I don't want to go to-day. It's too beautiful to miss."

Raymond reflected a moment. "Very well, but you'll want that stage-ride. It's one of the finest roads in the mountains. You rattle down the cañon to-morrow, sure thing; remember that!"

Together they went down towards the mine where a group of men were building a log-cabin. "Here is where we are to live, provided your sister consents," Raymond explained. "Now, throw off your coat, and I'll find something for you to turn over."

Thereafter Louis had no care. He handled tools, ran errands, and put his small palms to the rough logs with complete absorption, pausing only now and then to say, "Jupiter, but I'm in luck! I never expected to see a real log-house built." There was something in the pungent odor of the timber, and in the sound of the axes, which moved him — something he could neither understand nor measure. It was like the march of a great poem.

Kelly was the master - builder, and the flash and stroke of his axe, and his deft, yet unhurried, graceful movements won the lad's profound admiration. He was humble as a squirrel before men of that mould. They represented the unattainable, the majesty of self-poised, self-reliant, serene manhood. Altogether it was a glorious day, one never to be forgotten.

Barnett came riding up the hill about sundown, and immediately at sight of Louis began a jocose tirade. "You scamp! You young flyaway! A nice interlude you've given us. Ann hadn't slept a wink for a week till she got your message yesterday. How long have you been here?"

Raymond hastened to say, "I induced him to wire as soon as he turned up."

"Had you been here all the time, you young rattle-pate?"

Louis was not afraid of Barnett. "Yes, I was down there looking for Rob." He pointed towards the town of Bozle.

"Well, I'm to bring you home—instantly!"

Louis took shelter behind Raymond. "No, you don't. Tell him, Rob."

Raymond winked at Barnett. "He's going to-morrow, on a promise to me, Don. I've made a bargain with him. He can tell you about it on the way. Moreover, he is going by stage. He's on honor."

When they were alone Barnett said: "The most unaccountable of all things is the human heart. That boy is crazy about you. Now, I like you, Rob, and I think you're a fine figure of a man, but this boy considers you something quite supernatural. He is willing to leave his sister, the only real mother he ever had, and cleave to you. You're in for it. I don't see how you can shake him."

"It's a big responsibility," replied Raymond, gravely, "and I would shirk it if I could, but for the present I can only hope his enthusiasm will flag. He'll get tired of it up here after a week or two."

"I hope so, for Ann's sake. She was as near upset as I ever saw her. Did he tell you that the rupture came from his idea that she had mistreated you?"

Raymond faced him. "No; not a word."

"Well, Jeannette heard him shout something of that kind. Ann don't want to use force to control the boy, but now that he has tasted wild West freedom, he won't listen to any word of return, and as she hates the West and all it contains — barring the Barnetts, whom she tolerates—I see nothing but squalls coming. She wanted to scuttle up and get the boy herself, but I headed her off. By-the-way, how's the lung?"

"Almost as good as ever."

"Your constitution is a wonder. And the mining deal?"

Louis Finds Raymond

"Very promising."

In the talk that followed, Raymond learned for the first time of the proposed consolidation of the Red Star with two or three other heavy properties, and they fell into a discussion of the camp.

"If I had my way," said Barnett, "I'd have this meddling idiot Larned thrown out of the camp. What business has he here? He's a rank outsider, anyway, and this union is a breeder of war."

Raymond raised a warning hand. "Careful, Don! It don't do for you to say such things up here. This union has come to stay, and you who employ labor will do well to treat it with a certain measure of respect."

"But you're an employer, too!"

Raymond laughed. "Oh, my little crew don't count; they're all prospectors or cow-boys, and, besides, I work right with them, and am classed as a working miner. Your case is different."

Barnett went away calmly superior, but came back from a conference with Mackay, the superintendent of the Red Star, less haughty of manner but distinctly more acrid of tone. "Mackay says this confounded union is growing rapidly, and that practically every incoming miner joins at once. I told him to nip the thing in the bud, and he has begun to formulate a plan to do so."

"Wait a year," warned Raymond. "Wait till I pay for my mine." Then added, soberly: "And don't you go about saying rash things. You're not dressed for it. You look like one of those 'English dudes' the men hate so."

Barnett's sense of humor returned. "I suppose my riding-breeches do distinguish me."

"I wouldn't wear them through the street on Saturday night for a thousand dollars."

That night, as Louis sat before the fire in the centre of the unfinished cabin, his face shone with joy, and the heart of the tall miner grew very tender towards him. It was good to have this gay young brother of his love to keep him company. A new sensation arose from having some one to plan for and to protect.

The dreaming lad, outstretched on a pile of blankets, with his hands under his head and his small feet, clothed in moccasins, extended to the blaze, suddenly turned and said: "Rob, this is the kind of life for me. Wouldn't father have liked this? I'd be perfectly happy if I didn't have to pack off down the hill to - morrow. Why couldn't Ann come up here?"

A flash of warm blood crossed the man's face at the thought. "I wish she could!" he answered, quickly; then added, "But this is no place for her."

It certainly was not, for at the moment the cabin was merely a stockade of freshly hewn, pungent pine-boles, without roof or floor; though the promise of a goodly shelter spoke from the ample plan. With the stirring of some subtle, nest-making instinct, Raymond began to wonder how it could be made more acceptable to Ann. He imagined big settees here and a fireplace there. "We must have some rugs," he ended.

When the boy spoke again, his voice was grave and sweet. "If you won't tell, I'll let you into a secret, Rob. I'm going to have father's journal printed, and I'm going to make the illustrations for it. You mustn't tell Ann. She don't know a word about it."

Raymond looked upon the frail form and speaking

face flushed with the fire-light glow and wondered whether Philip Rupert's emotional concept of the West had not by some mysterious alchemy entered into his son's brain, making him the imaginative, mountain-loving poet-soul that he was; as widely differentiated from his sister as the flame of the ruby is from the frosty light of the diamond. When he spoke it was to say, hesitatingly, "Maybe, by-and-by, when we get our cabin fixed up, we will ask your sister and Mrs. Barnett to come up and visit us."

Louis started up. "Oh, will you? If Ann were here, I would never want to go back East again—never! I could live here always."

"How about the wild animals? There are no grizzlies here."

"Oh, I'm going to do a series of mining sketches first," he said, with easy shift of interest.

A foot outside disturbed Raymond, and a man's voice called, "Is Rob Raymond here?"

In the unfinished doorway stood a graceful young fellow in a white sombrero and a neatly fitting, dark suit. "Jack Munro!" exclaimed Raymond, and they shook hands. "Sit down. This is a boy friend of mine from the Springs," he said, indicating Louis. "What can I do for you?"

"Nothing, old man; just lined you out to-day. I heard that a man named Raymond had taken a lease with Kelly, but I didn't know it was you till I saw you with Barnett to-day. Well, this is wonderful! Where you from? What have you been doing since we—graduated?" There was something in his voice that eluded Louis. Raymond gave Munro a warning glance.

"Oh, a little of everything—cattle-ranching, hunting, mining. I saw you last night in Hanley's saloon."

"Why didn't you speak up?"

Raymond hesitated. "I didn't know whether you—"

"Oh, rats! I'm not one to dodge. What did getting fired amount to, anyway? I was ready to leave."

Raymond repeated his warning sign. "Have you been back—home?"

Munro smiled broadly. "You bet! I went back and swelled around in high feathers—told my side of the story—understand? I didn't let the institution get the drop on me; but, see here, come up to the saloon; I want to talk things over with you. The boys are bound to make me take a hand in this union." He winked and laughed in a sly way. "I stand in with the lads these days. First thing you know, I'll break into Congress as the miners' friend. But come out for a walk. I want to talk old times."

"Can't do it now, Jack; but come down again. Louis is going back to-morrow, and I'll be alone for a day or two, and then we can talk freely."

"All right. There are a whole lot of things I want to turn over. By the Lord! this is wonderful—our meeting up here." He was reluctant to go. "You bring up the old days. Well, so long."

When Raymond returned to his seat his face was grave and his eyes deeply reflective.

Louis was much interested in the stranger. "Who was that, Rob?"

"A chap I used to know. He's a lookout up in one of the saloons. Do you know what a lookout is?"

Louis laughed. "Do I? What was I doing all last week?"

Louis Finds Raymond

Raymond looked at him in mock sternness. "You young scalawag! Did you lose any money?"

It was like living a chapter out of a story to go to bed there on the chips and branches of the pine-trees (with the smoke of the fire rising through the cross-beams of the skeleton cabin), to see the stars wheel slowly past, and to fall asleep at last with a sense of following in the footsteps of a beloved father; and the boy's heart went out with growing love towards the masterful young man who still sat smoking his pipe before the flame, meditative as a Cheyenne and as self-contained.

When he woke, Rob was fanning the coals, and Kelly, scrutinizing the walls of the cabin, was planning the day's work.

Catching the boy's eye, he called out, "Come, now, Mr. Boss-carpenter, breakfast is waiting."

Stiff and sore, but happy, the boy leaped to his feet, yawning and stretching. "Oh, my shoulders!"

"Aha!" cried Kelly, "the frost got into your bones the night. Well, come now, the coffee is the cure for that."

After breakfast, notwithstanding his pleading to remain to finish the cabin, Raymond hurried Louis off down the cañon to the stage, and in his letter to Ann repeated his pledge to look carefully after the boy's health and to keep him out of mischief. "I hope you won't miss him too deeply, for he adds something very sweet to my life. I have never known his like. I am sending for some books so that we can do a little reading together. I don't want to seem only a rough old gold-hunter in his eyes."

Louis arrived at the Springs fairly hysterical with

joy over his wonderful day's ride, and set about to describe Sky-Town. He sketched with swift pencil Raymond's shack and the Kelly home. He outlined the butte behind it, and indicated, with a few waving lines, the great ranges to the west. He stammered with eagerness of description. "It isn't a bit like Switzerland—no chalets or hay-meadows—it's just big and primeval, and the men there have come from all over the world. It's settled I'm to live with Rob, and I'm to take back all my traps and some rugs and a few extra pillows. We're going to have a fine place—a regular bungalow—and, by-and-by, you're to come up and visit us."

It was impossible to be angry with the boy when this lyrical mood was upon him, and Ann forgot to utter the reproof she had formulated. Indeed, she was too happy over their reconciliation to even allude to the sorrow he had given her.

His absence had been a revelation of his value to her. She had not realized up to that moment how deeply his care was woven into her daily life. It was jealousy of Raymond's power—an acrid juice—which had turned her pity for him, while wounded and helpless, into resentment; and now that he was well and triumphantly drawing the boy to his side, her heart was bitter with hatred, but she gave her consent to Louis' return because she dared not do otherwise, and in a letter to Raymond she said:

"I resign Louis into your hands, because his happiness is more than my own, and because he no longer regards my wishes. I have heard much of the gambling and drinking of mining-camps. I beg of you to guard him. He is so fine and sweet now, and defilement is so easy."

Louis Finds Raymond

Upon reading this letter the camp suddenly became a dark and dangerous place to the young miner. Looking upon it with Ann's eyes, its ferocities and its shamelessnesses advanced, became appallingly salient. Accustomed to the rough types of Western towns, he had paid very little attention to the drunkenness, gambling, and disorder of the drinking-places. Their noise was as the wind in the fir-trees, but now he became impatient of every jest and uneasy over every open lure put forth for such as Louis, and the coarseness of even the reputable miners began to remove them from his sympathies. He found it harder to make excuse for profanity and foul jests, and he went less and less among them, and spent more of his time with the lad, watching him draw or listening to him while he read.

Their cabin became the centre of the finer spirits of the camp. Dolan and one or two of his friends often came in of an evening to smoke a pipe and play a friendly game of cards. "A visit to the bungalow always pays," said one young fellow whose weakness was drink. "They send a fellow away feeling respectable."

Mrs. Kelly supervised the housekeeping as well as she could, and the place was at least warm and cheerful. Once a fortnight Louis rode down the trail to spend Sunday with Ann, but Raymond steadily refused to join him, though he suffered keenly of loneliness.

"I am a miner now," he said. "I've taken myself out of that life." And Louis did not know when he carried these words to his sister that they conveyed a deeper meaning. Ann was aware that Raymond was holding aloof from her, and, while she respected him for his consideration, she was, after all, a woman, and resented his self-mastery a little. It touched her pride to think he could so easily put her out of his life, when, so far from losing ground with her, he filled a larger space each week; but this, she argued, was due to Louis' absurd infatuation, and not to any quality, any allurement in the man himself.

Meanwhile she was beginning to be bored to hopelessness by the narrow life at the Springs, under conditions which seemed to the outsider ideally beautiful. Surrounded by luxuries of food and dress, with a superb and ever-changing mountain vista, she grew restless, irritable, and moody, and horribly critical of every one she met. Had not Don been secure in good-nature, and Jeannette in long-suffering patience, they would have thrown her upon the street in disgust.

It was a small world, considered from the social point of view, and that was the only view Ann's circumstances permitted her to take. She knew, or at least had the opportunity of knowing, all about every one. The newly enriched were pointed out to her, and some of the more eligible of them were invited to dinner in order that she might hear their story of how sudden wealth had come to them, and see for herself how they bore themselves beneath their burden. It seemed that nearly every house on the avenue was built from the gold of Sky-Town.

Louis came down once a week, each time browner, more manly in bearing—almost comical in his assumption of the Kelly's walk and Raymond's impassive face. He always had exciting tales to tell, and seemed so entirely happy and so well that Ann had not the heart to ask him to return to the East with her. She

Louis Finds Raymond

even found herself listening with interest to his account of the doings of his heroes, for he had placed Matthew Kelly on the same pedestal with Robert.

Mrs. Barnett responded graciously to his invitation to come up and see the peak, but explained that the high altitude was destructive to her; and Ann shrank from meeting Raymond again, though she expressed to him in a letter a tepid sort of gratitude for his care of her brother.

XII

Ann Visits the Peak

ONE day Barnett telephoned to his wife that he would not take luncheon at home. There was nothing unusual in the words of this announcement, but Jeannette's keen ear detected restrained excitement in his calm drawl.

"What's the matter?" she asked, quickly.

"Nothing, my dear. Nothing," he glibly responded.

"Don Barnett, I know better. Tell me this instant!"

He was in for it. "Well, Mr. Mackay, our superintendent, was tarred and ridden on a rail by the miners this morning—"

"Gracious heavens!"

"And I'm getting off up the stage - road to meet him."

"What did they do it for?"

"Oh, it's the same old business. The men didn't like some regulation of his and struck, and—but it's a long story; I won't go into it now. I'll get back in time for dinner, probably."

"For pity sake, don't go into danger!"

"Trust me," he answered, with his familiar, mocking intonation.

"Oh, those savages!" exclaimed Mrs. Barnett to Ann

as she hung up the receiver; "they're always striking or fighting or something."

In an hour Millionaire Row was humming with news of the outrage. Reports, confused, conflicting, flew along the wires east and west, and the afternoon papers were filled with dramatic details of the opening of a big strike in Sky-Town, and the story of how the union leaders had mishandled Mackay, the superintendent of the Red Star Mining Corporation.

All this would have interested Ann very little had not her brother been in the midst of the disorder. She immediately wired him to come down, and got a reply from Raymond saying, "Louis is on the way—no danger," and the boy himself came riding into the yard at dusk, serene and jaunty, well pleased with his trip down the cañon with the infuriated members of Mackay's party which he had overtaken.

"They didn't hurt him much," he explained, referring to Mackay. "You see, the boys don't like his style, and so they gave him a little jolt."

Raymond's letter to Barnett took a much more serious view of the situation:

"I don't think Mackay the proper man to attempt to reorganize the working hours of this camp. Don't try to put him back, and don't make too much of this little affair. The whole camp is uneasy at this time. The union is getting very strong and likely to make it hot for independents like Kelly and myself."

"What is it all about?" asked Jeannette.

Don looked bored. "Oh, really now, don't ask me to go into the cause of a strike. A woman never understands such a situation. However, here is what Rob says:

"'Mackay posted his notices Saturday night, putting the new nine-hour schedule into effect Monday morning. Sunday the camp boiled. The union put forth its decree, and of course at the morning hour a big crowd gathered to see Mackay face his men. He came riding up (the jackass!) in tan-colored English riding-breeches and a little two billed gray cap—you know the kind. Of course they hooted him, and headed his horse back down the slope. He was red-headed, naturally, and, being a double-distilled idiot, hired a couple of desperadoes from Bozle as guards and came back. This time the boys jerked him and his men from their horses and hustled them down the cañon at the boot-toe. I did what I could to prevent this, but the men who had the matter in charge had been drinking, and the crowd was with them. My men are not in the union, but I hear ominous threats. I advise you not to attempt to put the new schedule into operation at the present time.'"

The effect on the valley of Mackay's recital of his maltreatment was most wonderful. The principal mine-owners of the Springs met to discuss their campaign. In a thousand Eastern newspaper-offices the click of the recording type gave permanent form to a distorted and inflammatory account of the miner's words and deeds. Mackay's schedule became an issue. The press took sides, playing upon partisan passions. It was overalls against leg-o'-mutton trousers; puttees against "chaps," and few saw any humor in the situation.

The valley called for the blood of those who had dusted the sacred person of their representative, and the sheriff was ordered to arrest and bring down the insolent "red-necks" who had humbled the proud and confident Red Star superintendent. "This spirit of lawlessness must be checked, or it will run into riot," said Barnett, who developed unexpectedly into a leader of the mine-owners by virtue of his large interests in the Red Star.

The sheriff valiantly responded to the call, and with a half-dozen deputies marched up into the glittering mist of the high peaks, and came down again empty-handed and sullen. A throng of men had met him and jocularly asked, "Why so high above the plains?" "Don't you know it's bad for your constitution?" "Heart-failure often comes from such sudden change of base," they said. "Go right back this minute!" and one young man, with solemn solicitude, took him by the arm and pointed down the valley, and the sheriff, being wise in the ways of such characters, bowed and retired.

A meeting of the officers of the Red Star and allied companies was called, Barnett presiding; most resolute resolutions were passed. Mackay was instructed to press his demands to the full. Barnett naturally opposed a conference with the miners. "Either they come to our terms or we close down the mines," he said. "It is our cue to be firm in this demand."

"But some of us small fellows can't afford to shut down," piped out a timid voice. "Some of us are working under bond, and we'll be wiped out by a prolonged strike."

"Well, you must suffer for the general good," Barnett replied.

The sheriff, who had been invited to be present and tell his tale, put in a warning word. "There's another thing, gentlemen," said he, "and that is this: you're dealing with a lot of free miners and prospectors—men who won't be driven and can't be scared. If it had been just a case of Micks and Dagoes, I would have brought 'em down; but they've got leaders that you can't monkey with. When Hob Smith, Denver Dan, and that devil Jack Munro met me with their holsters tied down, I threw up my hands. You are from the East, where things are different. About one-third of the men on the peak are old prospectors and free miners, and if they stay by the proposition, you've got to take a sneak or put up the fight of the age."

"We stand pat," said Barnett, "and we shall insist on your arresting the men who assaulted Mr. Mackay."

The sheriff made an elaborate bow. "Right you are, Mr. Barnett, but I'll want a hundred deputies to do it with."

"You shall have them," replied the prominent citizens, whose blood being hot were ready to go to war—by proxy, at least.

Moving with such secrecy as he could, the sheriff collected and swore in some ninety men—the boldest and hardiest to be found in all the towns of the valley. They were not sedate and considerate citizens, but they were brave, or at least reckless, and, without exception, experienced wearers of guns. They professed themselves quite able and willing to bring down anybody in the hills. After being armed and provisioned, they were to be sent round by way of a railroad which was building towards the camp from the south.

Barnett was heedful of his words at home, and made light of the probable opposition of the miners, but

Ann Visits the Peak

Louis, with a boy's ability to discern what was going on, soon acquired a pretty clear idea of the plan, and when Ann asked him not to return to the heights on Monday he was ominously calm, but asserted his right to go where he pleased, and when she brought Barnett's influence to bear, the boy became white and resolved and his big eyes glowed.

"Rob wants me and needs me, and I'm going. You can put me in jail, but that is the only way. If there is going to be war, I am going to be in it, and I'm going to be on the side of the miners."

Ann wrote a swift and fervent note to Raymond:

"I am intrusting Louis to your care because he will not stay. You have won his heart from us, and we are powerless to prevent his return. Guard him, for the sake of his boyish sweetness, for my sake—"

She wrote no further, for, as her mind dwelt upon that camp of ruffian miners and their desire for battle, a bitter resolution swept over her. "I will test his love for me." With cold intensity she announced her purpose. "If you insist on going back to that camp, I shall go, too."

His eyes widened in protest. "I don't want you to do that—not now."

"Now is the time you need me. I am going in order to keep you out of mischief."

"You mustn't do it. There is no place for you to sleep."

"No matter; it is my duty. As you will not stay with me, I will go with you. I came here for your sake; I went down to that ranch to watch over you; I am staying here for the same reason; and now, as you

173

threaten to run away, I know where you are going and I will go with you."

Listening to her quiet words, the boy visibly weakened. His eyes fell and his lips began to twitch as a sense of responsibility awoke in him, and he thought of the throngs of rough men and the possibility of riot with a new emotion. He saw his sister with new eyes. Her beauty, her dainty dress, her delicate hands!—how out of place she would be in Sky-Town!

"You must not go," he repeated. "It's no place for you."

"It is no place for you."

He asserted himself again. "I can take care of myself."

"Mr. Raymond has asked me to keep you here." She went to him and put her arm about his neck. "Stay with me, laddie, I am missing you these days."

In the end she seemed to prevail, but she took no pleasure in her victory, for he went about the house like a young eagle pinioned. Nothing save the news of the camp interested him, and when the time came for the sheriff to start on his new raid he became greatly excited.

"There's going to be a battle," he said to Ann. "I'm going."

"No! No!" she pleaded.

He turned upon her with resentful stamp of his heel. "I can't stay here like a kid."

She changed her tone. "Very well; when shall we start?"

He looked at her steadily, and into his eyes came a softer gleam. "I've just thought," he began, reflectively; "you can stay with Mrs. Kelly till we build a wing for you. She's a nice woman, and lives in the cunningest little log-cabin. That settles it! We will go right away, to-day!"

Ann was at a loss, but did not show it. "If you are determined to go, then there is no use in waiting. Let us start at once!"

Louis rushed away to secure a team.

Mrs. Barnett was appalled at the thought of Ann's going to live on the peak. "You can't do it! There are a thousand reasons why you shouldn't think of it. First, it's terribly high. You may have some kind of heart-trouble without knowing it—people often do—and the altitude is sure to bring it out. Then, we are filled with engagements for two weeks; and, finally, where can you stay?"

"I'd go now if I had to live in a tent or a cave. I am afraid to have Louis up there without me. Nothing will keep him here except force, and I can't be his jailer. Perhaps, when he sees the discomfort to which he is exposing me, he will relent. I should never have left New York in the first place, but now that he is here I must see that he does not rush into danger."

Barnett came hurrying home, his face showing deep concern. "You can't do it, that's all," he said to Ann. "The sheriff starts to-night with a big posse of men to go into the camp to bring down some of its chief conspirators. Say the word, and I will lock the young scamp in the cellar."

Ann was quite calm. "No, I am going. All I ask is that you go with me and help me find a place to live. He is sure I can stay with the Kellys, whom he likes very much. Perhaps I will enjoy the novelty of it."

"But there may be trouble!"

"All the more reason why I should be there. Do you suppose I could sleep, with that boy up there, crazily poking his nose into every street brawl?"

"Rob will take care of him."

"I cannot shift my responsibility to any one else," she said, firmly. "Father asked me to be a mother to him, and I am doing now what a real mother would do. He will tire of it after a time and want to study 'Injuns,' or the Grand Cañon, or something. At present he cannot be hindered from his will."

And so, while Mrs. Barnett suggested what to wear, Don ordered a carriage to take them to the train, and Louis saddled his horse for his return trip up the stage-road. "I'll beat you up," he shouted to Ann, and galloped away with shining face.

The railway which ran up Bear Cañon was still building, and had not yet reached the divide, so that a stage-ride of some twenty miles connected the town of Grand View with Sky-Camp. Ann and Barnett were noticeable persons in the car, which was filled with roughly clad workmen of all kinds, and Barnett's irreproachable sack suit, clear, pink-and-white complexion, high, glistening collar, and modest "Darby" drew many a thumb towards him. "See that English dood," was the oft-muttered remark of those who were going in to heave rocks in search for gold.

Ann was conscious of their admiration of her, and it deeply annoyed her. Two or three of the better-dressed men, who were on speaking acquaintance with Barnett, came up to ask him what he thought of the strike.

"I didn't know it was a strike," said he, ignoring their evident desire to be introduced to Ann.

Ann Visits the Peak

"Oh, it's a strike, all right. Your man Mackay wasn't much hurt, was he?"

"Not badly."

"He was a little too previous. I hope the sheriff won't try to do anything more about it. The boys up at Sky are a little sharp-set about that business. Ain't goin' up there yourself, are ye?"

"Yes; I've always been on good terms with my men. I think I can help to arrange some sort of a compromise."

The two miners looked at each other. At length the older of them said, in a tone that meant a good deal to ears accustomed to Western inflections: "Well, I reckon the whole thing has been exaggerated. My claim is just below Bozle, and so, of course, I don't know much more about Sky than you do. Still, I wouldn't advise your going in at this time."

There were three other women in the car, but Ann was not reassured by their presence. Two of them were hard-faced, chittering little hussies, and the third was a thin, wan, weary Swedish mother, who was kept busy securing and retaining, one by one, her brood of tow-headed boys, who were resolute in their determination to ride on the car-coupler at the rear. So, while the men drew Don aside for still more confidential talk, Ann looked out of the window at the frosty, hard, and glittering landscape. The train crawled slowly, painfully, like an overburdened mule-team, rising rapidly, following the course of a swift stream, which not even the air of that altitude could congeal. It was a vigorous, clear-cut, masculine landscape, inhospitable to women.

At Grand View a couple of stages met them, and as

Ann waited on the platform for Don to secure a carriage, she observed that on the seat of each of the coaches two guards sat, negligently nursing rifles which glittered in the sunlight. There was something sinister in this — or would have been could she have rid herself of the feeling that it was all a drama—that the country was on masquerade, living up to the novelists and their illustrations. She realized for a moment some of the charm which it had for Louis. "I wish he could see this," she said to herself. "It would make a superb picture."

The "alfalfa miners" were stowing their bags of clothing and rolls of blankets into the compartment behind the big coaches, their jocular words exploding in the thin air like torpedoes. The coaches swayed, battered, scarred, and covered with mud, seemed about to be crushed flat by the dingy-coated, brawny fellows who crowded the inside seats to the last inch and edged the top like a row of weather-worn crows on a wall. Soon the whips began to crack, and the coaches rolled away one by one, leaving Barnett to follow in a road-wagon which he had hired for their own especial use.

The sun was sinking to mid-afternoon, and Mogalyon on the left was in full glory of ermine and saffron. The air was keen and crisp, the sky cloudless, and the road, except for an occasional mud-hole, was very good. Barnett remarked, "We ought to pull into Bozle before dark, on these roads."

"That's right—we'd ought to," replied the driver, with discouraged inflection.

Barnett peered a little closer at the team. "Is that the best you could give me?"

The driver was apologetic. "Well, sir, the boss got

178

drunk the other day and put 'em down a hill too fast and lamed the gray."

"So I see," Barnett resignedly replied. The stages were soon out of sight—ahead of them. He turned to Ann. "We could have gone in the coaches, but you saw the crowd. It wouldn't have been pleasant for you."

"Don't worry about me, Don. I'm not afraid of the dark—with you."

"Thank you," he said. "It's all plain sailing, and if you're not nervous it doesn't trouble me."

Now that Ann was coming closer to the camp and its secrets, she began to desire a better understanding of them. She began to ask questions, but Don, with a sign of silence, indicated the driver, and so her questions remained unanswered.

Night came abruptly. A thin, gray scum rose swiftly on the western sky and suddenly grayed the brightness of the sun. The world grew instantly stern and cold. The road, after climbing a ridge, descended into a gorge with firs on either side, and when they came out upon the flat meadow to the northwest of Mogalyon only the lights of Sky-Town could be seen. The hill itself was a dim, mysterious mass bulging against the lesser dark of sky out of which the larger stars faintly shone. It recalled to Ann the loom of New York against the eastern sky as she last saw it from the ferry. This, too, was a mountain range—the reality.

At the moment that Don was pointing out the lights, two horsemen appeared in front and in the middle of the road.

"Halt!" cried a clear voice.

The driver pulled his tired horses to a stand so energetically that his hands rose above his head.

"Is Donnelly Barnett with you?" asked one of the men, as he rode nearer.

"Darned if I know," said the driver. "I got some kind of a valley dood here, and his wife or something."

"I'm Barnett. What do you want of me?" asked Don, coolly.

"Not a thing," answered the horseman. "That's just it. We have no use for you, and I've been watching to meet you and say that the boys want you to continue your quiet, uneventful life at the Springs."

"Who are you?"

"We're a couple of Sky-Town vedettes. Who is the lady?"

"That doesn't concern you. Go on, driver."

The driver took up the reins, but the voice of the vedette grew sterner: "Stay where you are!" Then, turning to Barnett: "I'm your best friend, Donnelly. The boys understand that you are backing Mackay in his plans, and it isn't safe for you to enter the camp. I advise you to turn around right here and go back."

Barnett laughed. "Do you suppose I'm going to take advice of that kind?"

The other vedette interrupted. "Swat him in the jaw; he's too funny."

Ann spoke up. "Please let us go on. Mr. Barnett is taking me in to meet my brother, and I am cold and hungry."

There was something thrilling in the calm, clear sweetness of her voice, and the first of the vedettes, pressing nearer, leaned from his saddle to ask:

"Who is your brother, lady?"

"His name is Louis Rupert. He is only a boy, and I am going in to care for him."

Ann Visits the Peak

"Rob Raymond's kid. I know him," replied the vedette. "But I thought he was visiting you in the Springs?"

"He was, but he went back to the camp to-day, and I am very anxious about him."

"He's all right, lady, so long as Rob Raymond has him in hand. You are welcome, but Barnett is on the outside and must stay there."

"I decline to acknowledge your authority," responded Barnett, now thoroughly angry.

The horseman laughed softly, irritatingly. "Manners don't go with us at the present time. I must ask you to camp right here or go back to Grand View till I can communicate with the president of the union. If you are here to talk compromise, the men will be glad to meet you; but my judgment is that you better retire to Grand View. I will see that this lady gets to her brother."

Ann was not a timid girl, but the thought of riding away into the blackness of the night with these sinister guards made her flesh chill and her nerves creep. "Don't leave me, Don," she whispered.

Barnett stormed at the horsemen. "It is impossible! If I am forced to go back she must go with me. What right have you to interfere with our plans?"

The answer came quickly, coldly, every word telling. "I'll tell you. The boys have learned that you have been chiefly instrumental in pushing the sheriff into another raid, and if trouble comes they'll kill you. It isn't safe for you to be on the hill to-morrow. Now you needn't be afraid to trust the lady to me." The vedette removed his hat. "I am not a man to be feared by women."

Ann again spoke. "I can't consent to your going into danger for me, Don. Turn back, and I will go on."

"It is madness!" he said, in a low voice. "These men are not fit escorts for you. We will both go back and wait—until morning."

Ann's teeth were chattering with cold. "I dread that long drive. We must be almost at our destination."

The two horsemen conferred together, and at last one of them returned to say: "Driver, you may come on until you reach the first cabin at the foot of the hill. There the lady will get out, and you will drive Mr. Barnett back before daylight to-morrow morning."

The driver chirped to the horses, and they began to plod across the meadow towards the base of the looming shoulder of Mogalyon. Ann's heart was small and weak in her bosom as she thought of riding that lonely way, behind that sinister guide; but she was suffering with cold, and the way of return seemed intolerably long and lonely.

As they drew up before the shanty door the leader of the vedettes rode forward and said, gently: "Lady, the road from here to the summit is lined with cabins, and no harm can possibly come to you while I have you in charge. Or, if you like, you can stay here till morning; but I would advise you to go on to Mrs. Kelly's. There is no cabin suited to your needs on this side of the peak."

Ann, stiff and weary and hungry, rose in her seat with a sort of desperation. "I will go," she said, with trembling voice.

The vedette, dismounting quickly, helped her to the

ground, while the second man, leaning low on his horse, entered into a muttered conversation with an unkempt man in the doorway.

Barnett argued and insisted on going on to Kelly's.

"Not one step farther!" sternly commanded the vedette. "But you can sleep here till daylight if you wish."

Ann interposed. "Don, I beg of you to go home. I don't want you to go any farther. I am not afraid now; this man will take me to Mrs. Kelly's. I'm sure of it, and Louis will be there by this time, and Mr. Raymond."

"Sure thing, lady; and it isn't late—not more than seven o'clock. We'll almost get there in time for supper. Can you ride a horse?"

"Yes."

"Western fashion?"

"I think so—if it is necessary."

"Well, I will put you on my saddle and I will walk and lead the horse." The light from the doorway fell upon him as he approached her, and the sight of his boyish face reassured her.

As Barnett saw her rise to the saddle, he burst out: "This is preposterous! You must not go up there; the boy isn't worth it. I'm going with you or fight!" He drew his revolver, but some one caught his hand from behind and twisted the weapon out of his grasp.

"Go on, Jack. We'll take care of him," called the man in the cabin door.

As the light of the lamp was left behind and the darkness settled round her, a convulsive terror seized upon the girl. The horse, stumbling over loose rocks in the road, which ran back and forth on the hill-side like folds of braid, passed now and again under dark and silent pines, and in one of these shadowy places her leader stopped to rest. By force of the violent contrast Ann thought of her box at the opera, when the lights go out for the overture. Surely if she had sought the whole earth round she could not have fallen upon a more appalling contrast than this experience. They were assembling for "Tristan und Isolde," while she was being led by masked highwaymen into the obscurity of a mountain. At that moment something took place in her brain—a mist cleared away—she felt herself in a new relation to the world.

She was not an imaginative girl; she was, on the contrary, given to taking a prosaic view of what to others would have been fervidly romantic and stirring; but this she admitted: the earth was larger, more vital, and more dangerous than before, and she of far less importance in it than she had permitted herself to acknowledge.

Once, as her guard came back towards her, something rose in her throat, some elemental dread, and her breath rushed hoarsely through her lips. "If Robert only knew my need of him," she thought, "he would surely come to me."

The man's voice was gentle as he said: "You see, lady, the camp is in a terrible excitement. We heard to-day that the sheriff was coming with a posse, and the boys kind o' hold five or six o' those one-lungers in the Springs responsible. They are particularly down on Barnett for putting Mackay up to that trick. But you'll be perfectly safe at Kelly's, and it's right close to Raymond's shack, so that you can see your brother as soon as he comes in."

As they resumed their way the lights thickened, and

great, angular buildings marked the location of the larger mines. Twice silent figures met them and passed, staring closely at the girl, and once a group of noisy miners crossed the road ahead of them, arguing blatantly among themselves.

At length Ann's leader turned towards a dark, high point of rocks, the trail began to descend, and a few minutes later they came to a warmly lighted cabin, on the door of which the guide resolutely knocked. The latch was immediately lifted, and a small, pale woman with a blur of yellow hair about her head appeared in the light.

"Mrs. Kelly, I've brought you a boarder," began the vedette.

Ann caught sight of a boy at the table and gave a cry of joy. "Oh, Louis! Louis!"

With a whoop the boy rushed from the cabin and flung his arms around her.

"Oh, Ann, but I'm glad to see you! Where is Cousin Don? Which way did you come? Rob has gone down to Bozle to meet you."

Ann turned to thank her guide, who was looking at her with undisguised admiration.

"It was a great pleasure," he replied, with an assumption of grand manner. "Introduce me, please," he said to Mrs. Kelly.

"I must introduce myself first," said the little woman. "I am Mrs. Kelly, and your guard is Mr. Jack Munro."

Ann gave him her hand. "I thank Mr. Munro; but I think he should have allowed Mr. Barnett to come into shelter. It seemed cruel to send him back on that long, cold drive."

Munro remained unmoved. "Oh, he'll stay at Clayson's overnight."

Mrs. Kelly put in a word. "I think you better come into shelter; you must be cold and hungry. Won't you step inside, Mr. Munro?"

"No, thank you. It is a great temptation, but I've work to do."

"Good-night," said Ann.

"Good-night, fair lady," he replied.

And so, chilled and hungry, Ann entered the pleasant home of the Kellys, and the terror of the dark ride became a part of the outer world, shut away by the strong, rude door.

"Rob has gone down to the stage office," explained Mrs. Kelly. "We thought you'd come that way."

"How did you happen to come with Munro?" asked Louis, still puzzled.

Mrs. Kelly put Ann down to some tea and cold meat, and, while she was still at the table and in the midst of her story, Raymond flung open the door.

"Here she is!" he called to some one behind him, and his white face and glowing eyes testified to his great anxiety.

Ann rose to meet him with a rush of trust and confidence that filled her throat and rendered her wordless, but she held her hand towards him.

He seized it. "I was greatly alarmed when I heard that you were coming alone. How did you come?— how did you find the way?"

Ann then said, "Your friend Munro met us, turned Don back, and piloted me up the hill."

"Don mustn't come here now."

"That is what Mr. Munro said."

Ann Visits the Peak

Raymond turned to a big man who stood waiting. "Miss Rupert, this is Matthew Kelly, my mining partner."

Ann gave her hand into Kelly's enormous palm with a look of admiration. "I am glad to know you, Mr. Kelly. I have heard Louis speak of you very often."

In the presence of these men Ann lost all sense of fear and weakness. They were possessed of something which Don, loyal as he was, lacked. Their very glances calmed and conquered. To be with them was like being befriended on the desert by the lion, in the jungle by the tiger—for they belonged to the wilderness and to the cabin, and knew the rigors, the rages, and the humors of the peak and its dwellers.

Raymond's eyes hardly left her face; but she no longer resented his interest. On the contrary, she studied him closely. There was a subtle change in him— he seemed older, gentler, but more manly and handsomer than before.

"It is a rude place for you to live, Miss Rupert," he said, "but there is no danger. The strike has not involved us. We are as peaceful as a farm here."

She smiled back into his eyes with more of liking than she had ever expressed.

"I am not afraid," she replied. "I am going to find the camp interesting. At any rate, so long as Louis is settled in his determination to be a miner, I must keep him in sight."

"It is a great pleasure to have him with me, and I am glad to be of use to him, for his own sake as well as for what you have come to mean to me."

Ann's lashes fell before the glow of his admiring eyes, and with this sign of weakness a flush of resentment again passed over her. "He must not look at me in that way," she complained to herself.

When Raymond left the house to walk back to his own cabin, he resented, for the first time, the presence of Louis. He wished to be alone with the mysterious emotion which had swept back upon him at sight of Ann. He faced the night, out of which every shred of vapor had vanished, and the blue-black vault, blazing with innumerable jetting globes of light, invited to high thoughts, to serious imaginings.

His duty plainly was to lay hands upon the lad and hustle him back to Valley Springs, and so put both brother and sister out of his life; but this was not easy. It was a deep pleasure to think of that delicate and cultured girl in the Kelly cottage — so near to him — fairly under his protection. "A few hours and I can see her again," was a refrain in his thought. "And yet this is no place for her."

He argued that she was in no danger, and that the change of air would do her good. "She will be interested in the mines," he went on, in formless debate with himself. "The scenery is magnificent; and then, of course, she can go down at any time we think wise."

Louis was too excited to go to bed. His eyes glowed and his lips trembled as he exclaimed again: "Isn't it good of Ann! I'm perfectly happy now. Wasn't it nice to see her come in?"

"Yes, it is wonderful to think of her—here so near us."

"She's a trump. I wish she'd fall in love with you," the lad ended, made reckless by happiness.

Raymond's face remained impassive, but his cheek flushed. "See here, youngster, don't you make any more such breaks as that or you'll invite trouble. Moreover, you turn in and go to bed or I'll buck and gag you this minute." Thereupon Louis fell silent, but his boyish frankness had made painfully definite the desire which Raymond had tried to keep unformed and unacknowledged in his heart.

Something softer, sweeter, more yielding had appeared in the girl's face, in her voice, and this phase of her character was more alluring than any other she had permitted him to see.

In this mood she seemed to approach her forgotten name—the name whose every letter was filled with poetry to her father. She became Hesper—star of the West—a part of the land the father found so imperishably beautiful a quarter of a century before.

XIII

Ann Touches Plank Floors

THE little room to which Mrs. Kelly conducted Ann was hardly larger than a steamer state-room and was very primitive as regards its furnishings. The walls were of unhewn pine logs and the floors of rough planks still odorous from the saw. A cheap wooden bed stood in one corner, taking up nearly half of the space, and a chair and a little wash-stand of Matt's making completed the "outfit," as he called it.

"It's a small place and a rough place for such as you, but it's the best we have."

Ann responded to the humility which shaded the hearty voice of her hostess, and, though she shivered in the chill air, answered, cheerily: "I'm sure this is very nice. The bed is tempting."

"I hope you won't freeze. I'll get another blanket for you. If I'd thought, I should have warmed the sheets."

"Please don't trouble. I do not expect all the comforts of a hotel on a mountain-top. I assure you I am a very healthy immigrant."

Hesitatingly, with many misgivings, Mrs. Kelly withdrew, and Ann hurriedly disrobed and leaped into the bed, which was white as snow and almost as cold. It was like a plunge into the breakers at Magnolia; it fairly took her breath away, and there was no escape from this icy contact, for the air was as bitter as the sheets.

As she lay with chattering teeth, her mind reverted to a visit she had once made as a child to the home of her grandmother — a Thanksgiving Day ineffaceably marked in her mind by the frost of an attic-room to which she and a maid had been assigned. She wondered if Mrs. Kelly's room were as cold as hers. Truly when one went out of one's proper sphere of life experiences lay in wait as eagles hover to devour lambs.

The courage with which she had faced the hardships of her trip and the amusement which she now drew from her struggle with the cold of her bed amazed the girl. Some latent force, some quality she was unaware of, rose to fortify her against discomfort and danger. Marvelling at this, she mentally retraced the mountain-road, dwelling upon the more salient incident of the ride. The loom of the horseman in the dusk thrilled her again with fear. She studied once more the differences in the voices of the two guards—that of the young man, jocular and cultivated, while the guttural snarl of his companion was like the threat of a wolf. The sinking of her heart at parting with Barnett came back, and when in this retrospect she abandoned herself to the guidance of her half-seen guide through the dark of the mountain-path, she shuddered with something other than cold. But the joy of the meeting with Louis, and the unexpected glow of confidence and pleasure with which she met Raymond's anxious, piercing eyes, came back to warm her heart.

How changed he was! How deeply brown! He looked as vigorous as she saw him first at the ranch, and yet different—years older; and with his strength, his resolution, something new was mingled—something graver and sweeter. He was handsomer in the miner's heavy boots than in the cow-boy's spurs and kerchief. His chin was fine—so firm and so cleanly carved—the chin of a man who would win his way, who would fight his way. And his eyes—

Her mind took up again the singularity of her position, lying there in a frosty bed in a miner's cabin two full miles above the city of her birth. She laughed. "Am I to meet my death by freezing?" But at last a glow of comfort began to steal over her, a delicious languor, and then—she was awakened by a grinding sound and by the shouting of cheerful children, and a few minutes later the gentle voice of Mrs. Kelly sounded at the door.

"Are you awake?" Ann threw back the coverlet to find the room full of sunshine. "May I come in?" asked Mrs. Kelly.

"Certainly," said Ann, and the pale and pretty little housewife entered with a pitcher of warm water.

"Good-morning. How did you sleep the night?"

"I don't know. I haven't the slightest idea where the night went to."

"It's quite cold this morning. Shall I bring your breakfast to you?"

"See my breath!" Ann cried, in astonishment. "It's frozen."

Mrs. Kelly laughed. "Ye're lucky not to have a nose frozen." Then she added, hospitably, "Don't get up till the fire warms the room. I'll leave the door open a bit."

After her hostess left her, Ann lay staring at the rough walls and the still more primitive ceiling in wonder. "It must be real," she thought, "for I couldn't possibly dream it." With a realization of her own sloth, she sprang out upon the cold floor and began to dress with a vigor and celerity she did not know she possessed.

She came into the little sitting-room, which served also as dining-room, to find Kelly with a youngster on each knee, trotting them "to Boston" so hard that their yellow hair flew in clouds about their shining eyes.

Pulling his horses to an uneasy stand, the big miner said: "Top o' the morning, miss. How did ye sleep?"

"Very well indeed, thank you."

"'Twas all I could do to kape these wild Injuns still. As soon as the sun comes in they begin the day—each day noisier than the rest."

The wild Injuns gurgled with laughter, and in the midst of their frolic Mrs. Kelly re-entered. "Oh, I'm sorry you got up, miss, I was about to bring your coffee to you."

"I'm among Spartans now," said Ann, "and I'm going to eat when the Spartans do."

During breakfast she studied Mrs. Kelly, and began to understand at last that the little mother had not merely washed and dressed the boys and cooked the breakfast, but had served as waitress and maid of all work, and now, calm and sweet and self-contained, was presiding over the table. If any dish needed replenishing, she sprang up to get it, and this put the robust daughter of wealth to shame.

"Don't you feel tired some mornings and lie a-bed?" she asked.

Mrs. Kelly smiled. "Indeed I do, but I can't afford to lie a-bed. When Matt makes his next strike, sure

I'm going to hire a girl and sleep till I'm weary of it, if it takes a week."

"You must let me do something while I am here," said Ann. "Let me provide a maid for you."

"Oh no; I was only jokin'. Sure you couldn't hire a girl on the hill to do housework; besides, the best of them are not fit company for you, and in a small hut like this you're cheek by jowl with your help."

Ann had not thought of them as company, but she gravely replied: "I might bring a maid from my cousin's house. At any rate, you must let me help this morning. I can sweep and dust—indeed, I can."

"Mighty little dusting the shack needs in this air," said Mrs. Kelly. "Good-luck to me, it's tiny."

"I must help or I will not stay," insisted Ann. "At least, I can amuse the children," she added, looking at Kelly, who had risen.

"Boys, mind the lady now," said he; "and you have a care they don't tear you to pieces. They are divils for breakin' bones."

Louis shot through the door like a stone from a sling. His eyes were dancing. "Good-morning, everybody," he shouted. "Haven't you breakfasted yet? Why, we've been done ten minutes. Isn't this bully— this life up here? How do you feel this morning?"

Ann laughed to see him so elate, so vigorous. "What a child you are!" she exclaimed, in wonder.

Raymond followed at a little distance. "Good-morning, Miss Rupert. Good-morning, Nora. Hello, younkers," and he gathered a boy under each arm. He looked very capable and entirely self-contained as he put the lads down and addressed himself to Ann. "I suppose your baggage went to Bozle, but we will get that to-day; and, Mrs. Kelly, if you need anything to make Miss Rupert comfortable let us know—to the limit of our resources command us."

Ann, with unaccountable lightness of spirit, quickly protested. "Now, please don't make company of me. I am going to earn my living by helping Mrs. Kelly about the house. My bed was very comfortable and my breakfast delicious. What else do I require? One needn't ask how you are; you look to be perfectly well again."

Louis stared at his sister, and was about to make some revealing remark when Raymond intervened. "We are very glad to have you in camp, but you must not suffer inconveniences."

"I've been thinking perhaps it would do me good to suffer hardship," she answered, with a reflective glance.

He considered a moment before changing the subject. "Everything seems quiet up street this morning, so our trouble may blow over. I am going up by-and-by and will report on what is brewing in the saloons. They are the storm-centres. I'm sorry Don started to come in, and I hope he will go quietly back and forget the whole incident."

As Ann helped about the table, clearing the dishes away, her senses seemed suddenly freshened, renewed. On the clean, rough floor the two sturdy, blond lads were playing with a small and battered toy engine. The sunlight streamed in magically clear and golden. There was a wifely charm in everything Nora Kelly did —in her deft handling of the dishes, in her unhurried step, and in her half-smiling, grateful face, which was often turned upon her visitor. The scene was homely —homely in the most primitive sense—and its spirit laid hold upon something long hidden in the girl. Her blood grew swifter in its courses; she returned to the joys of her grandmother's pioneer days in the Alleghany forests. The rough walls, the low ceiling, the slab chairs, the steaming tea-kettle on the fire, all these seemed at the moment more real, more vitally woven into her life than the furnishings of the city home in which she had lived since a child.

The cook-stove, the kettle, the busy housewife recalled the deep delight with which she used to visit, as a girl of ten or twelve, the ancestral home somewhere up towards the great hills — a gray, old farm-house wherein her father began his life. She was intoxicated with joy of her unexpected release from her indifferentism.

For years she had moved in a sort of gray cloud—a world in which the sunlight was always pale—a world of plenty, containing everything but zest, and deep in her secret heart she had begun to fear that she had gone past any real passion, any close-hand contact with life. She had said: "I've seen too much. I've travelled too much. I have destroyed my appetite, and nothing will ever taste good." Now, as she worked at the table with her gentle little hostess, a hope sprang up. She began to ask herself the meaning of this pleasure.

She found herself not merely liking Nora Kelly, but respecting her. She was work-worn and in a sense unlearned, but she had native dignity and a certain grave sweetness of temper which ennobled her, and the girl's heart went out to her. "Now, you're to call me Ann, and I'll call you Nora," she said, "and you're to teach me to work. I've been living a life of perfect idleness down at the Springs, and I need to work. You must get fairly dragged out with the never-ending duties."

Mrs. Kelly's face was wistful. "Yes, sometimes; but Matt is good to me, and the boys, with all their noise and worry of me, are a great comfort. Sometimes, when I feel ill of a morning, Matt gets the breakfast. 'Tis a sorry breakfast, but it does me good to see him moving about like an elephant pickin' up pins, leavin' a trail of dirty dishes behind him, the great gawk that he is."

Ann's heart warmed towards Kelly, and in imagination could see his kind but devastating figure lumbering about the tiny kitchen, followed by the lads. His giant frame made the whole cabin seem like a toy house. Thus far he had appeared rather silent and reserved; but this was shyness, so Mrs. Kelly said, though Ann could hardly believe her, so masterful was his head, so serene his glance.

"Have you always had to do this—I mean since your marriage?" asked Ann, a little later.

"Oh no. When we were first married we had a nice little house, and I kept a girl; but Matt is a restless one. He sold his claim soon after, and the house, too, and we began again in Sylvanite. We lost all we had there, and then we came here, and they made him chief, and we were just going to build a house when he found this vein, and put all his money into developing it; and now we're hoping to make a stake and sell, and go down to the Springs where the lads can get an education. Matt has roamed the hills long enough."

Here was the secret of her patience. Love made every hardship light—love for her husband, and pride and hope in the future of her boys. The girl rose to a conception that one might even grow old contentedly with cares and plans like these.

"I wish I could love like that," the girl cried out in her innermost heart. "I want to love and to suffer. I want realities—not this tepid, purposeless existence I now have," and the shaping of this cry in words helped her and cleared the way before her.

She had not always been so cold, so sluggish. She enjoyed her coming out, her first evenings at the opera, her tea-pouring at receptions. For some years these were pleasures—keen and joyous experiences—but by degrees they had come to be tedious, meaningless. Life had become flat, like champagne out of which the tang has fled. Her mother—she checked herself. "I will not blame my mother."

"Oh, if I could only give this poor, tired woman a little of my security and physical comfort," she thought, as she sat watching Nora put the boys into their out-door jackets. "I've been served too much," she said, aloud, to Mrs. Kelly. "I've had things done for me all my life, and I'm tired of it. It will be a real kindness if you will let me do things for you. Show me how to mend clothes and I will do it while you lie and watch me. I can do a little sewing of a sort. I can even learn to darn stockings and cook."

Something in her voice—but more especially in her eyes—touched the little wife to the heart. Turning, she put her arms about the girl's neck and gave way to tears.

"You're good to me. I've been so lonely up here. If you will only let me love you."

Ann kissed her. "You poor thing! I think I understand. Men are all very well—but we need our kind, don't we? Now, you get your work-basket and show me what to do, and I'll do it while you rest, you work-weary thing. It seems I am come just in time to keep you from breaking down."

"Sure, God must have known how lonesome I was and sent you to me," said Nora, fervently.

Raymond, looking in at the door, was wonderfully heartened by seeing Ann bent above a work-basket, with Mrs. Kelly sitting near in the attitude of teacher. "I'm sorry to interrupt important business, but Louis and I are impatient to have you see our bungalow. To tell the truth, we've been trying to tidy it up in preparation for your coming."

Ann looked up brightly. "Is it quite presentable at this moment?"

"Louis considers it in order. I am a little dubious myself."

She rose. "Very well; I will go now. I'll return to my work soon," she said to her hostess.

"Bless your heart, don't think you must hurry back," said Mrs. Kelly, and her look conveyed the gratification she felt in seeing the young people on such friendly terms.

"It is a source of chagrin to me that I was of so little service to you last night," Raymond began, when they were fairly outside the door.

"Oh, what a great, glittering world!" exclaimed Ann, catching her breath as the splendor of sky and peak rolled in upon her.

"You brought it. The sky has been gray for days."

When her eyes had absorbed the beauty of the high world, Ann permitted herself to observe the town beneath and the mines in the foreground.

Hesper

"It isn't a bit as I thought it would be," she said. "Where are the cañons and the rushing streams and the log foot-bridges and the cabins perched high on the crags? It isn't a bit as father described it."

"He was writing of cañon-diggings. Sky is a different proposition, as they say up here. We're above the cañons—above the streams, in fact. Saloon Row, over there, is almost above timber-line."

"How can you wash gold out of the rocks without water?"

"We pound it out with stamp-mills. You are thinking of placer-mining. There is no golden soil here. It's all quartz-mining."

"It isn't a bit as I thought it was," she repeated.

"Are you disappointed?"

"Yes, I am. I thought it would be more picturesque, more as father saw it. Still, it's superb—in the distance, at least."

"That farthest range is his Hesperean wall," he said, with a meaning glance.

Louis stood in the door to greet them. "I thought you weren't ever coming," he said. "I'm crazy to show our house."

"Oh, how fine!" cried Ann, quite sincerely delighted. The room was of good size, and the sun, streaming in at the windows, fell in a flood along the floor, while a big fire warmed the hearth-stone. It was color-full with rugs, and its rude chairs were in keeping with its walls. A big table showed signs of being the common work-bench, littered as it was with drawings and books.

"We have two other rooms," announced the boy, with pride, "a bedroom and a dining-room."

Ann Touches Plank Floors

"How luxurious!"

"The extravagances are mine," remarked Raymond. "Louis was quite content with the bare necessities—in fact, I think he resents comfort as being distinctly debilitating."

Ann could not but show a little surprise at each well-turned phrase in Raymond's speech. She turned suddenly. "Now, tell me about the camp. What is the trouble all about? I *can't* understand."

"It's quite simple," he replied. "The county is about equally divided now between the miners of the peak and the citizens of the plain. The peak's interests are not those of the Springs, and it has resented for a year the domination of the Springs. The owners of the mines are either residents of the plain or of the East, and violently opposed to the politics of the camp. Barnett's man, Mackay, attempted to reorganize the working hours of the camp and failed—you know of the mishandling he received."

"What are they going to do now?"

"I don't know. As the case stands, the camp is hot against any invasion by the sheriff and 'a mob of hirelings,' as they call his deputies; and his attempt to overawe the camp only created more furious resistance. I will be able to tell better what the outcome will be when I learn what the union has decided to do. Thus far it has been a game of bluff on the part of a dozen men who are not strictly miners at all, and the question of wages has had little attention. I am going up now to see what is going on."

She turned to Louis. "You must not go. You must stay with me."

Louis looked deeply disappointed, but Raymond

added: "That's true, lad; stay with your sister and keep her on the peak. We need her."

Louis smiled slyly. "Oh, she'll stay all right. She's going to like it as well as I do."

As they were walking back to the Kelly cabin, Ann said: "These are my brother's trial years, both physically and spiritually. If he lives these two years, the doctor tells me all danger of consumption will be over; and if he can be kept untouched of this vicious world up here—" She did not finish.

"I will do all I can to guard him—you know that; but I believe in breeding. Louis is a good boy, not because he has had no opportunity to do evil, but because his soul is naturally fastidious. He keeps his heart free of evil thoughts, just as he keeps his hands clean. He is a great joy and comfort to me—never a burden or annoyance."

Ann's eyes were softer in their light than he had ever seen them, as she put out her hand. "Thank you sincerely for those words. Henceforth I will not doubt your guardianship. You'll forgive me, won't you?"

"For what?"

"For distrusting you."

"If distrust of my care brought you here, I am ready not merely to forgive you but to thank you for it."

She turned her shoulder to him. "I don't like you when you pay labored compliments."

"Now, I beg your pardon," he answered, quickly. "I will not offend again."

"As it was a first offence, I forgive you," she replied, with a glance that exalted him and remained with him like a benediction."

XIV

Raymond Opposes Violence

AS Raymond entered the street, the peace and beauty of the Kelly home, and the vision of the two women bent peacefully above their sewing, stood away in radiant contrast above the reeking saloons, the reckless crowds of gamesters, and the rows of drink-inflamed men lounging along each bar. Slattern women leaned from shanty doors, blinking and yawning in the sun, garbed only in crumpled wrappers, their hair unkempt, careless of the sheriff's menace, careless of their future, careless of their God. Chinamen, sleepy-eyed, but mechanically swift and noiseless, looked out on the street sardonically while smoothing rough linen in the windows of their small shops. Compact knots of miners were grouped in the middle of the street, as if for greater privacy, talking earnestly, with many oaths. The searching light of the unclouded sun revealed the hard and unlovely lines of each face, and the town, utterly, inexcusably squalid, called fiercely for the shadow to cover its nakedness and filth.

The lover's senses, sharpened by Ann's presence in the camp, detected a most sinister change in the temper of the men. Up to this time all that had taken place had been jocular, at least on the surface, but the sheriff's threatened invasion, with a hundred hired thugs, stirred the red fires of wrath in men like Hanley, Brock, and Collingwood, who had hitherto been but on-lookers, and they were now the inciting centres of men talking loudly and with undisguised fury. Raymond began to see the striking miners as Ann would see them—abstractly they were oppressed workmen; concretely they were filthy and dangerous. "And yet this should not rob them of their right," he admitted.

Hanley, assuming a fine virtue, argued: "Why didn't he come up here *as* sheriff, alone. No one would have resisted the properly constituted authority of the county; but when he comes with a lot of battered bums trailing at his heels, he invites trouble, and he'll get it."

To this Dan Brock, surrounded by his cronies, merely winked and said, "We see his bluff."

Hanley, perceiving Raymond at the door, approached to say: "One of Munro's vedettes intercepted that kid of yours last night, and got word that Don Barnett was on his way up here. You better warn him off."

Raymond resented his tone, but coldly replied: "The boy was mistaken. Barnett turned back at Grand View."

Some one plucked him by the arm, and, following his guide, Raymond entered the room used as the office of the union, where he found Carter, the president, and Larned, the organizer, in the midst of a hot argument with Munro, Smith, and a group of others of their sort. Larned was shaking with excitement and rage, and Carter, the little president, looked white and scared.

"Keep out!" called Smith.

But Larned, who knew Raymond's mind, shouted:

Raymond Opposes Violence

"Come in! Come and talk to these fire-eaters; you're a man of sense."

Munro, with a grin, added, "Come in, Rob; this is a council of war."

Raymond entered calmly, his head a little bent, his keen eyes studying every face. "What's it all about?"

Larned explained, his hands quivering, the veins on his forehead bulging, his eyes restless and fevered. "If they do it," he said, "I leave—I get out. I will not countenance lawlessness of this sort. I'm not a fool, I know what the effect will be. If they turn back this posse, the State militia will be called out."

"The Governor is on our side," said Smith. "Our party has a majority in the State."

"Yes, yes; but that won't save you. Every decent, law-abiding citizen will go against you — your own party will desert you. I know. I know. I came to organize a union to meet the coming question of labor and capital. I did not come here to form mobs. I refuse to sanction it. I will not have a thing to do with it. If you make this raid, I leave the camp."

Smith leered. "That's awful; but I think the camp will stagger along."

Raymond spoke. "I'm not involved in the present disagreement, so that my advice is disinterested, but as you've ridden up and asked me, I give it as my opinion that Larned is right. You can stand off a sheriff once or twice, and you might even stand off a regiment of militia, but you can't stand off the United States army, and that's what you'll run up against in the end. Jack, you ought to have sense enough to keep out of this."

Munro smiled. "I'm only the military arm of government. I'm not making laws; I execute them."

"Why not call a meeting and put it to a vote?" asked Smith.

"I know why," replied Brock. "Larned is afraid it will carry."

Larned leaped to his feet. "I admit it! I don't want the word to go out that this raid has been voted on by the union. With the camp boiling with excitement, it might carry. Outsiders must be taught the difference between the action of the mob and the will of the organization."

Smith was brutally plain. "It isn't your say. You're only an outsider yourself. It's Carter's place to call the meeting and discuss what we are to do. A half-dozen of us have laid ourselves liable by doing duty for the union; now, the question is whether the union is going to stand by us or sneak and leave us to eat dirt in a valley jail."

"You had no sanction from the union."

"I know we didn't — no official sanction; but you know perfectly well that the men were with us then, and they are with us now, every one of them."

A rap on the door startled them all. It was like the tap of the finger of fate. Munro opened the door, and Dolan, the reporter, entered. "Hello, lads," he called, easily, "what's doin'?"

They all shouted, "Hello, Jim!" And Larned, starting forward, exclaimed:

"Any news?"

"Well, rather. The sheriff, with a hundred men and a special train, is at Trinchera. He means business this time, lads."

Raymond Opposes Violence

There was a moment's hush, and then Smith roared out: "He can have it! We'll meet him!"

A small Irishman leaped into the middle of the floor, wild as a hawk. "Mate him? By the piper, but we'll mate him! We'll make him *drink* blood!"

"Shut up," said Munro. "You howling Murphys make me tired. Think this is a clubbing-match? This is war, man—war!"

"Yes," said Raymond, "it is war, and the best thing you and Smith and the others named in the indictment can do for the camp is to hit a Western trail and touch the high places only."

Smith snorted. "Oh, h—! You farmers—"

A glint in Munro's eye stopped him as the gleam of a knife might have done. "Don't get gay with Rob Raymond, old sport. He grew up with a gun in his hand, and he's my friend."

The roomful of men now gathered into groups to discuss the certainty. Dolan, gay with excitement, drew round him Carter, Larned, and Collingwood. Smith and Denver Dan were the centre of another squad, while Raymond took Munro aside and earnestly pleaded: "See here, old man, you must keep out of this. It isn't your funeral, but it will be if you don't vamoose the ranch."

"I can't go back on the boys now, Rob. They need my military training; and, besides, I am in it. I won't sit back and see the district done up by these thugs who never earned an honest dollar in their lives. And your friend Barnett—what good is he on earth? Just a blood-sucker on the bare back of labor. I'm with the boys, and if my experience can do 'em any good, I'm ready."

"I know how you feel, Jack, but this is desperate

business. A fight with the sheriff will set the whole country against the miners."

Munro smiled contemptuously. "He won't fight. A round of shots in the air will send him hot-footing it back to the Springs. It's all a farce."

"Be careful. The farce may turn into tragedy at a moment's notice. These miners are idle and full of liquor. Men like Kelly who have women to protect—"

Munro caught at this. "By-the-way, who was the 'femme'? My word! she's a peach."

Raymond's tone was coldly indifferent. "Miss Rupert is from New York City—Barnett's cousin. She is here to look after her brother Louis. I was not thinking of her so much as of Mrs. Kelly and other women who can't get away."

"Well, she's a smooth piece of goods. I can tell silk from bombazine, even in the dark. Her voice was like satin; made me think of Allie Birbeck—you remember her; carried me back to 'Lovers' Lane.' I'm just as much of a 'spoonoid' as ever. How long does she stay?"

Raymond grew brusque of tone. "I don't know—a day or two, I reckon."

Larned's voice, rising high and cutting above the others, interposed. "Then I leave. You are crazy. You can't hold this hill with a million Gatling-guns. The national committee will not stand for it. Good-bye." Clapping his hat on his head, he walked out of the room, his white face set in a furious frown.

Brock roared out: "Call a meeting, Carter, and we'll carry it our way. To blazes with the national committee!"

Carter, however, was scared blue by Larned's despairing retreat, and refused. "We've got to go slow. We can't win without help. I won't make the call."

San Juan Smith, with flaming face, shouted, furiously: "Then we'll do it without your sanction. The executive board will act."

Raymond, on the doorstep, made a last appeal to Munro. "Jack, you can't afford to go into this thing with Smith. Keep out of it. It's bad business all around. It's one thing to strike, and another thing to resist authority. See this street!"

In some way word had already passed along the ridge that the sheriff was actually on the road, and that he would reach the end of the railway in mid-afternoon, and a great throng was packed round a man on horseback who was good-naturedly trying to force his way towards headquarters.

"That's one of my scouts," said Munro, "with news of the invaders," and he pushed off into the crowd, while Raymond, with serious face and slow step, went down the path towards his mine.

"They're going to fight," he said to Kelly.

"Fight? Of course they'll fight! They'll go down and drive the sheriff's men like sheep. But what then? The crazy jacks!"

"Do you think we ought to tell the women—are they in danger?"

Kelly was reflective. "Not now. The sheriff will hardly reach the hill this time. He'll go back. The authorities and the newspapers will chew the rag for a couple of weeks, and *then*—we'll be up against it!"

"All the same, Matt, I wear my guns from this on, and one of us must stand guard at night. The camp is filling with dangerous men."

Hesper

At Kelly's invitation, Raymond and Louis took noon-day dinner with him. It was a most delicious meal to Raymond, and a pleasantly exciting one to Ann, for she confessed to having cooked the eggs and potatoes. All reference to the trouble on the hill was jocular. The roaring savagery of the Golden Horn saloon seemed of another world, having no possible connection with the peace and sunshine and homely joy of the Kelly cabin.

The old mountaineer seemed to take it lightly. "They must fight their own battles. I had nothing to do with bringing on the strike, and I'll have nothing to do with stavin' it off."

"It is a regular strike?" asked Ann.

"It is, and it is not. The big mines are all shut down—so far, it is a lockout. But the men refuse to work shifts of nine hours for eight hours' pay. To that extent it is a strike."

"The trouble all springs from a small group of reck-less desperadoes," said Raymond. "The main body of the men are ready to submit to law, but men like Smith and Denver Dan and Brock must either fight or flee, and they prefer to fight. But what they do doesn't concern us. We are going right along in our small way. Our men are all outside the union."

Their calm and confident answers allayed all fear in Ann's mind, and she was girlishly gay as she brought in the pudding which she had made "all by herself," as Mrs. Kelly said. The men called for second helpings at once, and Louis asked for the privilege of scraping the dish. "You are over-acting your parts," replied Ann, but she flushed with pleasure nevertheless.

Mrs. Kelly spoke in praise of her to Raymond (she

Raymond Opposes Violence

had divined his love). "You should 'a' seen her—working every blessed minute this forenoon, Robert—"

"You must not compliment me too much," interrupted Ann. "Maids are sometimes spoiled by too much kindness. Are there shops near? We need a few things to make us comfortable; and my valises, when can I get them?"

Raymond replied: "I will take you down to Bozle to-morrow, if you care to go. The shops are better there and the streets less turbulent."

"I'd like to go very much," said Ann, on a sudden impulse. "I'd like to go this afternoon. Can we drive? How far is it?"

"We will ride, if you are not afraid of our broncos and steep trails. It will be more comfortable than a wagon."

"You need not worry about Ann," boasted Louis. "She's been riding down at the Springs. She's hardened to it."

"Very well," said Raymond. "After you've rested for an hour or two, I'll bring round the horses."

"Good-morrow, friends!" A clear voice made them all turn. Jack Munro, booted and spurred, stood in the door. "And how is the lady of the silken voice?"

Kelly greeted him coldly. "Hello, Jack; come in and eat."

"Much obliged, me lord, but I've already eat. I came round to see how the lady stood her ride with me up the hill."

Ann rose and faced him. "Are you the horseman who met us?"

"The very same, lady. I don't often hear voices like yours, and I wanted to see if the face and voice were of like quality. They are," he added, with a glance of unabashed admiration. "Introduce me, Rob."

Raymond reluctantly complied. "Miss Rupert, this is Mr. Jack Munro."

Munro stepped forward and held out a very handsome hand, and Ann could not refuse to take it. He was smaller than Raymond, and seemed hardly out of his teens, as he stood there smiling brightly, his bared head lightly poised on shapely shoulders, and some magic in his smile made Raymond and Kelly seem for the moment cold and reserved. His assurance, his frankness, amused her.

"I came to tell the lady that no harm befell Colonel Barnett, her escort. He was driven back to Grand View early this morning, and is at home ere this."

"Thank you for your good cheer," said Ann. "I was not so sure of your kindly intentions last night."

He smiled again, and his white teeth shone. "I must have seemed a bandit. I'm very glad I went to meet Barnett. Brock might have made you more trouble, and I would have missed the pleasure of being your guide and protector."

Kelly growled out, "Kape your murderin' scalawags as far from this cabin as ye can."

"I will see that you are not disturbed."

"You speak as one having authority," remarked Ann.

"I am captain of the vedettes," he replied.

"What are they?"

"A company of mounted police which I have organized to keep order here in the camp. The lockout leaves many men idle, and the local authorities need

help to maintain peace and quiet. My force represents the union and its desire to prevent violence in the
camp. You are quite safe here under our protection."

"You are very kind," replied Ann. "But aren't you
one of those for whom the sheriff comes?"

Munro laughed a silent, boyish laugh. "I believe I
am included in his list of notables, but, I assure you,
the honor is quite undeserved."

" 'Tis true he kicked Mackay down the hill, and put
the mouth of his gun to his ear," said Kelly, "but that's
a trifle not worth mentioning."

Munro winked. "A mere practical joke." He rose
and, with most richly modulated voice, said: "You
have made Sky-Town the most distinguished of camps.
Stay with us, for if I hear you are leaving I shall be
sorely tempted to put a cordon round the hill to keep
you in—"

"I am not thinking of leaving," replied Ann. "I
am this moment planning to stay."

"I'm glad to hear you say that. I repeat, there is
not the slightest danger, and I am entirely at your
service."

"Thank you again, Captain Munro."

With the punctilious grace of a dancing-master he
bowed himself out, swung to his saddle, and galloped
away.

Raymond and Kelly looked at each other a moment
in silence; then Kelly broke forth: "The smooth-
tongued little divil! Wouldn't that frost you? He's
to insure peace and tranquillity to the Kelly home—
you understand?"

"All the same, Matt," said Raymond, "I feel safer
for his presence in the camp."

Ann listened to these comments with interest. "Is he really so important?"

Raymond did not care to speak ill of him at the moment. "He has great influence among the men. In case of disorder he would be a valuable ally."

"Jupiter, but he can ride!" exclaimed Louis, who had watched him gallop away. "He must have been a cow-boy sometime."

"More like a cavalryman," remarked Kelly, shrewdly. "He holds his reins like a trooper, and his leg hangs not like a cow-boy's."

"When shall we start on our trip?" asked Ann, turning to Raymond.

"I will bring the horses round very soon." As they stepped outside, he turned to Kelly and asked, in a low voice, "Do you see any objection to this trip to Bozle?"

"Divil a bit. The sheriff will find Jack and his men waitin' for him on the road. He'll get no farther than Sage Hen flat this night. I'm goin' to ride down the hill meself, just to know what's goin' on. Go ahead, lad; only don't loiter." The big fellow smiled. "Get back before sunset, whatever ye do."

Raymond resented Munro's call and forced introduction to Ann more deeply than he cared to admit even to Kelly. It hurt him to think that Ann's hand had lain within the clasp of a man to whom women had ever been merely a lower order of life—to be used as playthings—even at that moment he was fresh from the kiss of a poor, doting woman who had renounced all the rest of the world for him, and with whom he made his home. Even Kelly, accustomed to the lawless sex relations of a mining-camp, was disturbed by Munro's uninvited entrance to his home at such a time.

Raymond Opposes Violence

"And yet I cannot say anything to her," Raymond said to himself. "I can't tell her what his life is. I dare not even hint at it. But I can stop his coming"—and his lips straightened grimly—"and that I will do!"

XV

Ann Rides with Raymond

THE prospect of a ride down the trail alone with a beautiful girl fairly unnerved the young miner. It was so much more than he had permitted himself to hope for. "What shall I say to her?" he asked himself, in wonder of his temerity in proposing such a trip.

Ann, on her part, became suddenly very thoughtful of Mrs. Kelly, and asked her if she did not wish to go.

"Saints alive, no!" answered the small wife. "The only horse I can ride is a burro, and I fall off that if it trots. I do not expect to leave this hill till I go in a carriage, and by that token I do not mean a hearse." She smiled brightly. "I'm a tough wan. Perhaps I'll live to ride in me own chaise yet."

"I sincerely hope you may," replied Ann.

At two-thirty, prompt as a groom, Raymond brought the horses round to the door. Ann was delighted with Kelly's big bay. There was something appealing in his eyes, so deep and brown, something trustworthy in the carriage of his head.

"I am not afraid of you, old fellow," she said, patting his shining neck. "You are not a bronco; you are a steed."

Even as she spoke, Tommy, the eldest lad, caught the horse by the tail, and, planting his bare feet on his gambrel joints, swung to and fro, shrieking with delight.

"Get down, you little monkey!" shouted Raymond; "you'll be kicked to kingdom come."

Mrs. Kelly only laughed. "He is used to the lads," she said. "They scramble all over him."

Mid-winter though it was, the sun was clear and warm, and as they went winding down the trail to the southwest Ann exclaimed over the exquisite quality of the air, the crystalline clarity of the distant peaks, and the cloudless serenity of the sky. "I have never been in a land where the sunshine was so abounding, so constant. Does it never snow here in winter?"

"Oh yes, indeed! Sometimes the snow-fall is immense, but it comes later."

After a short and steep descent they came out into a wagon-road, and were able to ride side by side, and Raymond's breath quickened as he looked into Ann's laughing face. Never had she seemed so simple, so girlish, and his courage came back to him.

"It has been a long time since I rode as escort to a lady. You ride well."

"Please don't think you must praise me. I am not a valiant horsewoman. I've only begun to ride since I came to the mountains." The novelty of the trip, the splendor of the way, and something in her escort's voice carried her quite out of her impassive self. She felt like giving spur to her horse for a wild gallop down the mountain-side.

Raymond, whose eyes scarcely left her flushed face and shining eyes, was bravely attempting to keep impersonal.

"You must be prepared for very poor goods and very

small stores. Bozle is by no means to be compared even with Valley Springs. Everything is temporary. No one really intends to live there; they are all just staying, and I fear the millinery is not of the latest fashion."

"What a power lies in the idea of gold! See the people who have come from all over the world! Don tells me that every European language is spoken here. Did I see Perry, the Mexican boy, at your cabin this morning?"

"Yes, Perry is here, and so is Baker. You have cause to remember Baker."

Ann laughed. "He was very amusing. It really was a first-rate farce, or would have been, only your rage at my coming was so real." Her glance at him was arch with humor.

She had not spoken so freely and so candidly since his illness, and he hastened to say: "To tell the truth, I was expecting to see an individual with glasses and a reticule. I really began to soften the moment you came in, though I didn't intend to show it."

"Your manner was quite reserved. Oh, what a singular town! What tiny houses!" she exclaimed, as they rounded a point and came in sight of the lower camp.

"Don't misjudge people for their homes," he warningly said. "In this log-cabin lives our chief banker. In this elegant aspen bungalow lives a celebrated gambler."

"Whose is the big house with the cupola?"

He was a little hesitant. "A certain Mrs. Rantoul. Her husband was a Mexican, I believe."

"She must be incredibly rich." Ann's curiosity seemed

satisfied. "Please take me to a shop where I can get some chairs and a small table. I am going to present Mrs. Kelly with an easy-chair."

"Very well," said he; "I know the very place, but please do not go about the streets alone. Of course you are perfectly safe, but you are a stranger and might wander into the wrong doors. Wait till I tie the horses and do one or two errands, then I will join you, and we can go where you please."

"Very well," she replied, with a feeling of pleasure in his care of her. "I will want to visit several shops."

The keeper of the furniture store was a portly Jewess. Her broad face shone with good-humor and the most recent application of a towel. The smell of fish was in her ample garments as she came forward to meet her customer.

"And what can I do for the lady?" she asked, alertly.

Ann referred to her list and named the small pieces she needed, while the Jewess stood with ears intent, her eyes securing every detail of the customer's dress.

"She is a New-Yorker," she thought, and at once put her thought into question.

Ann replied, coldly, "Yes, I'm from New York City."

"I t'ought so. We don't see such clothes out here, not very often. How did you get so far away?" She threw out her hands. "Ah, will I ever see Sixth Avenue again? Nine years we hafe been in the West. Benjamin is satisfied to be here among the mountains, but I—I am hungry for a sight of the good markets and the city crowds. If we had our little shop on Sixth Avenue once more, I would not leave it—no, not to be a millionaire. What business are you in?" she paused amid her lamentations to ask.

"I am visiting some friends on the hill," answered Ann, and smiled to herself as she added, "The Kellys."

"I know them. They are good people," said Mrs. Benjamin, in a tone which plainly indicated that her customer's social position had been bettered by her connection with Matthew Kelly. The humor of this appealed to Ann from moment to moment, as the saleswoman went on. "The Kellys buy all their furniture of me, and they pay cash, but I would trust them to any amount. Matt Kelly is good for every cent he promises."

The aristocrat found herself in a relation to this sturdy shopkeeper which she had never before occupied. Mrs. Benjamin treated her as a friend and an equal, and, as business was not pressing, seemed ready to gossip indefinitely. "The worst of it is, miss — I didn't catch the name—" She paused expectantly.

Ann reluctantly gave up her name: "Miss Rupert."

"Rupert? It is a German name. The worst of trade is here. You cannot be friends with all your customers. The women who come in, our best customers," she said, significantly, "are not the kind you can visit and be neighborly with. They live on the street back of here, and they are a nuisance. They drink, they swear, they fight; but they buy furniture, and so I must treat 'em right. But my children are now so big—Sammie is eight, and Sarah is ten—I feel we must move away to where we can give them good schooling and good society."

As she talked, Ann ceased to smile in amused contempt, and came to see the human side of this rule sagacious woman of business. "She is, after all a good wife and a faithful and loving mother." Her anxiety that her children should grow up good and clean dignified her—made even her gross curiosity, her tactlessness, of small account.

When Raymond came in, he was amazed to find the two women seated side by side in bright and shining new rocking-chairs, deep in a discussion of the duty of parents to their children.

The fact that Raymond, whom she did not know, was on intimate terms with Ann, caused Mrs. Benjamin to beam broadly on them both. She did not hesitate to say, "Will you have your man look at the tables, or shall we just go ahead?"

With a laughing look at Raymond, Ann demurely said: "I don't think we will need to trouble him. I see he has a newspaper; he can read that."

"Give a man a paper and he is deaf, dumb, and blind to his wife or anybody else," Mrs. Benjamin thereupon remarked, with conviction. "Well, now, come along, and I'll see what I can do on a table. Will you take ash or elm?"

Raymond would have been more highly amused had he not been filled with anxiety. The street was full of men drawn together by a report that the sheriff had stolen a march on Sky-Town, and was already on his way to intimidate Bozle and demand those for whom his warrants called. Horsemen were galloping up the hill to warn the miners, and the chief of police and mayor were mingling with the growing throng, pleading for peace. The whole camp resembled a nest of ants into which an ox had planted a hoof.

Ann observed Raymond's abstraction and restlessness, and asked, "Are you in haste to return?"

He answered, quite calmly, "Yes, we ought to start

back as soon as we can; but not till you make your purchases, of course."

Mrs. Benjamin seemed to love each article, and detailed its merits and complained of the high cost of freighting, all of which took time. Ann lost her sense of amusement at last, and cut short voluble explanations with a curt "Very well, I will take that. You will send them for me?"

Raymond stood at the door talking with a perturbed man in gray clothes, who carried a bandanna in his hand, and whose face was deeply lined with anxiety. He seemed to be in a profuse perspiration, and as Ann drew near she heard him exclaiming, in a choked voice: "My God, if they begin shooting I don't know where it will end. The whole town is mad as hornets, and some of the fellers are plumb crazy." Seeing Ann approaching, he bowed clumsily and edged away.

"Who was your nervous friend?" asked the girl.

"That was the mayor. He is scared blue by the news that the sheriff and his men are marching on Bozle. It stands us in hand to mount and get away at once."

Ann's face became grave. "Is there danger of shooting?"

"There is. Bozle is in sympathy with the miners, and hates the valley, and the sheriff's posse is considered a mob of outsiders. The streets are filled with men, and some reckless fellow may fire a shot and bring on a desperate struggle. I am going after the horses. Please don't step outside the door till I come back."

"What is that?" asked Mrs. Benjamin, sharply. "What is going on?"

Ann Rides with Raymond

Ann answered, "The sheriff is coming to arrest some men."

"He is! When?"

"Immediately, I think. Mr. Raymond said—"

"Oh, my little ones! They are playing outside. Keep the door while I bring them in," exclaimed the mother, and scuttled out like a distracted goose.

Ann stood at the door watching the miners as they boiled out of saloon doors like bees, and eddied and swirled into knots and close-packed circles. Here and there a man could be heard shouting a command, and horsemen began to clatter up and down the dusty street. It was all so unreal to the city girl, so like a shadowy moving-picture, that fear was not awakened in her heart. Strange to say, the tumult enthralled her—swept her out of herself. Near her on the walk men were snarling threats and curses, making use of phrases whose grotesque power thrilled her even though she could not understand why one man should call another such names. Once a decent-faced young fellow caught sight of her and struck the others into silence, then turned to her and said, quietly, yet with authority: "Go inside, miss. There 'll be hell to pay here in ten minutes."

She hurriedly withdrew into the shelter of the doorway till he had passed. Then, overcome by the hunger to see, she returned to her former position just as four men, inflamed of drink and belching terrible threats, turned and faced her. Beneath their gaze she shivered with a sense of her weakness, and her heart went out to Raymond in trust and longing, so that when she saw his impassive face and clear, brown eyes, she reached her hand to him with an impulse to be shielded. "Oh, these terrible men!" she cried out. "What are they going to do?"

Raymond was breathing rapidly. "Some one has borrowed our horses," he explained, quietly, "and I must ask you to wait a little longer while I secure another for you."

"Will they not return them?"

"I am afraid not. They have probably gone up the hill to join Munro's men, and they will be returned at the stable. If you are not afraid—"

"Oh no, I am not afraid!"

His manner was unconsciously that of the lover as he added, hurriedly: "I shouldn't have allowed you to come, but I had no idea that the sheriff would dare to visit Bozle. If anything should happen to you—"

"What can happen to me? If there is shooting, I will get behind the counter—that is the way the people all do when Alkali Ike begins to whirl his revolver—I've read the comic papers, you see."

He looked at her in admiration. "I don't believe you *are* scared. Well, now, stay here till I can see what I can do about a horse."

Again Ann stood alone in the doorway, watching a group of men crouching on the flat roof of a two-story building opposite. Two of them had rifles in their hands, and some man was shouting from the walk, "Keep them guns out o' sight!"

Mrs. Benjamin, glowering fiercely in maternal anxiety, came down the walk driving two weeping children before her. "Get on there! What do you mean by running away so? You shall go to bed now to pay for this! Did any one call?" she asked of Ann.

"No one—except Mr. Raymond."

Ann Rides with Raymond

"I must lock the door. There is going to be war. Oh, I wish Benjamin was here; he is gone to Valley Springs to-day. Keep my door for one minute while I lock these truants up," and she disappeared in the rooms at the back of the store, whence her loud voice rang in reprimand.

The girl began to tingle with a foreknowledge of violence. From a hundred sources she drew her fears. It was as if the voices in the street were the moan of leaves, the whistle of twigs, the creaking of branches in the storm wind. These men, who had amused her a few moments before, suddenly became squat and sinister and without pity. All that she had ever read of Western violence and mountain insubordination rose in her mind, and as she listened a wild cry went up from the roof-tops—"*Here they come!*"

The throngs below uttered answering shouts; men began to run to and fro aimlessly, filling the street facing to the south. In the back room the perturbed mother could still be heard expostulating with her rebellious children. Their wails added something uncanny to the roar outside. Men passed the door, pushing, trotting, their curses weak for lack of breath, but they all uttered the same grotesque phrase, the same singular epithet that to the girl seemed both vulgar and comic. It was evident that they intended this malediction to express their utter contempt and loathing for those who came up with the sheriff from the valley. In the hands of hot-heads, guns began to glitter. Their action was unreal, spectacular; but their voices shook her, benumbed her.

Raymond came hurrying back, his lips set and resolute, his brow frowning with anxiety. "I cannot find a horse that you can ride. I have ordered a team. We will have to go the back way to reach it."

A wilder yell arose. The leaders began to run down the street which led to the south. Ann took hold of Raymond's arm with nervous clutch. "What are they going to do?"

"It's hard to tell. I wish we were safely out of this."

"Can't we run?"

"Run! Dear girl, you couldn't walk four blocks in this altitude. If you will come with me we will cross to the barn and get our carriage there."

Unconsciously clinging to his arm, Ann went down the back street as in a dream. A row of mean houses stood close to the walk. A small and rather pretty woman in her night-gown leaned in a shanty door, laughing drunkenly, a toothpick in her mouth. An old hag next door was haranguing three or four di-shevelled female heads which were projecting from the windows of another wretched shack.

"Stay in, I tell ye! It's no good you're poking round. Stay in!"

Every door on that street seemed to have its slat-tern drab, just started awake like a lazy dog, aware of danger but not yet in terror. One of them, gay with the gayety of utter recklessness, cried out to Raymond, "Hello, Charley; what's all the row?"

Others, scared into respectful speech, stopped Ray-mond, asking, excitedly, "Is there going to be a fight?"

"I don't think so. Go inside!" he harshly replied, and hurried on, more eager to take Ann out of this defilement than to escape bullets.

Ann Rides with Raymond

Ann's lungs were aching, and a terrible pain was in her head and breast.

"Please don't hurry," she gasped.

He halted abruptly. "I beg your pardon. I hope I haven't winded you. We have only a few steps to go."

As the girl stood breathing hard and regaining her strength she looked about at the half-clad wantons, and said, "Are all the women of Bozle like this?"

"Oh no; this is the very street you shouldn't have seen; but it is our only chance to reach the barn."

They were already too late. The cross street was packed with men, and, looking down the hill, they saw the sheriff and his posse coming six abreast like a squad of cavalry, riding slowly up between the walls of stern and silent citizens of the great camp. Each deputy carried a rifle across the pommel of his saddle, and at their head, preceding even the sheriff, rode Matthew Kelly. His head was bare, and in his hand a long revolver gleamed. There was something in his face, in the lift of his head, that awed men. As he came he called out, not loudly, but every word could be heard:

"Aisy now, boys! Respect the law. Aisy, I say. This is no fight of yours. Down with yer guns; there are women and children to think of. Kape the peace."

Raymond looked at Ann with eyes whose light amazed her. "By the Lord, I wish I were by his side!" He spoke through his set teeth.

"Go!" she said. "Do not mind me. Go help him." Her voice recalled him.

"No, my place is here," and his look meant more than any word he had ever dared to speak to her.

In the square Kelly halted, and the sheriff, throwing up his hand, commanded silence. He was visibly trembling, but he blustered to his purpose. "Where is your mayor and your chief of police?"

The chief stepped forth. "Here I am! What do you want of me?"

"I want you to deliver to me the men who assaulted Mackay."

The chief waved his hand towards the hills. "They are up there; go get them!" and a roar of derisive applause went up.

Kelly raised his hand. "Boys, hear me! This is the sheriff, the properly constituted authority of this county. We are under the same laws, and we must obey the laws. I have on the hill yonder a wife and two babes. I came down here to do what I could to keep the peace, and I'll kill the first man that fires a shot. Be quiet, now, and listen to reason."

The sheriff, gaining courage, took up the theme. "I have no war with Bozle," he said; "I came to get the men who abused Mackay and who defied my authority."

"Well, go get them," repeated a man in the crowd. "What are you doing here? You came here to intimidate us, and you can't do it."

While they listened, Raymond stood shielding Ann with his body, ready to protect her from harm. The crowd pressed upon them so tightly that flight was for the moment impossible. His hand covered her shoulder as she sheltered herself beneath his arm. The touch of her soft flesh to his breast exalted him, gave him the courage of a lion. No one noticed them, so tense was the interest in the sheriff and his harangue.

Ann Rides with Raymond

"You came here to intimidate us," shouted the chief of police, "and it can't be done!"

The crowd, moved by some sinister impulse, closed round the sheriff and Kelly, cutting them off from the main body of the deputies. This movement opened a way of escape, and, expecting each moment to hear the crackle of guns, Raymond hurried Ann across the street and into the musty waiting-room of the livery-barn.

"Where is that team?" he shouted to the hostler, who was looking out of a side door.

"The boss took it."

"Well, get me another, quick."

"There's the mayor," gleefully shouted the hostler, ignoring Raymond's command. "And Kelly's speaking again; he's a good one."

"Whose horse is this with the saddle on?"

The hostler looked down for a moment. "Superintendent of Loadstone."

"Maynard's?"

"Yep."

"I thought so. Well, you tell him that Rob Raymond borrowed him for a lady." He turned to Ann. "Come, we must get out of this."

She obeyed like a child, all her imperious nature in subjection to his will. Lifting her to the saddle, he led the horse out the back way and through an alley into the main street, and so to the hills. As they reached a fairly level spot in the trail he turned and looked back over the roofs of the houses.

"The sheriff is retreating—wherein he shows good sense." He pointed above them, where, on Pine Mountain, Munro's vedettes stood waiting, backed by a thousand miners, jocular with battle-hunger, shouting faint defiance.

"I am sorry to be such a burden to you," said Ann. "I know you longed to be there with Matthew Kelly, and I have forced you to flight."

"I will be honest. I had that impulse. You see, I've been so in the habit of mixing in—but it was only a flash—for you were beside me"; and then he added, "And you are more to me than any other thing in the world."

She had no reply to this, no neat turn of phrase, no smile. She looked away in silence, her breath a little troubled, her throat contracted.

In fear of the effect of his words, Raymond hastened to the impersonal. "If this trouble is turned aside it will be due to Matt."

"Why should they obey him? Is he an officer?"

"Not now; but he was the first marshal of the camp, and afterwards chief of police. Everybody knows him, and his influence is as great as that of any one man. His presence here to-day undoubtedly prevented a desperate battle."

"I do not understand you Western people who want to shoot," said Ann, reflectively.

"The same impulse is at the heart of the city tough who heaves a cobble-stone. The difference lies in the Western man's weapon. Both want to kill, but the miner's gun is more effective. It carries out his will. If they had begun shooting to-day, no one in the town would have been safe. Those smokeless bullets ricochet frightfully." He looked at her again most penetratingly. "My anxiety was increased by my sense of guilt. I shouldn't have taken you down the trail

Ann Rides with Raymond

to-day, but the temptation of a ride with you w. s too great. I hope you'll forgive me."

She was recovering her self-command. "I have only to thank you; it has been a most wonderful trip. I wouldn't have missed it for anything, now that I am out of it."

"You have reason to be ironical."

"I assure you I am quite sincere. I am glad I saw it. I welcome these experiences, they are flashes of crimson in my dull, gray life."

"I don't understand you in that mood," he said, and started up the trail again.

Ann no longer realized her danger. The higher she rose in the clear, sweet air, the more incredible the whole miasmatic experience became. The sun, low in the west, made of Mogalyon a beacon to the world, and the far Crestones, pale violet in silhouette, were edged with golden fire. The horsemen above were as flies, the mob below like ants. The only realities were the mountains, the sun, and her protector, who climbed steadily, eager to set his charge in a place of safety.

The flight through that street of abandoned women, the crowd, the curses, the grotesque epithets, the march of the sheriff's posse, the ill-smelling livery office, the escape through the alley, all seemed like a specially vivid dream. The one thing that endured was Raymond's change of manner towards her. The clasp of his arm and his leadership seemed at the moment typical of that sovereignty which men of large mould impose almost unconsciously upon women.

As they neared the Kelly cabin Raymond stopped again, and, coming back, slowly said: "I am deeply chagrined by this experience. I really thought we were going away from disorder."

"Please do not trouble your mind with it any more," she answered, decisively. "It was an experience which will give me something new to think about."

Kelly did not return till late. At about nine o'clock he knocked at Raymond's door. "Get your gun," he said, quietly. "We're on guard to-night."

And together they paced to and fro on the hill-side, listening to the yells of drunken men up the street and to distant gun-shots as the storm of battle swept away to the south of them. By midnight all was silent. The sheriff's forces were either repulsed or captured.

Raymond was not without a sense of bitterness as he meditated on the events of the day. "I seem destined to play the weak man's part before her," he thought. There was something decidedly unheroic in being left afoot and skulking down back streets and dirty alleys, and not even the knowledge that he was thereby serving her to his best powers could salve his hurt. His had never been the passive part. On the contrary, he had always taken the rôle of leader, even in the games of his boyhood. Active, resourceful, and fearless, it was natural that he should rebel at a combination of events which seemed to make of him, in the presence of his love, a hesitating, sneaking coward.

XVI

Ann's Savage Lovers

NOTWITHSTANDING the excitements of the day, or perhaps because of them, Ann slept quite as soundly during this second night as on the first of her stay, hearing nothing of the tumult in the street, undisturbed by the furious rush of a squad of Munro's pickets tearing down the trail.

She was awakened, as before, by the sound of the little coffee-mill, but she did not rise as promptly as on the first morning, and was still dozing when Nora appeared with a piece of corn-cake and a cup of coffee.

"You feel tired this morning, I know. Well, now, take your breakfast in bed."

Ann was conscious-smitten. "No, no! You poor, dear thing, I am ashamed to have you waiting on me."

"It's so little—a mere step or two."

"Yes, but you have so many steps. After this I forbid you doing anything of this kind for me, and I've been thinking—why can't we hire a Chinaman to work for us? Unless I can do something to relieve you, I will not stay. You are tired. I wish you would ask Mr. Raymond to find us a helper to-day."

"Hello, sis!" shouted Louis. "Aren't you up yet? You'll never make a miner." Here he poked his head in at the door. "Jupiter! wasn't yesterday an ex-

citing day? It makes me sick to think I didn't go
down to Bozle with you. Rob has been telling me
about Matt's shielding the sheriff. It must have been
great. I was out on the hill-side. We all thought the
sheriff was coming up that way. But he didn't; he
turned back and went into camp, and last night Jack
went down and pitched into him, and they had a battle."

"They did? Was any one killed?"

"Ten."

Nora gasped. "Merciful powers!"

"So Perry says. Our side won."

Ann frowned. "*Our* side! You are not taking sides
with these lawless miners?"

"I'm not on the sheriff's side—sure thing!"

Ann studied him gravely. "Louis, you are getting
very slangy. I wish you wouldn't take on this rowdy
accent; it will be hard to shake off. I don't like to
see you lose your nice manners."

Louis wished to side-track this discussion. "Our
things have come."

"Have they? Very well, I'll get up at once and un-
pack. I want you to help me a little here."

"And I want you to help fix up our bungalow."

"Agreed. Now run away and find a hammer and
some tacks."

Together they worked to render her room a little
less bleak, and together they crossed the path to Raymond's cabin, where they toiled merrily. The weather
was deliciously clear and cool and golden, like October
in New England, and the girl responded to its influence as to some rare wine. She felt lighter and nimbler than at the Springs, and though her breathing was
painful at times, and a dull ache in her head troubled

her, she retained her vigor and her elation unaccountably. She was just leaving the bungalow to help Mrs. Kelly with the mid-day meal when Munro dashed up and flung himself from his horse.

"Good-morning, Lady Ann; how fares the day?"

Something unduly presuming in his tone irritated her, and she gave him a glance intended to check and humble him. "I am quite well, thank you."

He was not of those whom disdainful eyes abase. He hugged himself and shivered comically. "Wow! but that was a cold breeze. Some one must have left the bars down." His open-mouthed smile was like silent laughter. "Come, now, what have I done to deserve such a blast?"

Ann remained silent, yet she could not but acknowledge a certain charm in his effrontery. His was the beauty of the black leopard—rounded, swift, and changeable. Taking a step nearer, he added, with gentle sadness, "You're not going to draw the line on me, are you? What do you know against me?"

"I know nothing against you, or for you either," she replied, turning from him contemptuously.

"Don't go!" he called, and his voice became very frank and musical. "I didn't mean to offend. I don't want to seem fresh—I really don't. You've hit me hard. I came away from important business to see you this morning."

"You take too much trouble," she cuttingly replied. "You have my permission to return at once."

"I beg the queen's pardon again—I should have said this call was my most important duty."

"I hope the duty will not interfere with any pleasure."

He showed a little confusion. "You must take the deed for the word in my case; I meant to compliment you. I'm a little out of practice in repartee."

Ann relented a little; his self-confidence was amusing.

"Oh, if I can be of any service—in a conversational way—" she suggested, with most impersonal amiability.

Her tone and mocking inflection, both new to him, puzzled him. "You're having fun with me, but I don't mind so long as I can keep you standing where I can see your eyes."

Ann flushed with annoyance at this home-thrust, and was turning to go when he stopped her again, and his tone was hard and dry. "You were in Bozle yesterday with Raymond. Don't do that again. When you want an escort let me know; I'll send a man that knows enough not to take a lady into danger, and who has 'savvy' enough to keep his horses for the return trip."

Ann was trapped into defending Raymond. "I don't think my escort was especially negligent."

"He's a good fellow," the mocker went on to say in a patronizing way, "but he gets rattled when he's out with a 'femme'—he always did fall down in 'dragging' a girl around; you come to me when you are in trouble."

"Thank you, you are very kind; but I'm not in need of additional protection," Ann icily replied.

"Good-bye, till to-morrow," he called after her in mockery, his voice as musical as a bugle.

This interview, short as it was, left the girl with the feeling of having been grasped and shaken by a rude hand. This man neither feared nor respected her. He came as no other had ever dared to come— boisterous, confident, undisguisedly seeking to humble her. Her position, her parentage, her habitual reserve counted for nothing against him; her youth and beauty aroused only the instant, insatiable, devouring passion of the tiger. And yet her anger was not unmixed with admiration; his magnificent audacity and the grace and dash of his advance interested her.

"I wish I had asked him to tell me what took place last night," she said to herself after her anger had been transfused into amusement and her usual calm self-confidence had been restored. "It was silly to permit him to see that I was angry."

Raymond saw Munro riding away, and wondered what his errand could have been; and when Louis told him that the gambler had stopped and detained Ann in the path, his teeth set in anger. "The little hound!" he growled under breath. "I'll put an end to that!"

Immediately upon finishing his supper he went up the path to Hanley's to find "the lookout." Munro was in his place, sitting high above his faro lay-out, clicking a couple of silver dollars together, talking with gleeful intensity to Denver Dan, who stood at his shoulder broadly smiling. The saloon was packed with men all in high spirits over the precipitate flight of the sheriff.

Raymond was in a mood to suspect evil. "He may be boasting to Dan this minute," he thought, and his hands clinched. "If he is, I'll cut his throat."

Munro sighted him at last and called out, "Hello, Rob, how goes it?"

Hesper

Raymond did not reply till he reached his side. "I want a talk with you, Jack," he said, in a low voice.

Munro studied him for a moment, then turned to Dan. "Take my place a minute."

Dan complied, and Raymond led the way into the open air; and when they were well out of the crowd he turned and said:

"You intercepted Miss Rupert to-day?"

"I met her—yes. What about it?"

"Just this. You're not fit to shake the hand of a decent girl, much less a cultured, high-bred woman like Ann Rupert, and you know it!"

Munro was staggered. "The hell I'm not? What business is it of yours?" he asked, with instant anger.

Raymond's wrath was self-contained. "Keep your temper, Jack. We've summered and wintered together, and you can't make any mistakes about what I mean. I know the kind of women you live with and the kind of life you lead, and I tell you to keep away from the Kelly cabin, and when you're round where that boy is you keep a clean tongue in your head."

Munro did not snarl as Raymond expected. His voice became softly insinuating as he said: "Suppose the lady invited me to call? Suppose she was interested in my conversation?"

Raymond's hand clutched his shoulder. "Be careful what you say!"

"The lady had a chance to go. The path was open, but she lingered—she smiled."

"You're a liar!"

Munro was now very confident. "Am I? Ask

the boy, he saw her talking with me. I say the lady was gracious."

Raymond's hand fell away.

Munro pursued his advantage. "You're mighty hot, it seems to me. What business is it of yours who the lady talks to? Are you her guardian? Have you any claim on her? If you have, I withdraw. Come, now, has she made you her champion?"

Raymond was silent for a moment. "She has not; but she is here unprotected, and if you take her name lightly here among these gamblers and drunkards, or anywhere else, I'll kill you."

The gambler took on the air of an injured comrade. "Now, see here, Rob, you're away out of limits. I acknowledge I've known a whole lot of cheap women, but that's all the more reason why I should be able to tell when I meet the real thing. If you think I class Miss Rupert in with any 'rag' I've known since I left the Academy, you certainly do me an injustice. Her name is as safe with me as with you. Probably she's tied up back in the States, anyway, so that neither of us have any chance of interesting her. But it's an open course and no favors, and so long as she doesn't hand me out the 'icy mitt' I'm going to make the most of my chance, and from this moment "—he took off his hat—"I reform! I throw up my job at Hanley's, I cut off 'booze,' and I shake 'Eau Claire.'"

Raymond was impressed by his rival's manner. "You can quit gambling, and I hope you can leave liquor alone, but I see trouble when you shake Claire. But that doesn't matter. For the sake of old times, I want to avoid a quarrel with you, Jack; but I warn you that if Miss Rupert finds your presence disagreeable, you go, and you stay! As you say, she is probably engaged to a better man than either of us; but she is here because of the boy, and I feel a certain responsibility for them both, and the man who presumes on a chance acquaintance with her will answer to me."

"All right—leave it to her, Rob," said Munro, almost jocularly. "If she turns me down, I'll pull out of my own accord, lightning sure. Good-night!"

Raymond walked away with a sense of failure. Munro had adroitly writhed out of his grasp, and was probably exulting at his own cleverness. He was troubled, too, by the confident tone which Munro had taken in saying, "The way was open, she lingered." Was it possible for a man like that to win the love of a delicately reared girl like Ann? He recalled the case of Maud Elbridge, the stateliest, queenliest girl of his native town—a belle, surrounded by suitors —who won high social recognition in Cincinnati and later in New York, and yet remained unmarried till she was thirty years of age, only to be carried off at last by a miserable little rake of a man who had neither money nor honor nor grace, but who won because he broke through her barrier of reserve and laid confident hand upon her.

Munro had charm. He was undeniably alluring to women, and was fond of saying, "Any woman can be won by a little strategy and a great deal of gall." It was possible that such a man might interest, but quite impossible that he should win a girl of Ann's penetration and reserve.

Out of the tumult of his doubt he emerged with an accession of confidence in himself. "If it comes to a choice between us, my chances are as good as his. If she is being amused by us both, then, at least, I will have had the pleasure of her presence for a little space."

He really knew very little of her family history, for Mrs. Barnett had been careful in her descriptions. "Ann is rich in her own right," she said once, "and has had everything to make her happy all her life. Why she has never married I can't tell—nobody can. It's a mystery to her own family. She's not the kind of person to be interviewed on her love affairs, and she's not a confiding sort; and there you are."

"Her tolerance of Jack is due to ignorance of his real character," Raymond decided, as he walked slowly back to his cabin. "Mrs. Kelly must tell her."

He saw the light in Kelly's home, and its allurement was stronger than ever before, but he resolutely held his way to his own fireside, there to bitterly muse the entire evening over his poverty and the false position in which Munro had cleverly placed him.

He repented of his resolute passing of her door when he heard next day that a couple of the independent operators had spent the entire evening with Kelly, and that one of them talked a great deal to Ann. The sting of it lay in the fact that Tracy was a fine young fellow, studious and capable. "You are a fool," Raymond said to himself. "You threw away a chance to be happy. Don't do it again."

In the midst of Ann's return of mental health came also the delicious sense of mingled allurement and danger with which, as a girl, she had met the advances of her boyish lovers. There was something in these primitive surroundings, in the rocks, in the rough boards, in the lack of privacy and retreat within doors, and in the fulness of opportunity without, which renewed the mystery and charm of courtship. Conventions counted for less. Human emotions grew each day more vital, more compelling.

Every man who could by any excuse "drop in at Kelly's" did so in the hope of meeting "the Fifth Avenue girl." Several of the young mine-owners found it expedient to consult Kelly very often, and generally managed to have a word with Ann. These lean, brown men of the mountains were not given to ambiguous phrases. Their eyes met hers with frank and wholesome admiration. No half-way halting-places lay along the ways of their advance. No shadowy allusions existed in their speech. Their courtship, especially that of Munro, was as direct as a knife-thrust, as unequivocal as a pistol-shot.

And she enjoyed this, that was the amazing thing— even to herself—and she liked him and derived amusement from his singular methods of attack. She was mightily concerned to learn that her character was so largely a reflex of her environment. "Of course, it is only temporary," she wrote to Jeannette. "It's only a play. These people will soon fade out of my life, and I will go back to the old routine in the city, but at present I am actually amused by it all, and my health is amazingly improved. I never felt better in my life."

"The altitude seems to be doing her good," remarked Don, after Jeannette had read this passage of Ann's letter to him.

Jeannette sniffed. "Altitude! It's a man. She can't fool me with her talk about 'simple diet' and 'actual physical labor.' She's fallen in love."

Don dropped his morning paper. "No!"

"Why not? Wouldn't it be like that girl to interest herself in some perfectly worthless adventurer, after all we've done for her here? She was bored to death with us. She yawned in the faces of all the nice fellows we introduced her to. Now, who do you suppose *it is?*"

"My dear, I can't say. There are a lot of fine chaps up there doing one thing or another. Young Reese, for instance, is thick with the Kellys, or it may be Ben Tracy. It couldn't be Rob."

"No such good taste. She was perfectly brutal to him, fairly accused him of getting shot in order to win her sympathy. I want to see that girl taken from her high horse, but I don't want it done by some of those nasty little 'remittance men.'"

Don resumed his paper. "I'm not alarmed. Ann is no Maud Muller raking hay, if you think of it. She's a remarkably self-contained young woman." He lowered his paper again with the effect of delivering a weighty opinion: "She needs a lover who will box her ears. I'm going to give Peabody a line on her character."

"You keep out of this, Don. You are a failure when it comes to love affairs."

"Oh, I don't know," he gravely replied. "I secured you—and your millions."

"I was easy," she laughed. "And you sha'n't have the last word."

XVII

Ann's Humiliation

NOT a day passed that the captain of the patrol did not ride down to the door of the Kelly cabin and leap from his saddle with some fanciful greeting, carefully and ornately uttered. So much he retained of his Kentucky breeding.

Ann openly ridiculed his romantic phrases, and generally asked, "Have you killed any one to-day?"

"No, lady; but I robbed three," he would reply with a certain effective succinctness; and yet, with all this dare-devil assumption, he was never able to convince her of his wickedness. To her he was an actor playing a part, and doing it with joy and pride, and she did not care to discover his real self. He was a foil to Raymond, who had grown reserved and moody, and to young Reese, who was very practical and business-like. Munro, indeed, appeared to have little to do but amuse her by day and watch the faro-table at Hanley's by night. For while the valley grumbled and threatened, massing men and munitions of war, the miners of the peak loafed and laughed, and listened to the rattle of the leaping marble in the piebald wheel. The newspaper boys did all the fortifying, and planned all the campaigns which were to follow; and Munro's humorous account of these fictional preparations kept

244

Ann's Humiliation

Ann from taking a serious view of the situation, notwithstanding Kelly's growing uneasiness and Raymond's gloom. It was all a colossal farce to her.

"Well, the reporters put in a new system of torpedo-mines last night," announced Munro one morning, "and they've closed all communication from the south." And on the day following he gravely said: "We mounted another Gatling-gun this morning—so the papers say—and we are now invincible. The sheriff's army grows apace, but does not march."

Ann could not understand this humorous defiance of law—this colossal recklessness. "What will you do when it does march?"

"Meet it and bu'st it."

"What then?"

He laughed. "Sufficient unto the day is the evil thereof."

"Tell me, now," she said to him at another time: "what is your real motive? Why should you be the champion of the rights of labor?"

He astonished her by giving back earnestness for earnestness. "I'll tell you, my lady. Labor has got to fight. This union is the coming thing. The toilers have not only got to stand together, but they've got to drill. I happen to have a little military training, and I'm going to give Western labor its first lesson in the power of military organization. I want to show them that a hundred men trained to unhesitating obedience to a leader are better than ten thousand men whooping and yelling in a mob."

"I don't know whether I approve of that or not. Isn't it setting class against class?"

"There ought to be only one class."

"And that?"

"The toilers."

"Ah, you'd destroy us."

"Whom do you mean by 'us'?"

"The wealthy, the plutocrats."

"Are you a plutocrat?"

Ann smiled. "I suppose your brethren would call me that, Still, all this seems very strange in a gambler."

"I'll tell you something—I'm not a gambler. I am a judge."

"A judge?"

"Yes, I sit above the board to see that every man has a fair deal and a full count. I never gamble."

"Tell me just what you do. It is all so strange to me."

"There is a game, sweet lady, called faro. It is a pure game of chance when the dealing is honest and above-board. It is played at a low table round which the gamblers sit facing the dealer. Back of the whole 'lay-out,' and on a high chair, sits the judge looking down over the head of the dealer. He follows every motion and records every deal. I am a judge. It's a confining job, but it brings me in touch with the whole camp. The boys know I'm on the square—they've had occasion to test it—and when I want anything I get it. The dollars I earn are as honest as any of those your Eastern aristocrats make by bu'sting one railroad to build up another."

Ann's eyes were reflective. "That is a new avocation to me," she said, slowly. "And it is not for me to say that you are not doing good, and yet your wages come from the miners, after all."

Ann's Humiliation

"Can you sniff of each dollar you get from your father and not smell blood? All money is blood-money somewhere down the line."

Ann shrugged her shoulders. "Oh, this is getting too serious, 'Mr. Judge.' I didn't intend to stir you to an exposition of Nihilism."

"I'm only just trying to show you that I'm not so black as a lot of these 'dubs' would have you think. I want you to carry a mighty fine estimate of me. I claim that a man who is fighting labor's battles at the risk of his own life has some claim on your good opinion. I can see that Kelly and Raymond have set you against me."

"Quite the contrary, Captain Munro. Mr. Raymond is careful to speak well of you."

"Rob's a good chap, but he thinks I'm a lost one, all the same. You see he and Kelly both stand for the thing that is going out. They think any man has the same chance they have, but I tell you this union that they despise is the coming order — now, that's enough of war. I never explained myself to any one before, so you can know how much I think of you. You've made all the other women I know common as dirt—"

Ann stopped him with a gesture. "You mustn't begin on that again—I will not listen."

"You have listened, and I'll make you do it again," he said as he turned to go, and again he smiled, and while that look was on his face his plea seemed merely a subterfuge to win her attention—and he was very handsome at the moment.

In truth, Kelly and Raymond were watching Munro's rise to power with growing uneasiness. He was now in almost complete control of the camp, and though he still deferred to the union and its committees, his reckless bravery, his prompt execution of orders, and his knowledge of military forms had made of him the chief source of command, the only adequate regulative force on the peak. Those on the outside did not hesitate to call him "the arch-devil of the district," and the whole Western world was filled with his doings, his reckless speeches.

His fame had fired the hearts of all the dead-shots and restless spirits of the West, and from an irregular squad of twenty-five or thirty men his forces had risen to nearly two hundred heavily armed and hardy horsemen. This squadron the reporters (with intent to aid the camp) magnified into an army in their despatches to the outside world, making the valley leaders run to and fro in doubt and dismay, while the Eastern press cynically asked "What will those unaccountable Westerners do next?"

Raymond, though keeping keen eyes upon Munro, was unable to find cause for war in any word or act of the gambler, nor could he fathom Ann's mind either towards Munro or himself. She appeared to find Munro diverting, and spoke of him only in that way. If she understood his "home life," it made no change in her attitude. It was inconceivable that a refined girl should tolerate a man who passed from one ignorant and vicious woman to another, and yet Ann's greeting remained gracious, if not friendly. What it was when they were alone, he dared not think.

As for Raymond himself, he continued to punish himself by putting aside the many opportunities which came to plead his own suit, and took a morbid sort of pleasure in his renunciation. "There will be one man at least who will not persecute her," he said, savagely, and bent his best energies to the work of developing his mine.

One morning a great hunger to see her mastered his absurd pride, and, leaving the shaft-house, he returned to the bungalow at the precise hour when she came over (as he knew) to see that the rooms were put in order.

Ann stood in the centre of the room overseeing Perry and Louis, who were beating rugs and dusting. She wore a short gray skirt and a dainty shirt-waist, and was radiant with health and good spirits.

"Good-morning," she called, brightly. "You find us at the rugs again."

"You take too much trouble. I don't mind a little dust, and I don't think Louis does."

"It's demoralizing to be disorderly," she answered as she straightened the papers on his big plank table. "I haven't many virtues, but orderliness is one of them."

He stepped into the room. "Then let me help. I don't like to see you wrestling with this dust. Show me what to do, and I'll do it."

"No, I am well attended, and, besides, your mine demands your time."

"If this rug adjustment seems important to you, who have no call to do it, then it ought to be doubly important to me, who ought not to neglect it. Now, shall I shake this Navajo?"

In a spirit of concession she gravely said, "Yes, you may take that out and beat it; no, take it out to Perry, and I'll show you something else to do," by which it appeared that she wished him to stay with her. "You may move this table," she commanded on his return, "and take up that centre rug."

There was something deliciously intimate and domestic in this relationship, and he forgot mines and mining, while she put aside all reserve and laughed gleefully at his "woolling" of the rugs. "You look like a big St. Bernard puppy with a shoe," she laughed, as he went out with a big Navajo blanket.

"I'm sorry I appear ridiculous," he replied, mightily transformed by her intimate tone, "for my intent is knightly—I serve my queen."

"Now please don't you begin to pay compliments," she exclaimed, with a slight emphasis on the word "you." "I hate men who pay compliments."

"I beg your pardon—I promise not to offend again; only it does seem hard after the labor I had to put those words together. You can't prevent my looking compliments, can you?" This remark she ignored altogether.

At last she said: "There, everything is in order. And you can go back to your work. How is your mine getting on—or down?"

"Very fast, everybody says; very slowly, it seems to me."

"Are you so eager to be rich?"

"More eager than I care to acknowledge. I have a thing to do, a sort of restitution to make, which demands money; when I 'strike it' I will tell you, if you will listen."

"I hope you will strike it soon—you have awakened my curiosity." She turned towards the door. "Isn't it right weather? Is it always like this in winter?"

"Kelly says not. Every one calls this an extremely mild winter. I am very glad of it, for your sake as well as ours; it enables you to remain with us, which is a great pleasure."

She started slowly towards the door. "It has been a very healthful change for me. I was never so vigorous. I enjoy my work."

"I am coming to help you after this—every day— if you will permit me."

"Oh, I don't tidy up every day, I'm not so extreme as that. The rugs would go to frazzles at that rate. I come only on Mondays and Fridays."

"Thank you; you may depend on me. This has been the happiest hour of my life."

"I ought to come daily, after such a declaration as that, but I must not waste your time. I'm eager to hear what you are going to do when your million comes," she answered, archly. But somehow she left him in doubt even then. Her tone was too open, too frank.

On the afternoon of this serene day, as Ann and the little mother sat sewing and chatting together, a woman suddenly appeared in the open door. She was large and high-colored, her hat was awry, and there was a wild glare in her eyes and a look in her face that froze even Nora into silence. Both stared at their strange visitor in breathless apprehension till she pointed her unsteady finger at Ann and hoarsely cried out:

"So you're the one that's cut me out?" The muscles of one cheek contorted and her eyelid drooped like that of a paralytic as she fixed a baleful look on the astonished girl. After a moment's pause she stepped uncertainly upon the threshold and leaned against the jamb. "Well, you'd better watch out; if you don't give him up, I'll kill you!"

"She's crazy," whispered Nora.

The intruder fumbled in her absurdly flamboyant skirt, and at last drew out a pistol. "Now you better hop!" she said, with menacing calmness.

Ann rose, white and calm. "Who are you? What do you want?"

"Who am I? I'm Jack Munro's wife, that's who I am; and I want you to let him alone, that's what I want. You can understand that, can't you?" Her big, flabby face again contorted horribly.

Nora found tongue. "You go away, or I'll call Matt."

"Call him. What do I care for him. I ain't afraid of no man livin'. No, sir; let him come. But I got no war with you; you're all right. But that thing there, with her fancy dresses—I'll pink her with a bullet if she don't let my Jack alone."

If the drunken creature had swept a handful of mire into her face, Ann could not have been more revolted, more degraded. She understood now. This was one of those slattern female vultures from the street in Bozle. Fixing a look of disdain on the woman, she said: "You are quite mistaken. Your Jack is less than nothing to me. I despise him and all he represents."

The other wildly laughed. "Ah, yes, you can talk— you're smooth—but I know!" She began to bluster. "If you hated him, why do you talk and laugh with him? I saw you yesterday." She raised the pistol. "I tell you, I'll blow you into kingdom come if you don't promise right now to give him up!"

Ann's Humiliation

As she advanced, the two little lads at play just outside appeared in the doorway, and the sight of them steeled the little mother's heart. "Go away, darlin's," she called to them. "Quick, run for dad!"

The woman turned to see who was behind her, and the desperate Nora seized her by the wrist. "Give me the gun," she called.

"I won't! Le' go me!" shrieked the intruder, jerking hard in the effort to free her hand.

Ann seized the other arm. "I promise," she said, quietly, fixing her eyes full upon those of the infuriated woman, who ceased to struggle. "Now go away."

"You promise?"

"I promise!"

The woman again laughed harshly, drunkenly. "I don't trust you. I'll kill you, then I know. Let go me!" she called. "Let go, or I'll smash your face."

"Matt! Oh, Matt!" called Nora, as she clung desperately to that terrible wrist.

Help came from an unexpected quarter. Like the flash of a blue-jay's wing, Woo, the cook, rushed across the room and flung himself on the mad wretch. His long fingers encircled her throat. "Dlop it!" he curtly commanded. "Dlop gun!" For a few moments the woman struggled, then the revolver fell to the floor, and Ann snatched it up.

Woo turned the gasping, hiccoughing creature to the door and flung her out upon the ground. "You dlunk. Go home. Stop home. Me sabbe you—you sabbe me," he said, as he bent above her.

Ann interposed. "Don't hurt her, Woo."

He stood beside her while she slowly regained a sitting posture. "She belly dangelous. Me go tell Munlo. She fight—me kick."

The poor creature now seemed dazed and broken, and began to weep, and with her tears became as abjectly pitiful, as pathetically tawdry, as she had been hideous and menacing in her wrath. Ann shuddered with a bitter nausea, a disorder that was half physical weakness, half mental repulsion. There was something ghastly beyond words in this creature sitting in utter abandonment in her rumpled finery, which the pitiless sun dissected. Stooping, she took the miserable one by the arm. "Get up! You must not sit there."

Slowly the woman rose, all thought of revenge swallowed up in a wave of maudlin self-pity. "You're all agin me—all of ye! I guess you wouldn't like it to have your husband stolen by another woman—you let me alone!" she said to Woo, with a flash of anger. "You pig-tail! what business you got to lay hands on a white lady?"

Woo's impassive face betrayed no humor, but Ann thought she detected some mockery in his voice as he said: "Me belly solly. You fall down, me catchee you up. Me help you walk."

"I'll walk without any of your help, you yellow snake!" she malevolently replied, and sat down again.

Nora turned. "Go in the house, Ann dear. She is not for you to hear."

But Ann did not heed her. She had never seen an intoxicated woman before, and this sudden change of emotion fascinated her. It was like watching the convolutions of a serpent.

The creature began to pour forth a flood of vile

epithets, directed towards the patient Woo, who tried again and again to lift her, and was in the midst of a howl of wrath when Matt came round the corner of the house.

"What's all this?" he asked, sharply.

The woman suddenly rose to her feet, well aware that a man had arrived, and began to mumble and weep again.

Nora ran to her husband. "Oh, Matt, drive her away. She tried to kill us."

"Who is she? Who are you, and what are you doing here, anyway?"

The woman, quite dismayed, began to retreat. "It's all right. She promised. I'm going now."

Woo explained. "She Munlo's wife. Belly dlunk— allee same clazy. Take um gun—go shoot lady." He pointed at Ann. "Me choke um. She fall on glound. No get up. Nola (Nora) catchee gun."

Kelly followed the invader. "You go back to where ye came from, and stay there, or 'twill be the worse for ye, ye murderin' omadhaun."

Ann went to her room and flung herself down upon her bed in such abasement as she had never known in all her life. She could not deceive herself. She had brought this horrible assault upon herself by something more than tolerance of Munro. In this lay the sting, the stain of the woman's touch. All of Nora's hints and Matt's dark looks at Munro came back to her. "This is what they meant!" she exclaimed. "This is the kind of women he associates with. Oh, the disgrace of it!"

The woman's ignorance and tastelessness, her common voice, her badly fitting garments, her incredible baseness of speech, all came back. "Ann Rupert a rival to that being!" Of course she had *never* for an instant directly encouraged him, and yet he had appealed to her and she had listened.

"Rob should have warned me," she complained, her mind going back to the man she could trust. At the moment she could not see, or would not acknowledge that Raymond had ventured as far as he dared in revealing Munro's private life. She was too angry with herself and every one around her to be just. As her flaming wrath died, she grew cold and bitter. "This is what comes of going outside one's own proper world. I shall leave the peak at once, and I hope I shall never see it or hear it spoken of again."

She did not show herself at supper, and when Nora came to inquire if she were ill, she was calm enough to say: "Yes, I am sick with disgust. I wish you would ask Matt to keep this from Mr. Raymond and Louis. I want to put it all out of my mind as soon as possible." And she covered her eyes with her fingers.

Whether Nora divined the inner quality of Ann's grief and shame or not, she was tactful enough to withdraw without another word.

XVIII

Raymond Reveals His Secret

ANN'S disgust and bitterness of self-accusation wore away as she faced the resolving sunlight and measured her scars against the breast of mighty Mogalyon. In the dawn of the second day the incident, having lost much of its shame and terror, was debatable, and under Matt's kindly counsel she reached a certain resignation.

"No one but ourselves need know what took place," he said, in conclusion. "Woo is no tale - bearer, and when the woman herself sobers off, she'll not remember a word of it. Furthermore, I warned her that Jack would wring her neck if he knew what she had done. So I wouldn't give another thought of it—not one."

"I'll try to forget it," she promised, humbly, but she could not at once put the experience out of mind. She could only wait for that besotted face to fade into a grisly apparition. In the end, she pitied the poor woman who loved and was willing to defend her love.

Raymond was chilled by the change in Ann—by a return to the cold aloofness of her manner at Barnett's, and was profoundly troubled by it.

He spoke to Louis about it. "Has your sister any bad news?"

The boy stared. "No, I don't think so. Why?"

"She seems changed some way. She isn't so happy."

"Oh, you mustn't worry about that. She is always getting bored with something or other." There wasn't much comfort in this frank speech, and the keen-witted lad became aware of its implications. "But she isn't bored with you. She likes you now, all right. She's changed her mind about you."

Raymond knew that he ought not to probe deeper, but he did. "How do you know?"

"If you could hear the 'spiels' she gives me now about obeying you, and keeping at your elbow, I guess you'd see a difference. She used to talk against you to me—now all that is changed."

"Boy, you're picking up a deal of slang."

"I like it." His lips fairly smacked and his eyes shone. "It says just what you want to say. Father liked it, too. Don't you remember when he tried to put down just what a group of hunters said?"

"It is all well enough, if you don't let it get the upper-hand of you the way it has with me. I was well brought up in that regard, and now listen to me," and in this way he led the boy's mind into safe channels.

The day following Ann's visit, Munro rode down as usual to call, and seemed amazed when Mrs. Kelly greeted him coldly. "Ann does not want to see you or any one else this morning—you, least of all."

Munro whistled. "Another cold blast. It's sure draughty up here on the side-hill, isn't it? What do you suppose is the cause of it?"

Nora closed the door gently but firmly. "No matter; she will not see you." And the puzzled vedette rode thoughtfully away.

Two days later he came again, about the middle of

the afternoon, and, stepping into the open door, called out, jauntily: "Good-afternoon, Nora. Has the weather moderated down here yet already?"

Nora looked up from her sewing, and her big eyes grew stern. "Ye might knock like a gentleman, Mr. Jack Munro."

"I might, indade, but as the portal stood ajar I thought I might venture in. Is the Lady Ann Grey receiving to-day?"

From the inner room a clear, low voice, icy as a mountain-stream, replied, "Miss Rupert is not receiving Captain Munro to-day or at any other time."

He took a step towards the door. "What have I done to get a crack like that?"

The door closed with a decided jar and a bolt slid.

Munro bowed. "I understand. I take the hint; but some day when you are feeling jolly I'd like to know what has frosted the air down here among the aspens."

"I can tell you," said Nora, with the directness of a woman who has known rough men all her life. "Ann has learned the kind of life you live, and she despises the sight of your face."

For the first time in his life Munro was confounded. He stood for a moment revolving an explanation. At last he said, "You mustn't take an enemy's report of me."

"We do not," said Nora, calmly. "Your wife called on us a couple o' days ago."

"My wife!"

"The woman who calls herself your wife; 'tis all one so far as we are concerned."

Munro frowned. "Claire called! Here?" Then,

with a leer that was characteristic of him, he added, "I hope you had a pleasant chat."

"Ask her. She did all the talkin'."

Munro became very serious and very winning. "Now, see here, Nora—"

"Call me Mrs. Kelly," she interposed, shortly.

He was not smiling now. His heart was in his voice. "You tell Ann not to misjudge me. She must give me a chance to square myself. I don't claim to be a saint, but I've been open and above-board with every man or woman I've ever had any dealings with. Whatever my past has been, I'm living on a different plane now. I've cut off all my old habits for her sake. I'm trying to live up to her standard of things. I know she's better than I am, but I can climb. My family is as good as hers. I started right, and with the help of a good woman I can get back to where I was." His voice was tense with passion as he spoke. His jocularity, his insolence, had dropped from him, and he stood revealed, the passionate, unscrupulous lover that he was. "I claim the work I'm doing here is worthy her approval. Ask her to let me see her again."

Nora turned her face towards Ann's door, and both waited in silence; but no sound came from the inner room, and Nora, seeing suffering in the lines of his face, said, more kindly: "Ye may as well go. The door will not open to you this day nor any other."

Munro turned and went out with bowed head, and Nora could not doubt the sincerity of his pain.

With all these swiftly alternating flashes of joy and shame, Ann could not but exult over her recovered interest in life. It was as if the veil between herself and the world of men had burned away beneath the vivid sunlight of the peak. She rose each day to a closer touch with the ordinary emotions of ordinary people. Something within her rang in response to Raymond's voice, and his eyes resting upon her gave her pleasure. The whole world of human affairs freshened in interest precisely as the outer world — the world of peak and sky—grew each day more vividly beautiful.

"Living on this mountain-top," her father wrote in his journal, "is like being diurnally in the proscenium-box of a theatre horizon wide, in which clouds are the actors, electricity the illuminator, and thunder the trumpeter. It broadens a man's breast and expands his mental horizon."

At times every summit seemed to flare with fire, and the girl tingled with some mysterious dancing flame which invaded her blood and filled her with some subtle, magnetic power. Her hair rose beneath her toilet-comb as if fluffed by a crackling breeze. Her limbs felt lighter, nimbler, and she grew gayer of voice and readier of smile. Her work around the cabin became a pleasure as her arms grew firm and her hands deft, and with this return of perfect health, this content with her new world, the old life receded far. Only now and then, when some letter from London or Paris reached her, did she give a thought to the balls, receptions, and operas she was missing. She remembered this social Eastern world as an invalid recalls some scene, beautiful in itself, but inextricably bound up with disagreeable or painful memories. The splendors of New York and Paris were grayed by the cold light of her old indifferentism.

She spent many delicious nights beside the fire in

the bungalow, when, lying at ease in a big bear-skin, she listened to Raymond as he read from the journal, or to Matt as he related with delicious humor a chapter out of his adventurous life.

In answer to one of her correspondents she wrote:

"I am working with my hands, helping my dear little friend Mrs. Kelly cook and sew. The big strike which you read of does not trouble us, for we have strong protectors. It seems to have settled into a sort of siege, anyway. I haven't any idea when I am to return. I came West, as you know, for my brother's health, and he is so much happier here I cannot think of asking him to go home, and, besides, he is growing up rapidly, and I don't think he would go, and I daren't leave him, at least not till I make sure how the climate is going to affect him. Besides, I like it here. I am a 'bouncing dairy-maid' in appearance, so don't commiserate me. When I am bored here, I can go down to Cousin Don's."

One morning Ann rose to a singular light. In place of the clear, golden sunshine, which had so often glorified her room, a blue-gray mist lay thick against her window-pane. Raising the sash, she put her hand into it—it was like smoke, dry and cold! Dressing hurriedly she entered the sitting-room, where Matt was helping his sons to dress.

"What is going to happen?" she asked. "Does this mean a storm?"

"'Tis a curious cloud, sure, and fairly drippin' with electricity. Did ye feel it in your hair? The lads' crackled like cats."

"Yes, indeed! But isn't it grewsome? This light is so strange. Will it stay long?"

Raymond Reveals His Secret

"No tellin'. It's only wan o' them clouds of the peak settled down on us. It may hang about us all day, or it may lift and pass away in ten minutes."

She stepped to the door and looked out with vague alarm. The vapor had blotted out the world; nothing could be seen but the faint forms of one or two cabins and a clump of nearby trees, and she went back shivering and a little depressed. "I don't like to leave the peak on such a day," she said, at last. "I think I'll stay till the sun comes out. I want to think of it as it has been—radiant and inspiriting."

The cloud hung moveless for hours, impenetrable, yet resisting. A hush was in the air as though some disaster, concealed as yet, was about to be discovered. About ten o'clock, as she stood on the steps wondering whether to cross to the bungalow or not, Raymond burst from the obscurity.

"Good-morning," called Ann. "Isn't this a strange effect?"

His eyes were shining, his face pale, and his voice vibrant as he abruptly said, "Come with me; the time has come. I want to talk with you."

"What has happened?" she asked, in alarm.

He took her by the arm. "You promised to listen; you are not afraid of me, are you?"

"No, but I do not understand. Where is Louis? Has anything happened to him?"

"Louis is safe with Kelly. I want to see you, because things have happened to me. Come — I must see you alone."

They moved off up the path towards the overlook, and, notwithstanding her brave words, the girl wavered in the gust of this man's over-mastering excitement.

The mist closed round them, all signs of other human presence disappeared, and they soon stood alone in a world of gray light wherein neither sky nor horizon-line appeared. All that remained of the earth was a little strip of gravel beneath their feet.

Raymond stopped at last and held towards Ann a small, irregular piece of rock. "Do you see that?" he hoarsely inquired.

She took it wonderingly. "Is it ore?"

"Yes, and it's heavy with gold. Kelly's luck has won again. We've opened a vein that will make us both rich." There was no tremor or doubt in his tone.

"Oh, I'm so glad!" she cried out, with unaffected pleasure. "Now Mrs. Kelly can go to live in the valley."

"Never mind the Kellys now," he cried out, impatiently. "I have a great deal to say to you and I want to say it here. I have lacked courage; now I feel—you know what I mean—you know what you've been to me. I'm going to try and win you." His manner was exultant, his voice tense with passion. "I am bold to recklessness to-day."

"And all because you hold a little piece of yellow rock in your hand," she wonderingly said, trying to comprehend him. "You may be mistaken about the gold."

"I left Kelly on his knees trying to figure out the value of a car-load of the rock. Yes, all because of that little lump of ore I want to say that I love you, and I start on my third phase of life at this moment." Some mysterious potency emanating from the piece of metal seemed to flow into his veins as he shut his strong, brown hand upon it. He had never been humble; now he rose above her, masterful, an avowed lover, and his eyes burning down into hers made her shrink and shiver as if from cold.

He misread the movement. "Are you warm enough?" he asked, tenderly. " I hope you are, for I want to tell you — explain to you — why I am here. Let us sit here." He indicated a flat rock. "This is our only opportunity; no one will know — no one can see us. Will you listen?"

"I will listen," she said, quietly, and took a seat, drawing her cloak about her.

He took a seat a little in front, so that he could see her face, which was radiant as a rose in the mist. "I've been trying to write you a letter ever since you came. I wanted to set myself right with you on Louis' account. I love the lad, and I wanted you to know that I was trying to do him good."

"I know that. I trust you now."

"That assurance is sweet to me; but I want to tell you now that the only mystery in my life is this: I am a West Point cadet—I mean, I was—"

"Were you, really?" She looked at him with such unmistakable relief and gladness that he faltered.

"Wait. I was only there two years. I was court-martialed for breach of discipline and gross insubordination at the beginning of my third year."

Her face grew very grave. "I am sorry to hear that."

He hastened on. "You mustn't judge me hastily. It came on my return after furlough; that's the time when the routine and discipline pinches hardest on the men. After two years of grind that I hated, I had a visit home—a delicious, free time—and to get back into school, back into those cold, gray barracks, was like going into a strait-jacket. The first few weeks after the vacation are times of disorder—a period of boyish deviltry; and I took my share in it. My breach of discipline was nothing more than a boy's frolic. I should have been punished for it, and that would have ended it. But I hated one of the officers—the disciplinarian—and when he rounded me up he rasped me till I lost my head. Being a quick-tempered youth, I answered him. He abused me shamefully and I struck him in the face, and that ended my stay at West Point."

"Oh, how foolish! How wrong!"

"No; it was not wrong. I would do it again. The small sneak used a tone in addressing me which no man has a right to use to another. You wouldn't suppose a *tone* could hurt, but it did; it cut like a lash. Well, that ended my career as a soldier. My home was on the Ohio River, not far from Cincinnati, and my family still lives there. Our whole country is rich in traditions of General Grant, and my father had selected me out of all his sons to be the soldier of his family —you know how some men try to map their sons' careers. Well, he had trained me towards my career by putting before me biographies of the great soldiers and leaders of the world. How I hated those ponderous tomes! He was a proud man—a vain man—his neighbors said, and as our house looked down and over the town, so he looked down on business and politics. He had a theory that the United States was soon to enter on a war with all the world, and that his son's great brain was needed, and that I was destined to become a military genius. I considered all this tommy-rot, and that I was really being educated to go West and kill Apaches; but he was sincere." With a glance in which humor lay, he asked, "Don't you see, I couldn't go home?"

"Yes, I can see it was hard for your father. Was your mother living?"

"Yes, she's living yet. I write her every week; but not one word has passed between my father and me since my dismissal. Naturally enough, I drifted West and into cattle-ranching. I liked the excitement of it, and I'd been trained to ride and to shoot. I gradually became cow-boss and foreman, and so you found me, with a few thousand dollars saved up. Your coming changed every current in my life. I became ambitious to do something, to be rich. I came here, I bought this mine, and there shines my gold." He held it towards her again. "Now I can go home. My court-martial becomes a joke. Don't you see? My father is human. He would not receive me, poor and disgraced. With a big mine behind me the case will be different."

"Are we all purchasable with gold?" she asked.

His high mood sank a little. "Don't misjudge me. It's not so clear in my mind as when I met you at the door. Money *does* help — you know it does. It extends a man's power; it makes him effective for good, if good is in him. I was a rancher when you met me; we stood in a different relation from that which we occupy now. Isn't that true?"

"Yes," she slowly answered; "but it isn't because of your mine."

"What is it because of?"

"It is because you have been kind and considerate of my brother."

He looked disappointed. "Is that all? I hoped you liked me for myself."

"I do—like you," she answered.

"Can you not love me?"

"Do not press me." She spoke sharply, a flash of resentment in her eyes.

"I didn't intend to do so," he humbly replied. "I fear I've made a mess of it, just as I have with all the rest of my life; but this morning when we uncovered that vein it seemed as though I had a chance to recover my place in the world. Now—" He tossed the fragment of ore over the cliff. "There's nothing in it." The flippant bitterness of his final words touched Ann, but she did not speak, and he went on. "My excitement must have seemed funny to you, but I really thought my piece of ore would help me—" He turned to her again with a sterner line in his brow. "It is only fair to me to say that I am not in any sense apologetic for my family. I believe it to be as good as the best. I am proud of my father, of his unyielding democracy; although a natural aristocrat, he holds to the traditions that have made America great. My mother is of good stock. You may call me egotistic or anything you please, but so far as my people are concerned I believe them to be the equals of any one. I have gone wrong. I've wasted ten years of my life masquerading here and there, but that is finished. Since I saw you life began to be serious business with me. You smile, but you know what I mean, and if you would only give me time I would make you proud of me." He paused and looked about him. The mist seemed lightening, as if infiltrated with a golden vapor. It was in motion also, and far to the westward small patches of blue sky showed momentarily. "It is clearing," he said, in a quiet voice, though his eyes were wet. "The west wind is setting in."

The beauty of the girl as she faced him there in the mist was so shining, so all-conquering in its pulse and glow, that his lover's courage returned to him and he spoke again, almost fiercely: "I love you, and I want you to know it. Sometime I will ask you to be my wife."

"You must not do that," she cried out. "You must not think of it. You will only lead up to disappointment. Don't you see how impossible it is? You are of the West, I am a city dweller. Our ways of life are so different."

He remained unshaken. "Do you believe in fate? I do. Think how mysteriously we were brought together on that ranch. Why did that bullet cut me down at that time? It must have been for some purpose. To me it was a warning, a portent to lead me out of my foolish and trivial life. In those long weeks of confinement I took account of myself. I was at the bottom, but I was not dead. I said, 'I will climb.' I needed money first of all and so I set to work to win it. I had a conviction that I would win, and this morning when I took that piece of ore in my hand I knew that nature had answered my prayer; so I came to you to ask your help—your love—to make my life worth living."

She moved uneasily. "I am not fitted to help you. My whole life and training have been such that I am totally unfitted for the life you would lead. Please do not misread me, it is not a question of your wealth or your poverty. It's my own way of life, my own mind. I don't want to hurt you, but I must tell you that it is impossible to think of—quite impossible!'' and she turned away towards the cabin, now half disclosed.

She was cruelly effective in the tone of this reply, and the man walked silently beside her, benumbed by the finality of her inflection. Not till they reached the cabin did he recover his self-control.

"I accept my defeat," he said, slowly. "You are perfectly right. It was pure presumption on my part."

"I did not say that, and you must not put me in the attitude of scorning your — your regard. I simply say you are mistaken in me. I could not make you happy—because I don't expect to be happy myself. I have come to respect you, to like you very much; but you must not ask me to be your wife, for that would only lead to sorrow."

"Hello!" shouted Louis. "Where you people been? Have you told her, Rob?"

The door was open and Kelly and the two lads were on the floor picking at a small sack of ore. Mrs. Kelly looked up at Ann, laughing, with tears on her cheeks. "I don't believe it, not one word of it! And if it's true, Rob, I want you to keep it for us."

"Yes," said Kelly, "I've been of use to you in finding it, now do you be of use to me in keeping it."

"I will, Matt!" said Raymond, and the two men shook hands on a new compact. Both Matt and Nora were too engrossed with their new-found riches to observe the deep sadness of Raymond's face.

Raymond Reveals His Secret

"Now," said Kelly, "watch out for Curran; he'll bate us out of it if he can. I depend on you to stand off the lawyers and the gamblers."

"The mist is rising," called Ann from the doorway.

As she spoke a tremendous report arose from the obscurity where the fog still clung.

"Now what was that?" queried Matt, and all stood transfixed with surprise and vague apprehension.

Another and duller report followed — one that shook the ground. Kelly rushed to the door just in time to see a vast balloon-shaped cloud of smoke rise majestically above the mist, bulging into the blue sky above.

"Now they've done it!" he called, in a curiously reflective tone that was almost comic.

"What was that?" asked Ann.

"Some crazy divil under cover of the mist has dynamited the Red Star shaft-house."

Even as they waited, listening to faint cries, the wind swept the hill-side clear and Kelly's fears were verified. In ruins and on fire the Red Star shaft-house and mill lay scattered over its dump, and towards it the whole camp seemed hastening.

"Oh, the unholy jackasses!" muttered Kelly. "They've opened the door to the witches now. Come, Rob. We may be the next to suffer."

Raymond, as he was about to follow his partner, turned and said to Ann: "I hope you will not let my folly lose me what I had gained—your friendship."

"You have lost nothing by your frankness. I am glad to have had you tell me so much of your story."

"I promise not to return to it," he answered, and the finality of his voice sent a little pang of regret to the girl's heart. Of course it was best; but, after all, she would not have him put aside too easily the love that had shone in the depth of his quiet eyes.

XIX

Peabody Visits Sky-Town

THE blowing up of the Red Star mill and shaft-house shook the entire district with its possibilities of further violence, and concealed beneath its dust and smoke the rich discovery in the Kelly mine. Even faithful Jim Dolan did not know of it for several days, and the partners had time to calculate chances and plan for the buying-in of the property.

The din of controversy was deafening. The labor leaders disclaimed all knowledge of the outrage, and roundly condemned it for the foolishly destructive act it really was. Kelly marched in among them like a grizzly bear, and stormed thunderously. "You *are* responsible," he growled. "You sit here and send out appeals to the world while these hounds work their will. Where was Munro and his regulators?"

"They can't be everywhere," explained Carter. "No one supposed such a thing could happen in the daylight."

"Ye're all a set o' chicken-heads. Ye've created a power ye can't control. I give ye notice that if ye don't go after the thieves that did this work, I'll organize a vigilance committee and take charge of the whole gang of yez." And he strode out of the room, leaving the officers of the union disgraced and angry.

He confessed to Raymond on his return that it was a foolish action.

"It was, Matt. You couldn't have done a worse thing. A large number of these Dago miners already consider us their enemies, and this will confirm them. We might as well take steps to-night to get our party of the third part in some sort of organization."

All this excitement and worry aided Raymond in tiding over the day, but when midnight came, and the committee had slipped away into the night, his sense of loss and a feeling of loneliness took possession of him. Ann had announced her intention to return to the Springs at the end of the week, and though she had vaguely promised to visit the peak again, Raymond was not deceived. "She is leaving to escape daily contact with me. Our good comradeship is gone forever;" and with this conviction the gleam of gold in his ore grew dim and his confidence in the future less buoyant.

"She's quite right," he admitted to his better judgment. "A mining-camp is no place for her, or for Nora. Since the destruction of that mill it is even less desirable than before as a place of residence."

While on his way to the bungalow the following afternoon, he met Munro accompanying a stranger, a big, blond, handsome fellow in a gray travelling-suit and soft hat. His face was plump and his brown beard close-clipped, and, though he realized that he was more or less in durance, his eyes were smiling.

Munro called out, "Rob, do you know this chap?"

"I do not."

Munro turned to his prisoner. "I thought you were lying."

The stranger remained untroubled. "I didn't say

274

Peabody Visits Sky-Town

I knew Mr. Raymond, I merely said that I wanted you to take me to him. Mr. Raymond, I am Wayne Peabody, an old-time friend of Miss Rupert. Will you please explain to this knight of the hills that I am in no wise interested in his strike?"

Raymond looked at him keenly. So this was the Eastern lover—this fat, fair man. "I think I have heard of you," he began, slowly.

Louis' arrival relieved the awkwardness of the moment. "Hello, Mr. Peabody, how did you get here?"

Peabody caught at the boy's hand. "Well, well, Louis; I'm glad to see you. You save my life. How is Ann?"

"Fine! You ought to see her work. She's brown as oak. Come on, I'll take you to her. Gee! she'll be glad to see you."

As Peabody excused himself and made off, Munro, with a world of meaning in his tone, softly swore. "Well, by —— if I'd known *that*, I would have killed him and laid him away under a little rock. I wouldn't mind your getting her, but if that fat chump thinks he can come in here and run off our choicest one, he's mistaken. She turned me down flat the other day, and it hurt. It hurts worse now that I've seen the other man. I really hoped you were the winner."

"She's out of our world, Jack," replied Raymond, and a large part of his resentment of Munro's impertinence vanished with the knowledge that he was a fellow-sufferer in despair.

Munro went on, gravely: "She had *me* going, sure thing. Why, I stopped drinking—just as I told you I would—and I cut off Claire—— Say, boy, that was a severe job! She raised dust for a day or two, but when the queen of heaven gave me my jolt, I said 'w'at-the-good,' and slipped into my old ways." He made a queer little gulp as though swallowing a pill. "Well, Claire's happy, anyhow. Do you remember what old 'Coal-oil Sam' used to say? 'Life's a curious concatenation of categorical coincidents.' Think of us strutting around the parade-ground in front of 'the seats of the visitors' with intent to beat out old Grant, and here we are. I'm policing a mining-camp, and you're pawing dirt like a woodchuck. 'What a fall is there, my brother!'"

"Don't dig up mouldy bones, Jack."

"Do you know, that's the comical twist to it. I like to think over those days. I'd like to go back. I'm told we're a 'tradition' there now as 'the men who swatted a tac.' That's my one bitter memory, that I let you do the swatting. I ought to have *wallered* him."

Raymond did not enjoy Munro's tone, and changed the subject. "What are you going to do now?"

Munro ceased to laugh. "I am going to cinch this whole camp a little tighter from this on. I'm going to turn back every non-union miner. All you fellows who are friendly can go on working just the same, but your men must put themselves on record."

Raymond's face settled into stern lines. "Jack, I don't want to be mixed up in another man's fight. We are on good terms with our hands—they're a lot of cantankerous American citizens, anyway, and can't be coerced. I warn you not to monkey with our plant. We're good friends now, but don't try to round-up Kelly and our 'wild bunch,' or you'll meet trouble."

Munro laughed. "I'll fight shy, old man, so far as I'm concerned, but these Dagoes and Poles are getting watch-eyed, and if they stampede, they'll run over somebody. All they know is to herd, and they consider themselves a sort of outpost of the socialistic camp, and when they hear that the Red Star gang are going to run in a car-load of professional strike-breakers, they're going crazy. You don't believe in me and my cow-boys, but the time may come when you'll see that I'm about the only commander in this camp."

"I see that now, Jack; that's why I'm talking to you. But you've started on a line of action that means war with organized society. You had no call to join those jackasses who ran Mackay out of camp. It was none o' your funeral—had nothing to do with the question of wages."

Munro grinned. "He was such an ape."

"Yes, but it started you wrong. Now, I don't know who blew up the shaft-house, but if you do, your best plan is to cut those outlaws out and turn them back to the authorities."

"I don't know a thing. Of course the union had nothing to do with it. It was done by a few hot-heads full of peaches. These mine-owners have got to give up their nine-hour scheme. We've got 'em dead to rights, for I can drive every non-union man out of camp if necessary, and my advice to you is, have your men march up and sign our rolls double-quick."

"They can do as they please about that. I will bring no pressure to bear on them, but I'd like to ask you, as a friend, not to make it any harder than you can help for Kelly & Raymond. We've got all we can stagger under now, and the worst thing that can happen to us is delay. We've opened our vein and we're going to buy in our mine inside of six weeks if nothing prevents."

"I'll do what I can, old man, but Kelly mustn't go to making any more of his cracks about the union. They're getting ugly-tempered up there, and must be handled like glass."

Raymond walked on to his cabin with a heavier heart than he had carried since he left Barnett's home. Part of this was due to Munro's warning, but the larger part of it sprang from his meeting with Peabody, who was not at all the sort of citizen he had expected Ann's Eastern lover to be. He was a man of power, dignity, and decision, not an erratic idler like Barnett, and his air of quiet authority sprang from a strong personality securely placed in the world.

Louis came back to the cabin with a sly smile on his face. "What did you think of Mr. Peabody?"

Raymond strove to be jocose. "He'll lose some of his fat if he climbs round these hills. What's he here for, anyway?"

Louis dropped on a bunk and his face grew grave. "Darn him, he's here to get Ann to go back to New York. I don't go, I tell you that!"

"Maybe she won't go?"

"I'm afraid she will," the boy gloomily replied. "He's got some kind of a 'drag' on her. He's been trying to get her, oh, a long time."

Raymond's voice was calm as he asked, "What is his business?"

"Lawyer. He's rich, too. Ann wants us both to come over to the Kellys' to dinner. I don't want to go. Do you?"

Peabody Visits Sky-Town

"She's the captain," answered Raymond. "I reckon we'd better spruce up a bit."

"It makes me tired," the boy went on. "I wanted her to marry you and then we could all live out here."

A half-hour later Ann knocked. "Is any one at home?"

Raymond flung open the door. "We are all at home."

Ann introduced Peabody, who stood by her side, and the two men shook hands rather coldly, while she said to Raymond, "Can you take care of Mr. Peabody for the night?"

"With pleasure," Raymond politely replied.

"And will you come over to dinner? You need have no more scruples now that Woo is with us. We are ladies of leisure, and, besides, I have made a new pudding."

"You may expect us," said Raymond. "We let none of your puddings escape."

"You have subtle ways of flattering," she laughingly responded as she turned away.

Peabody was not in the least aware that Raymond stood in any lover-like relation to Ann, and his manner was direct and hearty. He was, indeed, full of talk.

"This is the most extraordinary development, this town on a mountain. What did that fellow mean by trying to turn me back?"

"I suppose he took you for a spy."

"A spy! What do you think of that, Louis? If he had known my office was in Wall Street, I assume that my troubles would have thickened. I don't understand why you gold-miners should be silver men. Yes, thank you, I would like to wash."

Raymond put his toilet articles at the Eastern man's disposal. "It's a rough outfit."

"Don't apologize. A man in a camp, twelve thousand feet in the air, can't afford to pick and choose."

At the dinner-table Ann studied the two men with highly amused interest. Peabody, easy, assured, and calmly tolerant, did the talking, while Raymond listened, a little sullenly, it seemed to Ann. The New-Yorker was most admirable in his consideration for Mrs. Kelly and his interest in everything about him, and yet he did not stir the one he hoped to please. He had always been commonplace to her, and was conspicuously so here on the mountain-top.

Kelly towered at the head of the table, clad in a dark-brown corduroy house-coat and blue flannel shirt, his grizzled head uplifted, a roguish shine in his half-hid, piercing eyes. Raymond ate in silence, replying only when directly interrogated. Louis, watchful for criticism against his beloved mountains, really found no cause for warfare, and Ann, possessed of a perverse desire to disclose some hidden trait in Peabody, touched on the prejudices of each man.

"Mr. Peabody comes direct from the money-changers, Matthew," she said to Kelly, "and can give you the latest news of the gold conspiracy."

"Can he? Well, I should like to have him tell me what he thought of that Englishman who took a walk through Wall Street a day or two ago and said, 'The faces I see here are criminal.' Are they so?"

Peabody hastened to be large and tolerant. "To me the faces are worn and anxious, not criminal.

Peabody Visits Sky-Town

The crush there is tremendous, and men are pale and haggard. I am an exception," he added, beamingly. "But I suppose the men who gather there are of the accipitral type, especially the 'hangers on,' the curbstone speculators. But, after all, it's the place where things are done—it is the heart, the financial heart, of the nation."

Kelly's eyes lost their twinkle. "I grant you things are done there, and great things; but are they for the good of the people, or are they just piracy? 'Tis easy to rob a man at a distance. If I can sit here and steal the wages of a hundred men in San Francisco, my sleep is untroubled; 'tis too impersonal, that Wall Street robbery, there's no chance for pity or remorse. 'Tis like our friends who sit below in the valley and try to regulate the hours of labor here on the peak."

Peabody was glad to turn the conversation into this channel. "I found them very much excited down in the valley. Indeed, I was warned not to attempt to come here; but I argued that if Ann could live here safely—"

"Ah, but she's wan of us," said Kelly.

Ann bowed. "I'm one of the toilers. Assistant cook and second girl."

"We've adopted her," pursued Kelly. "And Rob there is her defender in time of trouble."

Peabody turned to Raymond with undisturbed mind. "That is very good of you. The Barnetts told me of your kindness to Louis."

In all that followed he maintained this same large view, and Kelly grew to a manifest liking for the man.

Peabody did not attempt to conceal his intimate relationship with Ann and every tone of his voice when addressing her was torture to Raymond, who began to talk at last in self-defence, addressing himself to Mrs. Kelly as his hostess, leaving Ann free to listen unreservedly to her Eastern suitor. The girl understood this mood in Rob, and it touched her.

As they all re-entered the bungalow, Peabody rubbed his hands together in delight. "By Jove! this is something like! This chimney carries me back to my hunting - lodge in the Maine woods. Do you hunt, Raymond?" he asked, and the use of Raymond's name in that way indicated his liking.

"I used to. That bear-skin Miss Rupert is sitting upon is one of my trophies."

"Is it really! He's superb; where did you get him?"

"In the Needle Range."

Peabody was in the midst of a story when a knock at the door announced a visitor.

"Come in!" shouted Raymond, and Munro entered, entirely at his ease, graceful, jocose, making no account of the looks of surprise on the faces of Raymond and his guests.

"Remain where you are!" he called. "The house is entirely surrounded, and no non-union laborer will be allowed to escape."

Raymond mechanically gave him a chair, while Kelly nodded curtly. Ann bowed and said, "Good-evening, Captain Munro."

Peabody alone smiled. "Ah, you were my guide up the hill! My guard as well as guide I take it."

"I'd rather have been your executioner."

"For what reason?"

"Had I known you were coming to get the queen of the peak your blood had stained the heather."

"Good Heavens, what an escape! Am I quite safe now?" he asked of Kelly.

This fooling over, they took seats, and the conversation ran to the prospects of the camp, and Peabody, with a feeling that Kelly was the man of richest experience, persuaded him to tell something of his wonderful career as a trailer of golden pathways, while Louis lay at his feet in the blaze of the fire and listened as all the others listened. Peabody, looking round the room, was moved to repeat, most fervently: "Now, this is jolly—incredibly jolly. Will you believe it, they told me you were all murdering thieves up here in the clouds. I was especially warned against Munro's pickets. At this moment even they have no terror to me."

"There are others," said Munro, with a sly inflection, "who would charge a picket-line to see Miss Rupert's face lit by this fire."

Raymond sat in silence, scorning to take part in this flattery, while Ann awoke to a delicious excitement in the situation. Before her sat three very direct and forceful lovers regarding each other like tigers, instinct with hate, yet masking it, pretending to honor and good-will, while bitter jealousy raged beneath. She palpitated with unwonted, wicked joy, and never had she seemed more alluring to her lovers than at that moment. She provoked Munro to the most audacious sayings merely to see Peabody stare, and she flung an appealing word at Raymond now and again as if valuing his opinion above all others, though he made but curt answers, returning to his fire, mystified by her gayety and by her subtlety of by-play. Munro, so far from being depressed by Peabody's presence, was carried quite beyond his usual self, and his reckless compliments had a keen edge. In the end, Ann regretted her encouragement of his audacity.

Raymond realized that he was playing a poor part in this game, but, try as he might, he could not bend his tongue to any word worth saying. He was considering Ann's action, trying to fathom her intent. Her laughter and her shining eyes revealed to him an emotional exaltation of which he feared to know the cause. No one else had ever been able to make her eyes sparkle and her cheeks glow like this. He tried to be just to Peabody. "He is suited to her. He comes from the same walk of life, and is a mighty fine chap, physically and mentally." And the realization of his madness in the mist sent a burning flush of shame into his face.

Ann divined something of what was passing in his mind, but she did not realize how deep his depression was, for his face seemed stern rather than sad, and the light concealed the tell-tale stain on his brow.

His position as host enabled him to come off fairly well in his struggle, for when some intimate glance or word passed between Ann and Peabody and troubled him too sharply, he was able to rise and poke the fire or pass into the next room. His desire to be alone became at last insupportable.

His guests rose at last, and Ann and Peabody went away together. This cut deeper than all else, and Louis, who took a very pessimistic view of the whole affair, did not comfort him. "She'll go back with him.

I can see that," he said. "And she'll want me to go, too, but I won't."

"He'll not get away with her if a nine-inch gun is any bar," remarked Munro, in more than half seriousness. "Still, it's a fair test," he added. "She has had a chance to size us up, and if she can cotton to a pink-and-white slob like that, after seeing a couple of 'good ones' like Rob and myself—why, it's her own bet and her own coin. I'm still in the ring, however, as long as I can hear her voice."

Raymond could not jest, but he could be fair-minded. "Why should she consider any man on the hill, or in the West, for that matter? See what this lawyer offers—a good home in the big city, her native town. Right here the West takes a second defeat from Wall Street."

"Oh, I don't know. You never did understand women. She may be just fooling with him to let us know she's nobody's slave. How long has she known this lump of Herkimer County butter?" he asked of Louis.

Raymond stopped him. "There's a point where joking is barred, Jack. It's none of our business when or where or how she met him. We've got all the information we're entitled to right now."

Munro went away outwardly jocular but inwardly sadder than he had ever been in his life, for his love for Ann was mingled with respect for her mind, her character. Her calm and kindly attitude towards him that night had been a revelation to him. The women he had known would have been peppery, awkwardly silent, or nervously excited. She seemed amused, and her clear, searching eyes had abashed him. Her large tolerance of him, her easy forgetfulness of what he had tried to be to her, depressed him and in the end wounded his self-conceit.

"Jack Munro," he said to himself, in a voice of bitter scorn, "do you know what you are? You're a yaller dog in August."

Peabody, on his return, found Raymond sitting alone by his fire. Louis was deep in slumber.

"That man Munro is an interesting fellow. What do you know about him?" asked the lawyer.

"Not very much. He's rather secretive. He came here from Sylvanite, I believe."

"His jokes about getting under my ribs were a little grewsome. He struck me as just about mediæval enough to do it—under proper conditions. Tell me about yourself. Ann has only praise for you. I want to thank you most cordially for your kindness to her and to the boy."

"I'm not sure my influence has been a blessing to her or to the boy. Louis struck up a great friendship for me and followed me here, and that forced Miss Rupert to come. It is no place for a woman of her refinement, and I've felt all along a kind of indirect responsibility for her presence here. The boy ought to get out, too, for we are on the edge of war up here."

"You Western fellows are mediæval" (this seemed to be one of his pet words); "that's the reason you appeal to this boy. He's in the doublet-and-dagger stage of development. It seems a pity to take him away so long as he is so vigorous. He's much improved. Less nervous and more manly."

"I doubt if he can be persuaded to leave. He told me to-night that he wouldn't go."

"Well, I'm glad I met you, Mr. Raymond. I shall feel easier about the boy in case we do go East without him."

These cordial, frank, and manly words struck an icy chill to Raymond's heart. It was all over then. She had consented to go, and his life was laid waste. He rose unsteadily.

"You must be tired. Shall I show you your bunk?" he asked.

"I believe I will turn in," responded Peabody.

When the young miner returned to his seat beside the fire a big lump of pain filled his throat, and he owned a boyish desire to fling himself down on the floor and sob. He lost all shame of his weakness at length, and went out into the night—to be alone with the deepest grief of his life.

The darkness outside enabled him to close his eyes to outward things and fasten them upon interior scenes of haunting light and beauty wherein this queenly girl was the radiant centre. He deliberately called them before him—the picture she made on that first day at the ranch when, with heavenly pity in her face, she bent above him as he lay wounded. He dwelt long upon her as she appeared in evening-dress, her conventional guise, haughty, impenetrable, self-poised. Sweeter remembrances followed—remembrances of her girlish gayety in those intimate hours when they rode together or worked about the bungalow together, and these were the most deeply moving of all, and when he realized that they were gone, never to return again, he groaned like one in physical torture.

"Oh, my God! I wish I had never seen her!" And with that involuntary cry his tears came and he wept unashamed.

Hesper

When he returned to his cabin the fight was ended. He was outwardly calm. He went to his bed resolute to conceal his hurt. Longing for morning, that he might fling himself into the toil of the mine and so forget the clutching hand at his throat.

XX

Ann Sends Peabody Away

HE did not see Ann at breakfast next morning, but sent word by Louis that important work in the mine detained him, and the girl was hurt by the neglect. It was not a cheerful going at best, for Mrs. Kelly was broken-hearted and frankly pessimistic.

"You'll never come back," she said. "You'll forget the Kellys—you'll forget you ever lived in a log-hut and swept floors."

"Why, Nora, I'm only going to Valley Springs. Maybe I'll come back, and soon."

"You say so, but you are going far. I have two eyes and I can see. You've broken Rob's heart, too. I know why he isn't here this morning—he couldn't abear to see you go, and no more can I."

Ann's own heart received a wrench at these final words. "I haven't meant to give you pain. I've tried to help you."

"You're too beautiful, darling. You shouldn't go among poor people like us. Our love grows round you, and when you go you tear our tendrils off and it hurts."

The tears came to Ann's eyes. Never had such sincerity, such directness of affection touched her. "I'll come back. I promise you I'll come back, unless you come to the Springs to live."

"Come back!" shouted Kelly, who had entered the door. "Why, sure thing! She can't keep away. D'ye think Louis is going to leave the peak? Not for long. He has just been telling me when to expect him." Somehow, Kelly's tone helped Ann as well as Nora.

"I am not going back to New York till spring."

"Let me tell you something," Kelly resumed, with ponderous effort at being confidential. "Your Wall Street lawyer is all right. He's a man of substance, but Rob is going to sluice a stream of gold out o' this hill that 'll make the lawyer chap look like a worn dime— now mind what I say."

Ann laughed. "I'll remember; and now, you dear people, good-bye," and she looked back at the cabin with dim eyes.

They reached the Springs without accident and were greeted as if they had escaped from a robber's cave. Mrs. Barnett and her friends were all greatly excited over the events of the high country, which had been distorted, magnified by the shadows of the clouds, till they were of the most monstrous proportions. Munro was already a bogie—a sort of cow-boy Napoleon— and Ann laughed at the questions hurled at her head by the Barnetts when they found she had known and liked the captain of the patrol.

"Not at all," she replied. "I found him very amusing. No, he was not drunk, and I never saw any weapons upon him. Mr. Raymond considers him a dangerous force because of his zeal to serve the miners. I haven't any very clear idea of the situation, and, as I never went up to Saloon Row, as Matt calls the village, I saw very little of the disorder. I did see Matt when he rode at the sheriff's side to quell the mob, and he was magnificent. Yes, it is true that Mr. Raymond is the leader of the free miners and that he and Mr. Munro are friends. Yes, Kelly and Raymond have made a strike, but they are unable to get the men they need to work their mine."

It seemed good to get back to wardrobes and a bathroom and to the deft ministry of servants, and when Ann looked out of her window that night and watched a portentous gray cloud closing round Mogalyon she breathed a deep sigh of relief and pleasure. This world of competence and all comforts, these rooms with their dainty furnishings, seemed as far from the life she had led at the Kellys' as the earth from the moon. It was incredible that she had liked it and impossible that she should ever return to it.

Barnett came home looking hard and worn, quite unlike his jovial self, but he greeted Ann warmly. "I am glad to see you here. I want to know all about things up there. Where is Peabody?"

Mrs. Barnett replied: "Dressing for dinner. Hurry, Don, you're late."

After he left them Ann remarked to Mrs. Barnett, "He looks worried."

"He is worried to death. He insists on trying to be the head and front of this citizen's committee of safety. He's chairman of it and is away all hours of the day and night. Do you know the whole city is patrolled?"

"Patrolled! What for?"

"So that the miners cannot come rushing down here some night and burn us all up."

This amused Ann. "How silly! Why should they do that?"

"Because we mine-owners live here. It is not a

laughing matter to us. Word has come to us through reliable sources that your nice friend Munro has planned a raid, and every young man in the town has been enrolled in the 'home guard.' The women are so nervous they daren't be seen outside their yards after dusk. Everything has stopped. No one is giving any entertainments. The theatres are empty. You never saw such a condition. It's dreadful!"

"It would be dreadful if it were true, but I've been living up there in the midst of things, and I've never heard a word of this raid. I haven't once been scared, though it was exciting the day I went shopping."

"Yes, but you were protected by the chief devil of all—this man Munro. He's probably in love with you. Don said he was."

Ann laughed outright at this. "Jeannette, you people have been eating too much lobster-salad and ice-cream; you're all suffering from nightmare. There isn't a word of truth in what you've been saying."

When Don came down she continued to mock, and all through dinner she perversely defended Munro, and listened to Barnett's boastings of what they were going to do to open their mines, with entire lack of sympathy.

"I don't pretend to comprehend what you men call business," she said, "but it seems to me that rather than waste millions on a useless war I would allow the miners a few more cents pay, just as a matter of economy."

"But it's the principle of the thing. We don't intend to be dictated to by these 'red-neckers.' They must come to our terms."

"My grandmother would say that's like biting off

your nose to spite your face. Mr. Raymond is working right along."

"I've been deceived in him," Barnett burst out, interrupting her. "He and Kelly are playing a two-faced game with us."

"I beg your pardon, they are not!" she hotly answered. "They are doing just what you ought to do. They're paying their men good wages and treating them properly."

"When did you become a labor advocate?" he sneered.

"Don! Don!" warned his wife. "Don't mind him, Ann. Since this trouble came on he's lost his head. I'm afraid to have him come home, he's so irritable. He's perfectly savage."

Peabody put in a word. "If I might venture, I don't know a thing about it, except what Munro and Raymond told me, but it seems to me Ann is right. As I understand it, these chaps are contending that in making this change from three shifts of eight hours each, you shouldn't lay off a lot of men, and put the rest on two shifts of nine hours each at eight-hours' pay. Isn't that it?"

"Well, yes; but, you see, it's really a new system altogether."

"But in the change you don't intend to accidentally pay thirty cents or fifty cents or whatever it may be, for that extra hour?"

"The pay for a day's work will remain as it is now."

Peabody smiled. "A mere shuffle. Come, be frank. You fellows have fixed up a new deal in which the cards go against the miners. They protest, and now it is a matter of 'gun-play,' as you say out here."

Barnett broke into a grin, but he was irritated. "Have *you* taken out a brief for the miners?"

"Not at all. As the world goes now, wages are a result of bluff. You try to hire labor as cheaply as possible, and labor tries to sell its brawn as dearly as possible. It's a very pretty fight, and I'm an on-looker. Whether your bull gores the miners' ox or no is none of my affair, but it amuses me to see a faddist and a sport like Don Barnett involved in a far-reaching question of labor and capital."

Mrs. Barnett looked relieved. "I *wish* you'd talk him out of it, Wayne."

Peabody, with a lawyer's pleasure, went on with his analysis. "But there's a third party here which is of more interest to me than either you or the unionists, and that is Raymond's party of the third part. They are upholding the old traditions—that a man with an open door behind him cannot be coerced. These small operators who refuse to come into your combination are largely made up of the old-time miners and prospectors, so Kelly tells me. They are standing clear for the present, but if you crowd them to the wall, they'll take hold, and then, as Kelly said, 'you'll have a wild-cat by the tail.' I wish I could wait and see how you come out, but I've got a big case on for the 16th and must be in Washington."

"The whole thing will be settled in a day or two," declared Barnett. "When we go up there again, it will be with a thousand men and fully armed."

"That is a harsh arbitrament," said Peabody, with a gravity which was almost solemnity. "I would advise you to settle this case out of court."

Ann interposed. "I think you both take too serious a view of the whole thing. Mr. Raymond laughs over it."

"Mr. Raymond was probably trying to keep you unalarmed," answered Peabody. "And now that you are out of it, I do not think it well for either you or Louis to return to it."

Louis uttered indignant outcry. "Oh, see here! I've got to go back, I'm helping Raymond."

"I guess he'll have to stagger along without you, Louis," replied Barnett. "You better not go into this mix-up again."

"I'll go back whenever I please."

Ann laid a warning hand on his arm and hushed his boyish threat.

The dinner was finished with a pleasanter topic, and when the men were alone with their cigars Peabody carelessly remarked: "I'm going to take Ann back with me, if she'll go. I don't like the idea of this youngster dragging her into all this filthy turmoil. Why, I found her living in a log cabin with an Irish family—nice people, but no place for her."

"That's the singular part of it, she seems to enjoy it. She wrote Jeannette from up there pretty regularly, and she out and out said she liked it. And she is gay as a bird—she's lost some of her fat—I never saw her looking fitter."

Peabody mused. "She *is* changed. I can't quite make out why or how. She was like a school-girl for spirits last night. Do you suppose it's the high altitude?"

"Either that or some man. I'm told that this fellow Munro is a dashing kind of desperado."

"See here, Don, don't joke along those lines."

"My dear fellow, I'm not joking. Munro is just the kind of sport to appeal to a girl's romantic vein. He's handsome and audacious. I'm told he's at the Kellys' every day—"

Peabody became grave. "Yes, she told me that herself."

"Confound it, man, don't you know these things don't go by way of fitness? Something has happened to that girl. I hoped that Raymond would interest her, but it wasn't to be. She turned him down. Ann's a mighty curious girl and you don't want to get too confident. Now by all the laws of fitness and propriety she ought to go back with you, and I hope she will; but you don't want to guess at anything. Women don't like these self-contained lovers; they want fire and dash and mystery, and that's what she's been getting from this man Munro."

Peabody blew a whiff from his cigar; he spoke calmly, but his eyes were half closed in troubled thought.

"That's plain talk, Don."

"You gave me a full ration a moment ago, and now you listen to me. What are the facts? This girl came out here as white and cold as a statue. She was indifferent, or contemptuous of everything, except the kidlet, whom she idolized. Well, now you see the change. She's as full of color and 'gimp' as a girl of sixteen, her lips are red and her eyes bright. I'd like to think all this is due to the altitude and change of scene. But, my dear chap, I suspect it is a man, and I fear it is Munro."

"I hope not, for her sake."

"I do, too, and for your sake; but I've seen too many women go to pieces in that way to feel any assurance. It wouldn't have been so bad if she'd taken up with Raymond, for he is a fine fellow aside from his present stand; but there again, he was too respectful, too near her own type; it needed a wild devil like this cow-boy captain to stir her imagination. Did you notice how she defended him to-night?"

Peabody's cigar was broken between his fingers. "Don, you scare me! Merciful powers, man, I can't think of leaving her out here! She can't marry such a desperado. It would be horrible—horrible!"

Barnett having fairly crushed his friend, now tried to comfort him. "All this may be a wrong diagnosis, and I hope it is; but if I were you I would go to her and use words that would startle her. She needs the strong hand."

Peabody rose, all the quizzical lines of his face lost in a plexus of doubt and hesitation.

Don clapped him on the shoulder. "Cheer up, old man! Don't take my vaporings for gospel truth. This is my pessimistic night," and together they joined the women.

Ann wondered at the change in Peabody, but had no chance to speak to him for some minutes, for a couple of young men were detailing their stern plans for invading Sky-Town.

"But you mustn't tell me these things," she protested. "I am a sympathizer. I might convey your plans to the enemy."

This seemed very amusing to the young men, and one of them, Mr. Dan Morton, went on with his tale.

"You see, all the fellows have gone into this home guard or 'the dude company,' as the sheriff calls us. There are a hundred of us who are ready to march as soon as we have provisions and arms. We drill every night. Oh, it's great fun!"

Ann looked at the two young fellows and thought of Munro and his men. "Poor little lambs," she said, pityingly.

"What do you mean?"

"It's cold up there," she went on, "and those vedettes are very inconsiderate. It would not surprise me if they were to shoot at you just a little while before you shot at them."

"You're making game of us."

"You deserve it. Why do you go up there? As Mr. Munro says, it's none of your funeral, at least not now."

"We have to go. All the chaps are going. Those fellows must be taught their place."

They were so deeply stirred by their call to duty that her ridicule only rendered them stupid, and she turned away to Peabody. The library was soon filled with people who had heard of Ann's return from the peak, and the girl was profoundly amused to find herself taken for a fount of wisdom concerning the miners' war and their demands. The feeling against the camp was savage, and the men were loud in denunciation of the Governor of the State, who had refused to order out the militia. "He is as bad as Munro, an absolute anarchist," declared one man, whose strident voice dominated all the others.

Peabody studied Ann with keen and asking eyes. Her vivid color, her alertness, her instant humor were a revelation of beauty to him. She seemed five years younger. Youth was in the flush of her cheek, in the sparkle of her eyes, and in the firm muscles of

Ann Sends Peabody Away

her arm. She was radiant with the wine of health and happiness—a girl transformed. "In this I have had no share," he thought, and the conviction troubled him.

One by one the guests dropped away, and at last only the Barnetts and Ann and Peabody were left in the library.

"How absurd all this talk of warfare seems!" said Ann. "You men are strange animals, you fight for a fiction like demons. I never realized it before, but you are uncomfortable creatures to have around when your prejudices are aroused."

At a signal from Mrs. Barnett Don sauntered out of the room as if on some errand, and forgot to return. A few moments later she, too, begged to be excused "for a moment," and was seen no more.

Both Ann and Peabody understood these actions, but as he was intent on making an appeal to her, and she knew there was no escape from it, they faced each other with a tensity of emotion which seemed impossible a moment before.

Ann broke the silence. "How indelicate of them!"

"How considerate, say I, for I want to talk with you," he hurried on. ' I want you to go back with me, Ann, as my wife. I can't go back alone. I have missed you horribly. Dear girl, answer me, are you ready to go?"

Ann remained silent, her mind running over for the hundredth time the advantages, the duties involved, while his plea proceeded, earnest and manly, but leaving her cold. It permitted her to calculate, to criticise. He had much to give her; he was a man of large income, of unquestioned power, and his home was spacious. She liked him, she respected him **very** highly, she admired him, but—

The girl's dream was not yet faded out of her soul. She hoped—faintly, foolishly hoped—for a return of the glow, the mystery, the flooding, transforming power of a love that was more than respect, more than honor and admiration — a love that retained something of the elemental and the primitive; something not to be resisted, under which there was no current of self - interest — a passion not to be measured, weighed, and classified, but a blind, potent, irresistible, glorious force.

She found herself saying: "I know, Wayne, we seem suited to each other—all our friends would say so—but I'm not so sure of it. It is silly in me, but I am still wanting to be sure. I don't care for you as I ought to do. I'm no longer a school-girl; I know what marriage means, and unless I can feel differently from the way I do now, I shall not marry."

He was a little encouraged. "Can there be a better, a more enduring basis for marriage than respect and admiration? You say you like me—that you honor me—"

"Would you ask me to marry you if you only admired and respected me?" she asked.

"If you were you, yes."

She smiled. "You are evading; you said you loved me."

"I do. My whole life is bound up in you."

"Then you have what I have not and our marriage would be unequal. Oh, don't press me!" she cried, in sudden weariness and despair. "I don't want to make you unhappy and yet I must if you insist

300

on an answer. I cannot do it, Wayne! Please, please consider this final!"

"Take time to consider, Ann. You are crushing every ambition I have. Do you realize that for years I've struggled to win your love! Every victory I've won has been good to me because I hoped to have you share my honors, my home."

"Don't say those things to me; they do no good. Women don't marry men merely because they honor them. Marriage means something more to women than to men—something more than respect is necessary to sanctify it. If that something, that other higher impulse does not come, I shall not marry."

"Have you met any one else who rouses this other—emotion?"

She flushed. "I don't know. I am not sure."

He sank back in his chair, heavy and inert. The muscles of his cheeks drooped, giving him the aspect of a man of fifty. "Don't throw yourself away. Ann, for God's sake, assert your common-sense! If you cannot come to my home, don't waste your beauty, your culture, on some savage. It hurts me to see you out here, living among these sordid men—"

She interrupted him. "There is another inexplicable thing. This life has interested me. It has developed in me a capacity for physical effort that I didn't know I had. It's my good old Dutch grandmother coming out in me, I suppose."

"But you can't live here indefinitely, cut off from all your friends and the comforts of your home."

"I'm not so sure about that," she gravely answered. "I don't seem to care as much for our home and the city as I thought I did, and that was little. I've tried being a cosmopolite, and it has brought me nothing—it was like trying to embrace the east wind. I've reached a queer state—a sort of distorted epicureanism. I have decided to do that which hurts me worst for a time. If I don't want to do a thing, then I'm going to make it my duty and do it."

"Then marry me!" he swiftly interjected.

"No, no! I don't mean that—all but that," she protested. "It was your legal mind that trapped me. No, I daren't *marry* on the basis of my new philosophy —at least not now."

"You are glaringly inconsistent. I don't believe a word in your new philosophy. I begin to believe that you are taking a depraved pleasure in living in a shack and scrubbing dishes."

"Anyhow, I'm going to let happiness find me. For years, ever since I left school, I've sought pleasure. I've been everywhere—England, Egypt, Europe, Asia, Africa—you know how we have globe-trotted. What has it given me? A sense of failure here," she put her finger-tip to her temple. "So far I've lived like my mother, but my father was the flower of a duty-loving old Dutch family, and I hear his voice now after all these years. If he had lived, I would have been a different girl. It will seem absurd to you, but I have grown to love sweet, little, patient Mrs. Kelly. I like grand old Matt. I like the rude walls and the 'hand-made stoves,' as Matt calls the fireplaces—"

"And the tall young miner?" Peabody suddenly interrupted to ask, and leaning towards her, a flash of insight in his eyes. "Or is it the handsome, dare-devil Munro?"

A swift flush rose to her face, she lost speech, her

eyes fell. "Yes—I—I like them, too," she said. "They interest me. They are vital, unconventional, real."

"And would you marry one of them?"

"Am I on the witness-stand?" she asked, half resentfully, half in humor.

"I beg your pardon; I didn't intend an impertinence."

In this swift interchange of highly emotionalized thought they had forgotten where they sat, and all knowledge of time had failed them. Ann glanced at the clock and rose, but Peabody said: "Please don't go! We will never have a more important subject to discuss." She sank back into her chair and he went on quite calmly, his eyes very grave and sweet. "Ann, I want you to be happy. I am not the kind of lover who would make his bride a captive to her own sorrow."

"I wish you were," she said, under breath.

"It seemed to me when I came that I could make you happy. I doubt it now; but I must say a word of warning about this new light you are following. I believe in love, too; but can you afford to follow an impulse that has its seat in the organic? You know what I mean. In general it is a guide, but it is necessary to consider other things in order to avoid sorrow and pain."

"But have we any right to avoid sorrow and pain? Isn't my present condition—my uselessness—due to just that calculation? What right have I to come down to death saying, 'I've had a good time all my days'? There is something wrong in my life, Wayne. I've been eating whipped cream and hot-house fruit till my nature cries out for curds and whey. I don't know where I'll fetch up, but just now I am bruising myself against realities. My feet have touched planks, and I am better for it."

"Velvet is as great a reality as a plank floor."

"It may be, but it doesn't seem so to me just now, and velvet is only what it seems to me. The plain truth is, I am happier, healthier than I have been for years, and I dare not let go of what I have gained. I shudder to think what I was."

"If it is contrast you want, you could get it in the Tyrol, or even in the Adirondacks. Planks are planks. You might even scrub floors in a tenement on the East Side. I'll do anything to make you happy."

She shook her head sadly but decisively. "You do not understand me; but no matter. This you *must* understand. This talk has cleared my own mind. I admire you and I like you, but as I feel now I can never marry you." A little shiver passed over her at the thought. "No, it is impossible. I'm sorry, but you must go back alone."

He took his dismissal quietly, but he suffered. His voice was tremulous with passionate regret as he bowed over her hand. "I accept your verdict, Ann, and I can only hope that your new light may not lead you into a slough of despond."

She stood before him transfigured by some emotion he could not divine. "I have never been afraid of anything except my growing distaste of life. Now that the joy of living is coming back to me, I am as young as my years."

"Then good-bye, and God bless you," he said, with heart-felt sincerity, and left her transfigured by some inward light.

XXI

Raymond Receives Visitors

FOR the first time in his life Raymond was lonely, almost to the point of despair. To have both Ann and Louis taken out of his life on the same day left a painfully empty space. He did not permit himself to hope that Ann would return—he had, in fact, advised against it—and after his supper was over he sat beside the fire listening to the wind and pulling at his pipe like one deserted of his kind.

It had turned cold, and a great current of air was sweeping down from the peak—a movement portending some great change in the clouds. Kelly predicted snow; but as most of the outside work on the mine was done, he was not concerned about the weather. He was, in fact, taking account of himself and trying to adjust himself to a future without "Hesper." The glow of his pride had died out. The confidence which sprang from his possession of gold had dulled into doubt.

He found his evening unrestful and purposeless. Taking down a book he tried to read, but his mind wandered. He laid a scratch-pad on his knee and fell to figuring out his profits on the mine, and this proved a more absorbing business. He was intensely eager to own the mine, and so be rid of Curran and his spies;

and if the vein went on deepening and widening they could buy it in with a few good shipments, and then all that it yielded would be divided between Kelly and himself and his men, for some sort of profit-sharing plan was taking form in his mind as the outcome of the prolonged debates on the rights of labor. "They help lift the gold, they ought to share in it," he argued.

He carried his figuring on to the point where he could build a home and ask "Someone" to share it with him. Where this mansion should stand he left undecided, for the same reason that he did not permit himself to name the woman of its fireside. In this mood he was not so sure of the power of his gold as he had been on that misty morning, and the letter which he had fashioned to write to his father remained unpenned. "I will wait till the money is in my hand," he said.

As he sat thus, pondering over his problem, he heard voices, and a moment later a loud rap shook his door, ominous with its decisiveness of stroke.

"Come in!" he shouted, somewhat surlily, for he did not enjoy interruption.

Munro, Brock, Carter, and one or two others he didn't know entered, covered with snow.

"Good-evening, gentlemen." He indicated chairs. "What can I do for you this evening?"

Carter seemed very nervous and took a seat without looking at his host. Munro was smiling, but his eyes were aslant as he replied:

"Oh, we just called to pass the time of night and inquire about your good health."

Raymond glanced from Munro's waggish lips to

the frowning or troubled faces of the other men and braced himself for trouble.

"Out with it, Carter! What do you want of me?"

Carter fidgeted on his chair. "Well, you see, it's this way, Rob. We held a meeting to-day and we decided that, in view of the struggle that labor is making here, *all* the mines should either shut down or put their men into the ranks."

"You have asked my men to join, haven't you?"

"Yes."

"What did they say?"

Munro chipped in, "They said, 'Go to blazes.'"

Raymond smiled. "How impolite of them! Well, now, let me say once again, Carter, I am in sympathy with your main objects. I think a man should be paid for every minute he works, but I don't believe in any method of forcing men who are working, and want to work, into a strike. I can't afford to go into any such organization."

"You can't afford not to," growled Brock.

His tone angered Raymond. "What have you to say in this matter?"

"I'm a member of the executive committee."

"Since when?"

"No matter when. What I say goes."

"Does it? Well, you keep a civil tongue in your jaws when speaking to me."

Brock rose. "You'll close down to-morrow or we'll close you down."

Raymond faced him. "We will not close down, and you can't close us down. Carter knows, and you know, Jack, I've played fair in this. I have not believed in your methods. I stood with Larned, your own organizer, against violence. If you can't convince my men by argument you needn't come to me to dragoon them into your ranks. What difference will my hands make, anyway?"

Carter seized upon this. "It will make all the difference there is. There are a dozen of these small operators holding out because you and Kelly do. Your men are all strong men and ought to be with us. Besides, it weakens our discipline—"

Raymond interrupted. "We've been all over that before. I am not concerned with your discipline. I have no quarrel with my men. They are satisfied with our present arrangement."

"But we must take into account the solidarity of labor—"

"The solidarity of labor! I cannot afford to sacrifice my business for a mere phrase. You're going at this back-end to. If you would turn your attention to reforming mining laws and crushing out these speculative owners of mining lands, you would really be doing something; but your assault on men who are paying labor full wages weakens your case."

Kelly opened the door and entered while Raymond was speaking.

"What's the meaning of all this?" he asked.

Raymond coldly replied, "These men have come to serve a final notice on us to discharge our non-union men or shut down."

"Not at all!" cried out Carter, who feared Kelly. "All we ask is that you recommend your men to join the union—"

Brock sprang to his feet again. "Oh, rats! What's the use of beating around the bush. We know that you fellers are the backbone of the free miners' association, and that they would all come in if you said so, and we need you and your men. We want you to head 'em our way."

Kelly smiled. "Ye're not asking much. So far as I'm concerned, Carter, I don't believe a word in you and your school-boy, tomfool antics. From the very start ye've gone wrong. You began by defending a lot of drunken blaggards, and that queered ye with every decent man. Go back to camp, arrest Denver Dan, San Juan Jones, Hob Smith, and the rest of the bunch, and send them down to the valley as a peace offering; then serve notice on the men that blew up the Red Star that they'll be hung to-morrow morning. By that time I'll begin to believe in you and your love for the honest working-man—" Kelly turned to Brock and his tone cut like a frosty blade as he said: "Ye are dominated this minute by a man who ought to be thrown out of camp. I know you, 'Bloody' Brock. I know the hole in the ground ye are going to fill if ye don't cross the high range, and do it soon."

Carter, utterly unable to stem the flood of Kelly's indignant speech, sat with drooping head. He stammered, "You—you're a traitor to labor."

"I am a traitor to nothing that is good, but I am worn out and weary with your yellin', cursin', gamblin', drunken loons that assume to be workmen. I have more respect for the weak little Dagoes, for they do want work and need it; but the bums that fill the streets are a sorry threat to a decent man, let alone a decent woman; and here's Jack Munro"— Kelly turned, and the smile died out of the young despera-

do's face—"he's chief of a gang of hoodlum cow-
boys, and still pretends to be keepin' the peace. If
you want to help the cause of labor, Jack, me boy,
close the saloons while this strike is going on; protect
the women and children; arrest and throw out the
men that blew up the Red Star mine—you know who
they are—"

"I do not," said Munro.

"Then find 'em, you who are so sharp ye can find
a tack in the grass; but, by the piper! till ye do something to make the street less of a hell, ye shall kape
away from Matt Kelly and Matt Kelly's wife and
babies. The whole town is mad with drink this night,
and you here blowin' bubbles about their righteous
cause. Black shame to the gang of ye!"

He was lion-like in his wrath, and the group of labor
leaders cowered before him like revealed conspirators. Only Munro seemed unabashed.

"That's all well enough to demand, Matt, but to
carry it out is another story."

"Because ye're one o' them," answered Kelly.
"You boast of your power; ye're a man of education—
some say military education. You know what discipline is, but when it comes to controlling your men
from insulting strangers and abusing women you
set down. Now, listen to me. This is my last word
on this subject. We are neutral. We have had no
part in this row and we will take none. Go on, work
out ye're jackass plan, rouse the whole State, make a
political issue of yourselves, but lave Raymond &
Kelly out of it. Lave our men alone. They are
satisfied and earnin' good wages. As for my good
advice, take it or lave it. If you take it, ye win;

if you lave it, ye lose. I am for peace. I've done everything a man could do to kape the peace; I must do so. Everything I have in the world is here—the mine, me wife, and the babies. I want no quarrel with anny man, especially with a miner, for I have worked for wages half me life; but I tell ye once more, boys, this mob business must not circle round that little cabin over there. If wan of your loafers so much as puts his toe against my door, I'll kill him where he stands."

He ended with a hoarse intensity that silenced the men who listened, and after a pause Raymond remarked, very quietly:

"I stand with Kelly on this matter. Is there anything further you want to say?"

Brock shook his heavy shoulders, as if to clear himself of a weight, and clumsily rose. "I reckon that's all—you stay out?"

"We stand clear," said Raymond.

Carter fumbled for his hat. "Of course you mustn't think we blame you, Kelly; you are right enough from your point of view, but what would become of labor if we all stood aside?"

"I don't know," said Kelly. "There are wise men who have studied this problem — Hennery Garge, for instance—ye might look into his way. I'm dom sure your ways of violence will never cure the evil."

As they stood on the threshold Brock spoke with a vicious sneer, "We'll report your answer."

"Report to purgatory and back if ye like," replied Kelly, cheerfully. "'Tis a plain answer, and a man behind it."

As the door closed behind them, Raymond turned

to Kelly with a look of great solemnity. "Matt, this means war for us."

"Munro will stand between us and the union."

"I doubt it, Matt. His power will vanish the moment he goes against the wishes of the miners. He couldn't feed his men and their horses without the union; he is in their pay, for all his boasting."

Kelly looked thoughtful. "That is true."

"Matt, you better take the wife and babies down to the valley."

"I've spoken of that, but the little wife will not go without me."

"Then *you* must go. It is not safe for them here. The people below are in deadly earnest. They're coming up here with an army next time. You better take your little family and get out."

"I can't do that—I can't leave here. Do *you* take the wife and the boys down to the Springs while I stay here and see that the work goes on."

They tossed this duty to and fro, each arguing in favor of the other, till Raymond said, "Very well, let's leave it to the wife."

As they stepped out into the night Kelly cried out: "Here comes the snow. Munro's pickets have a hard night before them."

Lifting his face to the rayless sky, Raymond felt the feathery touch of snow upon his forehead, and looking towards the lighted windows, the thick-falling flakes could be seen in dancing swarm. "It will cover the grass—Jack will find his cavalry expensive."

Kelly's sons were fast asleep in their bed, but the small mother still sat at her sewing, her head haloed with lamplight. She had grown pinker and plumper since Ann's ministry began, and was the pretty centre of a sweet domestic picture as she looked up and greeted the two men.

"I'm glad you've come," she said. "My heart is lonely without Ann. Do you think she'll ever come back, Rob?"

"I hope so," he replied, but his voice had no heartiness of conviction in it.

"I'm glad she's away—just now," said Kelly, coming straight to business as usual. "And Rob thinks you'd better go down to the Springs also."

"And leave you here, Matt Kelly? I will not. You'd be sure to get into trouble at once. If I go, you go,"

Kelly looked at Raymond with a comical lift of one eyebrow. "That settles it—we stay!"

Mrs. Kelly laughed gayly. "I can't trust you two hot-heads."

"There's going to be trouble," warned Raymond, "and you ought not to be here."

"The fightin' will not be on the hill—you said so yerself, Matt."

"I did, and I think so still; but at the same time 'twould be safer far if you and the lads were in the Springs."

"What has happened to-night, Matt? You were not so blue when you went out."

He told her quietly while she rocked to and fro in her low chair. She seemed scarcely to listen, but at the end she said: "You did right. I am heart-sick of these drinkin', carousin' miners who go about making trouble for others. The most of them have no one but themselves, and they don't care what they do. If Jack Munro is the man he boasts himself to be all the time, he'll come in here and protect his friends."

"Jack is up against a hard streak o' weather. He's either got to stand in with the union or put up the money to feed and take care of his men and horses, and that's no small item when the snows have covered the grass. If he should join us, his power would be gone. He can't—"

A knock at the door brought a smile to Kelly's face. "Talk of the devil and he's at your elbow—come!"

Munro entered the room hurriedly, like a man pursued. His collar was rolled high and his hat pulled low. He shut the door behind himself quickly; but when he turned, his usual devil-may-care grin was on his face.

"Boys, this is on the q t. I mustn't be seen down here any more. This neutral game is up. They're going to make war on you independent operators—sure thing—and I can't hobnob with you. Oh, but they're wild up the street to-night! The report is that the sheriff has started up the old stage-road, and the lads are crazy to do 'em up. I've got to go down the cañon and see."

"It's another false alarm. The sheriff isn't going to march in on this camp even with ten thousand deputies."

"Anyhow, that's what they believe up there, and they're hot against you. This neutral dodge of yours won't work. I can't do much for you, but anything I can do to keep this little home undisturbed I'll do." He bowed to Mrs. Kelly. "But, as you said to-day, I can't maintain my men without the help of the miners, and besides, boys, I believe in organized labor. Labor is an army, and discipline is everything."

"Why don't you maintain it then?"

The smile dropped from his face like a mask, and a sinister, older man faced them: "Give me time. What this camp needs is a little Napoleon — the whiff of grape-shot. It needs a dictator, and I may be able to lay my hand on the sceptre yet."

"It's pure anarchy now," said Raymond.

"It was till I entered the game. I am in control of the situation to-night. If I could command ten thousand dollars to take care of my men, I'd bring order out of chaos, or hang about forty of these hoboes."

"If you'll make this camp law-abiding, Jack, you will be one of the great men of the State—even the valley will praise you. It's up to you this minute to show your power."

"Yes, but there are a whole lot of other considerations. I can't afford to play into the hands of those cursed, one-lung dudes. If it were a question of men like you and Kelly here—but it isn't. The Red Star company is made up of a set of pirates, who batten on labor like a lot of turkey-buzzards. They have no regard for any human rights—"

"These howling dervishes up the street are not concerned with rights—not even their own."

Munro was in deadly earnest now. "That's where you are wrong, old man. In their blind, fool way they are fighting labor's battles. They stand for the future. It isn't easy to strike a balance here, but I'm on the side of labor, and against privilege. The future belongs to the common soldier—no doubt of that. If those 'yaller-legs' come up here, I'll put up a fight that will make their noses turn gray. On that point my men are sound. They will fight till the last man. No, I'll be hanged if I play into their hands!"

"It's a queer mix-up," said Kelly, with a sigh. "I have a hatred of them dudes meself. They want to run our end of the county, and their own too. They despise a workin'-man. They dodge 'im as if he were a pole-cat."

Raymond rapped on the table. "Now wait a moment. You're confusing the jury. The immediate question is, 'How can we keep that mob of deputies from coming up here?' I'll tell you what I will do. I will volunteer to go down and meet the leaders and try to stop their advance."

Kelly rose with a spring. "Go, you! I believe you can do the trick. Barnett is your friend. The sheriff is mine. I would go with you, but I dare not leave me home."

"Never mind me, Matt," said the small wife.

"You're both taking a big risk," remarked Munro. "They may arrest you both."

"I have no fear," Kelly said; "but I dare not go— just now."

"I will go if the executive committee will authorize me to treat with the opposition," declared Raymond.

"They will never do that, but Carter may. You might take him. He's scared nearly out of his skin; but he might be willing to go. Come with me and we will see."

"Be careful where you step, Rob," said Kelly, anxiously. "The grass is full o' rattlers."

"I'll take care of myself," he answered, cheerily. "Good-night."

Raymond Receives Visitors

As he closed the door behind him he said: "I'm trusting you, Jack. If you lead me into a trap, I'll carry you with me."

Munro's voice had an injured tone as he spoke from the darkness. "You do me a great injustice."

"I said that as a test. 'Lead on, Macduff.'"

It required courage even with such a guide as Munro to walk the troubled streets that night. The town was filled with the most abandoned women and the most lawless men of the whole mountain West. Up to this time all the martial preparations of the camp had been half-hearted — underneath every menace had lain a vein of humor; every movement had been in the nature of a huge, rough joke, but now the camp was in fighting mood. Tongues clattered in hot curses, and with the sound of their own voices men were inflamed. The saloons echoed with fiery denunciations of the mine-owners. Gangs of armed desperadoes paraded the walks, calling for volunteers to assemble at the armory, and as Munro met and greeted these men, Raymond was made fully aware of his power over them.

Those who recognized Raymond burst into laughter and shouted, "Bringin' him in, are ye, Jack?"

One infuriate aimed a blow at Raymond's face, but Munro felled him with the butt of his revolver and walked on.

In the headquarters of the organization they found Carter and his staff loudly discussing measures, and answering and sending messages. Dolan, the friendly reporter, was there, and also the representative of the *Bozle Nugget*. They were both deeply trusted, and their advice was most carefully considered. Upon seeing Raymond with Munro, Dolan rushed forward. "What's the meaning of this? Have the independents come in?"

Munro said, quietly: "Boys, I want to be alone with the president. Clear the room, Sergeant Poole."

A tall young fellow in cow-boy's dress drew a big revolver, and, using it as a sort of baton, impassively drove every one but the president, his secretary, and Raymond from the room.

Munro put Raymond's proposition before Carter in a few words. Carter turned white with fear.

"I can't do that. They'd kill me. They hold me responsible for everything that's been done here. The Governor has wired me to meet him, but I daren't do it. It's suicide to do it."

"Then I will go alone," said Raymond, in vast disgust. "Give me a letter saying you would like to meet and confer with the sheriff to prevent bloodshed, and I will present it."

Carter was shaking with excitement over the responsibility thrust upon him. "I don't know what to say."

"I'll tell you what to say," put in Munro. "Tell him we are fully organized and heavily armed, but that we desire to avoid bloodshed, and to that end invite him and the president of the Red Star company to meet with us and Raymond, in the presence of the Governor of the State, in the hope of arriving at a compromise."

Raymond was pleased. "That's the first note of sense I have heard uttered in this whole row."

"I intend to take a hand from this on," said Munro, quietly, as Carter was writing the letter. "I shall have to kill a few of these loud-mouthed Weary Willies, who want to go to war by use of somebody else's relations."

When the letter was delivered to him Munro said: "Now, Carter, keep mum about this. If it works out you can have all the credit for it; if it fails I'll take the kicking."

The crowd in the outer room were consumed with curiosity as the two young men came out, but Munro said: "Get the recruits all together. I'll be back in half an hour and put them through the paces."

Mounting their horses, they set off down the trail in the thick-falling snow, guided only by the dim lights in the valley.

"It's a tough night to be out, Rob, but you're less likely to be interfered with on that account. If you meet any of my pickets the countersign is 'contact—porphyry—and slate.'"

They rode in silence till they reached the broad stage-road, which wound round the base of the hill and dipped into the cañon of the Bear River. No one was abroad, and their horses' feet made no sound in the snow.

Under an overhanging fir Munro pulled up. "I think you're all right now. You won't meet any one except, possibly, one of my men."

"Jack, old man," began Raymond, with feeling, "after all, we are classmates, and I don't want to see you run your neck into a noose. Why not ride on with me and get out of this business?"

"No, I'm going to stay right here, and prove that my aims are right. I've been working slowly to the point where I could take control. I'm pretty near there now, and when I do take hold, I'll make Brock and his hoboes hit the western trail or tread the air. I'm in this thing to win out, in spite of your 'dude' friends or Brock's gang."

"It's dangerous business, Jack."

"Oh, that doesn't trouble me. By-the-way, you'll see the lady from New York—present my regards, will you? Tell her that 'when this cruel war is over' I hope to call upon her in the Springs. Good-night."

"Good-night," replied Raymond, and for the moment both forgot their duties and the dark night in thought of Ann.

XXII

Raymond Meets Ann Again

RAYMOND'S descent of the cañon was singularly uneventful. He met neither the invading army nor the patrol. No living things but himself and his horse were roaming the world of snow, and he rode slowly, silently, so intent on keeping the road that little time was left him in which to ponder other possibilities. Happily the storm lessened as he descended, and by dawn he was once more trotting with the calm, close-adhering seat of the cow-boy, his horse's hoofs striking sharply on the hard ground beneath its thin, white coverlet.

The east was a dome of scarlet and saffron arching a pale-violet world of plain—a wondrously cold, clear, and inspiriting sky; and, tired as he was, he rose in his stirrups with a half-uttered cry of exultation. After all, his first love was the plain. The mountains fascinated and allured him, but the level lands filled him with wordless longing, for they were associated with his first romance.

He had planned to go to a friend's house in the lower town, but with the coming of light and the blooming of the rose of the morning, he resolved to ride directly to Barnett's. "My errand is an honorable one," he argued. "Why should I sneak into cover?"

No one was astir as he rode into the Barnett yard—
no one save the hostler, who received him with beam-
ing countenance and a word of inquiry about the strike.

"It's still on, Johnson."

"Is it true that they have the ground all planted
thick with bombs?"

"I haven't seen any such planting."

The housemaid who let him into the house also
smiled upon him in a most friendly fashion. "We're
glad to see you, sir. Shall I tell Mr. Barnett you are
here?"

"I wish you would; and tell him I wish no one but
himself to know of my presence."

"I understand, sir."

The beauty of the Barnett home smote upon him
freshly and with great power as he crouched in a big
chair before the fire, absorbing needed heat. He was
chill and stiff with his long ride, and the delicious
warmth, the harmonious colors, the repose of that
room, with its calls to reading and meditation, laid
hold upon him mightily. "I will have a library like
this," he said, "and I will use it, too. My books shall
be read."

He began to understand how easy it would be for
those who dwelt in such homes to hate the profane,
purposeless, gambling crowds at Sky - Town. Seen
from the vantage-ground of this reposeful, well-ordered
temple of literature, they were savages in very deed.

The girl returned promptly. "You may come right
up, sir. Mr. Barnett will see you in his room."

His heavy boots clamped loudly on the polished floor,
and he was forced to tread the stairs on tiptoe. The
foot-wear of the hills was as out of place there as a spade.

Raymond Meets Ann Again

Barnett was in bed, with a pot of coffee and some toast on a stand by his side, reading the morning papers.

"Hello, old man," he called out, when the door was shut. "I'm mighty glad to see you, but I don't know what to do about you. What's the row, anyway? Have you come down to see Ann?"

Raymond took a chair near the bed. "Not exactly —but of course—"

"I understand, and I don't blame you. She came back from up there looking like a rose of Sharon. Of course, you haven't had breakfast. Have some coffee. You've come on something important, but let's get some hot coffee into our blood the first off; we can think better. Touch that bell for me and we'll have something heartier."

"How is Mrs. Barnett?"

"Never better. I've got her locked in there"— he pointed at an inner door—"I had an idea you were coming with important news from the front. I don't know about your being here; the people have got you mixed up with Munro in this thing, and I've had the devil's own job to convince them otherwise. I'm not a bit sure they won't want to arrest you and hold you as a hostage."

"That would be a nice job."

"Wouldn't it? But they've lost their heads com-pletely. You see, these 'red-neckers' hit us on a weak spot—they broke loose just as we were trying to float our biggest issue of stock, and flattened out every deal till it looks like a square yard of nothing. Naturally, we're all red-headed as woodpeckers, and we're going to open these mines; we've *got* to open them or go broke."

Raymond's eyes twinkled a little. "That sounds rather farcical from one lolling in Babylonian luxury. You should come up and see how we 'red-neckers' live. There's horny-handed toil for you. It's a good thing Brock and Munro can't see you now."

Barnett's reply was a shout to the girl who knocked. "Christine, bring a good, big steak as quickly as possible, and a fresh pot of coffee." He turned to Raymond: "I'll make you share my comfort—I don't call this luxury. By-the-way, when did you come to town?"

"This minute."

"Ride! In this storm!" He rose on his elbow to survey him. "Great Scot, man, throw off those horrible boots and put on some dry socks and some slippers! Tumble the things out of that bottom drawer; you'll find all kinds there."

In the end he had his way, and so, in warm, dry foot-wear and a smoking-jacket, the young miner ate his steak and drank his coffee while his host looked on and commented on his looks.

"You've taken a hand to the plough, haven't you? That fist is a wonder. And you've really struck it? Well, I'm glad of it. But you want to watch Curran; I'm told he's been to every lawyer in town with your papers, in the attempt to break your grip on that vein."

"We are not worrying," replied Raymond.

When he had quite finished, Barnett said, "Well, now, Rob, what about it?"

Raymond was equally direct. "I'm here to try to persuade you not to send the sheriff and his men up the cañon."

"Whom do you represent—the union?"

Raymond Meets Ann Again

"In a way, yes. I have a letter to you, and I come on behalf of the independents, who don't want to see bloodshed. There'll be a horrible mix-up, Don— sure thing—unless your fellows are headed off. Munro's cow-boys and desperadoes will fight—don't make any mistake about that; and he's got the larger part of the whole camp behind him when it comes to 're-pelling invaders,' as they call your folks."

"Who is this man Munro?"

Raymond looked at his friend steadily. "Don, the time has come to tell you something; but it's a secret!" His voice ended in a rising inflection. "It concerns only you and me—for the present."

Barnett reached his hand. "All right, old man."

"Munro is really Jackson Hollenbeck. We were classmates and room-mates at West Point."

"What!" Barnett started up. "West Point! Were you at West Point? How does it happen? You didn't graduate?"

"I did not. Do you remember reading, some eight or nine years ago, of a group of six cadets being dismissed for hazing and insubordination? I don't suppose you do, but I was one of that gang. Jack was another. We weren't so bad as we were represented, but they fired us all the same. I lost all track of Hollie, as we called him then."

"So that's where Munro gets his military training— and his real name is Hollenbeck." He smiled slyly. "What's yours?"

"Oh, mine is straight. I never tried to conceal my identity. I'm Robert Huston Raymond, of Ohio, the man that 'swatted' his superior and got 'busted' for it. Since then I've lived a commonplace life."

"What was it all about? I never asked any questions before, but I'd like to know all about it."

"That's about all of it. I was a restless young cub and hated the discipline; but that's of no value. What is important is this — Jack Munro's military training is being felt. Now you mustn't ask me a single question as to conditions up there. I'm going back, and I must be able to say to Jack that I was faithful to my trust. If the sheriff will go back with me, alone, I believe I can get Jack to deliver the men that blew up the mine. Then if the Red Star people— you, in fact—will deal with the men fairly, I think the whole situation will clear."

"I don't share your optimism. Those jackasses must be whipped before they will yield a point. They'd kill you and the sheriff both."

"I don't think so. I *know* Jack will protect us. He practically controls the camp at this minute. I have the countersign and can pass the patrol at any time to-day, and the sheriff, if he has the nerve, can ride with me straight to Jack's headquarters. Then I want you to meet some of the head men and arrange a new scale."

To this Barnett would not listen. "Once you admit that these men can dictate terms, and where will their demands stop?"

Raymond spoke with some heat. "What I complain of is that you Red Star people are interfering with *my* business. You have inflamed the camp till I may be obliged to shut down at any moment. You have been unreasonable in treating with your men. It isn't so much a question of wages, it's a question of courtesy and decent regard for your fellows. Mackay was no man to make an issue of. He was, in fact, a conceited ass, and you know it. Kelly could have inaugurated your new system, and I think I could; but Mackay—the very walk of the man was an offence. His style of trousers would incite murder."

"He's one of the ablest men in the West."

"Able, but rank. Now, Barnett, you must 'back water' here. The camp is in a bad temper, and you can't cure violence with violence."

"Well, I'll tell you what I'll do," said Barnett, on sudden impulse, moved by Raymond's sincerity, "I'll call a meeting here of the sheriff, the mayor, and one or two others, and we'll talk this over."

"All right, only you must keep my presence here a secret and be mighty careful not to put me in a false position."

"I'll take care of you." As he rose he added: "You lie down for a while and rest while I collect my men. Follow me and I'll bestow you."

Raymond followed slowly and rolled into his delicious bed with a sigh of deep pleasure.

When he woke, Don was standing over him smiling. "The council is on. Dress and come down to the library. I was right about the indignant citizens; they were all for arresting you. They understand that you are a pal of this man Munro, and I was obliged to put forth all my influence to save you."

This did not appeal to Raymond's sense of humor. "It's just that blind sort of bucking at the wrong minute that tangles things up. Munro is the one regulative force up there, and yet you fellows want to kill him off."

"Save your eloquence for the committee; you'll need it."

As Raymond stepped out into the hall, Ann met him. "Good-morning," she said, and her fine hand closed strongly on his. "Don has told me of your mission. I hope you'll succeed." She turned to Barnett. "Do you know where Louis is?"

"No. Haven't you seen him this morning?"

"No; and I'm afraid he has gone back to Sky-Town. The hostler said he took his pony and rode away about eight o'clock." Her anxiety for her brother showed in the otherwise clear serenity of her eyes like a cloud in a summer sky.

"I am afraid to have him there when you are away," she said to Raymond.

Barnett moved on, leaving them alone.

Raymond hastened to reassure her. "I am going back to-day—to-night. Matt will take charge of him till I return. You must not return to the camp—at least, not while this invasion threatens. The turmoil is deepening up there."

Her concern augmented. "Is it so serious?"

"If these deputies move on the camp they will be shot down."

"Oh, these wild Western people!"

"Gun-play isn't confined to the Rocky Mountains. I can remember the riots in Pennsylvania."

"That seems different."

"It isn't. Wherever men reach a certain pitch of rage or desperation they shoot."

"Can you keep Louis out of it?"

"I think so."

"You must be sure, or I will go back. I could

keep him out of it to take care of me. Is Mrs. Kelly afraid?"

"Not a bit. I tried to induce her to come down here, but she refuses to make any change in her life. Even if the invaders storm the fort the Kelly household is out of range."

"They really have a fort, then?"

"I shouldn't have said fort; I meant the hill."

"You *said* fort."

"I am here as a messenger of peace, not to betray military secrets," he replied, with a smile in his eyes. "And I must be careful even with you."

"What do you hope to do?"

"I hope to persuade the authorities here not to send these deputies up the cañon. I want to arrange an armistice—that is, a wait of a couple of weeks in which to meet and consider ways and means."

"Your military training is coming out."

"I permit it to show in talking with you."

"Does anybody else know?"

"I told Don this morning."

She checked herself. "You must go. They are waiting for you below. We will see you at luncheon?"

"Yes, I may not start till dark to-night."

"You have my best wishes."

He went down the stairs with her last words lingering in his ears like song. She was very moving when she permitted herself to be gentle.

The men assembled in the library were a grim lot. Mackay was no less square-jawed than Banker Moore, and the squat, coarse-featured, scowling sheriff resembled a bull-dog. Don Barnett alone seemed not a part of the general massing of prejudice and passion, and yet he was one of the most pitiless of them all. The mayor, a large man with a plump and smiling face, seemed the one man likely to side with a peace messenger. The secretary to the committee was a tall young Swede, or Dane, with a most unexpected vein of humor. He was called "Baron," whether in joke or in earnest Raymond could not determine.

After general introductions Raymond took a seat, and at Don's request reiterated his appeal for a stay of the advancing hordes.

"You think they'll fight?" asked the mayor.

"I *know* they'll fight."

"How many men does this man Munro—"

Raymond raised a warning hand. "Now, your honor, and gentlemen, I am here merely as a peace envoy. I do not intend to utter one word which could by any force be twisted into revealing the camp secrets. If I betrayed these men my life wouldn't be worth a toothpick. They would quite properly mob me."

The mayor smiled as if it were all a joke. "Quite right, Mr. Raymond. I see the propriety of your attitude."

"I don't," said Mackay. "Raymond and Kelly have elected themselves into on-lookers. If they had taken prompt action with us in this whole matter trouble would have been averted."

Raymond looked at him with a glance that did not waver. "We did not take action with you because your ways were foolish," he coldly replied.

The mayor resumed his questions. "Who sent you? Whom do you represent?"

"Munro sent me."

"Who is Munro?"

"He is the adviser of the president of the union."

"He's the 'whole thing,' isn't he?" asked the mayor.

"That I cannot answer. He has the confidence of the committee."

"I don't suppose it will do any good to ask about the buried dynamite and the fortifications on the hill?"

"None whatever."

"Then what did you hope to accomplish?"

Raymond fired a little. "I came here to tell you that if you think you can overawe this camp with a thousand men or two thousand men you are mistaken. Since this trouble began hundreds of the most reckless and dangerous characters in the West have flocked to Sky in support of the miners; these recruits are accustomed to the sound of guns. Furthermore, Bozle itself—in fact, the whole western end of the county—is tired of the domination of the eastern end, and they will aid and abet the miners. Your party is in a minority in the State, and you cannot safely look for support to the militia; therefore, for all these reasons, and because I know Munro and his men, I advise, I plead with you to stay where you are. There is one other consideration: The party which I represent—the free miners and prospectors, like Kelly and Bingham and Reese—have stood aside from this quarrel. We have had no share in it. We have kept our men out of it; but if you march against the hill many of our fellows will join Munro; and I want to tell you, gentlemen, that one of these free miners—these rangers of the hills—is more dangerous than twenty little Dagoes. A hundred of them would stand off five hundred of your men. Some of you know the West—you know the kind of men these prospectors are. They are armed, every one of them, with the best guns that the market affords; they will not go out with mops and sledge-hammers. You are crazy to lead men up against a camp of this kind."

The sheriff sneered. "You don't seem to realize that we have a few good guns ourselves."

"Yes, only your men are hired to do their work. What is the history of the hired soldiers of all time? They failed when sent against men fighting from a sense of duty or in defence of their homes."

"This case looks like a lot of hoodlums defending their saloons," said Don.

"Well, I'll admit there isn't the same sublimity of sentiment that we found in the men of Thermopylæ, but all the same the sense of wrong is strong enough to make them all unite against you and fight like demons."

His deep earnestness impressed them all, and a silence followed his last words. At last Don said:

"Gentlemen, Raymond is not merely an acquaintance, he was in my employ for some years, and he is my friend. I am forced to give his words great weight. I suggest that we try to arrange a meeting between the miners and ourselves and the Governor and reach some peaceful solution."

The sheriff leaped to his feet. "That would make us the laughing-stock of the whole country."

"Better be that than a melancholy example of foolish pride and obstinacy," Raymond interjected.

At this point the argument stuck. Mackay, the county attorney, and the sheriff stood for war; the mayor and Barnett, being for the moment under the power of Raymond's earnest glance, pleaded rather spiritlessly for at least a stay in proceedings.

Raymond Meets Ann Again

The mayor suggested calling a larger meeting for Raymond to address, but to this he made instant objection. "If I cannot convince you of the folly of assaulting the peak, I cannot convince a convention of citizens. You have the power to call a halt. If you decide to go on you must assume the responsibility."

"I think it all a ruse to gain time," said Mackay. "I think we ought to hold this man here and march at once. He is known to be a friend of Munro. If we allow him to go back he will inform—"

"Rats!" cried Barnett. "What could he inform about?"

Raymond smiled grimly. "My services as a spy are not needed. Every movement you make will be watched by a hundred eyes, and back of the eyes will be a gun."

The mayor rose. "Well, gentlemen, I don't see that we can decide anything here. We have Mr. Raymond's opinion that our attack on the hill will result in disaster. The sheriff is confident he can win practically without a struggle. This is no place to take a vote on so momentous a subject—" Here he looked at his watch. "And it is lunch-time. I suggest that we go to lunch and meet at three o'clock in the committee-room."

They filed out quite promptly, only the mayor having the grace to thank Raymond for his efforts at peace-making.

After they were well out of the house Barnett said, "You see how it is, they are inexorable."

"I see that Mackay and the sheriff are letting their own poor, little, personal vanities rule their actions

333

towards a mighty serious matter. Mackay's pride is hurt; he was kicked and bruised. The sheriff has been humiliated, therefore he wishes to be revenged. I'm done. If they want to go up against those gun-experts on the hill they have my full permission. When they get back there will be bells tolling in this burgh. It's cold up there; the snow is deep. These men are not accustomed to camping—why, it's suicide —sheer, foolish self-destruction!"

"May I come in?" asked Mrs. Barnett at the door. "Luncheon is waiting."

"Certainly," said Don. "The council is over."

"You were all very quiet. I expected to hear loud voices and the sound of blows." She came towards Raymond, her face sweet with kindly interest. "How do you do, Robert? It's good to see you; how well you look!"

The sight of her kind face filled the strong young fellow with memories of her goodness to him, and a sense of guilt robbed his tongue of its wonted readiness. "I hope you haven't— I know I should have been down; but, as I wrote you, I have been busy—"

She stopped him. "We will accept your apologies for the moment and go out to luncheon, which is getting cold." As they moved towards the door she added, in a low voice, "I want to talk with you about —you know who."

She put him at her left hand and Ann next him, an arrangement which pleased him. The table was filled, as usual, with people "on their way to California," and Raymond felt himself to be the object of comment both above and below board, and it irritated him a little.

Raymond Meets Ann Again

"This is a long way from Sky," he said to Ann, as his eyes absorbed the shining, flower-decked table and its tasteful service. "You left just in time; it is white with snow up there to-day, and bleak and cold."

"The peaks were hid all day yesterday. I shuddered to think what might be going on beneath those clouds, and now I'm afraid Louis has gone back into them."

"Have you had no word of him?"

"No news whatever. I am sure he is on his way up to you."

"I am starting back at once, and I will take care of him. Trust him to me."

"I am very grateful to you," she answered, and her eyes spoke more eloquently than her tongue. "Your influence over him is wonderful. He talks of you constantly, and I feel that you have helped him in every way."

His face flushed with pleasure. "I fear I am a poor companion for such a boy. I would not like to be taken as a model for any human being."

Her eyes were enigmatical as she replied: "I have come to think your influence more valuable to him than mine. He is approaching manhood. He must learn of manly things by contact with life, and it is a deep satisfaction to me to know that you are interested in him."

"I love the lad."

"I know you do," she answered, with a tender and musing voice, "and he is worthy of it. There is no evil in his thought. I intended to say these things to you before I came away"—a gleam of humor came into her eyes—"but Mr. Peabody intervened; and then you didn't come to see me off."

He looked at his fork critically. "I am not very brave about some things. I hate—I dread 'good-byes.' I simply couldn't see you go away. It was, or seemed to be, final."

"What made you think it final?" She was looking at him with an amused side glance. "What reason had you?"

He rose to her humorous challenge. "There was a good reason—a bulky and convincing reason."

"What is the old saw about jumping at conclusions?"

"I am sure I don't know; but your going was too painful for me to witness. I preferred to seem boorish—"

Mrs. Barnett here interposed. "Will you have tea or chocolate, Ann Marie?" and something hidden in her tone appeared in her eyes, and Ann faintly colored.

"Tea, please," she said; and in this answer uttered a defiant word. Mrs. Barnett's glance seemed to say, "Oh, very well, if you want to monopolize him, do it; but, remember, I have some rights."

Raymond, receiving a covert signal from Ann, turned to his hostess. "It is a great pleasure to sit at your beautiful table again."

"After so long a time. Why didn't you say that?"

"I acknowledge my guilt; but you know why—I wrote you—and now I am in pursuit of gold. I am a man transformed. I am as hot after money now as I used to be careless and slothful. I have an aim in life."

"Ann has told me something of your story, and so has Don. Why am I left out? Am I not worthy of confidence?"

"All confidence; but I have not seen you since my confessions began."

Raymond Meets Ann Again

"I knew your people were nice—blood tells. I wish I could see the old father when his rich son drives up to the door in a tally-ho."

He was boyishly abashed. "I fear Ann has been laughing at me. I don't believe I like that."

He was a little hurt and she saw it. "Ann was really very nice about it, and she told me very little. I guessed at the rest. By-the-way, the big lawyer left very suddenly the other morning, and was not a bit cheerful."

"Indeed! Are you trying to tell me something?"

"I have told it."

"Then tell me one more thing." He was eager and bold at this moment.

"I can't do that, Rob. No one can. The person doesn't know her own mind yet."

Ann's voice sweetly interposed. "You shouldn't talk in riddles in the hearing of guests, especially when one of them has the key to the riddle."

Jeannette laughed, but was reproved. "I thought you were listening to Don."

"I was, but I have two ears."

"I beg your pardon—" Raymond began.

"Oh, it was not your fault. I will settle with the real mischief-maker after lunch."

"Ann Marie, turn your deaf ear this way. I've only this chance to talk with Rob, and I'm not going to let you interfere." And she boldly went on: "I'm glad your ambition is soaring, Rob. Why, you have *everything* before you. What business has a handsome, young, and successful man to humble himself before any woman?"

"I confess to the first two counts in the indictment,"

he answered, with some humor in his voice. "But as to the third, I plead not guilty."

"But it is reported that you have discovered a mountain of gold."

"There was a moment when it seemed all that to me. Now I am in doubt whether it will pay expenses."

Don was talking in a loud voice to a rather deaf old professor who had been lecturing on the subject of peaches and how to preserve them, and under cover of this thundering to and fro Raymond hoped to continue his conversation with Ann; but the learned man from the East, fixing his keen eyes on the miner, began to inquire what the men of the peak meant by their disregard of law and order; and when Raymond evaded this question, the old man started in on a discourse concerning the rights of capital to employ labor in its own way, and so the golden minutes were wasted.

When at last the hostess rose, the young miner's heart contracted with a sudden realization that his hour of grace was over, and that the time had come for his return to the stern realities of life. His cabin, the snow-covered peaks, the mines, and the strikers—all his perplexities came rushing back, and the beautiful dining-room, the ministrations of his hostess, and his delicious moment with Ann began to recede.

In the hall he extended his hand in fixed resolution to Mrs. Barnett.

"Good-bye. It's hard to leave you and this glorious home—"

"Must you go to-day?"

"Yes. I must hurry back. Kelly needs me; and then there is Louis."

"Well, if you must— But do come again, Rob.

Don't mind who is here; come to see *us*. It is always good to have you here."

The young man's eyes blurred a little. "I wish you knew how much you mean to me," he said. "Now that I am cut off from my own sister and my mother."

"I hope you won't be long. I think you should go straight to them—at once."

"As soon as this strike is over I will do so," he said, very earnestly.

Don followed him to his room, and while resuming his big boots Raymond said, "Don't let that sheriff head me off; keep him for a couple of hours and I'll be out of his reach."

"Don't worry about the sheriff, old man, and throw your whole weight against Munro's policy of resistance."

"I've done that from the first."

"I know you have, and some of the fellows know it and respect you for it. They aren't all like the crowd to-day."

Ann was waiting to see him as he came out into the upper hall. It was her first deliberate motion towards him; but her face gave him no hint of her quickened pulses as she said: "Give Nora my love, and greet grand old Matt for me, won't you? I feel as if I ought to go back—"

"You must not, much as we all need you. This is no time for you to be there. I wish Nora would come down—"

"I wish she would; and please let me know instantly that Louis is safe with you."

"I will do so. When do you go East?"

"Not till spring."

"Then I may see you again." His words formed a declaration as well as a question, and his glance meant more than his tone.

Her eyes fell. "Perhaps." And she added, with an upward glance, "If you visit us soon."

"That I will do. Good-bye."

"Good-bye, and please don't be reckless."

Jeannette followed him out upon the porch. "What have you been saying to Ann up there on the mountain-top? I never saw such a change in a girl in my life. It is incredible. She is in superb health, but that isn't what I mean. She is so different in her manner. I believe she is in love with you, Rob."

A fire glowed an instant in his eyes, then faded. "No, you are mistaken. I think she likes me and trusts me, but nothing further."

By this she knew he had spoken. "My advice is an old one, Rob; don't take the first no for an answer."

The air was balmy and the sky bright as he rode away towards the peaks round which the most portentous clouds were still rolling in stately blue masses.

XXIII

Louis Calls for Ann

RAYMOND looked back occasionally, half expecting pursuit. He could see in the valley below
the town the gleaming white tents of the little army
hesitant to march, and its plan of invasion seemed
born of folly and madness. Then, lifting his face to
the great, glittering peak, he recalled a line from a
poet, wherein a mountain asks, with scornful pity,
"Why so hot, my little man?"

The sun was low, half hid behind the Hesperean wall,
as he topped the divide, and the young miner caught
his breath with joy of the scene, profoundly regretting
that Ann could not have been by his side. It was an
overpowering spread of earth, richly glowing with yellow
and purple and deep blue, a vast, crumpled sweep of
lesser hills rising to the golden-haloed, pale-violet, serrate line of high peaks to the west. Almost beneath
him lay Sky-Town and Bozle, their houses mere flecks,
their teams slow-paced beetles, their footmen midgets.

With a last deep inspiration of its beauty, he spurred
his horse down the trail to meet the night which rose
to meet him from the valley like a chill, engulfing flood.
An hour's brisk ride brought him to the open, and just
at the edge of the peak he came upon a forlorn camp, a
small tent under a fir, and a group of four men sitting

about a fire. At their call he turned and rode up to them. They were an outpost of Munro's guard, a part of the cordon he had thrown round the peak and camp.

One of them knew him, and, greeting him pleasantly, asked where he had been.

He replied, with candor, "I've been down to the Springs to induce those 'yaller-legs' to put off their expedition."

"What luck did ye have?"

"None. They're coming."

The other men left the fire and drew near with incredulous oaths.

"You don't mean it!"

"Sure thing," Raymond replied.

Significant glances passed between them, and the firelight brought out stern lines on their faces. At length Brown, the corporal, said, solemnly: "Well, if they want fight, they can have it. But say, Rob, does the captain know you're on the road? There was a hullabaloo in town about you last night. A lot of the fellers think you went down to give away the camp, and some said if you ever came back they'd string you up. Now, I guess you better stay here while I ride up and tell the cap' you're here."

"I don't think that's necessary, but you might jog along with me if you want to go. Otherwise, I'll go alone."

"Well, I'll tell ye, Rob," said Brown, in an embarrassed way, "these monkeys on the peak have got an awful slant against you and Kelly, and they's two or three fellers who are working against you underhand right along. You don't want to take no chances; they'll do ye if they can."

Louis Calls for Ann

Raymond was impressed with Brown's earnestness and by the admirable loyalty of his fellows camped there in the snow. "Boys, what are you staying here for?" he asked. "This isn't a picnic. What do you do it for?"

Brown answered, "We do it because we want to help these miners stand off the 'plutes.'"

"But it's none o' your funeral. Why don't you let them fight their own battles?"

Brown shifted his quid in perplexity. "Well, you see, it's like this: these Dagoes are no good in work of this kind. They can't ride, or handle a gun—and then we've got it in for these thugs that's comin' up against 'em. We're down on them yaller-legged dudes from the Springs who want to own the earth and kick the rest of us off it. If they's goin' to be a scrap we want to be on the pore man's side—that's about as nigh as I can come to it. Ain't that the idee, boys?"

"That's about it, corporal."

Raymond mused. "But you're friendly towards Kelly and Raymond?"

"Sure thing. You fellers are all right. You've punched cows, and Kelly is an old bronco-buster himself. But let me tell ye this, Rob, we're goin' to need you and your men if these chaps come up here the way they talk o' doin'—with Gatling-guns and all that. The boys have been rollin' logs for a fort all day. You can just about see it from here—just on that point."

"Well, suppose we ride along," said Raymond, and as he took a last look around his heart warmed to these rough souls who had taken sides in a quarrel not their own, moved by a blind desire to aid

343

their fellows in a war against privilege and social caste.

Brown called another man out of the group to ride with them, and they started away. He said to Raymond, "I hope your guns are all in running order; we may bunt up against some of them wild - eyed cusses who want to hang you."

It was deep night, keenly cold and very still as they climbed the hill, and once, as they paused to give their horses breath, a distant shouting reached their ears.

"More slang-whanging," remarked the third man.

"They's a man a-yellin' and poundin' the air from a box 'most any time now," said Brown. "Oh, they're frothin' mad up there. I guess we'd better make a little side-play here and not disturb the meetin'."

On the hill east of the town and overlooking the valley, lights could be seen flickering. The corporal lifted his arm and pointed that way. "There they are building the fort."

Raymond's blood began to stir, his military instruction to freshen, and for a moment, as he paused there in the darkness, he understood something of Munro's joy in a defensive campaign; but he said aloud: "It's all a mistake, Brown; they can't afford to fight the sheriff. The law is on his side."

Brown grimly replied, "Well, we'll give him a little run for his money, anyway."

Raymond smiled at the boyish quality of this remark, but made no comment upon it, and allowed himself to be led by a roundabout path to the west side of the town. At last his guide paused. "You're all right now."

344

I wish you'd tell Jack I'm here and that I want to see him," said Raymond. "I'm much obliged to you."

"Oh, that's all right, Rob, take keer o' yerself," and the two men rode off.

"Good-luck, boys."

As he rode up to Kelly's cabin and called out, "Hello, the house!" Matt opened the door, and, with a lad on either side of him, peered out. "Is that you, Rob?"

"The very same, Matt."

"Well, now, wait a whist and I'll come and put out your horse."

Mrs. Kelly called, cheerily: "Rob, we're glad to see you safe returned. Are you hungry?"

He slid from his horse. "I am empty as a wolf in March," he replied. "Where's Louis?"

"Louis! He hasn't returned. Didn't you leave him at the Springs?"

"No; he left early this morning and Ann thought he had hit the stage-road for the camp. I hope he hasn't gone wrong."

This news took away a large part of his pleasure in the friendly hearth to which he was welcomed, and removing his outer garments he bent to the blaze in silence, while Mrs. Kelly spread some food before him.

Kelly listened to the news of Louis' disappearance with less concern. "He's run into some of Munro's men and is probably up at headquarters. He couldn't get lost—he knows the road. What's the word from the valley?"

"They're comin', Matt."

"When?"

"To-night or to-morrow."

"I've been receiving delegations and posters and all kinds of warnin's. It's been a lively day on the hill. They're building a fort."

"So Frank Brown told me. How do our men feel?"

Matt rubbed his chin. "They're a little uneasy, to tell the truth."

Mrs. Kelly interrupted. "Sit up and eat, Rob; talk afterwards."

Raymond could see that Kelly was disturbed, and that he had something to tell which he did not care to have Nora know. It was plain that he no longer minimized the danger, and his face fell easily into stern lines.

Seizing the moment when his wife left the room to put the youngsters to bed, the big miner laid a sheet of paper before his partner. "What do you think of that?"

Raymond looked at the death's-head warning, for such it was, with amazement. It seemed at first sight a rough joke. In one corner glared the conventional cross-bones and skull, rudely drawn, and to the right and beneath them sprawled the word, "*Beware!*" All this was amusing, but the logic of the argument which followed gave him thought. "This neutral business is played out," the placard went on to say, "either you are for us or you are for the dudes. If you are for the dudes, get out. If you are for us, send in your men to help us repel the invaders. This is our first warning. Remember the Red Star! (Signed) COMMITTEE."

346

Louis Calls for Ann

Raymond folded the sheet and returned it to Kelly. "You don't think that's a josh?"

"I do not. Battle is in the air. Yesterday and to-day have been wild days; nothing but guns will quell this mob now. Munro can't control 'em without using lead."

Raymond rose. "Let's go down to my shack; we can talk matters over there more freely."

"I'll be with you in a few minutes," answered Kelly.

On the path to the bungalow the young man stopped with intent to sound the night. The voices of his men on the dump, the roll and squeak of pulleys, the puffing of his engine, the clang of ore-cars came to his ears to testify that work was going on as usual, and he hurried on to his silent cabin. It was warm, for the faithful Perry had built a fire early in the evening; and after he had lighted a couple of candles and kicked the fire into a blaze the room resumed its cheerful glow, but he was too deeply disturbed over Louis' non-appearance to fully enjoy it. He took out his revolver and was examining it carefully as Kelly entered.

"Did ye meet with any trouble, Rob?"

"None. Some of the committee of safety wanted to arrest me and hold me as hostage, but Barnett stood 'em off. I didn't see a soul till on my way back I came on one of Jack's picket-posts, where I found four men camped in misery and eating snow-balls for supper."

"It's strange the power he has over them wild cow-boys. Drunk or sober, they do as he tells them. His trouble will come with Brock and Smith, who are neither miners nor cow-boys; for they are all tryin' to derive their power from Carter, who is dead sick of the business and likely to fly the coop at any minute. Where you goin'?"

"Up-town to take a look round for Louis."

"You go not! 'Tis a poor time for you to visit the street. They have it in their heads that you are playin' the spy."

"I must find that boy. He left the Springs at eight this morning, and his sister is worried about him."

"I will go for ye, Rob. It's too dangerous for you."

Raymond rose and laid a hand on Kelly's shoulder. "See here, Matt, I want to talk plainly to you. You've got to bundle up that little wife and the boys and get out of here. I'm going to take a hand in this game. I'm going to call the independents together and make a stand. I have no one, except Louis, depending on me, and if I'm snuffed out it won't matter —so much—but you must think of Nora and the lads every minute. They're worth more to you than all the mines on the hill. Now you pull out."

Kelly faced him. "I can't do that, Rob. If you make a stand, I must be beside ye. What is your plan?"

"I will not tell you unless you promise to take Nora out of danger."

Kelly's face grew stern and his voice fell to a level hoarseness that sent a quiver through the young man's blood. "See here, boy, we struck hands on this partnership. We share and share alike. Matt Kelly never shirked his end of anny load, and I serve notice to you right here that anny call you send out will be done touchin' elbows with the old man. Do ye think I'll sneak away like a scared puppy? 'Tis too much to ask of a man, Rob. I would not give them the satisfaction of seeing the broad o' me back. No, I am with you and so is Nora. I am ready to dig a hole in the ground and stand 'em off till hell freezes over. I'm worn out with their comin' and goin', whip-sawin' now on this, now on that side o' the question. They've declared war on us. Now, by the powers! we'll meet 'em half-way."

Raymond surrendered. "All right, Matt, here's my hand. We'll defend Nora and the mine, too. When your fighting blood is up I don't want any dispute be-tween us."

Kelly's eyes began to twinkle. "I begin to draw me breath natural again. For weeks I've been want-ing to put me fist beneath the noses of these rap-scalions, but for fear of Ann and Nora I could not."

"Very well, we'll send out a call for a meeting to-night; the quicker we move the better. I feel as you do—now we are acting a man's part. There is a big element here that is sick of this monkey-business. Half the camp will rally in our support. I know it. Then we will serve notice on Munro—" The sound of hurrying feet interrupted him, and a moment later Louis burst into the room.

"Oh, Rob, I'm glad you're here. Hello, Matt!" He shook hands, breathing heavily. His skin was flushed and his eyes shining. "You ought to be up-town. Jack is makin' 'em sit up. He shot one man. They were building a fort, and a drunken fellow—"

"Take your time," said Raymond, coldly, "there are several minutes left in the box. You might begin at the beginning and tell me why you sneaked away again without saying good-bye to Ann?"

The boy was not daunted. "As soon as I heard what the sheriff's plans were I wanted to leave, but it was so dark; that was last night. I was afraid to try it, so this morning I pulled out early."

"Where have you been all day?"

"I've been with Jack. I met his men way down the cañon and they took me to headquarters, where I told my story, and then I went to supper with Jack; and then this big row came on and I stayed to see that. Oh, but Jack is fine! He faced the whole crowd alone. One man wanted to clean out your cabin, he said it was a nest of traitors. He drew his gun on Jack, but he hadn't time to pull the trigger. Jack's bullet went through his arm."

Raymond, who had been studying the lad with softening glance, interrupted him: "Now, see here, Louis, you sit down here by the fire. Don't let your words all try to get out of the corral at the same time. We want to know all about it, but we don't want you to hurry. It's only ten o'clock, and you can get over a whole lot of ground by midnight."

The two men looked at each other with grave eyes. The boy was trembling with excitement, and his voice was high and strained.

Kelly said, gently: "My lad, 'twould serve your sister better if you kept out of this. I don't like to see you riding between the lines as a spy."

"I didn't intend to be a spy, but when I heard the trick they were going to play, I couldn't help hurrying back."

"What trick?"

Louis Calls for Ann

"Why, they're going to load all their men into freight-cars, and make them keep quiet; and then they're going to run them through Jack's guard at Boggy, clear to the end of the rails."

"That's a very nice plan," said Raymond. "When do they intend to come?"

"To-morrow night, if the guns arrive for which they are waiting."

"How did you drop onto this?"

"I heard Cousin Don tell Dr. Braide. He wanted Dr. Braide to follow next day in case of accidents."

"You've told this to Jack?"

"Yes. I wanted to come and see you, Matt, but he said I could tell you afterwards."

Raymond again looked at his partner. "Well, I don't see that there is anything for us to do now."

"Jack told me to tell you to be on your guard to-night. He said he'd come down and see you if possible. Oh, I feel so cold," he ended, drawing nearer the fire. "I'm all trembly over my chest."

"I reckon you better strip off your clothes and go to bed. This has been a hard day for you."

He seemed stiff, and was shivering convulsively. "I believe I will. Rob, I don't feel any good."

As Raymond helped him to undress, the boy's teeth began to chatter, and he drew his breath with a hissing moan. "I guess I've taken an awful cold, Rob; my breast aches so."

"Matt, go ask Nora to come over and bring her little medicine-case. This boy's got a chill right now."

"A swallow of whiskey will fix that," answered Matt, as he went out. "I'll be back in a jiffy."

Raymond bundled Louis into bed and heaped him

with blankets and furs, his heart deeply stirred with anxiety, for as the boy's mind turned from the excitement of his day's experiences to his condition, he became deeply depressed; he fairly collapsed.

"Oh, Rob, what is the matter with me? My bones ache like mad."

Raymond cheered him while rubbing his icy hands and feet. "You overdid it a little to-day, that's all. You'll be all right in the morning. You didn't take clothing enough."

"I wish Ann were here."

Raymond was silent, but beneath his breath he most fervently echoed this prayer, so slender and boyish did Louis seem at the moment.

Mrs. Kelly, with her "emergency case" of medicine, and a knowledge of sickness gained in years of maternal care in the rough country, was a great comfort to Raymond, but she could not keep down his growing anxiety. The boy's body was so small and frail when stripped of its clothing! Under their vigorous ministrations the sufferer ceased to shake, and at last fell into a hot, uneasy doze.

Raymond, seeing this, whispered: "You must go home. I will watch."

"No, Rob, you must sleep. I forgot you had no sleep last night."

"Oh yes, I did. I took a nap at Barnett's. Please go to bed."

To this arrangement she submitted, and, taking his seat close by the boy's couch, Raymond studied his flushed face, more concerned at that moment over his temperature and pulse than with the brawling crowds, the invading force, or the fate of his mine. When

Louis Calls for Ann

Munro knocked on his door he went out upon the threshold and reported the failure of his mission, while the captain of the vedettes listened with his horse's rein across his arm. At the end he merely said: "All right. Let them come; they will find us ready." Then added, "Did the kid turn up all right?"

"He turned up, but he has taken a chill and is burning with fever."

Munro seemed concerned. "He had nothing on but that little gray jacket. I tried to warm him up with some whiskey and a supper. I hope he won't be laid up. Well, now, old man, what are you going to do— help us or the dudes?"

"I can't decide anything to - night. I'm worried about this boy. If he is better in the morning, I'll have something decisive to say to you."

"All right; take your time — only don't take too long. It's up to you to decide. Good-night. Keep me posted on the boy's condition."

"What I do you'll know about," Raymond responded, quietly.

A half-hour later Jim Dolan and two or three of his fellow-reporters tumbled in, eager to know what Raymond had seen in the valley.

To them he said: "Boys, I haven't a word to say. I'm sorry I can't offer you a bed, for Louis, my boy friend, is very sick. Dolan, I wish you would send up the best doctor in Bozle. Tell him there's money in it, if he comes to-night."

Dolan was sympathetic. "I'll do it, old man. I'm mighty sorry about the kid."

To Matt, Raymond turned. "Go on with your meeting without me. I can do nothing till this boy dodges this fever." And Kelly went away, reluctantly, to meet with the leaders of the neutral party, robbed of half his resolution, for he, too, loved the sick lad.

At twelve o'clock, when some of the men were passing, he went out and called Baker and said, in the tone of one who has at last decided on a plan of action, "I want you to carry a message to Boggy, and see that it gets there."

And Baker, having a long training as cow-boy behind him, accepted his order like a soldier.

"All right, Rob, she goes."

Raymond pencilled the telegram and handed it to the messenger. "Tell the operator to send this to the sheriff, and ask no questions. See that he tears it up. You may meet Frank Brown—you remember him— worked for Williams one season—"

Baker nodded.

"If you do, tell him Louis is sick and you're going to wire his sister; but slip round him if you can. The counter-sign is 'Contact—porphyry—and slate.' When you've got the operator clicking pull out and ride back hard."

The telegram was addressed to the sheriff, and read:

"They're onto your box-car game. Look out!
"A PEACE LOVER."

At one o'clock Kelly returned with lowering brow. "I wish you'd been there, lad. They're afraid of Munro and voted me down. We are to do nothing."

Raymond, submerged in the rising flood of his anxiety, looked at his partner dully. "Well, perhaps it's better so, Matt. I gave my word to Ann

Louis Calls for Ann

that I would care for this boy as if he were my brother, and I'm going to do it, regardless of every other consideration. If he grows worse I shall send for Ann, and then I will have double reason to keep out of the movement."

Kelly was silent for a little space, then slowly replied: "I can't blame ye, Rob. She's worth more than the whole dom peak and the inhabitants thrown in. I'm on guard to-night, and I'll look in now and then. Let me know if I can help."

Raymond, waiting for the dawn, debated with himself whether to ask Ann to come at once or to wait. Now that he had seen her once more in the comfort and security of Barnett's home, it seemed cruel, almost criminal, to ask her to return; and yet the boy's restless tossing and moaning indicated developing fever, and towards daylight he called Kelly. "Send a message to Ann. Louis is a mighty sick boy and needs her care." And his face was white with anxiety as he spoke.

XXIV

Ann Returns to Sky-Town

THE morning paper, which the maid brought to
Ann while she still drowsed in her bed, contained the news of Louis' arrival at Raymond's cabin
and his collapse. It was only a curt paragraph in
the midst of wild head-lines about the mob, but its
wording froze the girl's blood. For a moment she
lay, while her mind ran over the possibilities of the
situation.

"All the early part of the night," the reporter went
on to say, "bands of clamorous men marched from
mine to mine, calling upon the gangs to lay down
their tools. Only two firms remained unintimidated
—Reese Brothers and Kelly & Raymond. In the
midst of all this turmoil," said the reporter, "Raymond, one of the men most concerned, was standing
guard over a sick boy, and would not leave his side
for a moment." Ann glowed with a sense of deep
obligation to that watcher.

Mrs. Barnett knocked on her door and called,
"Have you seen the papers, Ann Marie?"

"Yes."

"What are you going to do?"

"I am going up there."

Mrs. Barnett entered. "How *can* you go—with

356

that mob in possession. **You** must *not* go! It isn't
safe for you, and I will not consent to have Don go
again. Who will protect you?"

Ann flamed with wrath. "Have you no law out
here that will protect a girl who goes to nurse her
sick brother? I have nothing to do with your
idiotic wars. I am going up there as a citizen of
New York, not as a partisan of your side of this
struggle. I shall not leave **that** boy there to suffer
alone."

Mrs. Barnett reeled with the force of Ann's attack.
"Perhaps he isn't so ill—he couldn't be—he left here
perfectly well."

"I know he is ill—terribly ill—or Mr. Raymond
would not sit by his side all night when he was so
badly needed elsewhere."

"You surely cannot blame us — or even yourself—"

Then the reaction came and Ann reached for her
friend's neck. "Oh, I wish I had never seen this
barbarous country."

Mrs. Barnett, being wise, took proper measure of
this mood. As she went away she said: "I will
call Don and we will see what can be done."

As her indignation cooled, Ann's heart went out
to Raymond; his intrepidity, his loyalty, and his love
for Louis came back to her.

She imagined him sitting there alone through the
long night, hearing the tumult outside, knowing
Kelly's need of him, yet refusing to consider any
other duty. This gave her pleasure, even while it
indicated the seriousness of the boy's condition.
"And Matt and Nora — they were loyal, too," she

cried out, in a glow, "and Nora is such a good little nurse."

Mrs. Barnett re-entered a few moments later deeply disturbed. "I can't find Don; he must have gone down-town. Some one has just 'phoned a message from Rob. He says Louis has taken a chill, and that you are to come, if you can, but not to worry. He is well cared for."

"Can we reach him by telegraph?"

"The operator says there is no direct connection with Sky-Town, but that the wire from Bozle to the south is uncut. We can try."

"Tell Don to wire Mr. Raymond that I am coming at once, and that I will bring Dr. Braide, if possible," answered Ann, alert and self-contained.

She rang Dr. Braide's telephone a few moments later, and called, firmly, "Dr. Braide, I want you to go with me to Sky-Town—"

His cool, indifferent voice cut her short. "Who is it, please?"

"It is Ann Rupert—"

"Ah!" His voice changed—became swift, eager. "Certainly, certainly, Miss Rupert; I understand. I saw the note about your brother. It will be a privilege. I will run over at once and discuss the best plan for getting there."

"Thank you. Please come soon, for I am very anxious."

"I sympathize with your feeling."

Ann was eating her breakfast when the bell rang, and the maid, at her order, brought the doctor into the dining-room, looking very natty, very keen, and **very** much pleased. This too **obvious** enjoyment of his service cooled Ann's tone. "Have you had your breakfast, Dr. Braide?"

He bowed and smiled, a little too gayly. "As General Scott would say, I snatched a hasty chop."

She icily ignored his jocularity. "I am asking a great deal of you, doctor; I will gladly recompense you for any loss of patients, but this is a case—"

"Please don't trouble about my patients. It is a pleasure for me to serve you. I beg you not to bring it down to so mercenary a plane."

"That's very kind of you, but I must insist on making it a matter of professional service," replied Ann, for he, too, was a suitor, and she liked him, but at this moment she wanted his skill—his training as a physician, not his adoration. This he had insight enough to perceive, and, dropping all gallantry, made direct and practical suggestions as to the best means of reaching the camp.

"We can go by the Southern Railway, and drive from Sage Flat, or we can go over the stage-road. In either case we must meet and pass Munro's guard; according to all accounts he has a complete circle."

"I am not afraid of Munro or his men," she answered. "In fact, they will be our safeguard. I will telegraph to Mr. Munro that we are coming, and he will see that we are protected."

"If you feel that way, then the simplest and quickest route is over the old stage-road. With a good span of horses and a light cart we can drive to Bozle by four o'clock and reach Sky-Town before dark."

"Then let us go!" she cried, rising. "I will order a carriage at once, and call for you in half an hour."

"I will be ready," he alertly replied.

By means of the telephone Ann ordered the livery-man to harness his best span of horses to a mountain buckboard. "No, I do not need a driver," she sharply answered to his query. "Get them here quick!"

Before she left the receiver Barnett came rushing into the room. "What's all this? Jeannette tells me you're going back to Sky-Town to-day?"

"In twenty minutes I shall be on the road."

"Alone?"

"No, Dr. Braide is going with me."

"Impossible! You mustn't do it! Our attack is to be made to-night. The whole hill will be a battle-ground to-morrow."

"I can't help that, Don. I must go to my brother. He needs me all the more. Think of that poor boy lying there burning with fever and a battle going on! Put off your attack. It's all foolish, wicked, anyhow. What good will it do? You will only kill men, or get killed yourself. There is enough sorrow in the world without making more. I think you mine-owners are all acting silly—positively silly. Anyhow, I am go-ing."

He spoke in a calmer tone. "How are you going?"

"I've ordered a team from the livery."

"Why didn't you take some of my horses?"

"I don't want to take them into the cold and danger up there. Now please don't try to stop me. My mind is made up, the team is ordered, and you will only hinder me. Go on with your opera-bouffe campaign. Take no thought of Louis or me — that's the way Napoleon would do—all great commanders sacrifice life. Louis and I will try to escape somehow."

This strange mood in the girl puzzled him and daunted him, and, grumbling inarticulately, he retreated, seeking reinforcements, while Ann hastily ordered together the warm things she needed. When she appeared, splendidly robed in furs, she looked like a Russian princess on her way to her sleigh, though her anxious face belied her grandeur.

Barnett, now quite distracted, did his best to make her comfortable in the scant-bodied wagon, which offered very little protection from the cold winds.

As the driver leaped out, Mrs. Barnett shrieked from the piazza, "Ann, you're not going to drive?"

Ann kissed the tips of her gloves towards the house, nodded, and took up the lines. "They're not pretty," she said, speaking of the horses.

"They're chain-lightnin', all the same, miss. Can you manage 'em—think?"

"I'm quite sure of it," she said, and drew the reins taut. "Good-bye, everybody," and at her chirp the lank, yellow cayuses swung in swift circle and were off.

Dr. Braide was waiting as she drew up to his door. He carried a big bear-skin robe over his arm and held a medicine-case in his hand. "Have you plenty of wraps? It's cold up there, they say. Let me arrange this robe round your feet. Shall I drive?"

"No, thank you; I will drive."

He was a little longer tucking her in than she thought necessary, and her tone was a bit sharper as she said, "Come, doctor, we are losing time."

The young man sprang in with flushed face and shining eyes. "This is, indeed, a glorious enterprise," he gayly shouted. And it was. To sit beside a splendid girl on a journey towards a towering, storm-hid peak, hurrying towards a battle-field in the sky, does not come to many men in their lifetime. He was not discouraged by her curtness—that was probably due to her anxiety; and, besides, he was the leading physician of the town, of eminent family, and quite justified in having a very good opinion of himself. Ann had always been gracious to him; he had even permitted himself to fancy she admired him, and on this long ride in the wild, in the service to her brother, what might not happen?

Ann was deeply irritated by his presence, by some self-satisfaction lurking in his voice, and it was only by thinking hard upon his skill and how much it would mean to Louis that she was able to endure his touch. In the case of Wayne Peabody this feeling of repulsion amounted only to a mild distaste; with Braide it was actual shrinking.

The doctor, with carefully modulated voice (neither too gay nor too grave), discussed the probabilities. "We'll find the boy much better, I'm sure of it. It's rather curious, but I was pressed to go with the column to-night to be ready in case of accident; but declined, pleading my duties to my patients; now here I am going gladly, and my patients waiting." He said this with full intent to have her know with how much weight her lightest wish pressed upon him.

A realization of this indebtedness already troubled the proud girl. She was quite ready to face a money obligation, but she had asked something of this young man which he would have put aside disdainfully from any other person, and this fact rendered her resentful.

"However, Mr. Raymond would not even have hinted at my coming had he not been very anxious, and I will go on," she decided, though the thought of the long drive with this powerful young masculine and insistent personality by her side fairly frightened her. "What will we talk about?" she thought. "He must be careful."

"You're a wonderful whip," he began, after a silence.

"I used to do a great deal of it some years ago."

"I'm afraid you'll tire—let me relieve you?"

"No, I prefer to govern; it helps me bear the suspense," she added, a little more graciously.

"I can understand that," he admitted, with a keen glance of admiration.

The horses were, indeed, marvels; they pushed up the steep, winding road with steady stride, their awkward heads swinging. Not till they entered the cañon did they lag into a walk. The clouds hung low, in great, gray masses, covering even the secondary peaks. Patches of snow began to appear at the road-side. It was a bleak, inhospitable, and silent world. Not a branch was in motion. The wind, a slight, slow, circling current of air, remained high like a hawk, uncertain of purpose. Only the trickle of water dripping from the beds of snow could be heard as the horses stopped now and again for a rest.

"There is something ominous in this stillness," Ann said, at last.

"Where do you suppose we will meet Munro's men?"

"Anywhere after we leave the half-way house, according to report."

"You know this man Munro?"

"I've met him."

"Is he as terrible as people think him?"

"He seemed very boyish to me and not at all terrible."

"The morning papers stated that he had assumed absolute control up there and that his men were drilled in true military fashion."

"So much the better for us," answered Ann, "for he will see that we are protected."

After a pause the young doctor began again: "Raymond made a miraculous recovery. What a physique that fellow has. I shall be interested in seeing him again."

Another pause intervened. "It is singular what a passion a boy will sometimes conceive for a man of action like that. Don tells me that Raymond is Louis' exemplar, and yet to us he is merely a fine young rancher."

Ann refused to be drawn into a discussion of Raymond by this lure, and Braide went on, shying a little from the danger-point. "Still, these men of good, natural ability sometimes develop swiftly under favoring conditions. Raymond is a man of some education, and to strike it rich might send him to Congress. He has a strong following even here in the Springs. His course has been temperate all through this trouble."

Ann continuing unresponsive, he returned to the weather and to admiration of the magnificent cliffs round which the road ran, climbing steadily and swiftly. Once or twice they met a string of freight teams, whose drivers stared heavily at the sight of a pretty girl in superb furs driving a pair of bony broncos.

At about eleven o'clock they reached the wide mountain meadow out of which the Bear Creek fell.

Ann Returns to Sky-Town

The clouds hung just above their heads, a broad, seamless, gray roof, and as they drove across the level ground the landscape grew steadily bleaker and more desolate, and the wind, unimpeded by forests, cut remorselessly as it swept into their faces. Much as she disliked to do so, Ann was forced to yield the reins to Braide, her hands being numb with cold.

At the half-way house they found a stage-load of people and several freighters, and every man's mouth was agape. Braide sprang out, briskly calling to a slouchy individual who seemed a little in advance of the other loafers:

"Can you stable our team for an hour?"

"I reckon we kin, stranger; that's what we're here for."

"Very well, do so, and blanket them," he added, and Ann liked him for that.

The tavern was a survival of the days when railroads were of the far-away future; a long, low, log structure with a roof of dirt out of which dead weeds flaunted. The front room, which swarmed with men in rough clothing, seemed to be a country store and post-office as well as an eating-house. A small, active old woman met Ann with toothless grin. "Step right this way and get out o' the smudge."

Ann followed her into a minute bedroom which opened off the dining-room. The old woman began to clatter. "Put off your things here. My! but them's fine furs! Did ye drive up from the Springs? Wait a second, and I'll get some hot water." She was miraculously spry for one of her age, and soon returned, her eyes gleaming with a new thought. "Are you going on to the camp?"

"Yes."

"Wal, you'll find it lively up there! As near as I can learn they mean biz!" she whispered. "Some o' Jack Munro's men are in there now eatin'. They keep a mighty sharp watch on who comes in these days. Soon's you're ready I'll put you and your man down at my end of the table and I'll look after ye."

Ann laid aside her furs, but retained her hat, and as she re-entered the room made a dazzling appeal to those rough fellows, who eyed her with sly side-glances.

Braide, already seated, rose to meet her. "We have reached an outpost of the guard, and will be interrogated before we leave, I fear."

"I am quite ready to meet them," she replied, bending to her plate. "They can't refuse to let us pass."

The talk at the table was not illuminating. Each man apparently strove to fill his paunch before his fellow. Only one of them seemed to study Ann and her companion with candid interest. This was a small man with a chin-beard and an eye as keen as that of a bluejay. His voice was a drawling nasal and his manner assured. As the other men filled up and left the table, he came down and carelessly took a seat near Braide.

"I reckon I've seen you before," he began, pleasantly.

"I shouldn't wonder. I'm Dr. Braide, of Valley Springs."

The stranger glowed. "Why, sure thing! That's it. I heard you make a speech once in a county convention. You're the man that treated Rob Raymond, aren't you, out to Barnett's ranch?"

"The very same."

"Where you aimin' to go now, if it's a fair question?"

"To Sky-Town."

"People ain't travellin' that way much just now."

"Goin' to treat somebody?" asked the old woman, who was hovering near.

Ann interposed. "Yes, he is going up to treat my brother Louis, who is lying very ill at Mr. Raymond's cabin."

The stranger glowed again. "Well, now, I'm glad you told me that. I've heard of you, and I've met 'Raymond's kid,' as we call him. So he's sick, is he? Well, it's a bad time to be sick. He'd better be down at the Springs. Still, a feller can't always choose times to be sick. Didn't see nothin' of the sheriff's army on the way, did ye?" Here he winked at Braide.

The doctor smiled. "Not a thing. I don't think they've left the valley yet."

"I'd advise 'em not to. I'm glad you're going up. That's a fine boy, that brother of yourn, madam. I hear he can draw a horse and put a man on him natural as life. I'm going over to the camp myself, and if you don't mind I'll jest nacherly jog along a rod or two ahead of you—to show you the road."

During this conversation every one but a boy at the opposite end of the table had risen and walked out, only the old woman and the girl waiter seemed undisguisedly listening.

As he rose to go, the stranger said: "If so be it you folks have any influence with Rob Raymond, preach him into joining the movement. It 'll be a mighty sight safer for him, and a big help to the miners." There was a notable dignity and gravity in his face and

367

voice as he uttered this, and, as if in answer to Ann's unspoken query, he added: "Yes, I'm a mine-owner myself. I stood out for a while like Kelly. I'm one of the old-time burro-punchers—but, after all, the working-miner is my people. If I had a million I wouldn't fit in with Mackay and Barnett and their dude friends."

After the miner left the room, Braide said: "We're in the enemy's country. He was plainly warning us, and his going along is in the nature of an armed guard."

"His escort may be of use to us," replied Ann. "Who was that man?" she asked of the old woman, who fairly whispered her answer.

"That's old Steve Adams. He's boss of this squad. All six o' them men are Munro's pickets."

"We have fallen into good hands," said Ann. "I like that little man, he's so gentle."

"Gentle! Wal, if the yarns they tell of him is true, he is pizen as a rattlesnake, for all he's so low-voiced. We're all skeered to death of him."

"You don't sympathize with the miners, then?" asked Braide.

"Wal, now, sometimes I do, and then again I don't."

"Depends on the run o' custom, I suppose?" retorted Braide, rather cynically.

"How?" she asked, a little bewildered.

Ann put an end to this. "We must be going;" and the old lady never did understand the doctor's remark.

As Ann walked out through the front room, blue with smoke and filthy with spittle, her face was impassive as marble, but the lines of her lips were disdainful. "They are such nasty brutes," was her thought. The teamsters on their part became silent as she passed, and those in her path fell back against the counter as if fearing the touch of her sweeping cloak. But each man's eye, round, furtive, followed her stately stepping as if eager to fix in his brain this unexpected vision of superb young womanhood, and when she had passed from sight one man looked at the others, and, drawing a deep breath, uttered a low oath: "Man! She's a peach!"

Ann drew a deep breath also, but it was of the pure, outside air, in hope of driving out every least atom of the odor which had sunk deep into her lungs. She shuddered as though she had suffered some defilement from the glances of the loafers. By contrast, Dr. Braide was a dazzling creature, and she submitted to the touch of his hand to her elbow with less of the repulsion which filled her at the start. She also permitted him to drive, for her hands were tired.

The clouds began to lift, rolling slowly, ponderously, reluctantly upward from the timbered slopes, unveiling crag after crag of purple-gray rock, while far to the west a narrow gap in the hurrying ranks permitted the blue sky to be seen.

Their guide rode rapidly, signalling the doctor now and then to keep pace with him, and after nearly an hour of fairly level ground the road entered another cañon and crawled upwards along a prodigious wall, which beat back the clashing roar of a small but very swift stream of water. The tired horses lagged up this grade, and the horseman before them pulled up and fell in behind to talk a little disjointedly.

"Your brother passed through here yesterday, so the boys say. I didn't see him. He was all right then, but he weren't dressed for this kind o' weather. Likely he took a chill. He don't look overly strong. I hope it ain't nothin' serious. 'Peared to be a right likely kind of a boy."

Ann did not attempt to reply to his prattle, and he seemed not to expect it, and, after a few more disconnected remarks, rode ahead again and remained there, his graceful, small figure swaying most picturesquely to the motion of his horse.

"He carried a rifle under his thigh and a revolver under his coat," remarked Braide. "Did you notice them?"

"I saw the rifle," Ann quietly replied, and thereafter they rode practically in silence. It must have been about five o'clock when they rounded the base of the Black Cone at the head of the cañon, and looked away across the big camp and far out upon the valley to the west. The clouds still hung low on Mogalyon, and the shadow rested on Sky-Camp; but the mighty "Hesperian wall," as her father called it, was bathed in a flood of sunlight so pure, so dazzling, that each prodigious peak seemed translucent as a lily. The white mass rose into the deep blue of the western sky, as summer clouds loom after rain—sharply defined, yet soft as down.

The girl cried out with delight. "Oh, that wonderful range, always so beautiful, yet never the same. We are in the shadow, they are in the light. I am taking that as a good omen. There must be peace on the other side of this ugly contention between the valley and the peak." At the moment it expressed to her some of the magic, the mystery, and the allurement with which it called to her father a quarter of a century before.

Adams, their guide, was a considerable distance in

advance when a couple of horsemen encountered them. After a moment's conference one turned back and the other came on swiftly.

Ann's heart glowed with the hope that it might be Raymond with a message from the sick one. But it proved to be Munro. She recognized his mount and his way of riding long before she could distinguish his face. He came up swiftly, and, setting his horse upon his haunches, leaped cavalierly to the ground.

"Good-evening, lady," he called, as he approached the wagon. "Have you journeyed far?"

"How is Louis?" asked Ann, quickly, with instant revolt of his assurance.

He felt the impersonal rebuke of her manner and replied, simply: "He is better this afternoon, so I hear. I have not had time to call. It is a pleasure to see you again." He fixed his eyes on her companion. "I don't think I know you," he said, with a challenging inflection in his voice.

"I am Dr. Braide, of Valley Springs."

Ann explained. "Dr. Braide comes to attend to my brother."

Munro's face lost its reckless smile, and he looked worn and pale. "Doctor, I'm glad to meet you. I'd like you to attend a patient of mine. In a conflict of authority I maimed a man, and he needs skilled attendance."

"I'll do what I can for him, after my visit to the boy. What news have you? How is everything on the hill?"

"Very quiet, just now. We are waiting for the sheriff and his army. We are on the defensive."

"We must hurry on," interrupted Ann, warmly impatient of Munro's glances.

Braide chirped to his horses, and Munro swung to his seat and galloped after. At the foot of the hill he called: "Keep that winding road; it will bring you to the top, near Kelly's. I'll meet you there."

The peak was more than quiet, it was silent. No longer did the brakes of the ore wagons and the trucks cry out. The tall, iron smoke-stacks were stripped of their purple banners. The jaws of the stamp-mills idly gaped. The metal-cars stood in contemplative calm on the apices of their dumps. Around each shaft-house one or two watchmen moved listlessly. It was as if a palsy had fallen upon every able-bodied work-man, causing a swift-devouring decay to set in.

"What a change!" exclaimed Braide. "I was here just before this trouble began, and these hills teemed with men—"

"There is one smoking chimney; it must be the Ray-mond & Kelly mine." Ann pointed away up the hill.

"How do they keep going?"

"The strikers fear them, and, besides, Munro and Raymond are old acquaintances. I think he protects them."

As they rose the sun sank rapidly, and, short as the distance appeared, they were nearly an hour climbing to the foot of the overlook. Ann ached with impa-tience, but the horses were weary and too breathless to be hurried. The peak became each moment more inexorable, more sinister. With the thought of Louis and his needs, the physical barriers grew greater and more numerous—distances lengthened.

Raymond was standing at the Kellys' door as they drove up, his face sombre, his eyes clouded. He could not speak, so deeply was he moved; but, with a nod at

Braide and without a word, threw back the robes and reached a hand to help her. "How is he?" she asked, with a catching of the breath.

"He is very ill, but I think—" his voice failed him for a moment. "I'm glad to see you, doctor. He needs you."

Everything whirled before Ann. "If he should die— oh, if he should die! It's all my fault!" she wailed. "It's all my fault!" and her numb limbs refused to move.

"Don't say that," he urged. "I've gone over it a thousand times. I don't see that any one is to blame. I *know* you are not! Come, we must go to him."

In that instant something seemed to pass between them—some invisible, intangible bond was established. Ann put out her hand and he took it gently between his palms. "Be brave, dear girl," he said, tenderly.

She suddenly roused herself and hurried towards the cabin. Mrs. Kelly came to meet her with arms opened wide, her sweet face pale with pity. "Oh, Ann, darlin', we're needin' ye!"

Ann went to her for an instant, then put her aside and knelt beside the bed. Her heart grew icy cold with the horror and the pity of seeing that blithe, boyish face set and livid, the brows grave with the gravity of battle. His eyes were closed, and, at the moment, he appeared to be dying. She caught his lax hand and kissed it passionately. "Louis, speak to me! Speak to sister!"

Her low cry pierced Raymond's heart, and, while he stood helpless, sick with sympathetic pain, the doctor took Ann gently by the arm. "Please leave me alone with Louis for a few minutes. Trust him to me."

Ann turned blindly towards Raymond, her throat aching with sobs of remorse. "Oh, if I had only stayed here!"

Raymond turned comforter. "The doctor is right. His case is not decided yet. You must remember how strong and well he has been. He's not the pale slip he was when he came here. Please go over to the house and let Nora make some tea for you," he pleaded, and at last she yielded, and with a final look at the sick boy went out with Mrs. Kelly.

With that half-superstitious confidence which even the most intelligent feel when the doctor is present, Raymond soon followed. He was tired—tired! His long ride to the valley and back, his lack of sleep—but especially his anxiety—had worn upon him so that now, when he could shift some part of his responsibility, his steel-woven frame began to quiver and his brain to thicken. He sank into a chair and laxly looked at Ann.

"It is sweet to see you," he uttered, slowly—"doubly sweet because of Louis. We've done our best, Nora and I. I was in agony for fear you would not come to-night. I didn't want to shirk responsibility or labor—but—I—I wanted you. It's been a long day for me."

Mrs. Kelly explained: "Rob is dyin' for lack o' sleep. That's the truth. He wouldn't leave the boy, and after riding all the day and the night before. But come now, have some tea—both. My mind is easier since the doctor came. Sure I know he will check the fever, never fear that."

Raymond soon put down his cup and rose. "Your drink has done me good, Nora; I will go back to the doctor and see if he needs help. You stay here," he said to Ann, and his voice was intimate and tender. "I will report at once."

When he re-entered a few moments later his tone was cheerful. "The doctor has made his examination and is confident of heading off pneumonia."

Ann's face lit with joy. "Oh, did he say that?" She reached both her hands to him. "Now you can go sleep; I will watch to-night."

Together they returned to the bungalow, and Raymond, after a moment's conversation with Braide, threw himself on his couch. "Ah! this seems good," he exclaimed to Ann, and fell asleep almost instantly.

She drew the robe over him with careful hands and turned to Braide, "I'm so grateful to you, Dr. Braide."

"Don't speak of it. To serve you is a very great pleasure to me." His tone was sincere and manly and helped to reinstate him in her esteem. "I'm ferociously hungry," he added, "and the banging of pans in the shack back of us is suggestive, not to say tantalizing."

"You are to eat supper with the Kellys," she answered. "I think you would better go over to the house now. I will stay with Louis."

He protested against this, but she had her will. "In case he grows restless," he said at the door, "call me. However, I will return in half an hour, probably."

A suffocating throb of tenderness rose in Ann's throat as she bent above Louis' flushed face and listened to his troubled breathing. Life seemed a very feeble and evanescent power in his slender frame, and the persistence of his heart-beat a miracle. Raymond lay in profoundest slumber, his face in shadow, but his presence was most palpable and appealing. Somehow, since the touch of his hands to hers, he seemed nearer, less strange, and an impulse to stoop and touch his forehead with her lips came to her. She felt herself in the grasp of some new and searching power, an influence which she had resented, with which she now battled.

Nora came softly in. "Ann, dear, the supper is on the table; go you along and eat. You're needed to keep the peace."

"Peace between whom?"

"Munro and Matt."

"Is Munro there?"

"He's waiting to see you. Keep him from Matt; he's in a bad temper to-night."

Ann went out with a wrinkle of vexation on her brow.

Munro was waiting just outside the door in the clear, yellow dusk.

"How is the boy?" he asked, as she drew near.

"He is better, thank you."

"I'm mighty glad to hear it. I was worried about him on my own account. You see, he was brought to me by one of my vedettes, and as he had a great deal of information, I kept him with us."

"I hope you didn't ask him to betray his friends?"

"He was ready to talk."

"You shouldn't have listened. He is only a boy."

"It is no more than fair, lady, that one member of your household should be loyal to labor." His eyes burned into hers as he bent towards her. "What has changed you towards me?" he asked, with stern abruptness. "You give me nothing but 'marble

376

brows' these days. What have I done that you shut your door in my face?"

Ann experienced a certain helplessness in the face of this audacity.

"What you do is of no consequence to me, except so far as my brother is concerned."

He was too keen not to perceive his advantage. "No woman can play with me and not get cinched at some part of the game."

"What do you mean?"

"You know what I mean. You were amused with 'the wild man' for a time; you played me against Rob for the fun of it, and then pulled out with Peabody. Was that nice? Was that a square deal to Rob? This boy's sickness is a punishment. It brings you back where I count. You can't escape me so easily as that, my girl."

"You are beside yourself—I will not listen—"

He laughed. "Oh, I don't mind; I had a little fun out of it myself. I had never met just your kind before, and I thought you were a little different, but you weren't. You are like all the rest. I reckon you've played a hundred men in the same way, but you can't play me twice."

Ann recoiled before a certain savagery in his voice, and, with her hand on the latch of the door, answered, very slowly: "You interested me, I admit; you're very amusing at this moment, but you have no reason, no right, to say that I gave you the slightest encouragement to—to take this attitude towards me. It is the baldest presumption on your part."

At this moment Kelly opened the door. "Is it you, Ann?" He stepped aside. "Go in, girl, ye're supper's waitin'." Ann slipped in, glad to escape under the great arm which barred Munro's passage. "You stay outside," Kelly said to the young desperado, and his voice was dangerously calm. "I want a word with you. The blood of this night's work will be on your head, me lad. You can't excuse yourself by sayin' the committee demands it. *You* are the committee. Great God, man, you're crazy!"

The young leader laughed. "They're the crazy ones, to come up against my men on this hill with a lot of old soaks, one-lungers, and ex-policemen dead on their hoofs. But don't worry, there'll be no battle—the clatter of a tin can will scare 'em into bug-house fits. Now, Matt, let me finish what I came to say. We've been good friends, and I want to keep friends. You're a fair man, but, let me tell you, the boys are getting bitter against you independents in this fight. You have no business to stand out against the union."

Kelly harshly interrupted him. "I don't. I stand out against reckless devils like you, who think they can stand off the whole United States army. We've been all over this afore—"

"I know we have, and now let me say that I've stood for you and Rob a dozen times, but I'm done. If you want to go down to history as a traitor to the cause of labor—"

Kelly lifted his big fist in a gesture of menace. "Listen to me, Jack Munro; I've been a working-miner all me life, whilst you were at school—whilst you were playin' hooky and stealin' plums, and all the years you've been runnin' a roulette-wheel I was pickin' at the rocks. If any man is fitted to advise 'tis Matt Kelly, and not a play-actor and celluloid bunco-steerer like y'rself. Go yer ways, Jack Munro, but lave me and mine alone. This ends it. Ye'll have no welcome from the Kellys' door after this night's work, and if ye put so much as the toe of ye're boot across me path I'll kill you for the reckless, murderin' devil that ye are!"

Munro reeled under this gusty blast, but recovered himself. "You'll be coming to me for help inside of twenty-four hours, and you'll get it for the sake of Nora and the kids. Good-night."

And vaulting to his saddle he rode away, leaving Kelly bewildered and a little ashamed of his outburst.

"Was he intoxicated?" asked Ann, as Matt re-entered the cabin.

The old miner shook his big head in mystification.

"Drunk or sober, he's too flighty for the Kellys. He slips out o' me hand like sand."

XXV

A Day of Action

AGAIN Ann Rupert found herself confronting a question of life and death, and a sense of her own weakness and dependence brought her very near to the resolute young man whose silent presence comforted her during the long hours of watching. The knowledge that he was there within call, ready to serve her to the outrance, rendered her vigilance less lonely. Dr. Braide's manner towards her had also changed. It was evident that he considered Raymond an accepted lover. Therefore, he no longer paid court, and his care of the boy remained absorbedly professional. He spoke with positiveness of his ability to check the fever, and this confidence reached and influenced Ann, though she could not put away a sense of guilt and a weight of fear.

Louis came to himself just before midnight, and recognized her; and though his breath was labored and his face lined with suffering, it was good to feel his familiar self reaching out to her from his house of pain.

"How did you get here?" he asked.

"I drove with Dr. Braide."

"I'm pretty sick. I'm glad you came, sis," and he put his hand feebly into hers. "Where's Rob?"

A Day of Action

"He's sleeping. You must be quiet now, or you'll wake him."

"He's been good to me."

"I know he has, laddie."

"So was Jack. I was awful hungry, and I was so cold—"

"Sh! dearest," she pleaded; "don't talk now. Go to sleep."

"I don't want to sleep. I've slept enough. It makes my head ache worse."

Ann glanced at Braide, who came and bent above the boy. His voice was most admirably firm, yet gentle, as he began: "You want to get out of here soon, don't you?" The boy nodded. "Very well then; you must be quiet and do exactly as we tell you. Sleep is good for you. Besides, your sister needs rest, and you don't want to keep her awake."

In the end he prevailed, and the boy ceased to groan and twist, and at last slept; but Ann refused to go to bed. Her anxiety and the many questions pressing to be answered engaged her so deeply that she felt no need of sleep. Towards midnight, Braide, in despair of inducing her to sleep, stretched himself in a low chair and fell into a doze.

It was exactly two o'clock when a single gun-shot rang out sharply, like the voice of a sentinel questioning the silent night. As the girl listened tensely, three others, deeper-throated, answered in quick succession. Then silence again intervened for a moment, only to be torn by a fusillade—a rat-tat-tat of assault—which brought Braide to his feet.

Ann hurried to Raymond, calling, sharply, "Rob, they are shooting! Don't you hear them? Quick! Quick!"

Raymond rose to his feet dizzily and looked at her blankly, the mist of sleep thick in his brain. Other shots and cries followed, and though faint and far, they cleared his vision. Catching a belt of cartridges from the wall, and turning to Braide, he sternly asked, "Can you shoot?"

Before Braide could answer another shrill chorus of yells, fierce as the outcry of wolves, arose, a vivid light filled the room, and a second later a dull concussion shook the earth beneath their feet. Ann shrank and cowered, but Raymond, menacingly quiet, remarked: "Well, our turn has come. They've blown up our shaft-house."

"Oh no!" cried Ann. "They wouldn't do that. They daren't do that."

"That's what they've done," he bitterly assured her. Then a thought entered his mind which staggered him. "The men—the men were in the mine!" he shouted, and rushed into the darkness.

Ann heard his blows upon the door of the other cabin as he called: "Boys, roll out! The power-house is blown up! The men are in the mine! Quick, out with you! Buckle your guns!"

Then the girl recognized Kelly's great voice; he was calling as he ran, "Rob, are ye there?"

"Yes, I'm rousing the boys."

"It's the shaft-house."

"It looks that way."

"And the men, lad, the men?"

"I don't know, Matt, I've just got on my feet."

"May the fires o' hell blister the bones of the man—"

So much Ann heard before the sound of their feet

died away down the path. The sleepers in the bunk-house began to rumble and clatter about on the bare floors. One by one they emerged, slamming the door behind them. The distant wailing of Mrs. Kelly's scared children added a poignant note of fear, and a moment later the little mother herself came flying across the yard in her bare feet, her face white and distorted.

"Oh, saints above! What have they done now? Are you hurt? What is it all about?"

Ann caught her by the arms. "Where are your shoes? You must go back instantly; you can do no good. They have blown up the mine."

"Mother o' God! What mine? Our mine? Why should they do that? Oh, the fiends! What's the light? Is the mill burning?"

Braide, from the doorway, called out, "Yes, the wreckage is ablaze; the men are fighting it."

Once outside the door the women could see the flames growing each moment in power, licking with avid tongues at the confused mass of splintered beams, and on the curtain of red light the forms of Kelly and Raymond played in silhouette, as they strove furiously against the destroyer. Their workmen soon joined them, and each moment some hastening rescuer hurtled past the open door, and, as he ran, cursed in bitter frenzy.

"Ann!" called Louis from the bed. Faint as it was, the girl heard his cry and hurried to his side.

"Yes, I'm here, laddie. What do you want? How do you feel?"

"My head aches so. I can't breathe good. He moaned. "Oh, dear, I'm so hot." The voice of his anguish stung Ann to the soul. With a sign to Nora commanding silence, she closed the door, in the hope that no sound from the burning mine would penetrate to the bedside. If at that moment she could have set her foot on the swarming camp as on a nest of vermin she would have done it, so valueless were their lives in her indignation and despair. Of such revenges she had read; now here they were, breaking forth at her feet like fountains of blood and fire, imperilling the lives of innocent women and children.

Nora hurried back to her cabin, while Braide dropped some helpful drug upon the boy's tongue. When his patient had grown quiet, the young physician said: "If you are not afraid, I will go down. Some one may be hurt and my help required."

"Go; I am not afraid," she commanded. "Only, remember your first duty is here."

"I do not forget that," he answered. But even as he was collecting his outer clothing and his medicines, Raymond flung the door open and entered. His hands were blackened and bleeding, his head was bare, and on his face was a look that thrilled the girl. "Doctor, three wounded men are coming up the hill—they must be made comfortable. Ann, you would better go back to Kelly's; these victims must be sheltered here, and they are not pleasant to see."

Ann felt herself diminishing in power and importance as he spoke. His voice came from the man's world—harsh, inflexible—but she uttered a protest: "Louis!"

His face softened and his hand went to his brow. "I forgot; you are right, we must not endanger him. I will have the men taken to the other cabin."

A Day of Action

"Are the men in the mine all dead?"

"We can't tell. The engineer and some of the men on the dump were warned and escaped. The rest are below and out of our reach. We are working desperately to subdue the flames, but we are almost helpless for lack of water."

"It is horrible!"

His voice was very quiet as he said, "Munro shall answer for this!"

"Did he do it?"

"He did not prevent it!" He lifted his eyes to the sky. "It will soon be light, and then we can see to work."

He turned to leave without further explanation, but Ann called to him, "Send us word when you can, won't you?"

"As soon as we know the men are alive I will come and tell you," he promised, and hurried away into the gray dusk of the dawn; and his anger, his aloofness, his furious self-restraint raised him in the estimation of the girl. Gallantry at such a time would have been as noisome as drunken laughter.

And as she watched and waited, the day came leisurely, laggardly, over the hills, and swarms of excited men and slattern women poured from their shacks and tents and holes in the rocks to acquire in detail the news of this midnight assault on the leaders of "the independents." To do them justice, even the most virulent unionists were for the moment moved to sympathetic denunciation. The destruction of property was one thing — the murder of workmen quite another. As for the crews of the non-partisans, they were ready at the word of a leader to search out and lynch those who laid the train and fired the fuse; but to all of these Raymond gave the same word of command, "Save the men below."

On the heels of this tumult, as if to pile Pelion on Ossa, messengers came shouting through the sunrise: "The deputies have come! The sheriff's army is camped on the park!"

Instantly the throng of idle sightseers swept back towards the town, leaving not so much as a word of well-wishing to stand in their places. The ruin of the Kelly mine became a small thing to them, now that the real battle was on.

"Where is Jack Munro?" timorous people asked. "Where are the vedettes?" No one seemed to know, and the officers of the union were in a panic.

The sheriff had, indeed, stolen a march on Sky-Town, and was only waiting for daylight to discover his enemy. This was his capital mistake. Had he pushed against the enemy at that moment, with Munro and his men still on a wild-goose chase down the opposite cañon, he might have won the hill in a bloodless charge; but even as he dallied, the vedettes came toiling up the trail from the south, weary but full of fight, and lined out on the northern slope with the fort at their backs. And so at last the two forces of disorder—of passion and prejudice—were set face to face. Battle was now inevitable.

The storm that had muttered and rumbled and shifted ground, and dissipated itself again and again in echoing menace, had gathered head once more and was about to break in tumult. The "yellow-legs" had marched. They had arrived. They fronted the " red-necks," and their little, white tents gleamed like gravestones on the russet sod. In the darkness of the early night they had left the valley, and, to the sound of sobbing and cheers, had entered upon their winding upward course to the clouds and the snows. Only Raymond's warning had saved them from defeat and disaster in the cañon to the south.

Yet now that they were encamped in sight of the enemy they hesitated, for their leaders had been told that the entire hill-side was planted with dynamite— strange bulbs likely to spring up at any moment in destructive white clouds of bloom; and there was further menace—the muzzle of a great gun projected across the rude embankment on the hill and its dark lips seemed to utter a solemn warning; while above and beyond, and more deterrent still, were thousands of desperate men massed against the sky.

And over all — over Raymond and Kelly, dusty and bleeding, working with their men to rescue the imprisoned miners deep below — over the swarming groups of shivering women on the hill, over the bitter and savage ranks of the vedettes, over the whole great, silent range, the sunlight poured in splendor—warm and golden as October—and a soft wind from the west brought rose-tinted clouds sailing like gentle doves of peace from the far-off Crestones, impassive and serene. "What is it all about, my little men?" Mogalyon seemed to ask, concerned as he was with the affairs of geologic cycles and the return of waters to the sea.

XXVI

A Last Appeal

AT sunrise Raymond reported to Ann, his face a little softened. "The dynamiter Baker shot has died, but our men are going to live, the doctor says."

"I am very glad to hear that. What of those in the mine? Are they released?"

"No; but the fire is out and we have cleared the mouth of the shaft. The first level is blocked with rocks and beams. The murderers must have lowered a bomb into the mine with deliberate intent to kill."

"It is horrible to think of them down there in the dark. Did you hear that the sheriff had arrived?"

His eyes darkened. "Yes, the fool! Why didn't he attack at once. Now Munro is entrenched, and they are challenging each other like crowds of school-boys. The time has come for the Governor to take a hand."

"Will he do so?"

"He must, or be party to the bloodiest battle ever seen in the mountains. But I must go back," he said, and turned away abruptly, leaving the girl with a keen sense of the stress and bigness of his life.

He was, indeed, badly needed at the mine, for only the men of the second shift and a few of the crews of Reese and Earle remained to help. Each independent mine was held to be in equal danger and to require the

A Last Appeal

services of its most resolute men; and, besides, the certainty of a battle had drawn away the more excitable, even of their own men. Kelly was working like a Titan, and his presence, his concentration of effort, inspired every man to his best.

A messenger from Carter met Raymond, to assure him that the union had no hand in the outrage, and the young miner sternly answered, "As soon as I have rescued my men, I will demand that the officers of the union have something to do with finding the hyenas that did do it."

Munro sent a letter by Frank Brown, wherein he said, "I can't leave here—the attack may begin at any moment; but I am on the trail, and when I discover the scoundrels I will deliver them to justice."

To this messenger Raymond said: "Tell Jack I want to see him at the earliest moment. This is not a matter for long-range adjustment. I want to talk with him."

Brown, with true cow-boy unconcern, grinned and said: "Well, you see, Rob, Jack's busy just now. They's a ball on, and he's floor-manager for our side."

Raymond was in no mood to respond to humor. "Very well. Say to him that when I have dug my men out, I will come to him," and something in the tone of this answer stopped the grin on the messenger's face.

Reporters drifted up, made hasty notes, and passed on, lured by the more important material disclosed in the opposition of ranked and ready warriors on the hill. Only Dolan stayed, eager and sympathetic, fetching coffee from the cook-house and lending such other aid as he could—so deeply concerned with this tragic deed that he seemed wastefully negligent of his own affairs.

Seizing an opportunity for a private word, he began, in a low voice: "Rob, I know who led this thing. The union had nothing to do with it. It was done by a lot of Curran's spittoon-cleaners. The fellow that Baker killed is from the Springs. I've seen him round Curran's."

"Do you think so?"

"I know it. When you want me to tell you what I know, I'll do it—only not now. Wait till the militia takes possession."

"Will the militia come? Has the Governor ordered it out?"

"He's *got* to order 'em out now. He's a dead duck, anyway."

Raymond returned to his work beside Kelly, and together they tore at the rocks and beams—magnificent in their leadership. Kelly's head was bare, his face covered with soot, his arms bleeding, but his great voice rang out like a trumpet. The blackened timbers were cleared at last, but a painful delay intervened while a windlass was being brought from another shaft.

An hour later all was ready, and into the heavy, shifting smoke, which rose from the smouldering débris at the first level, Kelly and his young partner descended to extinguish the burning timbers, to clear away the fallen rock, and to signal to the imprisoned men below.

Again and again they were forced to lie flat on their faces with their lips touching the earth in order to breathe; but at last the smouldering material was all hoisted, the mine cleared, and they were able to look about them, dizzy but exultant. The iron beams had caught and held a huge mass of rock which the con-

A Last Appeal

cussion had shaken from the mouth of the mine, and to dig through this was the task that now confronted them; but the air of the shaft having cleared, volunteers thickened, and the exhausted leaders were able to rest their aching limbs and listen for signals.

They were mightily cheered by the faint but unmistakable sound of knocking. The imprisoned ones were calling in the well-tried fashion—by hammering on the rock with their sledges. They beat cheerfully, as if seeking to reassure their rescuers.

"Listen!" cried Kelly, his grotesquely be-daubed face lighting into a gleeful smile. "They're all right. I can tell that by their stroke. Ye see 'tis not like an explosion from fire-damp; they've plenty of fresh air. The mine is small, and has no gas in it."

An hour later, they could hear the voices of those beneath, and it was hardly more than mid-day before they began to lift them out two by two in the big bucket, and when they were all assembled on the surface in the bright sunlight, the worn and weary rescuers looked to be the victims of the dynamiters rather than those whom the bomb had sealed up below. Raymond and Kelly were especially damaged, almost unrecognizable through their covering of soot and clay, but they were jubilant.

Ann, hearing their shouts, came down the path with Nora to meet them. Kelly's eyes were dim with tears, and Ann's heart went out to him as he shouted, "They are all here, and unhurt."

"But you are hurt?" she asked of Raymond, with anxious, timorous voice, peering at his torn and trembling hands.

"No—only tired." He became almost gay now in

reaction. "Oh, the relief when I knew the boys were all right! The shaft looked worse than it was, with that pitchy smoke rolling up. But we're all right now. How is the patient?" he asked, as they started towards the cabin together.

"He is awake, but his pulse is still rapid and he is very restless."

"What does the doctor say?"

"He insists there is no danger. I think he means it. But, oh, that poor boy is so sick!"

He looked down at her tenderly. "These are stern experiences for you. I wish there was a way out of them. If only Louis could be moved."

"Do not trouble about me," she said. "I've been all over the problem, and I've made an end of fretting. I accept all this as my discipline. All the rest of my life has been wearisomely uneventful. Now I am to take my share of trouble." She checked herself. "This will be a very serious loss to you, will it not?"

He strove to answer lightly. "Oh yes; but our vein is there just the same. Luckily they couldn't blow that away."

At the door of the bungalow he turned. "I must leave you for a time. I must repair damages"—he looked at his hands and arms—"and I want to talk with my men."

"I hope you are not going into this battle?"

His voice suddenly acquired passion. "I must do something. I can't sit here and wait for these devils to dynamite me out of life!" He caught his breath, and ended in a calmer tone, "No, I shall not go into the fight; but I hope to take a hand in preventing bloodshed."

A Last Appeal

She put her hand on his arm. "Of course, Louis and I are small things in the midst of this warfare, and I suppose it is your duty to do something; but you must remember your mother; you owe it to her not to needlessly expose yourself to danger."

He turned, with an almost irresistible desire to take her in his arms. "It is to protect you and Louis that I must act. Don't mistake me," he added, quickly. "I don't mean to say that you are in danger—you must not be alarmed."

She saw that he had misspoken and that a deep anxiety lay at his heart. "I am not afraid," she said; "I can't make it seem riot; I can't even connect this outer tumult with our quiet life here in the bungalow. Go about what seems best for you to do. I have been a hinderance to you from the beginning—"

He passionately interrupted her. "If I could take you and Louis out of this accursed camp I would do it this moment. I would sacrifice my mine with joy; but he cannot be moved, and we must keep his room quiet and peaceful. That is my chief duty, now that my men are safe."

"Go to your luncheon," she said, gently; "you are hungry and tired." There was that in both her look and tone which made an answer an impossibility. To save himself from folly he turned abruptly away.

He found his men in the barrack, discussing with characteristic calmness the general situation while waiting for their dinner. And when Perry shouted "grub pile" in cow-camp phrase, each man bustled to his place with cheerful clatter. Raymond drew up with the rest, and for a few minutes no word spoken referred to the disaster. The master's face was

393

grave with his life's problem, and the men remained silent for sympathy. They were rough fellows, accustomed to keen winds and crusty fare, but they respected trouble; they waited for him to speak. Meanwhile they ate like hungry troopers expecting the bugle.

As the first man, well filled, pushed back his chair, Raymond called out: "Boys, I want to say a word before any of you go out. A council of war is necessary at this minute."

Those who had risen took seats again, and all faced his way. As he looked at them his throat filled with a realization of their loyal service, and he could not find voice for a few moments, but sat with bowed head, rolling a bit of bread between his fingers. At last he resolutely cleared his throat and began, harshly: "Well, boys, the game halts right here. You see where Kelly & Raymond are — they're flat. We've got a good mine if we could work it, but we can't. Just about every dollar we had to spare went into that machinery, and our ore shipments were just beginning. I've been doing a little figuring, and I find we can pretty near pay all that's due you, but we can't do any more. If this strike were settled we might get somebody to come in and help us put up a new power plant, but as things shape up at this present time, we're 'up a stump,' as they say back in Ohio. So I guess we'll have to let you go." There was a movement among the men which he felt as a protest, but he continued: "I hate to do this, especially now in the winter, but you can see how it is. Even if we had the credit we couldn't get the machinery on the grounds. If I were in your places I would go

A Last Appeal

to Reese and the other independents and stick by 'em, help them fight this thing through on fair-play lines."

His slight pause brought no response. When he began again his voice was softened. "And, boys, ride up and tell Matt a good word. He's hard hit. He's got to that time o' life when a man don't like to be thrown. He's been planning to kind o' sit back and let us younger fellows round up the stock, and it's sure hard lines on the old man—"

His voice trembled dangerously, and he was forced to stop.

The tension was eased away by Nary, one of the older men, who broke out with deep-lunged profanity in order to conceal his good heart.

"Well, I don't know how the rest of you feel, but I want to turn right in and put this mine into shape again, and lynch the sons o' dogs that blew us up!"

"That's the ticket!"

"Now you're getting wise."

Nary was encouraged. "They's a whole lot of work we can do ourselves towards putting up that power-house."

"Why, sure thing!" said Silsbee.

"I'm a jackass carpenter myself," Nary added.

"You're a jackass, all right—I don't know about the carpenter part," put in a wag, and the tension of the moment was relieved by laughter.

"That's mighty white of you, boys," responded Raymond; "and if I could see any way to do it, I'd take your offer, but I don't. However, if you want to stay in the shack for a day or two, do so; things may clear up by that time."

One of the men who had been imprisoned spoke with quiet menace: "Well, some of us who've been underground want to do something besides wait — we want to fight. We think we know the buzzards that threw the powder into us, and we're hot in the neck. If you say the word, we'll get a crowd together and go up and demand satisfaction. We're not in the habit of allowing a lot of sneaking coyotes to do us like that."

To this several shouted assent, "Let's go and race 'em up!"

"We know the beasts that did it."

Raymond lifted his hand. "Hold on, boys; don't be too quick on the trigger. Keep cool till I ride up on the hill and take a look around, and have a little talk with Munro. We must rally all the independents, which will take time; and, besides, you must remember I have a very sick boy on my hands, and there is Baker, who needs care. Don't rush. Let me go up and see what the sheriff seems likely to do. As I've told you before, I've no theory about the labor question. I never was up against it before, and I'm a little uncertain. I've always believed in the best man winning. I picked you fellows because you were likely chaps. I'm paying you the highest wages going, because you earn it. You're satisfied, you say, and I don't see why we are not privileged to go ahead in our own way. I haven't felt any need of going into this fight for the benefit of the crowd till now. It looks now as though we should take a hand. Anyhow, we'll give Munro another chance to do us justice, and if he don't—then— well, we'll try some other plan." He shook off this disagreeable cloak of doubt. "But be that as it may, boys, I shall never forget the good work you've done for me, when you knew the crowd was against you. It was noble, and I'm 'powerful obleeged,' as they say in Missouri; and if we ever open that mine, I shall consider you partners with me in it."

The men rose and went out two by two, but several of them came to him to say: "We mean business, Rob. Say the word, and we'll go up and get the gang that did for us. We'll rope and bind the whole outfit, if you say so."

He was again in deep thought, and only absently replied: "Don't be hasty, boys. Wait till I have a little time to work out a plan."

At last only Perry remained in the room, and Raymond, perceiving him, called out, "Well, Perry, what are you going to do?"

"Stay with you," he answered.

Raymond's face clouded. "I wish you were down on the ranch; you're in a cold climate up here."

"I wish you'd stayed there, too," cried the boy, passionately. "Let's go away; I don't like it here. It's no good, Rob; they are trying to kill you."

Raymond sighed. "It's all a big gamble, but I can't give it up. I've got to win out." He was talking half to himself, half to the boy. "I don't know whether I can pay you full wages or not, but if you'll stay I'll see what can be done for you. The men will remain here for a few days, anyway, and you and Foo can go on just as you are, for the present."

The boy's dark face lit with pleasure. "Si, señor," he gayly said.

Raymond found Kelly bending over Baker, his great face seamed with sympathetic lines. "Broken bones at your age," he was saying, "are soon mended. You'll be in the saddle all right for the spring round-up."

Raymond added a reassuring word. "Good thing we had a real, city-built doctor round the shack, don't you think?"

Baker smiled faintly and said, "How's the kid?"

"He's resting better. The doctor is hopeful of the whole bunch of you."

As they stepped out into the warm, afternoon sun, Kelly, with a jocular note in his voice, remarked, "Well, Robbie, we're gents at leisure; nothing to do now but play the nurse"—here his voice swiftly changed—"or do battle."

"If it were not for the women and the sick, I'd fight. We have nothing to lose now, and the boys are hot for it. Have you been up the street?"

"No, I have not."

"I don't see what we can do, with these two wounded men and the boy and the women on our hands. Matt, the real heart of this opposition is now in one man. If he were taken away, these rowdy miners would scatter like grouse."

Kelly turned quickly. "You mean Munro?"

"I do! I'm going up to have an interview with him."

Kelly laid a big hand on his arm. "You're takin' a big risk; let me go instead."

"No, you must stay here. I am going, and I am going unarmed. I am safer with empty hands, Matt. They will not shoot an unarmed man."

"I don't know about that. These wild-eyed Dagoes will mob a man with picks."

"No matter," the young man stubbornly answered, "I'm going to make one more appeal to Munro."

A Last Appeal

Kelly was bitter. "Lave him fight. His heart is set on it. 'Twill cool his blood to open his veins. Why trouble about it at all? Sure we've made wan appeal after the other from the start, and what good has it done? We're deeper in trouble than ever. The work for us to do is to find the men that destroyed our mine, and set 'em swingin'."

"We can do nothing till the strike is settled, Matt. We can neither raise money nor safely employ men, and we can't afford to be spectators. It's our business to step in and take a fall out of one or the other of these leaders. The neutral business is played out. Either we cut in and help Munro stand the sheriff off, or we join the sheriff and whip Munro."

"Ayther is the divil's own work."

"I know it is, and whichever we do, we endanger the women, your lads, and our sick; but we're up against it. I would urge you to take your family and get out, but that would leave Ann alone here with a very sick boy. We could rally the independents and make a fight, but that would endanger the ones we are bound to defend."

Kelly looked away over the pleasant, sunlit world gloomily. "All that is true, Rob; 'tis beyond the Kelly wits. 'Tis not me nature to retreat, but could the boy be moved, I'd say fer once in me life, 'Matt Kelly, put your hand over your mouth and sit down.'"

It was hard to realize that any danger lay concealed in the golden mist of that silent afternoon. The high peaks dreamed like gray Simons on towers of meditation. The sparse clouds were soft, slow, summer-like. The near-by snow-drifts had sunk into the ground.

Nothing remained to remind the observer of winter save the russet grass.

The two men stood in silence for a long time; then Kelly broke forth: "My curse on Mackay! Had anny other man taken the change in hand 'twould have gone through; but he, the brass-bound, double-jointed monkey, was just the one to set this hell's-broth boiling."

"I wish I were a good Catholic, too," laughed Raymond, as he turned away; "I'd add my curse to yours."

Mounting his horse, Raymond rode rapidly out along the ridge towards the hill on which the fortification stood. He passed now and then a group of men who knew him, and while one or two greeted him pleasantly, all the others met his glance with menace. He felt the hot breath of their hate, but passed on without haste, regretting his action in leaving his revolvers behind him. In the long years of life on the ranges of the West he had come to depend upon his gun as a Cornishman upon his fist, or an Irishman upon his shillalah; and felt helpless and ill at ease without it.

The camp had eaten its mid-day meal—for even in times of war men must eat; the miners had hastily devoured their rough food and were swarming on the hill-side overlooking the sheriff's encampment. Every movement of the little army below was noted and commented upon with boisterous laughter; the invading force seemed so ludicrously inadequate for the work its leaders had so confidently cut out for it. Far over to the left, on a smooth, low hill, a throng of spectators from Bozle was spread like a moth-eaten rug, and every soul was aquiver with impatience for the drama to begin.

A Last Appeal

The vedettes were bivouacked in a small grove of firs to the left and a little below the fort (which was merely a log corral banked with dirt), and Munro was directing the shovel brigade at work on the walls of the redoubt, which was growing rapidly under the brisk movement of chattering miners.

As Raymond neared the crowd of on-lookers he recognized Denver Dan and one or two other horse-men, but for the most part the spectators were strangers and plainly hostile.

He had drawn rein to pass to the left when Brock stepped forth on foot and roughly called out:

"What's your business up here?"

"I want to find Munro."

"Well, you go back to your shack and keep out of this."

Raymond smiled. "When did you become road-master?"

The ruffian's resentment burst out: "You keep out of here, I say. You're a traitor — that's what you are—and you need hangin'. Do you think you can spy round here and go and report your findings to Barnett? Not while I'm in town."

Denver Dan put in a word. "Now, don't be a fool, Brock; you've no license to run a court-martial. Munro will attend to that part of the business."

Brock raised his voice so that the rapidly gathering crowd might hear. "Here's the spy that warned the sheriff not to come on the freight-train; here's the man that ruined our plans. You can't deny that," he said, laying a hand on the horse's rein.

"I don't intend to deny it," replied Raymond, facing the lowering faces of the close-packed throng as a mastiff might face a pack of coyotes; "and, what's more, I don't intend to apologize for it." His promise to Ann came into his mind. "I must be pacific," he resolved; "I must not struggle." Then, very quietly, he added: "Take your hand away, Brock. I want to ride on."

"Lynch him!" shouted some fellow at the back. "Lynch the spy!"

A wave of gusty wrath swept over the on-lookers. They surged towards him like gray wolves, eager for his blood. Another of the leaders seized his horse's bit and held him as in a vise, but Raymond turned towards the horsemen on the edge of the mob. "Boys, I'm in trouble; some of you are old cattle-punchers. I'm unarmed—I haven't so much as a penknife. Stand these fellows off and give me a show. Let me have a fighting chance. Dan, call Munro."

Dan, half-heartedly, shouted out, "Hold on, boys, don't crowd the man," and attempted to spur his horse into the throng.

"No, you don't, Dan," cried those near him. "You stay where you are. We're going to do for this traitor right here."

The citizens of the peak were in motion, all centring towards Raymond as cattle respond to the wild call of a steer that has discovered a place of blood. From fierce mouths, distorted and malevolent, remorseless laughter broke forth. "String him up!" shouted Brock, and the hearts of the evil - doers fused together like drops of mercury, and the desire to kill submerged every other motive.

Raymond had been in danger many times in his life, but never had he looked down into such hate-

A Last Appeal

inflamed faces as now encircled him. The old, reckless heart came back to him. He lifted his voice in appeal. "Have I a friend here? If I have, let him throw me a gun! I want to go fighting!"

"Here you are!" called a stranger, and a big, glittering revolver came whirling over the heads of the mob.

Raymond caught it deftly, and with the touch of its handle to his palm his eyes narrowed and his white teeth set: "Now, let the dance begin! By the Lord, some of you will cross the range with me!"

Denver Dan attempted a diversion. "Look out, fellers; here comes Jack!"

Munro's name and the pistol in Raymond's hand induced a pause. The foremost of the assailants turned towards the captain of the vedettes, riding swiftly to the rescue. "What's going on here?" he shouted, as he reached the outskirts of the crowd. "What's all this about? Hello, Rob! Brock, what about this?"

Brock was ready. "Here's the man who has played with our plans all along, pretending to be neutral when he was nothing but a dirty, slinking spy from the very beginning—"

"Liar!" shouted Raymond, and his boot-toe caught the ruffian in the mouth and he staggered back among his fellows with a hoarse cry. For a moment he was dazed; then raging, furious, his mouth streaming with blood, he jerked his revolver from its holder, intent to kill; but a hand clutched his arm, and Munro, spurring his horse into the mass of irresolute men, called out: "Brock, I'll kill you if you shoot—this is a friend of mine — you know that! He's stood out against us all along, but he's been on the square. *I* sent him to the Springs myself."

Brock wiped the blood from his lips. "Mebbe you asked him to wire the sheriff last night. He admits he sent a messenger to warn him."

Munro turned to Raymond. "Did you do that?"

"I did! I wanted to see a fair fight. I didn't intend to let your crazy hoodlums wreck that train and kill those men like rats in a trap. You are insane, Jack."

Cries of frenzied rage broke forth again, and the crowd surged against the two horses. Furious, throaty cries broke forth.

"Kill him!" "Hang him!"

Munro blew a signal to his men, and his voice rang out clear and sharp. "The first man that reaches a hand out of that circle loses it. If any lynching is done, I preside over it. Dan, come in here—you, too, Cook."

The two cow-boys spurred their horses into the circle, and the four armed and resolute men faced the angry mob and held it at bay. Raymond, even in this hour of danger, regretted Munro's assistance; it put him under an obligation which weakened him. With his mind filled with conflicting considerations, he waited while the swift clatter of a hundred hoofs drew near, and a squad of Munro's picked men surrounded their captain, who called out as the mangy crowd fell back: "I want you to understand that I'm in command of this hill, and I won't stand for any more funny business. Open up there!"

When they were clear of danger, Raymond drew rein towards Munro. "Jack, you saved my scalp to-

A Last Appeal

day, and I'm grateful; that's why I don't want to see you in the hands of the sheriff. I want you to pull out this minute. Come, now, this is a last appeal. Fly the coop. If you don't, they'll hang you. What do you hope to accomplish? Face the situation. You are the one to hit the trail, and hit it like a wolf. What do you hope to do?"

"I expect to hold this camp until the syndicate yields to the demands of the miners, or until the Governor interferes."

"Then what?"

"Then I step down and out."

"Suppose the sheriff attacks to-night?"

"I will send him back a-whirling. And now let me take an inning. You mustn't come up here again. I can't answer for what would happen next time. You stay where you are, and—listen! take care of yourself." He laughed as he added, "Looks like this is my busy day, and I can't spare a guard."

Raymond mused. "Jack, you've got a wild-cat by the tail. You can neither let go nor hold on. You need some one to save you from yourself and the cat."

Munro's eyes twinkled. "I reckon you've hit it; but, meanwhile, there's nothin' to do but keep the cat's backbone straight. Well, now, so long, and take good care of the lady."

XXVII

Hesper

THE world of men had never before appealed to Ann's imagination. She had been quite content to let the predatory male go down into his jungles of trade and return at his leisure; but on the peak she was thrust amid the most distinctively masculine plans, and being measurably relieved from anxiety by Louis' subsiding pulse, she permitted herself a closer study of the brusque and ominous movements taking place in the scope of her window. She studied Raymond, in earnest but apparently unexcited conference with his workmen. No word of their low utterance reached her ears, but she observed that they organized into squads as if in obedience to some command, and that each man armed himself, and that each face was grim or recklessly smiling. That they formed her guard she knew, and this in itself ought to have been thrilling; but it was not—it seemed absurd.

Far up on the hill, Munro's horsemen (diminished to the size of swallows) swooped to and fro on aimless errands, and at a greater distance below, to the west, on the Bozle road, scores of teams and hundreds of footmen streamed along, each sight-seer eager to behold the first onslaught. It seemed as though every detachable thing in the camp was in motion—like leaves before an all - prevailing storm - wind — and that the place whereon she stood alone remained calm—dangerously, menacingly calm.

Dr. Braide's professional cheer irritated her during this time of waiting, and despite her acknowledgment of gratitude for his kindness, and her reliance upon his skill, she grew curt almost to the point of incivility; but she longed for a reassuring word from Raymond. "Why don't he come and let me know what is preparing?" she impatiently repeated, beneath her breath. "He has no right to leave me in the dark." And once she went to the door with impulse to call him, but her resolution sank away. He was a part of the man's world, and sternly busy.

He did not show himself again to her until about nine o'clock of the evening, when he entered the sick-room and said, quietly, to Braide: "Doctor, you better go to bed, if the patient will permit. You may be badly needed early to-morrow morning."

"Very well," acquiesced Braide, convinced that a closer tie than friendship united Ann and the young miner, and that they desired to be alone. "Our patient is doing well." As he was about to leave, he said, "You expect trouble, do you not?"

Raymond was evasive. "It's a good time to prepare for it, though it may drift round us."

The door had hardly closed behind the young physician when Ann turned to Raymond and imperiously said: "You must not try to evade *me*. I want to know what is threatening. Tell me!"

"The camp is wild," he admitted, feeling the resentment in her voice; "and I don't see how a clash can be avoided so long as Munro is in command and keeps his present temper. But you need give no thought to that. All my men are on guard to-night, and whatever happens, this cabin is safe."

"I like you to be honest with me," she said, more gently. "I'm not a child, and I'm not a timid person. I hate lying and evasions."

He smiled down at her. "I know you do; that is the reason I am speaking so frankly. If I thought you were in actual danger I would take you in my arms and carry you to safety, even against your own will; but there are twenty determined men between you and any violence that might wander our way."

"Thank you. Why didn't you come and tell me sooner?"

"I was very busy."

"What were you doing? What have you done? I want to know it all."

"You shall know," he answered, taking a seat before the fire. He had never been more admirable than at that moment. "My theory is that the sheriff's forces are eager to storm the hill before the Governor has a chance to interfere and 'protect his pets,' that is the way they put it. If the attack is made, a desperate struggle will follow. Probably the deputies will try to carry the fortification direct. Meanwhile, Kelly and I have drawn up and forwarded to the Governor a long telegram signed by the leading independents, reciting our disaster, and demanding immediate interference on his part, and we are hoping to hear from him before midnight. I have also wired Barnett to warn the sheriff of your presence here, and that we are guarding you. I think Don is with the deputies. If he is, he will see that this cabin remains outside the field of operation."

Hesper

"Where is Captain Munro?"

"His vedettes are camped on the north slope, but may engage the enemy at any moment, for Jack is quite as eager as the sheriff to win first blood. If it were not for the possible injury of innocent men and women, I would say let them fight it out. Each camp is quite as crazy and lawless as the other. Now you have the truth. I have concealed nothing from you. I will even tell you that Munro has promised to come down for a final conference with the independents, and that we are still hoping to persuade him to leave the camp."

Ann's face softened. "Isn't it an ironical turn, that Louis and I, rank outsiders, with no personal interest at stake, should be tied here helpless at the very centre of a miners' war?"

He stirred uneasily in his chair. "You touch my sore spot. I can't forget that you would never have climbed this peak only for me — I mean through Louis' friendship for me. In a sense I brought you here, and the thought of any harm to you or to him unnerves me."

The sick boy stirred uneasily and called faintly, and Ann went to him and bent above him tenderly. "Here I am, Buddie. Are you better?"

"Oh, I'm so hot! Take that blanket off me."

Raymond looked at Ann. "Shall I lighten his load?"

She shook her head as she put a glass of water to the boy's lips. "What time is it?" he asked, as he fell back upon his pillow.

"Going on ten o'clock."

"Has the fight come off yet?"

Raymond was cautious. "No, the camp is quiet."

He insisted on talking. "I hope they won't fight till I get over this cold. It's hard luck to be here. What day is it? How long have I been sick? You should have seen Jack when he rode up and stopped the man!" In this way his mind leaped and danced for an hour, but he grew drowsy at last, and went away into sleep, leaving Raymond and Ann alone together, each more acutely conscious of the other than before.

Ann spoke first. "Poor boy! He will always feel defrauded, to think he is missing all this drama."

"Your father must have been such another enthusiast. I have read his journal with the greatest pleasure. Some of it needs only capital letters to be poetry."

"Yes, my father was a beautiful character. I wish I had inherited more of his spirit."

"I liked his name for you," he continued in the same tone.

She colored. "That was the only thing I had to reproach him for. I reproach myself now for not acquiescing in it. I think it grieved him to have me side with mother against it."

"It is a sweet name to me—Hesper." He uttered it with the tenderness which dwells in the voice of a lover, and its letters sang together—but he dared not look at her. Ann sat silent with a rapt musing in her eyes, lost in wonder of the emotion this childish name, spoken thus, had awakened in her. Had this strong young miner chanted a love poem, he could not have conveyed to her so much of his frank and manly passion.

XXVIII

Raymond Silences Munro

RAYMOND was hastening to apologize for his temerity when the noise of a galloping horse cut short his speech and whitened Ann's cheek, so portentous was the sound of haste at such an hour. "I hope that is Jack," said the miner, and hastened to the door to meet and silence Munro, who entered with studied effect, and, removing his sombrero, bowed very low to Ann. "Good-evening, haughty princess. How's the kid?"

Ann, relieved to find the flying messenger an expected though unwelcome visitor, replied, pleasantly, "He's better, thank you."

A covert smile curled the handsome lips of the young leader as he glanced from Raymond to Ann, and something in his bearing puzzled the girl. When he spoke again, with a growing deliberation, she perceived that he was in liquor.

"You mustn't be alarmed—these are rough times, but you'll be protected. Battle's comin' off this time, sure thing. We move on the enemy at daybreak. Si-down. Don' stand in my presence," he added, with a comical twist of his lips.

Ann turned with a startled glance to Raymond, who genially said, "I'm glad you came down, Jack; I want you to hold a conference with the independents."

Munro stiffened. "No time for conf'rence. No time to talk with any one. I just came down to say howdy to the lady. That's all. Understand?" His voice rose.

Raymond lifted a warning hand. "Quietly, old man, don't disturb the boy. Let's go find Kelly."

Munro's face grew sullen. "Don't want to see Kelly—don't want to see you. I've come to see the lady." He faced Ann again. "I'm going into battle. May be killed to-morrow. Had to say good-bye. I may not see you again." He turned to Raymond and his voice was peremptory. "You go find Kelly; let me talk with Ann."

To Raymond's great relief, Kelly, who had heard Munro arrive, appeared at the door. His manner was easy and his voice low as he greeted the intruder. "Hello, Jack, how goes the Napoleonic business?"

Munro turned with darkening brows, and labored to be gloomily impressive. "Got 'em scared, all right. They're meditating retreat this minute. I'm only afraid they'll run too quick. If I see 'em moving out I'll drop down on 'em."

Kelly laid a hand on his shoulder. "Lad, you need sleep; you're worn out."

Raymond, with a significant look at Matt, turned as if to stir the fire—a movement which brought him behind his visitor.

Munro put his hands in his pockets and laboriously explained: "Been tryin' to keep awake on whiskey— trifle shot this minute, askin' Lady Ann's pardon. You see, the warm room makes my thongue tick—tongue tick." He laughed at his vain effort to speak these words. "Got a knot in it."

Raymond Silences Munro

Raymond's right arm encircled the young leader's waist, pinioning the deadly right hand to his side, while Kelly, seizing the almost equally skilful left, whipped the young desperado's revolver from his belt.

For a moment the fangless rattlesnake was bewildered. "What you mean, Rob?" he asked, ominously.

"Come outside, Jack. Don't make a row—for the lady's sake. We want to talk to you."

"Let go o' me," he retorted, writhing in Raymond's clutch. In the midst of this he grinned at Kelly. "I know these arms. What's your game, Rob?"

"Come outside and I'll tell you," pleaded Raymond.

"If 'tweren't for your company I'd cut your heart out," he replied, with calm malignancy.

Kelly, less patient than Raymond, broke forth: "Gwan out! Don't make a row here. Can't ye see you're disturbin' the sick boy?"

The sodden brain of the reckless leader was waking up again, and, with a bow to Ann, he said: "Sorry to 'sturb you, but I must take these men outside and kill 'em. See you again soon."

Raymond released his prisoner and stepped through the door in advance of him, but as Munro followed and stood for an instant on the step, peering into the darkness, Raymond seized him again, and with a furious twist threw him to the earth and fell upon him in a terrible struggle. Matt, mindful of Ann and the boy, closed the door. The girl, not daring to look out, could only stand with nerveless limbs and pounding heart and listen. Once the desperate man uttered a gasping snarl, but it was cut short by a merciless

413

hand, and all was still. Then her composure gave way.

"Oh, Rob, don't kill him!" she called, heedless of Louis. Opening the door she cried again, "Don't, please don't!"

Kelly was binding the captain's feet while Raymond, with a knee on his chest and one hand at his throat, looked up at Ann as she stood in the doorway, and said: "Please go in. We are doing this for his own good. We won't hurt him. He'll thank us for it when he understands our motive."

Munro, like a trapped wild-cat, snapped at his captor; but Raymond's long fingers prevented him. "Now listen, Jack. You did me a good turn to-day, and I'm going to do as much for you. I'm going to save you from State's prison against your own fool's will. You're going to leave camp to-night, dead sure thing! And you might as well go quietly. If you don't, we'll pack you on your horse like a roll of blankets. Will you be quiet? Will you ride your horse, or must we tie you on?"

Ann, appalled by this display of desperate fury battling with iron resolution, forgot to obey. Entering imaginatively into the captive's deep humiliation, she understood that he could not submit to such wills as those above him, even to save his life.

Braide appeared behind Ann. "What is the fracas?"

Raymond spoke again, and his voice was imperative. "Please go in; this is no place for you. Doctor, shut the door!"

They shrank before the authority of his voice, and withdrew into the house, and Braide closed the door.

Raymond Silences Munro

Louis was awake, his bright eyes widely opened, his ears alert. Forgetful of him for the moment, Ann listened breathlessly while Raymond pleaded with his captive. "Now, be reasonable, Jack. Go quietly with Kelly."

Again the frenzied man renewed his struggle. Blindly, ferociously, like an animal, deaf to all reason, acknowledging no law but that of force, he writhed, beating the ground. His gasping breath was painful to hear. At last Braide, who had been picking handily at his medicine-case, suddenly opened the door and ran out.

"Here is where the man of medicine comes in," he called, jovially, and thrust a folded handkerchief beneath Munro's nostrils. "Let him breathe, Raymond," he said, quietly. "It 'll do him good."

Munro's knotted muscles almost instantly relaxed, his hands fell inert, his head turned quietly to one side, and his face became as peaceful as a sleeping child.

"What have you done?" whispered Kelly, excitedly.

Braide laughed. "Hypnotized him. You can do as you wish with him now, but work quick."

"Much obliged, doctor," said Raymond. "Take him up, Matt. Let's put him away while he sleeps. He'll go by freight now." As they laid hold of the corpselike figure he added to Ann and to Braide, "Not a word of this to any one!"

The two men had hardly shuffled off into the darkness before a couple of men on guard came by. "Oh, it's you, doctor. I thought I heard Kelly's voice," said one of them.

"All quiet here," answered Braide.

Ann returned to Louis' bedside with a sense of having witnessed and condoned a midnight murder, and a knock at the door startled her as though it were a summons to trial. But the visitor was only one of Munro's men, deferential, almost timid, in her presence.

"Excuse me, but has the captain been here this evening?" he asked, politely.

The doctor quickly answered, "Yes, but he went away again almost immediately."

"If you see him, just tell him we need him on the hill."

"I'll do so gladly."

"Much obliged," The messenger withdrew, and they soon heard him gallop swiftly away, and all became silent.

At Ann's insistent request Braide went back to his couch, and she was again alone waiting for Raymond's return.

The situation in the great drama was now quite clear to her mental vision. She could see the small army waiting below, foolishly eager for the coming of the dawn, and it was not difficult to imagine the excitement and consternation in Munro's forces when their leader failed to appear. She understood also something of the panic in Bozle and in the valley, and realized that through the night the news of the impending assault on the peak was flying, loosed along aërial ways by the tapping fingers of a hundred deft, dispassionate operators. And though she knew the darkness outside was sentinelled by Raymond's faithful men, she could not rid herself of a feeling of impending danger. The air was surcharged with some invisible evil potency, and seemed about to crackle into a destructive tempest of pistol-shots.

From the outside point of view the entire campaign was farcical, a subject for ironical laughter; but from the position of a woman inside the lines and watching beside a sick-bed, it yielded no amusement; it was distinctly appalling.

XXIX

Ann's New Philosophy

RAYMOND was gone for nearly two hours, but when he did appear he was entirely self-contained and very gentle.

"You must go to sleep," he said, at once. "I will watch. I want to beg your pardon for seizing Munro in your presence, but it was necessary, both for his sake and to prevent bloodshed. I saw no other chance of disarming him. I hope you will excuse my harshness in sending you away."

"You need not apologize; I understood," she answered. "What have you done with him?"

"Kelly has taken him away out of danger. Have any of his men called for him?"

"Yes, one; but he rode away again. Have you any further news?"

"Something is going on in Bozle. I could hear cheering, and I thought I could distinguish the galloping of horses. Whatever is coming, my duty is here; and now let me take you to Nora."

"No, no! I can't sleep now. My brain is whirling with this night's events. I feel as if I were about to witness some great storm, some catastrophe. Sleep is impossible to-night."

He turned with low-voiced intensity. "What can

Ann's New Philosophy

I do to repair the injury I have done you and yours?
When I left Barnett's home, I was resolved never
to re-enter your life again. I honestly tried to get
away from Louis and to take myself absolutely out
of your world. When I think of you, sitting here
surrounded by these mobs, these violences, witnessing
such deeds as this to-night, I am in complete despair.
I see no way out. Each hour adds to my sense of
responsibility for you—"

She interrupted him with a gesture of protest.
"You must not blame yourself—it had to be. Do
you believe in fate?"

"I do not, nor in luck," he answered, slowly.

"Neither do I, but I believe in compensations. Since
I came up here I have worked out a theory of life.
I've been happy here; that should comfort you."

"It would, only I cannot rid myself of the thought
of what you have sacrificed to be here. Each day
has plunged you deeper into this lawless barbarism."

"There is where my theory helps me. One's life
has a general average like a weather report. Don't
laugh. I will explain what I mean. If one has too
abundant rains in June, one is likely to be dry and
parched in August; that is the law. As nothing ever
happened to me up to the time when I decided to
leave New York, so now events crowd each other's
heels. Don't you see what I mean? My life had
no real value to me, nor to any one else till I came
West. I bore no burdens. I demanded constant
pleasure. When I was tired of one place I went to
another, and yet I never got sufficiently weary of the
first to make the second a joy. So the time had to
come when I should sit as I do now, watching by a

sick-bed, unable to sleep. It's one of my compensations. As I lost interest in life by idleness and pleas-
ure-seeking, so now, perhaps, I am destined to regain
it by toil. Pleasures come to me now when I least
expect them. That is a wonderful thing to me. I
thought I had lost all power to vividly enjoy, but I
haven't. So you see, I am not accusing you or any
one. I have only reason to be thankful, if only no
harm comes to Louis or my friends here. I shall not
complain."

"It is very sweet of you to try to lighten my sense
of guilt," he replied, gently. "But I cannot absolve
myself so easily. I can understand your theory, but
I cannot understand how you find life a disappointment, you who have everything to make you happy."

She leaned towards him with eager face. "That is
just the point of my discovery. I have had too much.
Joy comes by contrast. You are hungry, and food is
good; you are tired, and rest is sweet. You can't over-
take the sweet joys on the road of life; they must meet
you—unexpectedly. All my life I've eaten when I was
not hungry and slept when I was not weary. I had no
duties; my wants were met instantly. That's why I
lost interest in life. It wasn't normal—it was as if
all the year were June. There were no compensating
pains, and so, to restore me to health, God took away
my sunshine."

He smiled a little. "I don't know whether I like
being a part of such discipline."

She went on: "I am, by heritage, a worker. I know
that now. My father's people were active and calculating folk, and my life in the city was unnatural.
I've been deliciously hungry and weary since I've been

here — life seems restored to its balance. I've been happier than at any time since my careless childhood. So do not blame yourself. I used to think I would go mad with the sense of my failure to grasp anything, to taste anything. Everything seemed slipping away from me. You have done me good—you and splendid old Matt and sweet Nora."

They had forgotten the warfare outside. They were face to face with the passion that forever rejuvenates the earth.

He sprang from his chair and faced her. "You mustn't talk to me so," he exclaimed, almost harshly. "I shall forget my promises and say forbidden words to you. You unseat all my good resolutions."

She heard but ignored his passionate words. A sort of mental and spiritual recklessness had seized her. "All my life in the East and in the old world, everything in the past, seems gray — as if covered by a mist. The realities seem to be here. I feel grateful to you, and I want to ask a favor of you."

"Anything you ask, except a renewal of my promise of silence."

She hesitated before the rising storm of his love. "I want you to let me — Louis and me — help rebuild your mine."

"What do you mean?"

"It's so simple. You and Matt need money. I want you to take Louis into your mine as a partner. Hush!" she warningly whispered, as the sleeper's head moved on his pillow. "If he lives, he will want to work with you; if he dies, I must help you for his sake."

"He will not die; he will live. But you—Ann, there is something back of this." He laid his strong hands upon her shoulders, looking into her face with such piercing passion that she shrank and grew timid. "You need me? Is that it? Am I one of your compensations?"

She tried to smile. "That would not be flattering—according to my theory."

He refused to be diverted. "I don't care what your Eastern world thinks of me, if only you are content with me. I accept your theory. I deserve compensation—some sweet return for my lonely, loveless life on the plain. Will you come? Is that what you mean?"

She was on the brink of the river now, and her heart failed her at thought of the strange lands to which it ran. "I don't know what I mean. Please let me go—you hurt me."

He was master now, stopping at no polite bar. "I will not let you go till you speak your mind." His physical hold on her arms softened, but his spiritual self closed round her. "Six months ago I was a rancher in the foot-hills, and you were in a great Eastern city. We were as wide apart as the poles. Now here we are! I don't understand it. This I know: you are here and I can't let you go. I accept your offer to go into the mine, but not for Louis' sake. I do it for my own sake, because I want you to be my partner—my wife. What do you say, Hesper, my star of the West?"

She put him away almost in terror. "I can't decide now. I must be sure — sure, and I'm *not* sure. I must have time to consider. I must go back into my old life—to my native city."

"Back into the gray shadow?" he asked.

"That is what I'm not certain about. I've been

wondering how all this would seem if I were to wake to-morrow in my rooms at the Westchester." She sighed, "Oh, it is all so complicated!"

"To my mind it is very simple. You say you are happier here than in the East. Why go back at all? Why risk the loss of this new-found health?"

"I will be honest. It is because by contrast the old life begins to glow. The change in me may be due to physical causes. Perhaps I could carry my recovered joy of life back with me. If this should be so, then I might never want to return, and that would be cruel to you. Don't you see?"

"Then you should go," he answered, quickly. "I want to make you happy. If I cannot, then it is better for one to suffer than two. Return to New York, and from that vantage-ground look back on this new life. If I do not then seem fitted to make you happy I will not complain. If any man stopped to count the reasons why he should not make a woman his wife he would live single all his days. You have raised my own doubts, and I insist no more. Besides, I have my own share of pride."

"Please—don't misunderstand me—"

"I do not. I understand, and I'm horribly afraid you are right—I have so little to offer you."

"A woman does not love a man for what he can offer in way of a home or reputation. No, it is not that; it is a fear that my mind may change—"

They were interrupted again, this time by Nora, who came in pale and troubled. "Rob, where is Matt? Sure he has not shown his face since supper."

"He's in command of the guard to-night. He's not far away. Don't worry about him."

"Ann, dear, I wish you'd come home. I need you. Rob will sit with the sick one—won't you, Rob?"

To this suggestion Raymond gave assent, and in the end Ann went away, her demonstration unfinished— the question of her future still unanswered.

Nora was fairly broken. "Dear God! how long are we to be kept on the edge of destruction like this? Sure my patience is worn out. In all my life in the mines I've seen nothing like this."

Ann comforted her as best she could, and at one o'clock, all being quiet outside, they went to bed, worn out with watching.

But Ann could not sleep—Raymond filled her inner vision. She loved him, that she now admitted, and yet she could not see herself adjusted to his world. It seemed like a complete abandonment of her old life, and gray though it had been she was afraid to put this new, strange, and tumultuous existence to the hazard. The charm of his voice, his clear eyes, the lines of his head, of his shoulders, she acknowledged. "His growth in tenderness, in comprehension of my life, promises happiness. And yet I must go back to my mother. I can't decide here. The temptation is too great."

She was awakened from an uneasy sleep by Nora's cry to Matt: "For love of Heaven, where have you been? What is that noise?"

Matt's voice, rumbling in reply, barely reached her ears, for a deep, trampling, continuous tumult grew each moment louder, and at last was distinguishable as the sound of horses' hoofs. Springing from her bed, she drew aside the curtain and peered out. In the clear, yellow light of the frosty dawn a regiment of mounted men was streaming up the road between the cabins, moving without word or bugle-note, as stealthily as a body of troops can move, gliding on a compound curve like a vast articulated insect, their movement giving rise to a steady, ominous, dull, trampling roar.

The picture took hold of her in a dim, deep-rooted way, and some elemental emotion, dating from the days of perpetual warfare, rose within her bosom and quickened her breath. All fear fell away, all surprise, and she was struggling with an impulse to open the window and cheer the warriors when Nora pounded on her door.

"Ann, dear, dress yourself — quick! The soldiers are here!"

For just a moment longer she lingered. It was as if she were looking for the ten-thousandth time upon a military picture by a master-artist. The earth was silver white, the sky vivid saffron, and now against the line of the rounded hill-top the capped heads of the men, the pointed ears of the horses were etched in purple silhouettes, and then they disappeared as mysteriously as they came; their going seemed each moment more furtive, more dangerous, and she strained her ears waiting to hear the sound of guns, but all remained silent.

Dressing hurriedly, she went out into the sitting-room just as Raymond came in, his face excited and exultant.

"Our reign of terror is over. The desperadoes are scattering like quail. The Governor, in a spirit of reprisal, has invoked federal aid, and Colonel Wood of the Fortieth United States Cavalry is about to take command of the camp."

"Oh, I am so glad! Now there will be no more fighting and you can restore your mill."

"You are right. Mobs do not fight the United States army," he answered, with the pride of a potential soldier.

They faced each other, even at this moment, with a knowledge that the most important matter of all remained unsettled between them; and all day, and the next, while the forces of disorder dissolved and the camp readjusted itself to military rule, Ann nursed her sick and brooded over her problem. At times she grew weary of the struggle and was ready to yield to his love; but the thought of the future, of the wrong she might inflict on an honorable man, came to torture her anew.

"Oh, if some one else could only decide for me!" she cried, knowing well the futility of the wish.

The second day passed slowly — even though she slept at times—and no further word of intimate meaning passed between them. Raymond came in from time to time with news of the changes in progress but did not tell her that the State was full of praise of the part he had played in bringing peace to the camp. He shrank from doing this, for the reason that, as usual, the press was extreme, loading him with compliments for his firm stand, for his influence over Munro, and for his powerful protest to the Governor; whereas, to his mind, Matthew Kelly was the leader of the free miners. "I was only the secretary—the clerk," he explained.

Dolan, however, brought to Ann a knowledge of the great light which had been turned suddenly on her lover's abashed figure, and the glow of pride which came to her brought a keen realization of how closely his success was interwoven with her good wishes. Nora, without a particle of jealousy for Matt's share of the honor, confirmed all that the reporter had said, and Louis, who listened to it all, quietly remarked, "Rob is the boss; I told you that all along."

Hounded and brought to bay by his admirers, Raymond made a speech bluntly protesting that he was not entitled to any credit in the matter. "I tried hard to keep out of it," he declared. "I'm not seeking honor of that kind." But his argument was in vain. His denials were called the excess of modesty; and at a meeting of the various factions looking to an adjustment he was amazed to find himself put forward as chief arbitrator of the contention, mainly by Barnett and the mayor of Valley Springs, and the news of this was brought to Ann by Barnett himself, who came into the bungalow during the afternoon as *debonair* in dress and manner as he were at Casino Park. "Somebody must be the hero of this victory," said he, with dubious meaning. "Kelly won't have it, I don't deserve it, and we can't afford to let it go to Carter. I don't see any way but this—Rob must wear the laurel wreath. He ought to get the girl," he added, with sly side glance. "But I infer that she's under lease and bond to Peabody."

Ann did not rise to this jest. "You are mal à propos. We have not found our situation humorous."

"Oho!" responded Don, "then he *does* get the girl."

As the news of what had taken place slowly filtered into Louis' consciousness, he wept with vexation. "Have I missed it all?" he wailed. "Now, I call that mean."

XXX

Munro's Last Word

LOUIS had not missed it all, for just at sunset, as Ann, lingering at his side, was about to cross to the Kelly cabin, Munro, wild, white, and breathless, burst into the room.

"Where's my gun?" he demanded. "Where's Rob?" He was a hunted man in every look, in every gesture. "My gun!" he demanded, sharply, and ran into the inner room. When he reappeared his face was set in a grim smile, for in his hand dangled a shining weapon; his panic was at an end. Whoso faced him now must give account of himself.

"Good-bye, girl!" he called, and his voice was wildly tender. "Don't forget me!" With a bound he reached Barnett's horse and rose to the saddle just as a stern voice called, "Halt!" and a blade of fire reached out of the dusk and pierced his side.

Spurring his horse in a swift, rearing circle, he flung from his right hand an answering puff of smoke, and a tall man with a rifle in his hands dropped at the corner of the cabin; but from his knees again took aim, and the beautiful horse went down, flinging his desperate rider over his head.

Horrified, frozen into immobility, Ann stood in the doorway, while Munro shook himself free from the saddle and dragged himself clear of the groaning horse. Resting himself on his elbow, with the face of a calm panther he confronted a second armed officer. His right arm was useless, but his mind was clear, his eyes steady; and, as his new assailant approached, he shifted his weapon to his left hand and rolled upon his useless right arm, and the bullet intended for his heart went wide then. Lifting himself with terrible effort, he fired again, and put a bullet into the very heart of his pursuer, who fell in a heap just as Raymond and Barnett, followed by Kelly, came rushing to the scene of combat. Raymond bent above the fallen leader. "How is it, Jack; are you hurt?"

"Hurt! I'm shot to pieces. Raise me up. I want one more crack at that—" His persistent malignancy was appalling, like that of a splendid mangled serpent.

"No, no, Jack! He's whipped. He's gone."

"Is he dead? There's another—let me get him." He struggled again to rise.

Raymond pushed him gently to the earth. "Never mind him now; you need help. Where's the doctor? Why didn't you jump the camp as Kelly told you to do, Jack, old man? Why didn't you?"

"How could I—no horse—no gun. I'm no jack-rabbit to go slinking into the sage-brush." He raised his voice querulously. "Some o' you boys get me a drink—I feel weak."

A half-dozen started, but Braide put a glass to his lips. Munro looked at him with a steely gleam in his eyes. "I ought to kill you," he said, slowly, "for doing me last night." His voice rose to a stern command: "Take hold and stop this blood. I can't stand this very long. Don't you see that?" he ended, with a note of fierce impatience in his voice.

At Braide's orders they took him up and carried him into the bungalow, where Louis lay watching, listening, with Ann close beside him trying to shield him from the sight and sound of this tragic end of a gambler.

The dying man suffered the doctor's examination in silence for a while, then quietly asked: "Well, doc, what's your verdict? Do I hit the long trail?"

"It looks that way, Jack," Braide replied, with a good deal of feeling.

Munro closed his eyes and his face quivered. At last, when he had regained control of his voice, he said: "One o' you boys find Father Halloran. I need him to outfit me for this big trip. Be quick about it. I was raised a Catholic," he explained to Braide and Raymond, "and I need a priest—" He tried to raise his head. "Ann," he called, imperatively, "I want you—here— till the priest comes—"

She obeyed his call, sustained by her great pity, and, kneeling at his side, asked, quietly, "What can I do?"

He looked at her with wide eyes, whose expression filled her throat with aching sorrow. "I'm leaving camp on a long trip," he said, quietly, "and I want you to say a good word for me; maybe it 'll make it easier for me where I'm going."

At these tender words Ann's fear and hesitation passed into a sort of awe. He was so piteously young, so boyish, to take that lonely journey into the night. She took his hand in both of hers and whispered a little prayer, to which the dying man listened intently. At the end she added, softly: "I have faith that the great

Judge will deal with you mercifully. He knows all your motives as well as your temptations. Surely His forgiveness is greater than man's."

"I take my chances," was his indomitable reply. "I want to live, but I'm not afraid to die. Rob, I want you to stand by at the funeral. You can tell about me better than any preacher. You know the worst of me. I got you into trouble at the academy, but I didn't intend to—you know that."

"I never marked that up against you, Hollie," replied Raymond, using the name he bore among the cadets.

"I know you didn't. Doctor, give me something. I don't want to go just yet. . . . I want a few words. . . . Give me breath, can't you?" he demanded, sharply.

Braide shook his head, and the dying man closed his eyes, and his hands shut convulsively. When he opened them he could only whisper, "Girl—your hand." Ann gave her hand. He pressed it hard. "You're the best —I ever met. Stay with me. It's a dark trail—and no blazes in the green timber. Good-bye—"

With throat choking with emotion, Ann bent and touched her lips to his cold forehead.

"You're good to me. So long, Rob," he breathed, and Ann turned away, shaken with sobs, unable to witness the struggle as the unquenchable spirit loosed itself violently from the mangled body.

The funeral of the young leader was the most impressive ceremony ever seen in the camp. It seemed that every man and nearly every woman in the district had assembled in the street before the Golden Horn, and Raymond's succinct oration, delivered in a conversational tone—he scorned to make oratorical capital of the moment—was inaudible to those in the outer circles. "Jack was wrong-headed, but his heart was right." That was the substance of his plea. "He never cheated or lied or deserted a friend, but he lived defiantly and died violently. Of his life between the date of his leaving the academy and our meeting here I know no more than you. It was reckless and roving, no doubt, of a piece with what we know of him here. He would have made a notable character in the Middle Ages, when a man could range freely up and down the country and accuse or defend at his pleasure; but these are not the Middle Ages. Such lives as his lead to just such abrupt ends, for disorder is not the rule. Society to-day hates disorder.

"Jack was not a hypocrite. He knew his failings. And when he asked me to stand here and tell a good word for him, he knew I would not lie about him. He was my friend. He proved it the other day not far from here, and it was to save him from just this stern business that Matt and I took him and tied him. He refused to flee like a coyote—he preferred to die fighting. I am not here to preach—to draw lessons from his life—I am only here to say he was my friend, warm-hearted, ready to serve in time of trouble, and fair and above-board in every contest. I hope the great Judge when He enters up the charges against him will not forget the credit side of his account. Till that day of reckoning," he concluded, brokenly, "may he sleep soundly; and if he dreams, let it be of the days when we were happy cadets on furlough down the river, in the glory of June."

With face still deeply lined with emotion, Raymond

made his way through the silent crowd and down to the bungalow, eager to return to Ann and Louis.

"It is a strange thing," he began, as soon as he had closed the door behind him, "how an erratic, disorderly life like poor Hollie's appeals to us all. Theoretically, we believe in order; but when a man is brave enough, or reckless enough, to ride across lots, how grateful we are to him. At bottom, we are all gypsies and feudal knights and Comanches. That's the fact. What other man in this district could have brought forth such a crowd?"

"I was thinking of that, too," replied Ann. "From every reasonable point of view, he was a destructive force, and yet my heart bled to see him die. He and his like are the Robin Hoods of our day. I suppose there were a great many people at the funeral?"

"An immense number—the whole camp and surrounding country. Every cow-boy within fifty miles is here. The procession will be well worth your seeing. Louis must see it."

When the sound of a triumphant march announced the coming of the funeral train, Raymond folded Louis carefully in his blankets and bore him to the window, and there held him in order that he might see the passing of the captain of the vedettes.

Louis, wide-eyed, absorbed, intent, uttered no word, but gazed in silence, one slender arm flung over Rob's neck. He hardly breathed, so deep was his interest.

Ann looked upon it all with steadily expanding comprehension of life's mystery. In the clear sunlight the band appeared, stepping alertly, glittering in brass and gay with scarlet and silver. Behind them, two and two, leading a host of horsemen, rode nearly a hundred of the dead man's guard, a look of stern melancholy on each brown face, proud of their place of honor, proud of their shining weapons, their horses, their dangling latigoes and decorated bridles. They ceased to fight when their leader died, but many of them were of a mind with him—they scorned to flee, they remained to do the last honors to their captain, reckless of law.

Behind these cavaliers of the plain rolled a few carriages, with Hanley and Claire and two or three others of the dead man's intimates in position as mourners. The officers of the union were conspicuous by their absence, but an army of miners of all nationalities and all characters, led by Kelly and Adams on horseback, tramped behind. Many of them could not speak the dead man's name, but each dimly felt that he had somehow died in their service, and that he was a good man, and so they lent their work-twisted bodies to the deeply significant pageant. Last of all came the sight-seers from Bozle and the Springs, in all sorts and conditions of vehicles, vulgar and insincere for the most part, but adding, to Ann's eyes, a final touch of tragic pathos.

"I hope Jack can see this," she said, almost involuntarily. "He would enjoy it so."

"He can," replied Louis, without taking his big eyes from the scene outside. "I know he can. How they loved him!" he sighed. "I wish I had known him better."

Raymond exchanged looks with Ann. "You see— the heart of the lawless!"

It passed at last, and the stillness, the brilliancy of the springlike afternoon settled back upon the peak as the air closes behind the flight of an eagle. The heart of

the revolt went away in Munro's small, straight body.
The vedettes broke up into squads of twos and threes
and rode away, never to reassemble. The miners
climbed weakly back to their haunts on the street, there
to chant in sad or furious voices the praises of their dead
leader. The sight-seers returned to their own petty
affairs of the day, putting aside the warning, the significance of the ceremony; but on the sensitive brain
of a dreaming boy the lights and shadows of that procession fell with lasting power, and some day the world
may learn how much of the mystery of life and death
he drew from that ludicrous, picturesque, and solemn
intermingling of mourning miners and bronzed and
reckless mountaineers.

XXXI

Ann Returns to New York

IN a few days Louis was able to be removed to the valley, but his recovery was slow, and notwithstanding imperative letters from his mother, Mrs. Allard, Dr. Braide strongly advised against his return to the East. As a proprietor in the mine, Louis was now doubly anxious to be on the ground, but, being prevented from that, he called on Rob for frequent personal reports, which the senior partner was very glad to make.

These visits were delicious experiences to Raymond. There was joy in laying aside his miner's clothes for a day, to loaf in shining linen and patent-leather shoes. It was a delight to be a guest at Jeannette's well-filled table, but to sit beside Ann in the cart, or to take dinner with her at the Casino of a Saturday night and listen to the Hungarian band, restored his youth; and Ann, to her astonishment, found an almost equal pleasure in these simple entertainments. There was so little to criticise in her lover's attitude — his self-restraint was most admirable, his reserve a satisfaction. It was plain that he would wait for her decision in this way indefinitely, and this deep-seated courtesy and reasonableness touched her; and yet she grew no nearer to a decision as the weeks went by.

At last the day came when she decided to leave Louis

in his care and return to her mother, desperately determined to test her new-found happiness and her love, though she did not put it thus.

Raymond received the announcement of her plan with outward composure, though he said, sadly: "Now that I know more about your life in the East, I am not so sure I can make you happy, even with a million. I've lost my ambition to be rich, for what could I give you, who have had everything?"

"I am not the great heiress you think; and, besides, I've eaten too much honey and preserves."

"Very well. Then you know where you can feast on corn-bread and bacon." Then he became very grave. "I am going to flee to my mountain. I can't bear to see you take the train, and I will not say good-bye. I will wait as patiently as I can till you send for me, and if you feel that you—that I am not fitted to make you happy, I will not complain." And they parted with only a clasp of hands.

On the journey eastward Ann had a great deal of time to think, and the farther she descended upon the plain the more certain it seemed that she was leaving it all behind—Raymond, the good Barnetts, and all— and a sadness which lay beyond tears seized upon her. She felt, too, that Louis was growing out of her life— her control. He would soon be a man in the world of men.

However, she approached New York on a glorious morning in May, and the North River was a glittering spread of leaping wavelets tossed into the sunlight by a brisk southwesterly wind, and her spirits rose with a bound.

Hesper

With a sense of boldness and daring she pushed forward amid a crowd of working-folk on the upper deck, her eyes fixed on the irregular mass of the city looming against the misty sky, notched, jagged, like a line of sand-worn cliffs speckled with the holes of some rock-piercing sea-birds. The innumerable water-craft starting and returning to the base of these walls were like intent beetles in pursuit of prey.

Hardly more than half a year of sidereal time had rolled between her going and her return, but, measured by the changes within herself, ten times the length of these days had passed over her head, each laden with experiences so transforming that she had now the aloofness of a traveller returning to his native land after long wanderings in strange countries. New York Bay, opening to right and to left, teemed with suggestion, took on new grandeur. It was now a glittering gateway—not the end, but the beginning of the republic. Its relation to the vast interior States stood revealed.

She had never seen the city at this early hour, and the types of worn and hurrying women crowding the gang-plank, the throngs of working-men, sallow and a little sullen, menaced her as she mingled with them for a moment before entering a carriage.

"How dispirited and sickly they all look," she said to herself.

Raymond was in her thought constantly. "How would all this seem to him?" she asked herself. "After the plains, these crowds would be intolerable. I can't think of him here. He belongs out there." In such wise her thought ran on in a tumult of readjustment.

The morning was deliciously cool and very brilliant

with sunlight, and as she rolled through Madison Square and entered upon the lower avenue the girl's throat filled with a sob of joy. The generous, good mountains had not merely lured her to themselves, teaching her to love them, they had restored her sanity and the power to enjoy the glint of sunbeams anywhere in the world. She was elate, throbbing with recovered love of life, with the regained joy of being young, and, best of all, she found herself looking back each moment with undiminished affection to the high peaks. The wealth and power of her native city could not dethrone the sovereign majesty of Mogalyon and the Hesperean wall.

The shopkeepers were drawing the curtains to disclose their innumerable jewels, their exquisite pottery, their rare carvings and weavings from all over the world; but these heaped wares did not lessen, they only enhanced, the beauty of the fir-tips traced against the sunset sky. These rugs, the choicest work of the Orient, only served to make the more exquisite the turf of the mountain-peaks, and to enrich the brown carpet of needles beneath the cañon pines. Into this moment of elation the thought of her mother intruded with chilling effect.

The complete lack of sympathy between mother and daughter dated from the day of her birth, for she had never known maternal care. From the time she could speak, paid servants and teachers guided her in feminine ways—the cold and smileless woman who gave her birth was a being of another world. No caresses were ever invited by the mother and none were ever offered by the child—even the companionship of the gentle, impulsive father was cut short, or interdicted altogether, during melancholy periods by his wife's exacting demands.

When Louis came the father revolted, refusing to be forever at the whim of his wife. He gave up attendance upon her and devoted himself to the children. This, Ann afterwards recalled, was the beginning of her mother's morbid seclusion. Then came boarding-school, from which she was called to receive her father's last words, and these admonitions, gently spoken, with a sad sweetness of tone, like the dying hum of a bell, she had never forgotten. She *had* been a mother to Louis, and she was coming back now with the consciousness of a duty well performed; but as she approached the towering wall of the great apartment hotel in which her mother made her home, she lost courage, and the resolution she had made to forget their differences and to confide her perplexities died away.

Mrs. Allard received her in bed, reading—she was forever reading useless books—and impassively said, "What an unearthly hour to arrive!"

Ann took her lax hand and bent and kissed her chill lips. "How are you feeling, mother?" she asked, tenderly.

"Miserably, and Mr. Allard is away, as usual," she replied, with a bitter frown. "Your letters were very few — very unsatisfactory. Why did you not return sooner?"

Instantly Ann's old feeling of sullen anger and resentment resurged like a tide and threatened to bury all her good resolutions, but she struggled with and rose above her resentment and said, gently, " I didn't intend to neglect my duty— I wrote as often—"

Ann Returns to New York

Her mother interrupted her as she entered upon a more extended confidence. "Go to your room and bathe, and get your breakfast. We will talk over Louis' extraordinary plans afterwards."

Her own rooms, at the back of the suite, faced the morning, and the sun was flooding them with light as she entered. The familiar sense of reaching a safe harbor returned to her as she closed the door behind her. Everything was in place, even her maid Sarah, who responded to her cordial greeting with words of admiration. "How well you are looking! Your color is wonderful."

"Thank you, Sarah. How have you been?"

"Not very well, miss. It's been lonesome without you. I do hope you'll not leave me behind again."

Each article was as Ann had left it; even the book she had put down last had been lifted, dusted, and put back in the same spot every day. Her return was like a return of the dead, so devotedly had the room been kept against her need.

First of all the bath allured, and when, refreshed and rerobed, she yielded herself to the care of her maid, she seemed so settled, so deep in her old-time way of life, that the peaks and their shadows began swiftly to recede. The immediate future troubled her. At about eleven her mother would send for her and ask for a confession. This would not be an easy or pleasant interview, but it was coming.

" She will, of course, sneer at Robert, and deny every one of Louis' requests. She has probably included me in her plans for the summer. If we go abroad, it will be the same wearisome round of noisy hotels, the same complaints, the same controversies. If we stay at home, it will be Lenox and Bar Harbor — and mother. It is shameful of me, but she depresses me. And how lonely and wretched she is now! She is so strong and yet so inert, she saps my very life. And so the summer will pass—to what good purpose? If I could influence her—but I can't. Oh, I wanted to tell her everything —I need her love—but I am afraid."

With a tap on the door the maid announced a telegram.

Ann clutched at the little yellow envelope and tore it open swiftly. It was from Robert.

"Love and greeting from all. Louis quite himself. Wants to go back to the mine. Will hold him at the Springs for a week longer—miss Hesper horribly.

"ROBERT."

Instantly the heart-sick girl returned in memory to the Springs. Closing her eyelids, she lifted an inward gaze to the glory-covered head of old Mogalyon. The vivid sunlight was smiting fierce against his breast, but on his brow, like a vast turban of purple and snow-white, a cloud rested. They were all on the wide, vine-clad veranda which opened upon the west— sweet Jeannette, jovial Don; Louis, impatient, restless, lyric of speech, and Robert— How sympathetic they all were—how good and loving! "I have no other friends so vital to me," she admitted.

Opening her eyes to the present, she again took thought of the coming interview with her mother, whom at the moment she pitied. Her step-father was away—he was always away—but, as he had never presumed in any domestic matter at any time, the discussion lay between her mother and herself. "How can I make her understand that this journey in my father's footsteps has developed in me the saving grace of his legacy to me. The old, purposeless routine is waiting for me. I feel it. This high-colored, artificial hotel is a malign influence. I cannot, I must not sink into my groove again."

The interview with her mother was quite as painful as she had feared. She began by demanding to know why Louis was not with her, and when Ann re-explained bluntly that he would not come, Mrs. Allard looked at her daughter in cold silence for a full minute, and then said: "There is something about you that I don't understand. You look well; but Louis should come home. That climate doesn't agree with him."

"On the contrary; his illness is due to his own impetuousness in riding up into the mountains without sufficient clothing."

"What's the meaning of this talk of his about buying a mine?"

Ann explained this as patiently as she could, and when Mrs. Allard contemptuously said, "He shall do nothing of the kind," Ann broke out:

"Mother, you don't seem to understand that Louis is no longer a child, and that he is growing very difficult to manage. I used my best powers to persuade him to come home and consult with you, but he refused; furthermore, the doctor advised against his coming just now."

"I don't care what the doctor said; my plans are settled. I am to spend the summer in the Tyrol, and I want Louis with me. The air there is better for him than the raw winds of that crazy mining-camp. I wish you would write him or telegraph him at once to come."

"You are not asking me to go with you, I hope?"

"Certainly you are going."

Ann turned white and tense and sat for a long time in silence, a deep humming sound in her ears, well knowing that the hour of revolt had come. Her voice was hoarse with emotion when she spoke, "Mother, you must not make any more plans that include me."

Mrs. Allard's eyelids opened in surprise. "Why not?"

"Because I am to be married very soon."

Mrs. Allard seemed stunned for a moment, but she recovered and asked, ironically, "Are you, indeed? How very considerate of you to tell me! May I ask to whom?"

"You may. His name is Robert Raymond."

"One of those Western miners?"

"Yes, a miner, but an Eastern man."

"Now I understand Wayne Peabody's glum face. I infer that this Mr. Raymond is rich?"

"No," replied Ann, quite simply; "he works with his hands among his men."

"It's like you to throw yourself away. Do you think I will consent to such a piece of folly?"

Ann was coldly calm. "Fortunately your consent is not required." Then the thought of how all this would sound to her lover moved her, and with tears of entreaty in her voice she cried out: "Oh, mother, don't let's quarrel, wait till you see Robert! You cannot help but admire him—he is so big and manly. I came here to ask your help, your advice. I wanted to confide in you. I want your love, your sympathy."

"You have it—my profound sympathy. But you cannot have my consent to such a foolish act."

Ann Returns to New York

Ann rose, wounded, bleeding, but no longer in a mood for confidences or entreaties. "Further controversy is useless, mother. I have given my future into Robert's hands."

Once more in her room, she caught up a little framed portrait from her desk. "Oh, my beautiful, poetic, dear father, now I know why you loved the mountains, and why you sickened and died here in the city! You gave me a precious heritage, and I have only just found it. I will live as you would have me live, dear." She touched the picture to her lips as a sign of her dedication of herself to the new life. "You would have liked Robert, and I love him!"

With bosom heaving with passionate resolution, she hurried to her desk and wrote a telegram in big, strong letters, as if to make an imperishable record:

"Robert, come for me. I am waiting.   HESPER."

THE END

S